BLOOD
LEGACY

Book 1 of The Divine Elements

Copyright © by Daman

For any inquiries, please contact damanknightley@gmail.com

CHAPTER ONE

Prologue

"I'm sorry, Elaine."

The old midwife spoke sorrowfully as she gazed down at the pale woman lying on the dirty mat. Splotches of dark blood pooled around this frail woman, and she appeared to be on the verge of her last few breaths.

Gently holding the stillborn baby in her bloodstained hands, the old midwife slowly laid the child into its mother's arms. Meanwhile, a small, wiry boy was currently kneeling next to the dying woman while firmly grasping one of her hands.

It was as if the boy was afraid that he would lose her hand's warmth forever.

The young boy had hair the color of midnight and eyes equally dark. With streams of tears rolling down his cheeks, he scrunched up his childish face in an attempt to look brave, but his facade collapsed immediately when he saw his mother struggling with her next breath.

"Mother..."

The boy choked on his words, causing his voice to croak.

Tendrils of light blue essence slowly coalesced around the old midwife's hands as she desperately tried to heal the dying woman with her element. After a few seconds, the blood seemed to cease to flow out of the pale woman, but there was no preventing the inevitable outcome that would soon occur.

"Calron, come meet your little sister."

The dying woman gently whispered as she slightly tilted her head to look at her sniveling eight-year-old son beside her.

Reaching out a trembling arm, the woman warmly grazed her palm against her son's wet cheeks. She felt her soul crumbling from knowing that she would soon leave her son as an orphan in this cruel world.

The boy stopped crying the instant he felt his mother's touch on his face.

This was the woman who brought him into this world and who showed him the true depths of love and compassion. Noticing the motionless, blood-covered baby within his mother's embrace, the boy felt his heart being slowly crushed with agony.

Robbed of the chance to take a single breath in this world, his sister would never know who her brother was or experience what it felt like to be alive.

Abruptly, the boy's mother started to cough uncontrollably and struggled to catch her breath.

"Mother!"

The dark-haired boy frantically yelled in panic.

"It's alright, Cal... mommy's fine... She just needs to rest a bit."

The woman spoke softly, trying to reassure her son. With her hand trembling, she reached out to wipe away the tears from her son's cheeks.

"Cal, leave this place after mommy's gone... Those *people* will soon come here to torment you. Just like they did to your father..."

The boy slowly nodded in response to his mother's wish, but a fierce determination spread across his face when he thought about the *people* his mother was talking about.

After the death of his father a few months ago, the boy had already experienced the sensation of loss at a tender age, and the grief in his tiny heart could not bear the pain of another loss so soon.

How could he simply leave this place?

Those *people* had not only caused the deaths of his parents, but also denied his little sister the warmth of her family.

Fate was cruel.

Destiny was worthless.

Only strength is everlasting.

The dark-haired boy tightly clenched his tiny fists together, drawing blood as his nails pierced into his skin.

As the small drops of crimson liquid dripped onto the floor, a seed of vengeance took root inside the boy's heart.

"Keep the locket safe, Cal. It was the heirloom of your father's family."

His mother's soft voice abruptly shook the boy out of his raging thoughts.

The dark-haired boy tightly gripped the dangling bird-shaped locket on his neck and slowly nodded his head to his mother while wiping away the tears on his shoulder.

The pallid woman tearfully clutched the small baby to her chest before raising her head slightly from the mat to plant a gentle kiss on her son's forehead.

Lovingly gazing into his eyes, the woman gingerly patted her son's head for the last time. Slowly closing her eyes, the boy's mother took her very last breath of life.

All time seemed to stop.

Silence.

A heartbreaking cry from a young child echoed throughout the area as it shattered the silence of the world.

CHAPTER TWO

New Destiny

thak

thak *thak*

In the blazing sun's heat, an eight-year-old boy stood panting with bloody fists at his sides.

In front of him was a tree with blood-smeared bark. No matter how many times he punched or kicked, the anger and grief he felt would not leave him. The boy twisted his head towards his family's modest farm behind the tree and forlornly gazed at the three graves.

The villagers helped him dig the two new graves, but they did not continue to help him further as they knew exactly who would come for the boy later. They did not wish to gamble with their lives for a mere orphan.

With pity in their eyes, the villagers left for the safety of their own homes and families.

The boy was truly alone now.

The child looked up towards the bright blue sky while squinting his eyes as the sun's flare bore through his eyelids. How could such a beautiful and yet cruel world exist?

As he pondered these thoughts, the boy looked away from the sky.

With only a few weeks remaining until he reached his eighth birthday, the child knew that his element's awakening was drawing near. However, when one's family and friends would normally rejoice and celebrate would only serve to bring further pain and anguish to him.

Especially if he awakened to the same element as his father: the element of lightning.

Lightning was said to be the weakest of all the elements, as a lightning elementalist could only paralyze an opponent.

It was too weak to land fatal blows, and against a stronger opponent, the paralyzing attack would hardly deter them for longer than a moment. Without the power to kill an opponent, who would ever be afraid of a lightning elementalist?

His father used to say this was not always the case for lightning elementalists in the past, but even he had only heard stories through his grandfather.

Although using an element was not the only method for killing one's opponent, against higher-ranked cultivators who had bodies stronger than steel, normal weapons were completely useless. For this reason, on the continent, lightning cultivators were always looked down upon.

Throughout recorded history, there had never been a human lightning cultivator who had ever managed to breakthrough to the rank after Spiritual stage.

Breakthroughs required an immense amount of elemental essence, so cultivators would have to go to an environment where their element's essence was rich in quantity. A lightning elementalist, therefore, could only cultivate near thunderstorms, as an enormous cloud of thunder was the only time lightning would appear.

Five elements exist in the world: fire, wind, earth, water, and lightning.

Other elementalists could cultivate without fear, as their elements were not as naturally violent like lightning. They could cultivate a fire element near fiery places like a desert or, in later stages, near a volcano. There were not a lot of risks involved, as a desert was a relatively safe environment, although there was a danger of thirst and scarcity of water. If fully prepared, it would be completely safe.

Even for the volcano, they could choose a dormant one at the earlier stages of cultivation rather than a fully active one. The fire cultivators could still absorb the purer fire essence without having to put their lives at such a risk.

This held for the other elements as well, but lightning was never dormant, as its unpredictable nature denied any chance of safely cultivating. A lightning elementalist could never know where the next bolt would strike or how powerful the bolt would be. Even the weakest of lightning, when in contact with a mortal body, would completely disintegrate the cultivator within seconds.

Many hopeful youths and a few elders with the lightning element had tried to breakthrough during thunderstorms to escape their fate and life of servitude, but only ended up staring at the face of death under the vicious torrents of lightning.

The tyranny of the lightning that exists in nature is not as meek and powerless as the essence of lightning cultivators. With both speed and power under its dominance, even nature trembles when hearing the roaring sound of thunder.

With this, the lightning elementalists were forever doomed to a life of servitude. In a world where the strong ruled, the weak were only looked down upon and continued to live as they kneeled before the strong.

Strength was glory.
Strength was authority.
Strength was everything.

With power, one could have any riches or wealth they wanted, as powerful sects would try to rope them in with further prestige and influence. The higher your cultivation, the better life you will live.

Expectedly, lightning elementalists were at the bottom of this social ladder.

Calron's mother was a second rank at the spiritual stage, and his father was a fourth rank at the same stage. This was considered being especially weak for an adult.

There were four elemental stages, beginning at the spiritual stage, followed by the vajra stage, where the body would fuse with the elemental core, which would make the physical strength of the cultivator reach immense heights.

After that came the saint stage, where the soul of the cultivator would awaken and allow godly feats with their willpower. The next stage was the heavenly stage, but not much was known about this realm, as very few cultivators had managed to achieve it.

Calron's family worked in the local lord's mansion as servants. Even though the Lord was only around the fifth rank of the Vajra stage, the difference in power between each stage was comparable to the difference between heaven and earth.

Furthermore, breaking through each stage would become increasingly difficult. The citizens in the city of Vernia were mostly at the fifth rank of the spiritual stage, and the common soldiers were at the seventh rank.

As servants, Calron's family had little 'free will' of their own, but under the oppressive power of a Vajra stage cultivator, who would dare to argue against injustice? His father, as a lightning cultivator, was forced to fight for the Lord against the magical beasts that plagued the border between Vernia and the mountains. The local citizens soon called the mountain ranges "the desolate mountains".

This coalition of numerous mountains was surrounded by an unending forest full of magical beasts, and the deepest part of the forest was said to be the home of beasts in the Vajra stage.

There was even a legend that the Desolate Mountains was ruled by a beast in the Heavenly Stage.

Very few cultivators willingly went inside the mountains, but the cores of magical beasts were the primary source of Vernia's economy and its immense wealth, so warriors and cultivators were actively recruited to take part in beast hunts. As a lightning cultivator, Calron's father had no choice but to follow the commands of the City Lord.

Even the core of a beast in the first rank of the spiritual stage was worth at least one gold square, and a single gold square could last a poor family for an entire year.

With his father's strength of a fourth rank, the paralyzing effect on lower magical beasts was a tool that the Lord of Vernia would never cease to exploit, as it would save both the lives of his soldiers, and Calron's father being a servant to his family, the Lord would not even have to pay much for his services and would rake in most of the profits.

Although lightning elementalists were looked down upon in society, they were extremely rare, as only a few children ever awakened to the lightning element. The reason for the rarity of the lightning element was unknown; however, the world did not seem to mind this fact.

Another reason was that sometimes the parents would abandon the child once they discovered the lightning element inside them. Eventually, that child would meet his or her death, as without the shelter or support of an adult, it was immensely difficult for an eight-year-old to survive on their own.

The greed of the lightning elementalist's paralyzing ability led the city lord to hunt higher-ranked beasts deeper into the forest.

However, one day, when a sixth-rank beast suddenly appeared, it decimated the entire regiment of soldiers, along with Calron's father, who was forced to be at the very forefront of the formation.

Calron's father was the first one to be killed, as his paralyzing attack did not deter the beast at all, but only seemed to make it angrier as it charged toward him.

A few soldiers survived the aftermath of the attack, as the beast did not give chase to the ones that escaped, but over twenty soldiers of the seventh rank were killed that day.

Although the magical beast was only a rank lower than them, magical beasts were generally stronger because of the toughness of their bodies and the fact that they were already born with awakened cores, allowing them to fight against human elementalists two ranks above them.

With a last punch to the tree, Calron kneeled in utter exhaustion. No matter how much rage his little heart contained, his body was still that of an eight-year-old.

Calron slowly walked back to his home, and he suddenly felt a few wet drops on his cheek. He stopped to touch his cheek in confusion and looked up at the sky.

He had not realized it in his previous daze, but the sky was darkening as the number of gray clouds increased by the second.

Having decided to make a run for it, Calron knew without a doubt that there would soon be a downpour of heavy rain.

The sky was now filled with gray clouds as streaks of light flashed within the clouds. Calron ran as fast as his tired legs could handle, and after a few minutes, he could spot his humble hut within a few steps away.

Just then, the rain poured down in a vicious frenzy, and the clouds rumbled as bursts of light flashed above.

Calron hurried to enter his hut and panted with lack of breath until he found some water to gulp down. The loud rumbling continued outside as the sounds of the rain hitting the ground echoed within Calron's hut.

Calron collapsed on the straw mat as he reached the end of what little energy he had. Closing his tired eyes, Calron lay down uncomfortably on the mat while his thoughts kept coming back to his mother and father, and even the small baby sister that he would never get to spoil or play with.

His anger at the city Lord increased every second, as he knew it was his father's death that eventually led to the weakening of his mother's health, and combined with the pregnancy, she became too weak to give birth to his sister. Calron then looked down at his chest as he noticed the piece of metal hanging there and clenched the rusty, bird-shaped locket within his fist.

This was the last memento from his family.

Intriguingly, the locket felt warm to the touch, but Calron figured it was due to the running and his body's heat warming it up, so he paid little attention to it. With the increased rumbling outside, Calron was worried for a brief moment, as he had never felt rain this powerful before and it sounded like the beginning of a terrible storm.

He stopped worrying and let his exhausted body collapse back on the mat as he fell into a deep sleep.

RUMBLE

Outside, the rain continued to pour, and just at that moment, the very first lightning strike struck the ground.

The villagers were all terrified, and the sounds of small children crying could be heard in the vicinity while the parents tried to soothe the kids. Waiting in the protection and comfort of their homes, the villagers waited until the sounds of thunder finally stopped.

After the first lightning strike, every few seconds another one would strike constantly as the sound of its crackling echoed in the surroundings.

In his small hut, Calron kept uncomfortably turning around on his mat as his clothes stuck to him under the sweat. Calron did not know what was happening to his body.

He thought it was his awakening, but an awakening was not supposed to hurt, and he still had a few more months until his eighth birthday.

It felt like his blood was boiling and his muscles twitched now and then. What Calron did not feel through all the pain was that the once-warm locket on his chest was now scorching hot and stuck to his skin, further increasing the torment he felt.

Calron silently screamed as he felt the angry heat surging through his body, but the agony had no intention of going away.

The sounds of thunder stopped for a moment, but if anyone had dared to look towards the sky, then they would have seen the most terrifying scene of their lives.

In the middle of the clouds, a pale azure light slowly glowed as small bursts of blue lightning crackled around it.

The world seemed to turn deaf.

Even though the rain kept falling, there was no sound from it.

It was as if time itself had frozen in space.

RUMBLE *RUMBLE*

CRACK

A single bolt of deep azure lightning came crashing toward the ground as it carried the power and might of the heavens.

And if anyone had dared to look outside, then they would have seen that the place where the blue lightning struck was exactly above Calron's small hut.

....

The pain never seemed to end.

Calron felt like his blood would burst out of his veins, and with tears pouring from his small face, he kept silently begging for the torment to end.

Just then, he felt something strike his body with the force of a small building.

The pain abruptly stopped.

Although Calron felt the force of something striking him, mysteriously, there was no trace of pain anywhere. Feeling around for where that mysterious force might have struck him, Calron swept his hands over his body and felt the bird-shaped locket on his chest.
Rather than a locket, the metal was now firmly lodged in the

middle of his chest, as the surrounding chain had long ago melted under the intense heat.

Calron tried to remove the bird-shaped locket from his chest, but it would not even slightly budge. Intriguingly, there was no pain from it. Calron looked closely at the locket in wonder and saw that it was no longer rusty and that it seemed to emit a pale azure light.

The bird appeared to be almost alive, but Calron figured it was just his mind playing tricks on him. He further noticed that the locket was in the same place as where his core would have been after he awakened to an element. Did he already awaken?

He hesitantly touched the locket. It was just a whisper of a touch, but just at that moment, a bright azure flashed inside the hut, and Calron felt an intense amount of essence emitting from the locket. His blood boiled again, but this time the azure blue essence from the locket seeped into his blood, and Calron felt a shock of lightning running through his body.

If someone had seen Calron at this moment, then they would have seen a boy with bright blue lightning surging and crackling around him.

He felt power.

Raw, unfiltered power coursed through his veins.

However, suddenly, he heard a voice. It was a soothing sound, as if a whisper were traveling through a cool breeze.

"So, you're the scion of his house, huh?"
Calron abruptly looked around but could see no one.

Even the rain outside had slowed to a faint drizzle as the gray clouds slowly retreated.
Seeing no one near him, Calron put his thoughts aside and sat

down to stare at his body. The locket had disappeared, but Calron could still instinctively feel that it was still inside his chest.

It had not merged completely with his body, as it still retained its shape, but from the outside, there was not a single trace of metal on Calron's chest.

Calron gaped at his chest as he saw the elemental glow.

He had awakened.

As he saw the elemental glow on his chest, it looked no different from others, besides the fact that rather than the usual gold color of the lightning essence, the glow was a bright azure blue.

Calron initially thought that it might have been the water element, but water's essence was a light pale blue color, and it had a gentle and soothing aura. In contrast, this azure lightning was tyrannical, as Calron felt the violent bursts of lightning crackling around his core.

Wanting to test out his new element, Calron raised his right hand and concentrated as much as he could to make the lightning appear.

Nothing.

Silence.

"Pfft, what is with that pose? Are you trying to strangle someone?"
Calron heard a snicker inside his mind, and he knew it was the same voice that he just heard before.

Stunned, Calron looked around his hut as he asked in a trembling voice.
"Wh-who are you? And why can't I see you?"

No answer.

Calron tried to release his lightning again, but just as he was raising his hand, Calron felt slightly embarrassed as he remembered the previous snicker of the voice and quickly withdrew his hand mid-air.

"Kid, first release the elemental essence and then release the lightning."

There was no ridicule in the voice, as it sounded sincere, so Calron tried to release his essence. Suddenly, an azure wisp of essence coalesced around him. Calron tried to release the lightning next, but it still would not come out.

He clenched his fists and tried again, but no hint of lightning appeared.

"Relax your body, kid... Feel the essence coursing through you... Imagine the shape of lightning and will it to come outside."

The voice abruptly spoke again, but there was a slight hint of amusement in its tone.

Calron unclenched his fists and sat down on the floor in a meditative pose. Breathing deeply and closing his eyes, he pictured the Azure Lightning in his mind: a bolt of blue lightning crackling with unrestrained power and violence.

crackle

Calron opened his eyes and saw the blue lightning sizzling around his body. He smiled at his success, but suddenly Calron felt an abrupt shock of pain as he coughed up blood on the floor.

His tiny body trembled as both the lightning and the essence vanished into thin air.

"Guess it's still too early for you..."
The voice sighed.

"What happened? Why does it hurt so much?"
Calron rasped as the pain racked through his body, and he momentarily forgot that he was just talking to air.

"It's the Azure Lightning, kid."

And then Calron lost consciousness.

CHAPTER THREE

Red Boar School

Just as Calron woke up, he saw the sun's light bore through the window as it pierced through his eyes.

Scrunching up his eyes, Calron quickly got up as he remembered the events that had happened last night. Looking around his small hut, he was surprised that it was still intact, with only a few objects jumbled on the floor.

Other than the mess on the floor, there were absolutely no signs that a lightning bolt had struck this feeble hut.

Worried that it was all a dream, Calron attempted to release his essence.
Wisps of bright gold light surrounded him as Calron sighed in relief, knowing that he had finally awakened to his element.

However, Calron was suddenly hit with the realization that his essence last night was a unique azure blue color and not the normal gold of other lightning cultivators.

This gold essence felt a lot weaker than the azure essence Calron had experienced yesterday, as he remembered the feeling of unrestrained power that surged through him. Where did it go?

Calron let out a disappointed sigh.

"It went back into the locket, kid. The Azure Lightning puts a lot of pressure on your body, and if you had continued to channel it any longer yesterday, you would have died instantly. Just be glad that it protected you."
The voice abruptly stated it with a lazy tone.

"Are you a ghost?"
Calron asked, his voice quivering.

He was in extreme pain yesterday, so naturally, he paid little attention to the origin of the voice, but with his mind clear now, Calron's childish thoughts could not help but remember the ghost stories that his mother used to tell him.

"Haha, I'm not a ghost. But more importantly, why is the son of the House Raizel living in this dump, kid?"
The voice inquired in a peculiar tone.

"House Raizel? What's that? I've never heard of that name before."
Calron curiously responded.

The name was unfamiliar to him, as only the most powerful families were titled by their house names, so why would a servant's family ever have one? For as long as Calron could remember, his parents just had a single name.

"Never mind."
The voice sighed. He seems to do that a lot, Calron inwardly thought.

"I heard that!" The voice exclaimed.

"Wait, so you can hear all my thoughts?"
Calron thought inside his mind to test the voice.

"Yes, I can hear your thoughts loud and clear, kid."
The voice responded lazily.

"What's your name?"
Calron sent his thoughts to the Voice. He started enjoying talking to this voice as it filled a lonely part of him that was empty after the death of his family.

Although Calron could not listen to the thoughts of the voice unless it intentionally talked to him, he could subconsciously feel that the voice meant him no harm, and he even felt a slight feeling of affection from it.

"Well, for now, just call me Teacher."
The voice spoke lazily, but there was a hint of excitement in his voice.

"Why would I call you a teacher?"
Calron already called old Ronny his teacher, as she taught him history and numbers along with the other village kids.

Since his parents worked at the city lord's house, Calron had lots of free time to spend, so he usually tried to make friends with the other kids. However, despite Calron's best efforts, the village kids always seemed to either ignore or condemn him.

Calron saw no reason to call a voice in his head "teacher", and besides, he hated Ronny; she always ridiculed him in front of other kids because he could not remember the dates in history, and he abhorred counting numbers.

Calron simply did not like teachers.

"Stupid kid, do I look like I want to teach you how to count numbers?"
The voice retorted in Calron's mind.

"I'm going to teach you how to cultivate your lightning element, so you can finally use that Azure Lightning in the future. And one more thing, kid: never tell anyone about that blue lightning, alright?"

For some reason, Calron trusted the Voice, as he knew instinctively that his blue lightning was different from his father's or any other element of the other cultivators. Calron simply nodded in response to the Voice's request.

Calron wondered if the voice saw his nod or if he only responded to his thoughts. Calron knew the voice was a 'he" as no woman would ever have such a rugged voice that sounded like two boulders grinding against each other.

"I can see just fine, kid. My soul is connected to yours, so anything that you see, I can see as well. By the way, the ladies back in my day swooned over my deep, manly voice."
The voice sulked before quieting down.

Calron just smiled at the Voice's behavior, but right at that moment, he saw them.

....

A trio appeared outside his hut and stared intently at him.

Two of them wore the uniforms of soldiers, while the other one was an older, gray-haired man who stood in the middle of the trio. The gray-haired man wore a simple light brown robe but based upon his distinguished aura, it was clear to anyone that he had the highest authority amongst the three.

With the city lord's insignia of a black bear on their chests, the older man stepped forward towards Calron.

He raised his eyebrows at the frozen smile on Calron's face, but choosing to ignore the boy's expression, he simply said to the boy in a stern voice,

"Come."

Calron knew they would come for him eventually.

He tried resisting by sprinting away, but immediately the older man counterattacked by releasing his elemental essence.

A thick brown essence constricted Calron's body as it exerted intense pressure on his mind. With the muddy brown essence coalescing around the robed man, Calron knew he was a cultivator of the earth element.

Calron's small body trembled under the pressure, but he refused to give up as he glared at the older man with his bloodshot eyes.

What tremendous willpower! The robed man inwardly thought and couldn't help but sigh in pity, as he knew this boy would soon be taken advantage of, just like his father.

Just then, Calron released his elemental essence, and the bright golden essence surrounded him as it warmed his insides and relieved the pressure from the older man. The constricting aura was still there, but it was at a bearable level for Calron.

Surprised that the boy had already awakened, and that it was to a lightning element, the older man felt giddy in his heart, and he knew that the city lord would be ecstatic as well, especially after their previous lightning cultivator died in their last hunt.

Although the lightning element was the weakest of all, it was also the rarest, as few children awakened to it. The chance of awakening to a lightning element was one in a thousand.

"Go with him, kid. You are too weak to resist him, and it doesn't look like they'll kill you, so don't worry. I'll make sure you'll get your revenge against them soon enough."

The voice soothingly comforted the mind of his latest young student.

Calron abruptly stopped resisting and withdrew his elemental essence. Calron did not know why, but he started to trust the voice.

The robed man was astonished. He was sure that this boy would resist, and eventually, he would have to drag him by force, but the kid abruptly stopped resisting. Suspiciously, he beckoned the young boy to follow him.

Stepping outside his home, Calron turned back to take a last look at the place he grew up with his family, as he had a feeling he would never return here again. He had no material possessions to take with him besides his locket, so he simply left with the older man.

Walking behind the gray-haired man, Calron clenched his fists as he vowed to make the city Lord and his people suffer for tormenting his family. He would go with them now, but on the day that he gained enough power, he would hunt every one of them like dogs and save the most vicious death for the Lord himself.

Meanwhile, the voice inside Calron silently observed the events unfolding. He knew everything that happened in Calron's life, as their souls had linked long ago, but the violent thoughts of this boy, who had yet to reach adulthood, made him wonder just how this world would react once this boy grew into a man.

Unbeknownst to others, the Voice knew that once this boy reached the Vajra stage, Calron would become a terrifying power, as this was the stage where the Azure Lightning would merge with his mortal body.

Calron stepped into the simple wooden carriage and sat across from the older man, as one soldier sat next to him while the remaining one sat ahead in the driver's seat.

"What is your name, boy?"
The robed man brusquely asked Calron.

The older man had dark coppery skin as if he had stayed out in the sun most of his life, but it was his piercing dark green eyes that evoked fear in others. The cold aura emanating from him shook Calron's heart, but he forced himself to keep his calm expression.

Seeing no reason to refuse or be hostile from the beginning, Calron simply answered.
"Calron."

"Nice to meet you, Calron. I'm Warrick, a ninth-rank earth elementalist of the spiritual stage."
Warrick tried to sound polite, but the coldness remained in his tone.

He knew that if he could influence this boy, who had yet to mature, then he could use him to hunt magical beasts on his own. The greed of the elemental cores was too great for any person, regardless of their cultivation or power.

Calron simply nodded at the older man's introduction, but he didn't say another word.

Seeing the boy's attitude toward him, Warrick couldn't help but frown.

What's with this kid? Even though he's a weak lightning elementalist, he still dares to disrespect me. However, Warrick did not say those words, as he still wanted to use Calron in the future.

"Do you know where we are going, Calron? The city Lord has ordered me to take you to the Red Boar School to train your cultivation for two years. The Red Boar School is one of the middle-tier schools of Vernia, and their founder was a famous fire elementalist in the Royal Army. You should be grateful to the Lord for giving you such an opportunity to be one of their outer disciples."

Calron once again only nodded at this new piece of information.

He knew that the Lord only wanted to use him and to do that, Calron had to cultivate to reach a higher rank; otherwise, even first-rank spiritual-stage beasts could kill him with just a scratch.

thadak *thadak*

For the next few moments, they could hear only the sound of the carriage.

This brat. Trash like him is even allowed to step foot into Red Boar School, and yet he shows no reaction. Just wait, boy; once I get my use out of you, I'll whip you for your insolence. Warrick couldn't help but inwardly fume as his thoughts raged on, but he maintained the outwardly aloof, stony expression on his face.

After a full fifteen minutes, the carriage finally stopped.

The soldier sitting next to Calron stepped out first, followed by Warrick and then Calron. In front of them was a courtyard full of young people between the ages of eight and twelve, as well as some older youths.

"Those gray robes show they are all the outer disciples of the school."
Warwick pointed it out as he stood next to Calron.

An elderly, hunched man in a black robe stood in the center of the courtyard as he addressed all the gray-robed disciples. Calron could not hear the words, so he stopped paying attention to them and instead focused on his surroundings.

The school was quite large, as his entire village alone could fit into just one of the school's gardens.

The gate had the insignia of a red-headed boar, which Calron assumed was the symbol of the school. Calron could also see a range of buildings that spread around the area, along with a few smaller batches of huts, which he guessed were the living quarters for the disciples.

Just then, it appeared as if the black-robed elderly man had finished talking to the disciples as he calmly walked around the courtyard.

The old man suddenly noticed Warrick and smiled as if he were expecting him.

He calmly walked in Calron's direction. Although the old man had a slight hunch in his back, he walked with no difficulty, and his movements almost seemed as if he were slicing through the air currents.

He only had a few white wisps of hair around his head, as the rest of his head was completely bald.

The old man's wrinkles crinkled around his eyes, and his lips slightly curled upward as he continued to walk forward.

It was obvious that the black-robed man knew that Warrick was coming due to the lack of surprise on his face and his furtive glances at Calron, indicating that he knew very well why this child was here.

Warrick slightly bowed to the elderly man as he finally reached them, and Calron guessed this old man probably had much higher cultivation than Warrick; otherwise, this cold snob would not be so respectful towards another person.

"Welcome, welcome, my friends. Warrick, I trust this is the young man who was sponsored by Lord Regis?"
The old man questioned Warrick, even though he knew the

answer.

"Yes, Elder. He's the lightning elementalist that Lord Regis wants to cultivate. He has already awakened, so he can begin his cultivation immediately."

Warwick respectfully replied to the elder.

The elder nodded and then turned to look at Calron as he examined him. Calron looked back at the old man, and for the first time, he didn't see any sort of contempt in someone's eyes when they looked at him.

As a family of servants and, furthermore, a family with a lightning elementalist, people usually looked at Calron either with pity or disdain, knowing that in the future the boy was destined to be weak no matter what.

Seeing none of these reactions from the Elder, Calron was a bit taken aback, and the Elder seemed to guess what went through Calron's mind based on his reaction, as he very well knew the life of a lightning elementalist.

"Boy, what is your name?"
The elder asked gently.

"Calron."
Calron timidly replied.

"Very well. Let's be off then, young Calron."
With that, the elder started walking away, and Calron hesitantly walked behind him.

The old man had not even looked back at Warrick or wished him a farewell. This only seemed to further infuriate Warrick, but he just clenched his fists and rode back in the carriage with the two soldiers quietly following him.

……………

After walking away from the courtyard, the elder took Calron towards a large building while providing him with a few details on the nearby building.

The massive building in front of them was called the Foundation Building, where the outer disciples gathered to receive a spiritual pill every week and receive training in martial arts.

Although elementalists did not have to practice martial arts for cultivation, a true expert on the continent of Agatha would always practice at least one form of martial art, as it provided greater destructive power when combined with the elemental essence.

So every aspiring school in the world would have mandatory martial art training for the young cultivators, as which school would want to be known for having weak disciples?

"Since this is your first week, I'll let you have your first spiritual pill now, and I'll teach you how to cultivate your elemental essence. Spiritual pills are not necessary for cultivation, and sometimes they might affect your foundation if you consume too many of them, so try not to depend on them. It seems that you've just recently awakened, so you need to learn the proper methods to cultivate, understood?"

The elder instructed Calron while still walking towards the foundation building.

"I understand, Elder."

Calron immediately responded. He was a bit more respectful towards this old man, as he did not look down upon him, and Calron would repay any goodwill with his sincere respect.

They entered the Foundation building, and right at the center was a small shack, currently maintained by a middle-aged woman who looked to be in her late thirties with just a hint of gray on her hair.

"A cultivation pill for the lad, Gretha."

The elder said while indicating Calron to his side. Without hesitation, Gretha took out a green pill from a small jar and handed it to the elder.

The old man thanked her and then started walking towards a room on the corner of the building. Calron nodded towards the woman and followed the elder, while the woman went back to her work, wondering who the boy was.

Obviously, she did not dare ask the elder.

Although the elder was kind to everyone around him, it still did not change the domineering power he had at his disposal. The absolute requirement for being an elder of the Red Boar School was that the person must at least be in the first rank of the Vajra stage.

....

Calron entered the room behind the elder and then sat down at the place directed by the old man. The elder soon followed, sitting in front of Calron in a meditative pose.

"I'm going to teach you the proper way to cultivate your essence. First, sit in a meditative position with your hands forming a teardrop shape with just your fingertips touching. Place both hands near your navel and start breathing in a three-step variation, with the first breath being deep, then exhaling quickly, and finally taking in another deep breath."

A green glow emitted from the elder's entire body rather than just the wisps of essence, and Calron finally knew why Warrick was so respectful to this old man.

The elder had the cultivation of a Vajra stage expert.

Only in the Vajra stage does the body fuse with the essence, so the essence would emit from the entire body rather than a few wisps swirling around. The Elder suddenly stopped and gestured for Calron to imitate his movements.

Calron took the meditative pose as well and constructed his hands in the same shape as the elder as he started the three-step breathing technique.

However, after the third breath, there was still no sign of his essence gathering around his body.

"Draw your essence towards your core every time you breathe in, as this will direct it from your surroundings and into your body. Try again."
Elder explained calmly.

Although this three-step breathing appeared to be simple, combining the sequence of breaths with the circulation of essence made it simply too difficult to comprehend on the first try.

The hand gestures had to be extremely precise to direct the essence, or else it would just gather around the body but not be absorbed inside the core.

Calron immediately started again, but this time he drew in his essence each time he breathed in.

Faint trickles of golden essence slowly coalesced around him as he felt the light brushes of the essence against his skin. It was a pleasant and warm sensation, as the essence was being slowly absorbed by Calron, and each time it entered his skin, small bolts of lightning would softly crackle at that place.

The elder abruptly drew in a sharp breath, as even his calm exterior could not contain his surprise.

He had just wanted to show Calron the procedure for cultivating, so the boy could practice until he perfected his forms and then finally start to absorb the essence, but this kid copied his hand gestures almost perfectly.

The boy's control over his essence at this stage was simply too extraordinary for an eight-year-old.

It would normally take a few weeks before a child could start absorbing the essence from his surroundings.

"Now take the cultivation pill and resume your training."
The elder said this as he came out of his daze and handed out the green pill to Calron.

Calron instantly swallowed it and started the cultivation process again.

Just after a few seconds, the essence gathered around Calron again, but this time, the golden wisps were slightly thicker than before. The Elder patiently waited, as he knew it would take about half an hour for Calron to absorb all the essence.

If this boy had awakened to any other element besides lightning, then he would have been a genius. However, with his lightning element, his future was sadly restricted to the spiritual stage. *A pity.* The elder thought inwardly as he shook his head in regret.

crackle *crackle*

The Elder suddenly looked towards Calron.

CHAPTER FOUR

Disappear

While Calron was still absorbing the essence, the voice suddenly sent out a thought toward him.

"Curl both your first and fifth fingers against each other and then spread all your fingers as wide as you can, with the tips still touching."
The voice sternly commanded Calron.

Calron immediately complied, and within a few seconds, he felt a sudden rush of essence being absorbed into his body at an alarming rate as the lightning around his body became much more active.

The Elder stared in shock at the pace of essence being absorbed by Calron.

The astonishing fact was not the amount of essence Calron was cultivating, as any other cultivator could gather this amount of essence, but that was only for the other four elements.

The amount of Lightning essence was naturally scarce in the environment, and this was one of the main reasons Lightning cultivators were considered to be the weakest, as they would always be unable to gather the immense amount of essence needed to make a breakthrough from the spiritual stage.

However, this rule did not seem to apply to the boy.

A genius. An authentic genius had appeared.

Meanwhile, Calron continued to cultivate while completely unaware of the Elder's excited thoughts. The voice remained silent after having given the advice, as it did not want to distract Calron during his cultivation process.

This was an important moment for the boy, as this would be the start of his journey into the cultivation world.

His body would slowly become familiar with absorbing essence and the feeling of it circulating through his spiritual veins. Any mistake at this point would affect his future cultivation and advancement.

After a full fifteen minutes, Calron finally opened his eyes, and just for a fraction of a second, a surge of blue lightning flickered across his dark black eyes.

Fortunately, the Elder did not notice the change in the boy's eyes, as he was intently staring at Calron's current hand formation.

"Why did you suddenly change the position of your hands in the middle of cultivation, Calron?"
The elder inquired with a tinge of surprise and excitement in his voice.

Calron did not want to mention the existence of the voice in his head, so he innocently replied.

"I don't know, Elder; it felt easier to put my hands in that position. I'm sorry if I did something wrong."

Pretending to be meek and clueless so as not to arouse any suspicion, Calron's eight-year-old mind was already on the verge of entering the path of cunning.

"No, my boy, you did nothing wrong. I was just surprised."
The elder responded in a gentle tone as he sensed the boy's nervousness.

Looking at Calron's current innocent and chubby face, who would suspect him of being capable of deceiving others?

"You have a natural talent, Calron. With the aid of cultivation pills, I'm sure that you would reach the peak of the spiritual stage."

The Elder knew that no matter how shocking Calron's talent was, to break through to the Vajra stage, a cultivator would require an immense amount of essence, and as a Lightning cultivator, Calron would never have that opportunity.

A water elementalist at the spiritual stage had to immerse himself in a lake or a river and continuously let his body absorb the water essence during the point of breakthrough to successfully advance to the vajra stage.

A lightning cultivator, on the other hand, could never achieve this, no matter how talented they were, as a mortal's body was incapable of enduring the vicious and violent power of lightning.

"I'll ask Lord Regis to sponsor an extra cultivation pill for you every week, as it will increase your pace of cultivation by leaps and bounds, allowing you to at least be able to compete with the other outer disciples at the spiritual stage. Even if the Lord does not sponsor you, I will do so."
The Elder sincerely conveyed this to Calron.

Calron was utterly astonished.

He knew exactly how expensive a single cultivation pill was, as it could easily sell for ten gold squares a piece. Only the wealthy could afford to use these pills for cultivation, as which commoner would even have five gold squares to spare?

Seeing the expression on Calron's face, the elder guessed what was going through the boy's mind.

"I'm sure that Regis would accept when I tell him you will be able to reach at least the third rank of the spiritual stage in the two years you'll be studying here. Now, wait for a moment, and I'll call one of the outer disciples to take you to your lodgings."
The elder gently stated this as he exited the room.

Calron was sure that Lord Regis would not hesitate to sponsor another cultivation pill for him, especially if it meant that Calron could advance much faster and work sooner for him.

Although a single cultivation pill was expensive to a commoner, an amount of ten gold squares was not even worth mentioning compared to the wealth of the city lord.

The elder soon returned after a while and introduced an older boy in a gray robe to Calron.

"Calron, this is Tal, and he will take you to your lodgings now. He will also show you the buildings you need to familiarize yourself with and the important rules of the school. You are free to train however you want, but I suggest finding a martial master. There will be a tournament at the end of every six months, and all disciples are required to participate in it."
The elder finished his speech and gestured for Tal to take Calron.

Tal signaled Calron to follow him and started toward the end of the building.

"So, your name is Calron, right? The guards at the entrance gate said you were a lightning elementalist; is that true?"

Tal curiously inquired while walking towards a series of small huts, while a few gray-robed youths were chatting near them.

"Yes, my name is Calron, and I am also a lightning elementalist."
Calron calmly replied as he took a quick glance at Tal.

The older boy appeared to be thirteen years old, with short blonde hair and dark green eyes. From the way the older boy carried himself, Calron guessed Tal came from either a wealthy or noble family.

Hearing Calron's response, Tal had a shocked expression on his face.
The reason for Tal's shock was that they seldom accepted lightning elementalists into any influential schools.

Only the lower-tier schools would bother to accept them, and sometimes not even they would accept Lightning elementalists.

The Red Boar School was a middle-tier school in the city of Vernia, so it was extremely surprising that they would have taken in a lightning cultivator.

All schools and sects on the continent were in a constant struggle to be the most powerful force in Agatha and to reach the peak, they needed the elite of the elites, and this was only possible through nurturing talented disciples in their schools. So, which top-tier school would even take a single glance at a lightning elementalist?

Tal had just assumed Calron being a Lightning cultivator was just a rumor, but when the very person in question confirmed it, how could he doubt it?

After a few minutes, they finally reached an empty corridor with shabby-looking huts on the side. Tal gestured toward one of the small huts and said,

"This is your room, Calron. Your disciple robe should be inside as well, so wear it soon, as all disciples must wear them. You are free to do what you want, but I suggest getting a meal in the gathering hall before all the food is finished."

However, just as Tal was about to leave, the older boy spun around and quietly stated,

"Not that it's any of my business, but stay clear of the other disciples, Calron. They have a lot of pride, and many of them come from influential families, so they won't take well to a lightning elementalist in their midst."

With that abrupt warning, Tal left Calron to his thoughts.

Calron slowly entered his hut and closed the door behind him.

The hut was completely bare, as only a single bed and a mat on the rough floor were placed in the hut. Although it appeared shabby and small, for Calron, it was perfect, as he did not have to share it with anyone.

Calron immediately jumped onto the bed and let out a content sigh as he reveled in the soft feeling of the mattress.

"Hey Voice, how did you know about the hand positions you told me about earlier?"

Calron curiously asked the voice, as they were finally alone.

Although Calron did not understand the reason why the Elder was so astonished, he instinctively guessed that it was because of those specific hand positions that the Voice had taught him.

"Kid, you really need to stop calling me "voice". Call me "Teacher" instead. It makes me sound sophisticated.

The voice irritatedly interjected.

Seeing that the Voice knew a lot more about cultivation than the Elder, Calron decided it was all right to call the Voice his "teacher.".

The voice was hardly anything like that of that fat Ronny, who had taught him numbers and counting in the village.

"Alright, I'll call you Teacher from now on. So, teach me more about cultivation."

Calron whispered with excitement to his new teacher.

"Hmph, since you called me Teacher, I guess I can instruct you for a bit. But right after that, you have to go eat something. I can hear your stomach grumbling, and it's disturbing my peace. Now, get into the meditative position again."

The voice sternly stated this within Calron's mind.

Calron noticed that although his teacher sometimes acted arrogant and lazy, sometimes his demeanor would completely change into an attitude that demanded respect and admiration from others.

The boy did not know what his teacher's real identity was, but he guessed he had once been a very powerful cultivator, as only cultivators at the peak of their existence had that naturally arrogant attitude.

Calron rushed to the mat and quickly closed his eyes while sitting in the meditative pose.

"First, let me tell you how cultivation works. Hand gestures are very important, as just a slight deviation in their position can completely alter the entire cultivation process. The one that I taught you before was a fifth ranked cultivation technique called the Thunder-Bird technique, while that elder's technique was only at the third rank."

While waiting for Calron to absorb all the new information, the voice continued.

"However, the higher the rank of the technique, the harder it is to comprehend it. I created the Thunderbird technique, and I doubt any other elementalists are cultivating this technique."

Calron curiously listened the entire time, and he was dumbfounded when his teacher mentioned the rank of the Thunderbird technique.

He knew the importance of cultivation techniques in his world, as they determined how fast a person's cultivation would be, especially in the early stages. His father had cultivated using a first rank beginner cultivation technique.

"My technique has three stages. The first is the hand gesture, which you have already perfected, and the next is the breathing technique. However, your body is not yet ready to endure the strain of this stage. Wait until you reach at least the second rank of the Spiritual stage before even attempting it."

Calron listened attentively to what his teacher was saying and mentally noted down the name of this technique.

The Thunder-Bird technique.

Calron just realized that his teacher had only explained the first two stages. He was wondering what the last stage was, and just as he was about to inquire about it, his stomach growled.

"Kid, the last stage is not something you have to worry about now. Go get some food, as I can't bear to listen to your stomach's grumbling."

Calron mumbled in embarrassment at his stomach's growling and turned to search around for his new gray robe. After finding it neatly folded at the foot of his bed, he quickly put it on as he prepared to leave the hut.

Closing the door behind him, Calron started walking towards the gathering hall he had seen earlier when he had first entered the Foundation building.

However, just as he arrived in the adjacent corridor, he saw a group of three female disciples casually chatting with each other.

The girls were roughly around Calron's age, while two of them were a bit taller than him and the last one was just about his height. At first glance, they all seemed really cute, but for Calron, food was of higher importance than the beauty of these girls at that moment.

Although all disciples wore gray robes, most of them had several designs and patterns etched into them, as they were accustomed to finer clothing back home.

From the girls' robes, it was clear to see they were young daughters of wealthy families, as their robes were etched with gold and silver threads. What kind of commoner's family could afford gold or silver stitching for their children's clothes?

Ignoring the girls, Calron continued to walk forward.
Just as he was about to pass by them, one girl looked directly into his eyes.

Her piercing ice-blue eyes tore through him, and Calron could not help but be startled by the stunning color of her irises.

They were breathtaking.

Her pale face and her ice-cold eyes bore into him. Although the other girls were also cute in their own right, standing next to this heavenly girl, their looks only appeared to be average.

Calron could only stare at her in a daze, unable to look away from her piercing eyes. The other girls soon stopped talking when they realized their friend was looking at something, and they turned their heads in unison until they saw a boy their age with dark hair and pitch-black eyes.

His gray robes indicated he was also a disciple like them, and besides that fact, there appeared to be nothing special about the boy. With a plain chubby face and a slim build, he was like any other scrawny eight-year-old.

"Who are you, boy?"
A clear and sweet voice sounded out from the beautiful girl Calron was staring at.

This brat—how much older than me does she think she is?

Although her bewitching eyes had captivated Calron for a moment, he was still not at the age where the thoughts of pretty girls could influence his mind.

So when the girl talked condescendingly to him, he decided he did not like this spoiled girl and any previous thoughts of admiration were instantly crushed.

He continued walking towards the gathering hall without responding to her; however, this only seemed to further infuriate the girl as she shouted back at him.

41

"How dare you ignore me? Don't you know who I am? Apologize for your rudeness this instant and I'll think about forgiving you."

The rude girl shrieked in her high-pitched voice.

The sweet voice from before was gone like the wind, and the voice of a shrill harpy replaced it. The ice-cold feeling Calron got from her was completely wrong. This brat had a raging hot temper.

Being yelled at by a girl the same age as him, Calron simply could not maintain his calm, and also after dealing with Warrick's condescending behavior this morning, he frankly had no more tolerance at this point.

Although he had forgotten the anger and grief of his family's death after meeting the Voice, those burning emotions were still there, lying in wait to be ignited again.

Calron abruptly stopped walking and slowly turned around to face the girls. His pitch-black eyes suddenly bore into the spoiled girl, and she immediately closed her mouth after seeing the convulsed expression on the boy's face.

Before his family's death, Calron was one of the most timid boys in the village, as he found it hard to make friends and usually played alone by himself.

However, that shy boy died the moment he picked up a shovel to dig graves to bury his family in the ground.

A barely visible trace of azure lightning suddenly flashed across his eyes.

The time of the world seemed to halt as if it were waiting for this boy's next command.

The boy simply said a single word.

"Disappear."

CHAPTER FIVE

Element-Less

Seeing the wrath and anger on the boy's face, the girls felt a profound fear surge through their hearts, while their knees quivered uncontrollably.

Suddenly, all three girls turned around and burst into motion as they tried to flee from the boy. They were not thinking rationally about the situation and were just acting purely on instinct.

If they had taken some time to consider, then they would have realized that the boy was just as young as them and that he could not possibly be a lot stronger than them.

If they also knew that he was a lightning elementalist, then the girls would have died in shame at that moment.

After a few seconds, the blue-eyed girl's knees suddenly gave out, and she fell with an abrupt yelp. She frantically glanced back to see if Calron was still following her.

Seeing the boy continue to stand there while exuding such great killing intent, she painfully struggled back onto her feet and immediately sprinted to catch up to the other girls.

Although her heart was still trembling with fear, a small ember of anger started to slowly burn within her chest when she realized this boy had dared to publicly humiliate her like this.

Vowing retribution, she swallowed her pride for the moment and continued fleeing.

Meanwhile, Calron desperately tried to restrain the pain shooting through him, as veins popped up all across his body.

"You need to control yourself, kid. You are not yet ready to control the Azure Lightning, and if you try to force it out like this again, your life could be in danger. Your current body is simply too weak to endure the strain. Now, try to steady your breathing and force the lightning back into your core."

Under his teacher's guidance, Calron painfully forced the Azure Lightning back into his body bit by bit until the agony truly stopped.

Breathing a sigh of relief, Calron wiped the sweat off his forehead while looking down at his sweat-soaked robe. He promised himself that he would not call out the Azure Lightning until he was ready in the future. The gut-wrenching pain it brought was too unbearable for eight-year-old Calron.

In truth, Calron was not angry with the girls, as they were simply spoiled and rude. It was just that his emotions were extremely unstable at the moment, as it had just been a day since he had to bury his family. He was now completely alone in the world.

He was an orphan.

Furthermore, the azure lightning that awakened inside of him was utterly unfathomable and seemed to bring more destruction to him than his enemies.

"Kid, no need to fret this much over that Azure Lightning. It does not truly wish to harm you, but its very nature is violent, and until you reach at least the peak of the Spiritual stage, using the Azure Lightning would just cause you further torment."

The Voice stated in a consoling tone, as it tried to ease its student's worries.

grumble

"Enough of this. Go eat, NOW!"

The Voice's yell immediately jolted Calron out of his stupor, and he quickly rushed towards the gathering hall while ruffling his robe into a presentable form.

....

Arriving at the entrance of the hall, Calron saw that quite a few disciples were already seated in groups at the tables as they chatted with their friends.

Calron walked towards the lady who was handing out the meals.

Although all disciples could order various luxurious foods; however, they had to pay extra money out of their own pockets to request them. The prices of those luxurious foods were simply too exorbitant for commoners like Calron, so it was only the wealthy who could afford them.

"Excuse me, Madam, may I please have a meal?"

Calron politely asked the lady behind the counter. He recalled that this was the same woman who had previously handed out a cultivation pill to the elder.

"Of course, young man. Today's meal is a cut of pheasant, a loaf of bread, and some sweet cider."

The lady said while handing out Calron a tray full of the specified food.

"And here's a little extra meat for a cute, polite boy like you."

The lady said sweetly while pinching Calron's cheek.

Calron thanked the lady for her generosity as he gingerly rubbed his reddened cheek. Giving a slight bow to the woman, Calron set out to find an empty table to eat his meal.

Calron might act indifferent toward others or even lash out in anger, but to the ones who treat him kindly, he would always pay back that kindness ten times over.

Calron soon located an empty table and started slowly walking toward it. After sitting down, he immediately began wolfing down the food on the spot while lightly listening to the gossip from the other disciples' conversations.

Most of the chatter was about their training and boasting about their progress, but some were about who the strongest Martial Masters were, and who was the most beautiful girl in the school.

Calron tuned out of their conversations and thought about his current predicament. He needed a Martial Arts teacher and as a lightning elementalist, most of the Masters would not even bother with him.

Which Martial Master would want to pass down their fighting Arts to a weakling?

He could ask the Voice, but getting mental information about Martial Arts and physically learning it were vastly different.
Martial Arts required a cultivator to practice the same movements repeatedly in conjunction with the essence, as they adapted their body to remember those movements instinctively.

Although the Voice could teach him those movements, it would still be impossible for Calron to properly train without having a physical partner to spar, and to correct any minor errors he might make in the stances.

While contemplating this predicament, Calron had nearly finished all the food on the tray when he heard a sudden *click clack* sound of a wooden stick tapping against the floor.

Glancing up from his tray, Calron saw an old man who was reaching out his hand to grab a chair on Calron's table.

After the old man grasped the top of one of the chairs, he slowly sat down and groaned in relief. He had seated himself on the chair directly across from Calron.

It was at that moment when Calron finally looked into the old man's eyes and realized that the elderly man was completely blind.

The old man's pupils were a dull gray color and looked faded, as if there were an opaque layer of film covering his eyes.

The blind man also wore a gray robe, but it was much lighter than the ones the disciples wore. Calron curiously wondered who this old man was, as he clearly was not one of the Elders, who were easily recognized through their black robes.

The blind man's robe also looked worn out with several torn patches, and it was evident that this elderly man had been wearing this same cloth for many years.

"Young man, will you please fetch a meal for this blind old fool? Gretha knows me, so don't worry about her thinking you're stealing an extra. I'm afraid these old bones just don't have any spring in them anymore."

The blind man gently requested Calron.

Being asked by a handicapped person, how could Calron deny fulfilling the request of this blind man?

However, what Calron had failed to notice was that this blind man, who was supposed to be unable to see, clearly called him a young man. How did he even know how old Calron was when Calron never even spoke a single word?

"Please wait here, sir, and I'll go get you your meal."

Calron politely responded as he stood up and walked back towards the lady.

Gretha had already noticed the old man enter and chat with Calron, so she knew the boy was coming for the old man's meal. She immediately started to prepare the tray as soon as Calron arrived in front of her.

Handing the tray to the boy, Gretha sincerely thanked him.

"Thank you, little one, as few disciples bother to help old Elias. I usually have to give him his tray at the end of my work hours, as I cannot leave my station here, so the poor man has to wait for hours until he can finally eat."

Gretha was visibly sympathetic to Elias, and Calron could sense that it hurt the woman to watch the old man wait for hours in hunger. Although it would only take her two minutes to walk ahead and give the tray to the blind man, in a society that followed the strict hierarchy of power, she had to first feed the disciples and the elders before giving out the food to the weak and crippled.

"Why won't the other disciples help him?"

Calron inquired angrily.

Not helping someone weak and disabled was despicable, according to Calron's ideals.

"Well, Elias is an Element-Less."

With that one word, Calron immediately understood why no one would help the old man.

In this world, the only other person who was said to be weaker than a lightning elementalist was a person who did not even have an element, an Element-Less.

"Rumors are that he was injured and lost his essence in a war long ago. Only the school's head knows the actual truth about Elias, as it was the head who saved his life after the war and brought him back to the Red Boar School. However, the head is rarely at the school, so everyone just mistreats Elias. Without an element, or his sight, how could the poor man even fight back?"

Gretha sorrowfully explained it to Calron.

Although the technique was now forbidden, during the age of war, elementalists would sometimes sacrifice their entire cultivation for a single moment of tremendous power.

The technique was now forgotten, and only the last survivors of the war remembered it. However, none of them would teach that technique to their disciples, as it would destroy their future.

The forbidden technique had the potential to raise one's cultivation by an entire realm. If a Vajra stage expert used this technique, then he would be able to directly enter the Saint stage for a brief moment. However, it came at the price of never being able to cultivate again.

"You should take the tray to Elias now and tell him that I'll come visit him after I'm done with my shift."

Gretha softly stated this as she handed out the tray to Calron.

A few disciples in the waiting line were impatiently glaring at her for the delay in their food, so Calron quickly grabbed the tray and started walking back to his table.

The old man had hardly moved from his seat and simply sat there with his eyes closed. He was humming a tune when Calron returned to give him the tray of food. Gently placing the tray in front of Elias, Calron softly whispered to the old man.

"Sir, I placed your tray of food in front of you."

The old man suddenly stopped humming as his eyes slowly opened.

Dull gray eyes stared back at Calron, and he felt as if this blind man's eyes could pierce straight through his very soul.

"Such a polite young man. What is your name, child?"
The old man asked Calron in a calm voice.

"Calron."

"So Calron, judging from your polite tone, and that you were even willing to chat with me, I'm guessing that you are a new servant here?"
Elias inquired as he slowly chewed his food.

Although the old man was blind and appeared shabby, there was a certain grace in the way that he cut his food and elegantly chewed. It reminded Calron of the elegant Noble families of the city.

"Actually, I'm a new disciple at the Red Boar School."
Calron tentatively answered Elias.

Calron guessed why the old man would think that he was a servant, as only people with weak cultivation would be polite to an Element-Less like Elias.

"What? You're a disciple of the school? Did they really let a lightning elementalist enroll here? Boy, you're not messing with this old man, are you?"
Elias asked in a disbelieving voice.

Calron was stunned when Elias mentioned his Lightning element, but after thinking for a while, the only explanation he could come up with was that the old man had probably heard the rumors around the school. Otherwise, how else could the blind man know about his element?

"I was sponsored by Lord Regis as a disciple here for two years. I will be under his command after that time is over."

Calron stoically replied to Elias's barrage of questions.

Hearing the emotionless tone in the young boy's voice, Elias felt a tinge of pity in his heart. He knew exactly the type of lives Lightning elementalists lived, and there was nothing that could change their fates.

After that, the two stayed till midnight as they chatted about their lives. Calron talked about his family and life in the village, and Elias about his time serving in the Royal Army. Calron talked little besides mentioning the death of his family, to which Elias gave a sympathetic pat on his back.

What Calron enjoyed the most were the tales of combat from Elias's war stories. Calron was still an eight-year-old boy, and stories of battles and war excited him to a great extent.

Although Elias's stories were vague on what his actual position in the army was, Calron figured out that Elias was once a Fire elementalist and at least at the peak of the Vajra stage, or even at the Saint stage.

Calron stared in awe at this blind man without even a hint of doubt in his eyes.

When the other disciples in the room overheard Elias's tales, they scoffed in ridicule at Elias's claims of once being a mighty figure in the Royal Army. Calron paid no attention to the other disciples' sneers or mockery and instead continued to listen to Elias's tales.

Elias never mentioned how he got blinded, or the point when he became an Element-Less, but Calron did not truly care. It was the first time he felt such a close connection to someone else besides his family, and he simply wanted to talk to someone.

With the moon brightly glowing in the starry sky, a young boy and a blind old man exchanged their stories, as they just enjoyed each other's company.

Only a few disciples were remaining in the gathering hall, and they soon dispersed as well, as some went off to cultivate in the night, or just go to sleep in their huts.

Seeing that it was getting late, Elias finally decided that it was time to go back home and brought the chat between him and the boy to an end.

"Calron, it has been many years since this old man had someone to talk to, and I thank you for listening to these tales of mine."
Elias sincerely conveyed to the young boy, as he gently grasped his shoulder.

After losing his ability to cultivate an element, Elias had been constantly ridiculed by others, and besides a few servants like Gretha who pitied him or the school Head, there was no one else who bothered to talk to him.

Giving a slight bow to the old man, Calron happily responded.
"It was my pleasure, and thank you as well for listening to my story. I wish you a good night."

Hearing the politeness of the boy, Elias let out a low chuckle as he turned around and started walking away.

Hearing the click-clack of the wooden stick, Calron also turned around and trudged back to his hut. After his very first cultivation training, and the strain of using the Azure Lightning, it had completely exhausted Calron's small body.

Just as Calron had left the gathering hall, three shadows separated themselves from the surroundings, and stealthily followed the boy in the darkness.

....

Elias's eyebrows suddenly flickered as he stopped in his tracks, and tilted his head back towards the direction of the gathering hall. Throwing away his wooden stick to the side, Elias abruptly vanished from his spot.

....

Calron was feeling slightly drowsy from all the apple cider that he had a while back, and he was ready to crash into his bed for a good night's sleep. Just as he entered the corridor of the disciples' huts, the Azure Lightning within his body suddenly sent a shock to his brain.

"You really should not have insulted Lady Felice, you little brat."

A cold voice whispered in the darkness, as a mysterious person sent a thick killing intent towards Calron.

Two more shadows coalesced next to the mysterious person, and their features slowly became clearer as they stepped into the moonlight.

A veil of dark fabric obscured their faces, as only their cruel eyes gazed at Calron. The three people all wore the same stygian-colored uniform, and under the pale moonlight, Calron suddenly noticed the glimmer of metal in their hands.

For the first time in his life, Calron felt afraid.

Calron slowly stepped backward, as if that small distance would be able to protect him from these assassins. With his heart and mind in turmoil, Calron completely forgot to use his essence, but even if he did, he was pretty sure these assassins could still thoroughly suppress him.

The assassin in the middle suddenly moved.

All Calron saw was the shine of the metal coming closer and closer to his face. He shut his eyes tight as tears started to flow down his cheeks.

At this moment, Calron was not afraid of death or pain. It was the thought of not being able to avenge the deaths of his family that brought these tears of anger and helplessness.

Regret.
Anger.
Vengeance.

"I'm sorry father, I'm sorry mother...I'm sorry..."

Just at that moment, another shadow flickered across the scene, and a trail of blood sprayed into the darkness of the night.

Drops of blood splattered onto Calron's face as the boy slowly opened his eyes.

Without stopping his rhythm, the unfamiliar shadow suddenly flashed behind the second assassin, as another stream of blood sprayed under the moonlight.

A severed head silently thudded onto the ground.

The last remaining assassin's face was contorted in anger and fear as he gazed at the killer of his brothers.

Two assassins had been killed within seconds, and neither the last assassin nor Calron even had the time to see who the new mysterious shadow was.

Meanwhile, the last assassin's mind was full of shock. Both of his companions were in the eighth rank of the Spiritual stage, and they had been slaughtered like chickens, without even getting the chance to release their essence.

This man was a supreme expert.

What both Calron and the last assassin had failed to notice was that this mysterious shadow had not even released a speck of essence from the very beginning.

"You shouldn't have tried to hurt the boy."
An icy and deadly voice resonated in the air.

Shock.

Calron recognized that voice.
It was the same voice of the person with whom he had just shared his life stories a while ago.

swish

Another lifeless corpse fell to the ground, as it stained the grass with dark crimson blood. All three assassins had been killed within barely a minute.

What kind of power was this?

From start to finish, Calron could not even see the movements of the old man. How could the old man even see where his opponents were?
Wasn't Elias blind? Or was it just a pretense?

"Hahaha, that was fantastic. Don't worry, kid, he's truly blind, but he's only blind in his vision, as he sees the world through his Divine Perception. Hahaha, to think there was someone like him here. This is truly fascinating!"
The Voice excitedly exclaimed within Calron's mind.

Drops of blood slowly dripped onto the floor, as Calron realized he was covered in blood as well. It was the blood of the first assassin.

Before Calron could wipe away the blood, Elias slowly turned around with his gray eyes mysteriously glowing under the moonlight and solemnly addressed Calron with a slight smile on his face.

"Boy, do you want to inherit my Legacy?"

CHAPTER SIX

Twin Demons

"Commander Elias, the army is ready."

A lone silhouette stood at the edge of the cliff as he stared down at the multitude of masses stationed below the cliff. With his dark red hair fluttering in the wind, the expression on the man's face was one of calm and absolute authority.

Wearing dark blood-red armor, the man was an imposing figure as he stood on that cliff.

A soldier was currently kneeling behind the red-haired man as he patiently waited for further commands from his commander.

"Where is Marcus?"
Elias asked the soldier without turning around.

Faced with this question, the soldier let out a faint smile. Although the soldier could not see Elias's face, there was also a hint of amusement in Elias's expression when he asked this question to the soldier.

"The prince is... well, uh.... contained by the... ehem, female soldiers."

The soldier hesitantly replied with a red face, as it was mostly his squad's female elementalists that were the ones who were pestering the prince.

Elias could not contain himself anymore and burst out in a belly full of laughter.

"Hahaha, that kid. No matter where we go, he still has his female followers pestering him. Anyway, this will lighten the mood before we set out for the first battle, so it's fine. Marcus needs to solve this problem on his own, otherwise, once he gets married, I'm afraid his wife will leave him after the first day. Hahaha!"

Seeing the Commander himself laugh, the soldier let out a grin as well. He knew how popular the Prince was with the ladies of the court, and that seemed to extend to all young females of the kingdom.

At sixteen years old, with milky-white skin and raven-black hair, along with his dark emerald eyes, Marcus was more of a beautiful male than handsome.

Combined with his compassionate personality and amiable attitude towards others, Marcus found it difficult to directly reject any female's advances.

step *step*

Hearing the soft footsteps, both men turned around to look at the newcomer.

Seeing who it was, the soldier quickly saluted Elias and returned to his post. He knew that these two powerful men would like to be in private, so he swiftly departed.

"It appears that wherever we go, carnage and bloodshed seem to follow us, old friend."

The newcomer stated as he continued to slowly walk towards the cliff where Elias was standing.

The newcomer had dark purple hair mixed with strands of gray, and eyes the color of black jade. With a thin face, he had a sharp jawline and excluded an aura that was no less authoritative than Elias's.

He was just as tall as Elias, but lacked the muscular structure of his friend.

In response to his companion, Elias simply looked toward the sky and said.

"This war feels different, Solin. Our enemy this time is the Kingdom of Gastron, but we've always been on peaceful terms with them, so why did they suddenly declare war on us? It just makes little sense."

Elias did not feel the need to hide anything from Solin, as he was his closest friend since childhood and they had both fought together in countless battles.

"What does your brother say about this?"
Solin inquired as he wrinkled his eyebrows.

"My brother is suspicious as well, but as the King, no matter how false of a threat, he has to send an army to defend our Kingdom of Xuria and its people. He fears that someone is trying to cause unrest in Xuria, but with no proof, he does not dare to accuse any of the Nobles."
Elias solemnly responded as he gazed at the horizon.

It was not surprising that in a world dominated by power, even Kings had to be wary of their subjects, as the moment they showed weakness, was the moment they would be overthrown.

It was well known that familial lineage was integral in determining both one's element and talent they would have in cultivating it. That was why, as a general rule, most Royal families nurtured many gifted children under their care.

Solin silently stood next to Elias without saying a single word and simply waited for his friend to finish pondering his thoughts. Solin was the son of a servant working in the Royal Palace, and would usually play by himself in the courtyard, when one day, a red-haired boy suddenly approached him.

The red-haired boy had an enormous grin on his face as he cheerfully introduced himself to Solin. Although Solin had been wary of the boy's noble status, it soon became apparent that the red-haired boy did not care about Solin's background.

Once Solin awakened to his element, they discovered that he had an extremely high talent for cultivating, despite his commoner's blood. So, Elias begged his father, the King at that time, to allow Solin to train in the cultivation techniques of the family.

Usually, when faced with such a request, the King would have denied it even if it was his son asking him, but with Solin's talent in the Wind element, he knew that his son would have a powerful companion once they grew up.

Soon, the two boys developed an unbreakable bond and entered the Royal Army together.

Many years had passed with countless battles and skirmishes, which led these two men to stand here. They were the veritable geniuses of their Kingdom and with the strength to back it; they eventually became one of the most feared duos in the Royal Army.

....

"Uncle. So this is where you were. I was looking all over the barracks for you."

Hearing the melodious voice of his nephew, Elias broke free from his daze and turned around to face Marcus with a mirthful smirk on his face.

Solin similarly gave a faint smile at the spectacle in front of him.

"The barracks are only so small, and you should have been out of them after a few minutes, so I wonder what could have kept you there for so long?"

Elias inquired with an amused tone, as he raised a single eyebrow.

Marcus's face suddenly turned bright red, and he stumbled on how to respond to his uncle.

Seeing the blushing Marcus, Elias stopped his teasing for the moment. He was glad that his nephew still had the innocence of youth and not the mindset of a power-hungry cultivator.

He would have kept his nephew away from this war, but his brother wished for his son to experience the brutality of war. Otherwise, Marcus would never have that ruthlessness and would be devoured by the nobles in the Royal Palace.

"Hahaha, I was just teasing you, kid. Just remember to stay on the other side and just observe the battle. There is no need for you to get involved, as you are still in the Spiritual stage. Make sure to stay safe, and I will also dispatch a contingent of guards for you."

Elias chuckled as he patted Marcus on his shoulder.

"Uncle, I would like to fight as well."

With this one sentence, Marcus's entire demeanor changed.

While everyone would think of him to be a shy youth who would often get harassed by girls; however, within the boy ran the blood of the Royal Family, so how could he not have the same power as the rest of his family?

Although he was only sixteen years of age, he was already at the ninth rank of the Spiritual stage with half a foot entering the Vajra stage.

He was almost at the point of breakthrough, and if not for the war suddenly spreading across the kingdoms, then Marcus would be currently training to break into the Vajra stage.

"Sigh... Marcus, I know exactly how strong you are and I'm sure that none of the elite soldiers here would even be a match for you, but you're still the prince. The future of this kingdom is within your hands, and unless absolutely required, you should not carelessly charge into battle. You still haven't mastered our family's legacy, so just observe for now. Is that understood?"

Hearing the stern voice of Elias who had drilled Martial Arts into him, Marcus subconsciously nodded and bowed his head in acceptance.

A loud horn abruptly sounded in the air, as it startled everyone.

"Elias, it is time."
Solin quietly whispered next to Elias.

"I think it's also time to remind the world who the Twin Demons are."
Elias muttered, as a savage grin spread across his face.

With the horn blowing, everyone knew it was finally time for the battle to start and waves of killing intent could be seen spreading throughout the camp. Elias's gray eyes flashed with a strange glow as he released his essence into the air.

This was what he lived for, the thrill of the battle and the slaughtering of people. He was not royalty, not a commander, not an uncle or a brother, but simply a man who wanted to test the limits of his Martial Arts in the blood of his enemies.

"Get ready Solin. We will depart once the sun sets."
Elias quietly whispered to his brother-in-arms with a slight smile on his face, as he eagerly awaited the start of the battle.

....

While the red sun was slowly setting, a massive army silently stood at the edge of the terrain as it faced a similarly sized opponent. Although it was eerily quiet, the bloodlust in the atmosphere could not be mistaken.

At the forefront of one of the armies, stood a mighty onyx black warhorse with a tall rider dressed in a dark blood-red suit of armor.

Another warhorse with a pure white coat stepped up behind Elias, with its rider carrying a monstrous long bow behind his back. This was Solin.

Elias silently unsheathed his massive sword and raised it toward the rumbling sky. He spoke a single word, but that word echoed throughout the entire battlefield, causing the hearts of the soldiers to tremble in fear.

"SLAUGHTER!"

....

Meanwhile, Marcus silently watched from the sidelines. He restrained himself from charging towards the battle behind his Uncle, and instead just observed the two armies. His guards remained on high alert behind him.

....

It was a complete massacre on the battlefield.

It had only been a few minutes since it started, but the smell of blood and gore had deeply infused the air.

Desperate cries of agony and amputated limbs could be heard and seen everywhere, as rivers of blood flowed around the corpses and turned the ground to a dark crimson hue.

It was as if hell itself had descended upon the mortal world, and in the center of this carnage stood two figures bathed in the blood of their enemies.

While one figure cruelly butchered the soldiers apart like meat, another one used his vicious bow to puncture the throats of men.

They were aptly named, for they were given the title of the Twin Demons.

There was no sign of humanity within their eyes, and one could only guess how many people the two demons had killed to achieve this level of brutality and savagery against their kind.

Within the detached consciousness of Elias, he could not help but think that something was very wrong here.

The Kingdom of Gastron should have known that both he and Solin would definitely be dispatched to the war, but they still sent common soldiers against them.

Elias continued to slaughter his enemies, but the unease within his heart continued to grow.

....

On the other side of the enemy headquarters, a mysterious trio silently walked toward the center of the battlefield.

No signs of emotion flashed across their eyes as they walked through the carnage and bloodshed. The most shocking fact was that whenever a loose arrow or an elemental attack came their way, someone quietly incinerated it before it even reached a foot from them.

The trio wore bright silver robes, and against the darkness of the night, their robes shone brightly like a collage of moons. Hidden under their robes, it was plain to see that all three of them were completely armored in metallic plates.

Two of them were male, while the third one was a female from her slight figure and the shape of her body.

They did not exude any aura, so it was difficult to tell what their cultivation stage was.

The trio stopped after a few seconds, and in the woman's hand, a slim longbow appeared from thin air.

The bow was decorated with intricate patterns and edged with a silver lining. The string was taut and extremely thick, and one could imagine the extraordinary strength that would be required to draw that string.

Condensing her essence into the shape of an arrow, the woman silently aimed while the essence around the arrow increased by the very second. The air around the arrow distorted at the sheer amount of essence being gathered.

Suddenly, the earth quivered and the surrounding wind screeched as if being pierced by a thousand needles. The knees of every soldier on the battlefield trembled under the suffocating pressure, and even Elias and Solin were frozen by this oppressive display of power.

Their hearts felt like they were being crushed from the inside, and for someone to suppress them both to this extent, it meant that the enemy was at least at the Saint stage.

The hearts of everyone on the battlefield suddenly froze.

Even the enemy Commander of Gastron did not know who these people were, and he hesitated to give any further commands to his soldiers, so he simply awaited the next actions of these ultimate experts.

Once the elemental arrow was buzzing with raw power, the woman quietly took aim and released the arrow.

BOOOM.

The sound of a loud explosion erupted once the arrow was released from the bow.

It was right at this moment that Solin realized just where this arrow was aimed at. The only reason he could tell was because of his extraordinary talent in the cultivation of the Wind element.

Solin felt numb to his core as he thought about the repercussions of what would happen to his kingdom if the arrow pierced through its intended target.

All blood drained from his face as he realized that his closest friend would soon die, and he would have to helplessly watch his brother fall.

Just as the elemental arrow was about to pierce Elias, Solin forcefully shattered his elemental core.

CRACK

Solin's blood started to violently surge through his veins, and his soul separated from his body as it developed a separate realm of its own.

His purple hair wildly floated in the air, as his emerald eyes flashed with an intense light.

Solin's heart pounded against his chest when he felt the uncontrollable amount of power flowing through him.

He had just entered the Saint stage.

This transformation had all happened within a fraction of a second, and with no time to lose, Solin instantly rushed in front of Elias just in time to take the full-blown might of the elemental arrow.

BOOOM.

Even with the might of the Saint stage, Solin felt a soul-crushing amount of pain wreck through his body.

"ARGGGHHH!!"
Both of Solin's arms were bent at odd angles, and even the bones of his legs could clearly be seen against the dark red blood covering his body. Solin coughed up a mouthful of blood before spitting it on the ground.

What was this?
Solin thought while hanging on to his wavering life force.

This was not the might of an expert in the Saint stage, but the absolute domination of a Heavenly stage elementalist.

This whole time, Elias had not even realized that he was the actual target of the elemental arrow.

As he looked down upon the almost lifeless body of the man whom he called brother, and the one who risked everything including his life to protect him, Elias's heart burned with rage at the person responsible for this.

"Run...Eli...as... Heav..."
Rasping these words as he struggled with each breath, Solin weakly reached out his hand towards Elias, but suddenly collapsed as his soul left his mortal body.

When he saw his brother take his last breath, Elias felt raging wrath churn his insides, as the fury within his eyes burned with an inextinguishable will.

"UNCLE!"
A youthful voice suddenly boomed in the silence of the battlefield, as it shook Elias from his murderous thoughts.

He knew the enemy was powerful if they could so easily defeat Solin, even when he had sacrificed his core in exchange for the tremendous boost of power. Elias guessed the enemy was at least in the Heavenly stage to kill Solin in a single strike.

And there were three of them.

If all of them were at the Heavenly stage, how could Elias even dare to hope of surviving this battle?

His first and foremost thought was to immediately escape with Marcus.

When Marcus had abruptly bellowed, it startled the mysterious trio of the supreme experts.

They guessed that he was also a member of the Royal Xurian Family, as he referred to the other man as his 'uncle'.

Another elemental arrow swiftly appeared within the woman's hand and she immediately released the arrow the moment it formed, giving no one the chance to register what was happening.

Obviously, for a person still in the Spiritual stage, the woman did not have to spend as much energy as before.

The arrow flew straight and, in an instant, it brutally drilled through Marcus's skull.

The boy's head exploded, as parts of his brain and blood splattered onto the guards behind him. The guards did not even realize what had happened until the blood smeared their faces.

The prince of the Xurian Kingdom had just died in a second.

Silence.

There was absolute silence on both sides.

CRACK

The sound of someone's core being shattered resounded throughout the battlefield.

"ARRRRGGGGGHHHHH!! YOU BASTARDS! I'LL KILL YOU! I WILL SLAUGHTER EVERY ONE OF YOU!!"

Any trace of sanity left his body, and Elias sacrificed everything for a chance to kill this woman: the murderer of his nephew.

This was the first time Elias had truly wanted to kill someone out of pure hatred.

Taking the life of that woman was not only his duty as a soldier, but the righteous revenge of an uncle seeking retribution for his beloved nephew.

Just at that moment, Elias heard a snort.

"Haha, you will kill us? Do you even have the capability to threaten us? I will show you the power that separates us."

Immediately, countless blades of wind coalesced around Elias and pierced through his skin, as it shredded his flesh like paper. Blood freely seeped from the cuts and even the body of a Saint stage cultivator could not protect him.

"Die like the insect you are. I can't believe HE sent us out to dispatch you and your family."

With a wave of her delicate hand, a hammer of wind formed above Elias and crushed him deep into the earth. Sounds of bone shattering and the painful screams of a man could be heard before a deep empty crater was formed in the center of the battlefield.

The last thought Elias had before he lost consciousness was, *Who were these people?*

Floating above the ground, the trio looked down upon the crater, and seeing no sign of life below, they quietly turned around and gradually vanished without a single trace.

No one knew who these people were, but they knew that on this day, the entire Xurian Royal Family would be massacred in their city.

....

Sorrowfully opening his eyes, Elias looked at the carnage in front of his eyes.

The three assassins he had just killed lay unmoving on the ground while their blood stained the soil beneath them.

He had somehow miraculously survived the war back then, and woken up the next morning with his entire body broken, and with half a step into the world of the dead. Without the help of the school's Head, Elias would not have survived to this day.

Gazing at the young boy who reminded him so much of Marcus, how could he simply walk away when others tried to harm this boy?

He could not save the life of a child that day, but he would not make the same mistake twice.

He did not know what came over him, but on the spur of the moment, he pivoted his head around and quietly asked the shivering child.

"Boy, do you want to inherit my Legacy?"

CHAPTER SEVEN

Axier Family

"Boy, do you want to inherit my Legacy?"

It was a simple question, but the words reverberated through the darkness of the night.

Two figures stood in the open corridor as a gentle wind breezed past them. No sounds could be heard, and it seemed as if all life quietly waited to hear the response of the boy.

The world seemed to stop, and time slowly trickled as it froze the scene of the two figures: an old man solemnly looking down at a shivering young boy with blood smeared across his face.

Calron's mind was blank.

What he had just witnessed should have been impossible, unless it was an expert at the Vajra Stage. But the old man clearly did not even have any essence to begin with.

Moreover, he was blind.

No matter how one would look at it, this situation should have been impossible.

However, Calron was clear on one thing: that this man was

definitely a Martial Master.

"Accept it, boy. You need a legacy of your own and seeing as you have no other blood relatives, this is a fortunate opportunity for you."
The Voice quietly sent his thoughts to Calron.

Elias stood still as he patiently waited for Calron's response. Not a hint of emotion flickered across his face.

Calron was on the verge of collapsing, as this was his first time experiencing senseless murder and the metallic taste of blood in his mouth. He knew he should be afraid at the gruesome sight of the massacred corpses, but deep within his soul, a feeling of hope started to bloom.

If the old man in front of him could easily kill men like those assassins, then he could teach Calron his Martial Arts and give him the strength needed to avenge his family.

Power.
That was the only thought running through Calron's mind.

"I, I accept...Master."
Right after rasping those few words, Calron immediately lost consciousness.

....

Elias grinned while gazing down at the unconscious boy.
Carefully picking him up from the ground, Elias quickly located Calron's hut, and soundlessly opened the door, as he gently placed the sleeping boy on the mattress.

If any of the other disciples or Gretha had seen the previous scene, then their jaws would have immediately dropped. This old man was supposed to be blind, but he could evidently see where the boy was, and the exact location of the bed.

This was simply too shocking.

But, how could anyone know Elias was a practitioner of the God Class Technique, known as the Divine Perception?

This was a technique that had even astonished the Voice in Calron's body, so how could it be so simple?

Divine Perception was an omnipotent ability to sense essence in nature and all cultivators. This was how Elias knew Calron was a Lightning elementalist, even though he could not physically see him.

Everything in the world has traces of essence, including inanimate objects such as chairs or rocks. Elementalists could normally detect essence if another cultivator released it, but if the cultivator chose not to release his essence, then it would be very difficult to determine his true strength.

The Divine Perception technique was an exception to this rule.

With the power of the God class technique, one could detect every kind of essence in nature, and know the exact cultivation of any elementalist. Its main ability lay in the fact that practitioners of this technique did not even have to use any form of energy or essence to activate it.

This was the secret of how Elias could see, and if the fact ever got out that he practices one of the God class techniques, then there would be countless elementalists at his doorstep trying to glean the information out of him.

God class techniques were a mystery and in a league of their own, as even ninth rank techniques could not compare to them. Not much is known about what the various God class techniques were, but traces of their vast power were recorded in the books of history.

Each of the God class techniques had its limitations and

requirements to activate them, and it was unknown what the conditions were for the Divine Perception.

Elias carefully covered Calron with a warm blanket and quietly left the room. Stepping out into the open night, Elias tilted his head up as he looked at the bright moon floating in the sky.

"Sigh... the boy already made enemies on his first day. This will be troublesome..."

Elias murmured as he looked back down at the bloodstained ground, and the cold corpses spread there.

....

—The Next Morning—

Calron groggily woke up from his sleep as the sunlight burned through his eyelids.

Standing up from his bed, Calron lightly yawned as he felt the essence in his body recover from last night.

Smelling something rotten and vile, Calron slowly sniffed around the room as he tried to locate the source of the smell. He realized that the pungent smell was coming from him. Or more specifically, from the blood-soaked robe he was currently wearing.

"Ugh!"

Calron exclaimed with disgust as he looked down at his robes.

In a sudden daze, he abruptly remembered everything that had happened last night, from the ambush to the brutal killing by Elias.

No, his Master.

Calron quickly discarded the robe he was wearing and looked around to find his previous clothes. Although he was supposed to wear the gray robes every day, he rather not let anyone know about yesterday's bloodbath.

Searching for his old clothes, Calron soon spotted a mysterious bundle under his bed and slowly placed it on top of his bed. There was a small note next to the bundle, so Calron grabbed it and read the eloquently written handwriting.

"I found a spare robe for you, so wear it and burn the other one as soon as you can. I will teach you how to not get blood on you later in the future. Meet me at the back of the Foundation building after you finish your breakfast."

Although the handwriting was immaculate, there were still several words overlapping with each other, and Calron assumed that even though Elias could see through a mysterious technique, his actual eyesight was nonexistent.

Even without any signature on the note, Calron knew that this note was from his new Martial Master.

Swiftly opening the bundle, Calron grabbed the new clean robe and immediately donned it. After doing so, he washed his face with the pitcher of water outside and started walking towards the gathering hall for a quick meal.

When Calron stepped out his door, not a trace of blood appeared on the floor.

It was perfectly spotless.

....

"Good Morning, Gretha. May I please have some breakfast? Anything on the menu is fine."

Calron enthusiastically greeted the cooking lady and requested some quick food before he had to meet up with his new Martial Master.

After responding to Calron's greeting with a cheerful response, Gretha quickly prepared his tray as she hummed to herself.

She also seemed to be in a pleasant mood as she patted Calron on the head while handing out the nearly full tray to Calron. She playfully shooed him away before handing out the trays to the disciples behind Calron. Finding an empty table to sit down at, Calron quietly ate his meal.

The tray had a plate of warm eggs with some mushrooms, along with a loaf of bread and a small glass of milk. Munching on this delicious food, Calron happily greeted the Voice in his mind.

"Piss off, kid! Let me go back to sleep."

Wondering if ghosts could even sleep, Calron decided not to ponder on this matter and immediately gulped down the entire glass of milk, before setting off to meet Elias.

....

Going around the Foundation building, Calron tried finding any sign of Elias being there, but could barely find traces of the blind old man.

While walking, Calron heard many of the disciples whispering amongst themselves as they shot glances toward him.

"Hey, I heard this kid was a Lightning elementalist, is that true?... What? They honestly let those kinds of people in this school?.... This school's reputation is going down the drain.... But, he is kind of cute though..."

Ignoring all the whispers around him, Calron continued walking towards the back of the building. The number of disciples slowly decreased the further along he went, and once he finally reached the end of the block, the scenery in front of him stunned Calron.

It was a forest.

Calron was utterly puzzled how a forest could appear here when he had not once seen anything resembling wildlife while he was walking around the building.

"It is one of the precious Artifacts of the school, Calron."
A calm voice sounded out from behind Calron.

Turning around, Calron faced the sight of Elias leaning against the wall with a walking stick in his hand.

"Master."
Calron greeted Elias as he gave a slight bow.

Pleased with the inherent respect displayed by this young boy towards him, a faint smile spread across Elias's face.

"Come, your first training will start inside the forest. Do not worry about anyone disturbing us, as it is a separated spatial plane that even the Elders are not allowed to enter. I was only given special permission by the school's Head, as he was worried about the discrimination I would face, so he temporarily allowed me residence here."
Elias stated calmly as he tapped his wooden stick against the ground and began walking toward the forest.

Calron soon followed behind him, but just the moment that he stepped into the forest's entrance, he felt an unexpected sharp jolt and stumbled back onto the ground.

What was that?

Calron curiously wondered. It did not hurt him in the slightest, but the electric jolt certainly surprised him.

"Ah, I forgot. Here, hold on to this and enter again."

Elias turned around to face Calron as he flung out a circular wooden token at him. Calron deftly caught the small disk while slowly getting back to his feet.

Observing the token, it appeared to be a regular wooden disk with no special features. The only abnormal thing about the wooden token was its texture.

It felt soft to the touch, unlike any wood Calron had felt before. It was almost like caressing a piece of velvet.

Calron placed the token in his pocket and attempted to enter the forest again. Just as he took his first step into the forest, Calron felt a small tendril of essence emanating from the wooden token before it promptly vanished.

Looking around the forest, Calron was in a complete daze.

The illusion felt way too real. The sound of birds chirping echoed in the surroundings. There were countless trees spread across the forest and hints of a small lake in the distance shimmered within his sight.

Calron had never heard of an artifact with an unheralded ability to contain an entire dimension within it. But then again, in his world, Artifacts were objects of legends, and few people even had the chance of seeing one, let alone experience it.

"We have wasted enough time already. Hurry up, this place has no small amount of magical beasts and with the nearby lake, some of them ought to be hovering around. I can tell that you are curious about this artifact, so wait for a while and I will educate you in everything you need to know from Artifacts to Martial techniques."

Elias placated Calron as he threw away his wooden stick to the side and walked with a confident gait.

His Master now emanated the same powerful aura that Calron witnessed during last night's failed assassination.

This was his Master's true demeanor.

Since there was no one around, Elias didn't care about putting on the cripple act and started walking toward the lake while Calron kept on his heel.

The young boy couldn't help but stare at the marvelous forest during his brisk walk, and he was sure that he saw the silhouette of a magical beast, but couldn't be certain. Calron burst into a sprint when he realized his Master was increasing his speed.

After a while, a small shape of a hut gradually grew more and more visible as they drew near. The hut was small but looked extremely well taken care of. It was surrounded by a lush garden with a small patch of growing vegetation behind the hut.

"Calron, come sit here. It is time to finally begin your very first lesson."
Elias stated as he gestured for Calron to sit on the grass in front of him.

Sitting in a relaxed posture, Calron eagerly waited for Elias to continue speaking.

"Before we start your Martial Arts training, you need to learn something about the so-called legacies."
Elias stated in a serious tone.

Calron immediately straightened up, as he knew how mysterious the legacies were, and the power they held within the martial world. Although he did not know the whole details of the different legacies, it was widely known that only the most powerful people possessed them.

Every single legacy was unique, as each one followed a different path of martial training like the path of fist, sword, spear, etc.

Although many elementalists might practice Martial Arts, only the most talented and the direct disciples of their Masters could inherit a legacy.

In a fight between a Martial Artist and a legacy Inheritor, the one with the legacy would always win regardless of how weak his or her legacy was. This was the might of inheriting a legacy.

"Child, you might've heard various things about legacies before, but do you know the real reason legacy inheritors are so much stronger than their peers?"

Calron shook his head in response to the question.

"It is because a legacy cultivates your battle spirit and killing intent."

Calron's eyes dilated as he stared at his Master.

He knew exactly what this meant. To cultivate your fighting spirit or killing intent, one would have to experience life-threatening battles on a daily basis and kill without mercy.

For an eight-year-old, it was a horrifying thought that he would eventually have to kill his enemies.

Just then, Calron realized why a wild and violent atmosphere occasionally surrounded his Master, as it was because even without releasing his killing intent, Elias had already reached a stage where his mere presence released the unrestrained bloodlust in him.

Seeing the blood visibly drain from his disciple's face, Elias could guess the direction of Calron's thoughts, but he made no move to comfort him. The boy had to overcome his fear of killing others right now; otherwise, in the future, his hesitation could cost him his life.

Although he felt pity looking at his disciple, this was the path of his legacy and Elias had been even younger than Calron when his father had first trained him.

Even the Voice inside Calron's mind stayed silent through this. The mysterious entity naturally understood the boy's dilemma, but he knew that in Calron's future, there would be countless massacres and powerful people after him, so he could only hope that Calron would be prepared by then.

Meanwhile, Calron's thoughts were running wild and his horror at seeing the assassins killed yesterday surged through his mind once again. Despite his occasional cold and indifferent demeanor to others, he was still only an eight-year-old boy.

Could he really kill people? Could he genuinely stare into the lifeless eyes of the ones he had killed?

No, he couldn't. Absolutely not.
While these thoughts wildly ran through Calron's mind, Elias patiently waited for his student.

Father... Mother... What should I do?

Suddenly, a bolt of blue lightning surged through Calron's mind and shattered all his hesitant thoughts. His mind immediately regained its composure as his previous thoughts abruptly cleared up.

He had long ago vowed to seek revenge against the ones who harmed his family, and he had already embarked on the path of bloodshed back then, so why was he hesitating now?

Would his enemies give him a chance at life? Did they stop themselves from exploiting his father?

No.

In this world, how many would look down upon Calron and his Lightning element? Would they show him mercy, a person born to be a servant?

NO.
There was no place for mercy in this cruel world.

The strong made the rules, and the weak followed them. If this was the path that he would have to take to get his revenge, then he would gladly throw away his humanity: the humanity that deserted him and his family, and the same humanity that was never once shown to them.

Slowly, a determined expression formed on Calron's cherub face and Elias smiled at this sight as he knew that the one who would inherit his legacy was finally here.

Kneeling on the grass in front of the boy, Elias slowly placed his right hand on top of Calron's head and gazed fiercely into his disciple's pitch-black eyes. Seeing unmistakable resolve there, he stated in a somber tone.

"From today onwards, you will walk in the path of blood. Destruction and Carnage will be your sworn brothers and follow wherever you go. May the God of War bless and look favorably upon you and give rise to your valor. I, Elias Salazar Xuria, hereby acknowledge you as my Inheritor and pass on my will and legacy to you. Do you accept?"

"I do, Master."

Elias then cut the palm of his hand with a small knife and placed his bloody palm on Calron's forehead, the blood droplets steadily slithering into the young boy's eyes.

"The first blood has been shed, and from this day forth, you will walk the path of my family's legacy; the Legacy of Blood. Let's begin."

....

Meanwhile, at the Axier Household, a commotion could be heard from inside the family Head's room.

CRASH

"What do you mean they just simply disappeared?"
An ice-chilling voice threatened the man that kneeled on the floor.

The kneeling man was dressed in very similar clothes to the assassins that had tried to kill Calron previously.

The regal man on the throne had a head full of silver-gray hair and a trimmed beard. His face was cut like a stone sculpture, full of sharp edges and no softness. Although the man could not be labeled as handsome, there was a certain dignified nobility in his stature and aura. However, at this moment, only a chilling anger could be seen on his face.

Trembling under the pressure that the gray-haired man exuded, the assassin could only gulp down his saliva and pray to any of the gods listening for one more day of life.

"My Lord, they were all guarding the little lady, but the three never reported back the next morning. The others stationed at the school also did not know where they went. But..."
Under the glare of the giant man, the assassin hurriedly spoke.

"But there was a commotion regarding Lady Felice, where a boy humiliated her in front of her friends. Even if the little lady was safe, it was after that incident that the three who were guarding her vanished. Since we can't detect them, I'm afraid that they probably died a while ago. I suspect an enemy knew of the Shadow Corps stationed there and took action."

Silence.

Finally, the man spoke.

"Investigate the ones responsible for this and bring them to me. Use as many men as you need. As for the boy, leave him alone. Felice needs to learn how to be on her own, and I cannot always indulge her whims. Now, leave!"

Under the intensity of the blazing arctic-blue eyes of the man, the assassin shakingly bowed once, and then immediately disappeared into the night.

If Calron were here, then he would have instantly recognized those ice-cold eyes as they were almost exactly the same as the pretty girl he had humiliated the night before.

CHAPTER EIGHT

Legacy Of Blood

shua

Calron abruptly opened his eyes and saw the smiling familiar face of his Master. His vision was still tinged with red from the blood, but it started to slowly return to normal.

Calron sensed that the foreign blood was seeping deep into his body, as it merged with his muscle tissues and into the bone marrow. His cells multiplied at an alarming rate, and jolts of pain flared through his body as the transformation begun.

Although Calron could not see this phenomenon, his internal muscles and bones were currently emitting a faint crimson glow.

Consumed with an unbearable agony, Calron doubled over on the grass, as prayed for the pain to leave him.

His heart was furiously pounding against his chest, while his muscles continuously stretched and contracted, as they became denser by the very second. Although the size of his muscles stayed the same, at Calron's current muscle density, he could lift a large rock twice his height, without even the aid of his essence.

Calron's transformation continued for a full two hours until finally, the pain subsided slowly as it left a completely sweat-soaked boy in the middle of the garden.

Throughout the boy's transformation, Elias patiently waited at the side as he observed the changes happening in Calron. After losing his ability to cultivate essence, Elias' major worry had been that his family's legacy would die out and that he would be its last Inheritor.

Although every legacy inheritor went through the same initial transformation, the extent of one's transformation would vary according to how compatible one was with the legacy itself.

The Legacy of Blood resonated with violence and carnage, and since it had taken so long to transform the boy, it seemed as if within the depths of his soul, Calron subconsciously sought for a life of violence.

Elias had been the same when he was young, and this was the reason the Legacy of Blood had chosen him as its Prime Inheritor.

Whilst multiple practitioners could inherit the same legacy, its power dwindled as the number of Inheritors increased because of the sharing of the legacy's source pool. The only exception to this rule was the Prime Inheritor.

In a family that possessed a legacy, the head of the family would be the Prime Inheritor, and he would then pass this on to his eldest son. If the legacy did not designate his son as a Prime Inheritor, then the head of the family could only try for his next son or daughter, as the will of the legacy could never be forced.

When Elias's family had been exterminated on that fateful night, he felt the death of all his family's Inheritors, especially his father, and brother. Since they all shared the same source pool, their consciousness was linked and they could faintly detect each other's location and life force.

Once all the previous Inheritors of his family's legacy had died, Elias had felt an immense power flooding through his veins, as waves of source energy crashed into his body. This was one reason Elias had survived the onslaught of the silver-robed woman.

The source energy had constantly replenished his lost blood and regenerated his muscles and bones back to normal. Due to this, Elias could maintain his consciousness until the Red Boar School's Head coincidentally encountered him.

It wasn't till the next morning that Elias realized that yesterday's sudden surge of source energy was because of the death of his family members.

There could have been other surviving family members who were not legacy Inheritors. However, Elias had no hope for such a thing, as who could protect the other members from those monsters when the strongest of his family were all crushed so easily?

At this moment, within Elias's consciousness, he felt another bridge forming in the legacy's source pool. This new bridge was much thicker and stronger than his own. Elias felt an immeasurable joy at seeing this scene unfold; as it meant that a new Prime Inheritor was finally being born.

....

At the same time within Calron's consciousness, a similar scene was occurring, and this was his first time seeing the mental manifestation of the Legacy of Blood.

It was truly breathtaking.

It was an ocean of thick red blood surrounded by endless darkness. The crimson waves violently crashed against each other, and Calron felt the raw energy contained within them.

Just at the corner of the blood ocean, Calron noticed a decaying bridge connected to the blood ocean.

Sending his consciousness into the worn-out mental bridge,

Calron promptly entered the foreign entity. Delving deeper into the core of the bridge, Calron discovered another consciousness within that bridge.

It was his Master.

Right then, a tremor ran through Calron's mind.
Rumble

Another bridge slowly materialized in the opposite direction of the decaying bridge. The new bridge was much thicker and stronger than the other one and it seemed to burst with a limitless vitality.

Calron felt a mysterious connection with that new bridge and curiously sent his consciousness into it.

A ball of essence shot from Calron's core and rushed into the bridge, as bright blue light illuminated the entire construction. Soon, the light dimmed down as it revealed a faintly glowing azure-blue bridge.

The other decaying bridge seemed to lack this glow, and now there were no further doubts in Calron's mind that the worn-out bridge belonged to Elias, his Master.

"It is quite a sight, is it not?"

Hearing Elias's calm and gentle voice, Calron jolted awake from his inner consciousness and groggily opened his eyes.

Seeing the bewildered look on the boy's face, Elias smirked with fondness. Calron's Legacy of Blood had awakened today.

"Master, that red ocean... was that really all blood?"

Hearing Calron's question, Elias could not help but hesitate a bit. The truth was that even he did not know the answer to this.

"It is called a source pool, and every legacy has a source pool of its own, as this is where we Inheritors draw our strength from. The source pool differs greatly from the essence in your core, as you can draw the source energy regardless of what your elemental affinity is, or even the level of your cultivation."

Checking to see whether the boy was still listening, Elias continued his explanation.

"However, the greater you draw from the source pool, the greater the stress your body will have to endure. I am currently incapable of drawing upon the legacy's source pool for extended periods, and even when I do, without my essence I can only draw a minuscule amount from it…"

Elias finished speaking as a forlorn expression flickered across his face.

Calron could feel the regret and solitude emanating from his Master when he talked about the loss of his essence.

What was an eight-year-old boy like Calron supposed to do in this situation?

Realizing that his demeanor slipped for a brief moment, Elias quickly composed himself and started explaining more about the Legacy of Blood to Calron.

Elias felt it was too early to let Calron know the Legacy had chosen him as the Prime Inheritor, but the elderly man knew it was only a matter of time before the young boy would eventually discover it.

As the Prime Inheritor, the Legacy of Blood would influence Calron's mind more than usual, and he could also draw upon a tremendous amount of source energy. Deciding to contemplate this matter later, Elias resumed to explain the secrets of his family's legacy.

"Now Calron, I am sure that you have already guessed that the Legacy of Blood altered your physical body. I can sense your muscles coiling in tension and let me warn you before you do something irreversible: under no circumstances are you allowed to reveal this legacy or its power to anyone."

Elias's words dropped like an anvil in Calron's mind and killed all the excitement he had earlier.

Calron thought he would finally be on par with the other disciples, and not be so helpless as before, but with his Master's previous words, he would have to hide his strength and couldn't fight back.

How could Calron stay calm after hearing this?

Although Calron was born as a servant, deep within the depths of his heart, there was a small seed of arrogance and pride, which was just waiting to bloom. Or could the legacy already be influencing his personality?

After being attacked by those assassins yesterday, a shred of unknown fear lurked in the corner of Calron's mind due to experiencing the terror of realizing that his life was no longer in his own hands and he hated the feeling of being at the mercy of others.

This was unacceptable.

Calron had embarked on a path of revenge, so how could he cower like a coward when others were challenging him?

Seeing the indignant look on the boy's face, Elias could not help but feel like trouble would soon be on its way if he did not restrain Calron right now.

He knew that once Calron started training in the Legacy of Blood, his anger and rage would be uncontrollable, and if not restrained right now, then it would lead to an irreversible catastrophe in the future.

All Legacy Inheritors of his family had undergone a similar situation. It wasn't a coincidence that his nickname back then had been one of the "Twin Demons".

"Child, the Blood Legacy is brutality in its purest form, as it pushes the Inheritor towards violence and chaos. If you cannot control your emotions, then you will only become a tool for its destruction. The legacy has no motive or purpose, as it simply seeks violence in any form."

Elias seriously stated as he gazed deep into Calron's eyes.

"The Blood Legacy is neither evil nor good, it just exists. I am only telling you to restrain yourself until you can control its power. After you achieve that, I will give you the freedom to decide whichever path you wish to take."

Elias was intimately familiar with the savage bloodlust that his family's legacy possessed, as even he could not completely control it during a battle.

This was another reason why Elias did not want Calron to reveal his new strength to others right now, as the boy was simply too weak to deal with all the trouble that would follow him once he was exposed.

Meanwhile, Calron could only swallow his indignation and follow his Master's instructions, as he knew Elias was right.

"Now, let us begin your Martial Arts training."
Elias said with a slight smile on his face.

Hearing his Master's statement, Calron immediately sat up straight and focused his attention on Elias, his heart softly thudding against his chest.

"Stand up and copy the movements I am about to execute."
Elias spoke as he promptly moved in a slow, rhythmic pattern.

His arms moved in harmony with each other, as they sometimes punched, jabbed, or swept the air. The stances were akin to a musical melody as they flowed with Elias's entire body. Soon, he moved faster and faster, as Elias's arms became a blur of shadows, with the sound of wind whistling around the surroundings.

After a few minutes, Elias paused mid-movement and beckoned Calron to execute the stances he had just shown.

Calron excitedly stood up, as his eyes twinkled with a bursting enthusiasm.

Closing his eyes, Calron tried to recall the earlier stances and movements he had seen his Master execute and slowly began moving his arms.

Although the movements were clumsy at the start, they soon flowed in rhythm as Calron punched the air. However, just as he came to the part of switching between the stances, his legs and arms could not coordinate together.

The movements initially appeared to be simple, but in reality, they were intricately complicated to execute.

Elias had been momentarily stunned when Calron could perfectly grasp the rhythm of the arm movements, and he could not help but inwardly praise his disciple. Judging from his student's astonishing ability to comprehend Martial Arts, Elias was sure that Calron's future growth would be even more frightening.

These arm movements were part of the First Layer of the Blood Arts, and also the easiest one to comprehend. The further along you went in the layers, the higher the difficulty level. Even Elias had been unable to master all the layers of the Blood Arts, and he was known as a martial genius within the Xurian Kingdom.

Only his first ancestor, and the original Prime Inheritor of the Legacy of Blood, had ever reached the twelfth layer and experienced the ultimate power of the legacy.

Taking in a deep breath, Calron slowly entered a trance as he repeated the movements. His arms sped up, and they soon became a blur like his Master's.

swish *swish*
Elias stared in shock at the scene in front of him.

What is this? This is too abnormal.
Elias inwardly exclaimed, with a stunned expression on his face.

"This… is this the talent of a lightning elementalist? Or is it just Calron?"
Elias had initially taken in Calron as a student because of how much the boy had reminded him of Marcus, so he expected little from him.
However, Elias had been elated when the Blood Legacy chose Calron as its Prime Inheritor, as it meant that at least his family's legacy would not die with him.
Realizing that the boy he selected as his student turned out to be a martial genius, Elias felt a surge of hope rise within his heart.

Meanwhile, Calron continued executing the movements, as the newly strengthened muscles in his arms coiled like a dragon.

At that moment, Calron's skin emitted a faint crimson glow.

Calron was unknowingly drawing the source energy from the legacy's pool for the first time.
Not realizing that his eyes were glowing a deep blood-red color and that a savage aura had erupted around him, Calron remained in his trance.

The smell of blood languidly permeated the surrounding air.

"Hmm?"

CHAPTER NINE

Defiant

His body was aflame.

Anger. Rage. Wrath.

He wanted to destroy. To kill, and to kill even more. He stood above all beings, even the Gods themselves feared the power he held.

Life was meaningless in front of him. He was its natural reaper. A farmer, a soldier, a general, all perished under him.

An endless terrain of blood-soaked sand surrounded him, and it was unclear whether the sand itself was red or it was stained with real blood. The scorching sun rays burned through the sand and the countless corpses lying around him. Some bodies were skewered with spears, some with necks full of arrows, and countless more with missing limbs.

However, it was the smell in the air that exhilarated him.

It was the smell of blood.

He stood still on the deserted plain for over millennia as he waited for an opponent to test his might against. Blood dripped painstakingly from the tips of his fingers, making the already blood-colored sand appear more sinister.

His mighty chest rose and fell with each breath he took, meanwhile maintaining a mysterious smile etched onto his face.

Gazing at the multitudes of corpses surrounding him, a low chuckle escaped from his lips. What were once beings that stood at the peak of the heavens now lay lifeless around him.
Even the flow of time on this plain was under his domain.

Immortality was tedious.
Time was tedious.
Only the flow of blood was eternal.

He wanted to end his immortality and return to his past when he could still bleed mortal blood. Back to when he was still a human.

Back when he was not known as the Blood Ancient.

………………………..

Cough *Cough*
Calron abruptly spat out a mouthful of dark blood onto the grass below him. He continued to spew globules of nefarious blood until he felt like there was none left in his body anymore.

Each time he coughed, a stream of fresh blood would replace the old blood, and the process seemed to continue endlessly until not even a speck of his old blood remained in his veins.

Calron felt like several pores on his body were being forcefully opened, and the feeling was akin to the sensation of a thousand needles piercing his skin.

Elias calmly observed the changes around Calron, and he knew the boy was currently undergoing the opening of his meridians. This process would bring upon a mind-crushing agony, as this was the stage when the meridians would slowly connect to the spiritual veins within one's body.

The meridians were essential in letting an Inheritor draw the source energy from the legacy's pool.

The blood purging also expelled any impurities within one's body, but usually, it was only a small amount of blood that was expelled. However, Calron was perceivably spewing out large quantities of dark blood. Just the sheer amount of blood on the grass would have caused any grown man to die twice over, but Calron remained standing.

Too many abnormal events keep revolving around this boy.
Elias inwardly thought while observing the boy.

Even Elias was startled by the current scene unfolding before him. Was it because the power of the legacy was too much for Calron? The Blood Legacy's power had usually been shared among multiple Inheritors, and this was the first time known to Elias that the Blood Legacy's Inheritors had dwindled to only two members. Maybe this was causing an extra strain on Calron's body.

Meanwhile, Calron stared absentmindedly at the puddle of blood underneath him and was just as confused as Elias about what was happening within his body. What were those images he just saw? The scenes soon became hazy in Calron's mind, but he instinctively knew that the figure in those images had something to do with the Blood Legacy.

"I think this is enough for today. Get some rest to recover your body and meet me here again tomorrow morning."
Elias gently spoke to Calron and dismissed him for the day.

....

Calron painstakingly dragged his body away from the forest and slowly trudged towards the gathering hall. His thoughts kept revolving around the person he saw in the earlier images within his mind, but his brain seemed to freeze every time he tried to recall the person's face.

"Hmph, you forgot about cultivating your essence after all that Martial Arts crap. Kid, although the power of a legacy is great, you would still need a high enough cultivation to contend against tougher opponents. Hurry up to your room and let us begin. No eating until you finish cultivating today!"

The Voice strictly stated within Calron's mind as it urged the boy to resume his cultivation training.

Calron let out a depressed sigh and changed his walking direction towards the disciples' lodgings. After reaching his hut, Calron immediately sat down on the mat in a meditative position and started training under the first stage of the Thunderbird technique.

With his hands properly aligned, Calron began the rhythmic breathing of the technique and sensed the surrounding essence slowly being absorbed into his body.

With every passing second, his elemental core felt fuller and fuller, as tendrils of lightning essence gradually entered it. Calron continued to absorb the essence until he felt like his body could not any more essence.

After storing all the absorbed essences, Calron began refining it. When one absorbs the essence from the environment, it contains many impurities within it and if the essence was not refined to its purest state, then it would affect the future cultivation of the elementalist.

Calron felt like he was very close to reaching the peak of the first rank, but he still needed to refine all the essence before attempting to break into the next rank.

The purer one's essence was, the more powerful one will be compared to other cultivators at the same rank.

....

"Good, good. Although your speed of refining your essence is slow, we can work on that later. Alright, go get something to eat now, as you have been cultivating for hours."

The Voice amiably conveyed to Calron within his mind.

It had been several hours since Calron had first started cultivating, and after his strenuous transformation by the Blood Legacy, the Voice felt like Calron finally deserved some rest.

crackle

Suddenly, multiple bolts of Azure Lightning crackled around Calron's body.

"Haha, I was wondering whether or not it would help you. Seems like the Azure Lightning is slowly awakening as well, kid. Just relax your body and let it enter your core."

The Voice exclaimed with exhilaration when he saw the blue lightning flicker across Calron's body.

Calron then relaxed his muscles and sent his consciousness into his elemental core to observe what the Azure Lightning was doing. Bolts of blue lightning enveloped his entire outer core, while the gaseous golden essence was slowly rotating within the inside of the core.

Within seconds, the surrounding blue lightning instantaneously charged into the inside of his core and then began merging with the gaseous essence.

The young boy opened his eyes and cried out in alarm. This could not be happening. Was he really going to lose all his cultivation at this moment?

Seeing the essence being absorbed by the Azure Lightning, it appeared to Calron as if the blue lightning was gradually devouring his entire cultivation by force.

"Sigh... You need to trust it, Calron. Stop crying like a little girl, and pay attention to what is happening inside your core."

Calron sulked at his Teacher's comment, as he obviously was not crying and there was no need for the Voice to throw a personal jibe at him.

Shaking his thoughts away from his grumpy teacher, Calron turned his attention toward the current changes happening inside his core.

drip *drip*

While the bolts of blue lightning continued to crackle within his core, the surrounding golden essence was slowly dissipating. However, when Calron scrutinized the scene, he saw that small golden-azure drops were forming at the bottom of his core.

Sensing the raw energy contained within them, Calron was momentarily shocked. It was apparent that those golden-azure drops were his lightning essence.

"You can close your mouth now, kid... Sigh, you indeed have the luck of the heavens. Truly worthy of being a disciple of someone as great as me!"

While the Voice gloated over its own superiority, Calron continued to observe the golden-azure drops forming in his core.

After a few minutes, the drops had ceased to form, and there were about a few dozen golden-azure drops pooled at the bottom of his core.

crackle

Calron then felt his muscles quivering uncontrollably, as a steady stream of the liquid golden-azure essence flowed out from his core and into his blood and bones.

Am I breaking through right now?

Calron thought inwardly as he felt the new sensations bubbling up inside his body. He remained in a daze as he realized he was indeed having a breakthrough right now.

It had not even been a few days since he had awakened to his element, and he was already advancing again?

This was a cultivating speed that even big city geniuses would be jealous of.

A steady stream of the liquid golden-azure essence surged through his veins, as it strengthened his muscles and bones. Meanwhile, Calron's core also went through a huge qualitative change as it became denser and shone with bright golden-azure light.

After a few minutes, the essence fluctuations around Calron abruptly ended as a new strength surged within his body.

"Teacher, why do I feel so much stronger now? Even though I broke into the second rank, I feel ten times more powerful than before. The second rank is quite impressive."

Calron softly whispered while curiously detecting the changes within his new body.

Calron had a sudden feeling as if the Voice was currently smirking at him right now. Although he could not see his Teacher, Calron had begun to sense the Voice's emotions and thoughts as the bond between them solidified with each passing day.

In Calron's mind, his Teacher was a fat, grumpy old man who liked to make snide comments at little children.

"Brat, if I was alive right now, I would smack your bottom until it turned red like a baboon's backside. Hmph, I will let that comment slide right now because of the crybaby comment I made earlier."

Calron snickered at his Teacher's sullen attitude, but he could not let the Voice bully him all the time.

"By the way, kid, you did not break into the second rank; you broke into the third rank."

"I broke into the third rank?"

Calron's mind was in complete shambles as he realized that he effectively skipped a rank in his cultivation. This was something that should have been impossible.

One must understand that Calron's mother was only a second rank cultivator of the Spiritual stage, while his father was at the fourth rank. Currently, at eight, Calron had already surpassed his mother and was probably even physically stronger than his father.

Calron tightly clenched his fists and faintly felt the new power thrum through his muscles and bones. After his transformation due to the Blood Legacy, Calron's physical strength was already on par with a third rank elementalist, and now with the aid of his purer liquid essence, his present attack potential was on a completely different level.

Within his age group, almost no other child would be a match for Calron's strength, and even the geniuses of large clans and renowned schools would be hard-pressed to find an advantage against Calron in terms of simple brute strength.

However, when it came to the battle strength of his essence, Calron would still be at a disadvantage with his golden lightning. Things might be different if he could use the Azure Lightning, but he was still too weak to use its violent power. The Voice had previously said that Calron would only be able to slightly control the Azure Lightning once he reached the peak of the Spiritual stage.

"Mm, good, very good. Looks like we can finally begin training in the second stage of the Thunderbird technique. Get some rest and we will begin early tomorrow morning."

The Voice mumbled as if it was already preparing to fall asleep.

"Teacher. You still haven't told me why I suddenly broke into the third rank rather than the second rank?"

Calron frantically yelled when he saw that the Voice was slowly withdrawing.

Although Calron was ecstatic about this recent development, he still did not understand how or why it happened. Any normal cultivator would have to first break into the second rank, then into the third rank, and continue following that chain.

However, Calron had somehow broken that normal chain and directly broken into the third rank. No matter how one would look at it, this breakthrough should have been impossible.

"Damn pesky kid. Don't you know that it's time for me to sleep right now? Where is your respect for your elders? Don-"

Sensing that the boy was on the verge of tearing up, the Voice hastily stopped mid-sentence. Although it knew that Calron was probably just playing him and using his cuteness to get his way, the Voice still succumbed to his student's childish charms.

"Sigh... Alright, brat. Tell me what the state of the essence is around you?"

"The essence is like air. It's light and flows around you."

Calron enthusiastically answered.

"Correct. When you cultivate the essence and absorb it into your body, it's in the form of gas. Even when you refine it, it will only become a purer form of a gaseous essence, but it will remain a gas in the end. What the Azure Lightning aided you with is that it converted all the gaseous lightning essence directly into pure liquid essence."

Calron recalled when the golden-azure drops were forming inside his core. He still had not tried channeling the liquid essence yet, but from the aura it was currently giving off at the moment, Calron was sure that its power would not be weak.

"When a cultivator tries to break into the Vajra stage, he will have to convert all his essence into a liquid form before letting it merge with his body. This is the reason most cultivators cannot step into the Vajra stage, as refining and condensing that gaseous essence into a liquid was very difficult."
The Voice calmly stated to his young student.

"Wait, so every time I experience a breakthrough, I will advance an extra rank?"
Calron asked with childish joy.

"Rascal, you think the heavens are so unfair in their treatment? For every miraculous advantage you get, there will always be an equal drawback to it. You only broke directly into the third rank because your core had undergone a tremendous qualitative change. Your next breakthrough will be into the fourth rank and not the fifth. Since your core already contains liquid essence for every future advancement you face, you will have to gather a monstrous amount of essence to even have a chance of breaking through."

Calron's face immediately fell when he heard his Teacher's words. He understood that although it might not be difficult to advance to the third rank, what about trying to advance to the eighth rank or even the Vajra stage? The amount of essence required to break into those stages would be simply colossal.

Other elementalists had their methods of gathering the required essence: fire elementalists could go to a desert to safely absorb purer fire essence, water elementalist could go to the sea, or in the case of a wind elementalist a high mountain. But what about a lightning elementalist?

Places like the desert, lakes, or mountains were relatively safe and cultivators could easily absorb the essence from the environment. A desert will have naturally stored heat under the soil, thus large amounts of pure fire essence could be absorbed pretty easily.

Although that fire essence would not be as pure as compared to the fire essence coursing inside an active volcano, it would still be enough for breakthroughs within the Spiritual stage.

However, for a lightning elementalist, where in the world would he find an environment that contained a large amount of lightning essence besides under a thunderstorm?

Lightning is a creature birthed from the heavens, and it does not burn in a single place like fire, or flow continuously around the earth like wind or water.

Lightning is swift and strikes viciously without mercy. A bolt of lightning disappears almost as soon as it strikes, and its speed is second to none in this world.

Many desperate lightning cultivators have tried to absorb the lightning essence under a thunderstorm hoping to escape their fate, but what mortal could tame the violent energy contained within a bolt of lightning?

Only one thing followed lightning: Death.

This was why lightning cultivators had always remained in the Spiritual stage, and none of them could breakthrough into the Vajra stage, because what human could hope to contain and channel the lightning essence under a merciless thunderstorm?

It was madness.

"Looking at your face, it seems like you understand the difficulties you will face in the future. Don't be so down, kid. The heavens may often put obstacles in your life, but who says that you cannot defy the heavens themselves?"

The Voice responded as it tried to lift the spirits of its only student.

It knew that the path would be torturous for Calron in the future, but it did not have the heart to drown the hopes of this eight-year-old kid. Although it had never been done before, the Voice knew that if Calron inherited the same bloodline as his ancestors, then he just might have the potential to tame nature's lightning.

Wiping away the tears on his shoulder, Calron sniffed twice before getting up from the ground.

"Will you sleep with snot covering your face like that? Geez, don't start the waterworks every time you face a difficulty. Do you want to sit down and bawl like a baby whenever you meet a stronger opponent later? All hail Calron the Sniffle Face!"

The Voice teased Calron, as it knew that these childish jabs always got to the boy.

Calron might have a raging temper, and an almost perfect perception of Martial Arts, but despite all that, he was still a kid.

If there was too much seriousness in Calron's life, then his future would be lonely, and this was something that the Voice promised to never let happen.

"I wasn't crying. All this moving on the floor just made the dust rise. That's right, it's dust. I definitely wasn't crying. Stop making up lies and go to sleep. Isn't that what old people do?"

Calron hurriedly retorted, proud of his counter against his Teacher.

The Voice inwardly smiled with relief that the boy was back to normal. It was worried that with a past such as Calron, with him losing almost everyone and everything in his life, he would wallow in depression and misery forever.

It was nice to see the occasional childishness in the boy, as who knew how long it would last?

"Goodnight, kid."
The Voice whispered tenderly.

....

With the full moon illuminating the dark night, a cold and gentle wind breezed through the trees. Insects crawled around the ground while small predators hunted for easy prey.

Just at that moment, several shadows darted across a series of huts, as they caused numerous blurs to appear in the blackness of the night. The shadows made absolutely no sound and continued towards their destination at the back of a building.

"How is the little lady?"
A cold and deep voice asked the kneeling shadows on the ground.

"She is asleep, Captain. Currently, there are four guards stationed outside her room."
One of the kneeling men responded in a low voice.

"Any information on who killed our men that night?"
The Captain icily inquired.

"All traces of them have completely disappeared. Without the bodies, we do not know whether it was a Martial Artist, or an elementalist who killed them. However, only someone at the level of an Elder could possibly defeat peak Spiritual stage cultivators, so we are discreetly tracking the movements of all the Elders present in the school."
After hearing the report from his subordinate, the corner of the Captain's eye twitched. This task from his Lord was more daunting than he had expected.

The Captain was the only Vajra stage expert from their Shadow Corps here at the school, and the possibility of a conflict against several Elders at the Vajra stage was not a very comforting thought.

"Continue to observe their movements and inform me if you notice anything suspicious. However, do not engage them without my permission."

Just as the Captain was about to turn around, he abruptly gave another command.

"On second thought, although Lord Mort said to leave the boy alone, I'm curious about who this kid is. Give me a report on him tomorrow after you gather some Intel. Disperse."

"Yes, Captain."

A series of faint murmurs filled the quiet night.

CHAPTER TEN

Explosive Strength

chirp *chirp*

The sun slowly rose on the horizon, as it colored the sky with a mix of red and orange. The servants were quietly sweeping the school grounds, while a few disciples groggily rose from their beds for the beginning of an early morning.

—In Calron's hut—

snore

A little boy was still peacefully sleeping with a blissful expression on his face. A slight smile was etched on the corner of his lips and one could only guess the content of the boy's dream.

Suddenly, a mysterious dark smoke drifted out from the boy's body, as it slowly took on the shape of a large eagle-like bird. Bolts of golden lightning crackled around it and soon the bird changed its shape again, as it finally revealed the shadow of a kneeling man.

The translucent figure of the man stood up from the floor as he gently gazed upon the sleeping boy. Tucking away the strands of dark hair from the boy's forehead, the man bent down to gingerly touch the child's face.

Although the translucent figure appeared to be formed of smoke, surprisingly, it had a real physical touch.

"You remind me of him so much, Calron, and it pains me that his descendants have to bear the agony of such a torturous life. I do not have the power that I once used to, but I will make sure to guide you to the peak of power that you desire. Even those senile Ancients and Gods will tremble at the mere sight of you once they discover your existence."

The man chuckled softly.

At that moment, the boy suddenly stirred with his eyelids faintly flickering.

"Your heart is still soft, my child. You will need to get stronger soon, as there will be countless battles ahead of you. Unfortunately, I will have to leave you for a while in order to give you the chance to survive. I will explain it when you wake up, so stay strong until we meet again."

After whispering those words, the figure then exploded into bursts of smoke and re-entered the boy's soul.

....

"Wake up, kid!"

Calron mumbled various incoherent words in annoyance, but the Voice persisted.

"Calron, we need to start on your breathing technique before you go out there. We cannot have anyone know the current cultivation rank you have reached. It will simply bring too much-unwanted attention. Wake up now!"

"Alright, alright, I'm getting up. Geez."

Calron annoyingly muttered under his breath, as he gingerly rubbed his eyes to force the drowsiness out of him.

Getting out of his bed, Calron slowly sat down on the mat below and meditated. However, his eyelids soon started to slowly close.

thwak

Calron instantly sprung back into position and winced at the pain in the back of his head.

"This is important, you punk. Do you know the dangers you'll face if the world finds out what your current cultivation is at that age? Sleep again, and I will smack you harder the next time."

The Voice said in a threatening tone.

Sensing a tone of urgency in his Teacher's voice, Calron promptly became serious and focused his attention on the breathing technique. What he had failed to realize because of his sleepiness was that the Voice had actually inflicted physical pain on him.

"The second stage of the Thunder-Bird technique aids you in gathering large amounts of essence into your body and then circulate it within your spiritual veins. The reason why I had you wait until now was that with the absorption of massive amounts of essence, your physical body would not have endured that strain and would have instantly broken apart."

Calron attentively listened to every word his Teacher spoke and tried to ingrain them into his memory.

The Voice continued with its lecture.

"The other benefit of this technique, and the one which is most useful to you right now, is the ability it provides in camouflaging your cultivation. It will give you complete control over the flow of your essence, and you can use that to disguise your cultivation rank. Even experts at the Heavenly stage would be unable to uncover your cultivation if you do not want them to."

Calron was astonished by this information. A technique that even Heavenly stage experts could not see through? This was simply an inconceivable thought for Calron.

"Now, I will directly imprint this technique into your soul. We do not have the time for me to teach you step-by-step, and even with your unusually perfect perception, it will still take a very long time to comprehend this technique fully. Since we already share souls, I can easily imprint this technique onto you, and once it is engraved into your mind, you will be able to use this technique as if you had been practicing it for decades."

The Voice then turned silent for a while after it said those words as if composing itself for the next stage.

"I'm ready, kid. One more thing, once I imprint this technique onto your soul, I will need to recover for a long time, and cannot advise you until then. The connection between our souls is still unstable, so I will have to depend on my soul energy to recover my vitality. After you receive the technique, immediately start practicing it and only leave the hut after you've completely comprehended it. Stay safe, child."

The Voice gingerly whispered as its presence begun to slowly vanish within Calron's mind.

Sensing the absence of his Teacher, Calron unknowingly felt more lost and alone than ever. Sorrow built up within his tiny chest, and just as his eyes were about to get misty, Calron remembered his previous resolve to stay strong and forcibly suppressed the tears.

He missed his Teacher terribly, especially since he was the only one that he talked to besides Elias. But he knew that the Voice would soon return after recovering, and until then Calron would just have to endure.

Within seconds, Calron felt a jolt shaking his very soul.

Streams of foreign energy circulated through his body until it finally reached the center of his mind. Calron saw flashes of images as various sensations exploded within his nerves. He closed his eyes and absorbed the technique being imprinted on his soul.

* * *

After what seemed like years and years, Calron finally opened his eyes. Small bolts of golden lightning crackled around his pupils for a second before gradually fading away.

Currently, there was an intense aura surrounding the boy, as if the very essence around him trembled with an unrestrainable excitement.

The room was undoubtedly still.

There were no sounds, except the soft breathing of the boy seated on a mat in the middle.

Golden essence rippled around him as it rose and fell to the rhythm of the boy's breathing. The essence orbited him in waves akin to the rhythmic pumping of a large heart.

The birds continued to chirp outside while the servants remained busy with their sweeping.

shua

The waves of golden essence around Calron finally dispersed as he let out a deep sigh.

"So that is the second stage of the Thunderbird technique... formidable."

Calron then rotated his essence around his core to mask his true cultivation rank. The key aspect of the technique lay in its ability to convert some of the liquid essence back into the gaseous state and spread it outside of his core to make it appear as if one's cultivation was much lower.

Calron could also change the amount of essence he wished to reveal while hiding most his essence within the center of his core.

It seemed simple in theory, but was extremely difficult to execute, as how many cultivators would have the ability to maintain both liquid and gas essences at the same time? It was only thanks to the

Thunderbird technique that Calron could achieve this extreme control over his essence.

After disguising his cultivation back to the first rank, Calron breathed out a sigh of relief and hoped that the masking was perfect.

"Ah, I'm going to be late meeting Master Elias if I don't leave right now!"

Calron exclaimed after he glanced outside his hut and saw the sun beginning to fully rise on the horizon.

....

In a lush garden surrounded by lively vegetation, an old man sat at the edge of a lake with a small fishing rod resting in his hand.

None of the fish appeared to take the bait, but it did not seem to matter to the man as he simply reveled in the tranquility of nature.

Elias quietly hummed to himself while he enjoyed the sensation of the warm sunlight on his skin.

pant *pant*

"I'm sorry Master, I was running late."

Calron wheezed out the words after he caught his breath. He had rushed to Gretha for some quick breakfast and wolfed it down as fast as he could before sprinting here.

"Hmm, Calron? No worries. Come here, child. We will shortly begin your training, but you have to get your mind calm and lucid first. Sit here."

Elias gently stated without turning his head.

Calron obediently walked over to the lake and slowly sat down right next to his Master, while trying to regain and steady his breath.

The moment Elias turned his head and glimpsed toward Calron, he abruptly dropped his fishing rod as his hands trembled.

plop

The rod sank toward the bottom of the lake while Elias's hands continued to tremble.

"Huh? How did you..."

Elias struggled to get his words out due to the immense shock that he felt, but how could he not see through Calron's true cultivation with the legendary Divine Perception?

Divine Perception was a God-class technique that stood at the peak when it came to detecting the changes in essence, as no other technique or ability even came to a close second.

No kind of illusion could ever hope to deceive one who practiced this technique, and it was no wonder that Elias saw through Calron's masking of his cultivation.

Calron's heart started to frantically pound against his chest.

He could not have found out, could he? Teacher said not even a Heavenly stage expert could see through my cultivation.

Calron inwardly thought in panic.

How could Calron know that the technique his Master practiced belonged to that of the God class?

"Child, how did you suddenly advance to the third rank? It has barely even been a day since I last saw you, and you were only at the first rank. In a few hours, you have advanced by two whole ranks out of nowhere!"

No matter how one looked at it, it was simply impossible to advance that quickly in a matter of a few hours. How would the other cultivators feel if they found this out? They had to cultivate for years to reach the same rank as a boy who was just in his eighth year.

After his Master spoke those words, Calron knew without a doubt that his secret was revealed. He felt slightly anxious about revealing the Thunderbird technique, as it would raise questions of who taught it to him, but at the same time, Elias had always been kind to him and had even saved his life before.

Elias was the only one besides the Voice that Calron felt a kinship towards. His new Master shared the same loneliness as him as they had both lost their families and were orphans in this world.

They shared the same pain of loss and it was that bond that brought forth their unlikely friendship on the first day they met, as they could subconsciously sense each other's tormented past.

"It is alright, Calron. You do not have to say anything. I already knew you were an unusual boy from the moment I met you, and everyone has secrets they do not want to reveal to others."

At the end of the last sentence, Elias's mood turned somber as a tinge of pain suddenly flashed within his eyes before he instantly suppressed it. Elias turned to give the distressed boy an assuring smile hoping to soothe Calron's anxiety.

Calron's cultivation had shocked him to his core, but looking at the troubled expression on the child's face, Elias decided to leave the matter alone. Calron was a good kid, and that was all that mattered to him. The boy was now the Prime Inheritor of his family's Legacy, and since it had chosen Calron, Elias had the utmost trust in him.

"Master, I..."
Calron hesitantly started to mumble out words as he did not know how to address his Master.

"Child, I said to leave it. Let us begin our lesson now. Look out far into the lake and tell me what you see."
Seeing the stern look on his Master's face, Calron dropped the issue as well and observed the lake in front of him.

"It's very calm and peaceful. It's really beautiful, Master."

Calron said in wonder, as he reveled in the peaceful and soothing presence of the lake.

"Look closely and answer me again. Observe the creatures in both the sky and the water."

Elias calmly replied, as he told his new student to pay closer attention.

Calron tried to discover something amiss, but he could see nothing noteworthy besides the birds flying in the sky or the fish swimming in the water. There were various species and sizes of fish and animals, but nothing appeared to be unusual within Calron's sight.

"I don't see anything out of the ordinary, Master."

Calron responded while shaking his head.

"Nature, Calron. You see nature, but you only notice its beauty and fail to see the cruelty hidden within it. Look at the fish; they are swimming right now to escape from a larger fish behind them. The big animals hunt the smaller ones. The strong eat the weak. This is an unbroken rule of this world."

Elias stated softly as he continued to gaze at the scenery in front of him.

"There is nothing fair in this world, Calron, and only the power you wield will decide your fate and that of those around you. Remember these words, child."

Calron subconsciously steeled his mind, as he knew Elias was right. Calron himself was living proof of nature's brutality, after experiencing the loss of his entire family, and being constantly oppressed by stronger cultivators like the city Lord.

Even now, the only reason Calron remained alive was so the city Lord of Vernia could exploit him.

"Your disciple will ingrain this into his heart, Master."

Seeing the resolved look on the boy's face, Elias did not doubt Calron's words for a second.

"Let us begin your training now. Stand up, and start drawing the source energy from the legacy's pool, but remember to start slowly to reduce the strain on your body. Close your eyes and just listen to my voice. Nothing exists in this world besides you and my voice. Begin."

Calron swiftly stood up and started the same movements he had learned before. Slowly drawing the energy from the source pool, Calron felt his muscles bursting with power. However, Calron stopped drawing the source energy once he felt a bit of pressure from it.

He recalled the first time he drew from the source pool, and the pain that he had experienced from drawing too much source energy was simply agonizing.

"Good, you are learning to control your intake. Now, continue those movements while adding more power to your fists, and start circulating the source energy within your blood vessels."

Elias strictly instructed when he saw Calron was steadily controlling the source energy within his body.

Calron felt strong. Very strong. He did not know whether it was because of the recent breakthrough he had, or the source energy coursing through his veins, but he felt an unlimited amount of power surging within him.

"Now, enter the lake and continue those movements underwater. The water is quite shallow at the edge, so you should still be able to breathe. You will feel some resistance as the water will constrict your movements, but persevere through it."

Elias calmly guided his student.

Calron slowly entered the lake and resumed his training. It was noticeably more difficult as his movements were slowed down by a large margin, but Calron continued to push his arms through the resistance while drops of sweat formed on his forehead.

"Draw more energy from the source pool, and continue the movements."
Elias's soft voice sounded out from behind Calron.

Following his Master's direction, Calron started to slowly draw more source energy from the legacy's pool. His body suddenly began to rapidly heat up, but he still did not feel that he was in any danger.

This was because his body had grown immensely tougher after his breakthrough to the third rank, and could now endure more pressure than before.

"Not enough. Draw more. Your body can withstand it now, and without any extra pressure, how will you ever get stronger? Push through your body's limits, Calron!"
Elias yelled as he tried to get his student to break past his natural limits.

Without hesitation, Calron now drew colossal amounts of source energy with vigor. His body was filled with violent energy, as waves of heat could be seen radiating out from above Calron. His body's temperature was extremely high right now, and steam burst out from his skin.

The water circulating him started to sizzle and boil, but Calron did not feel any discomfort from the changes happening within his body. It was as if the boy's skin was completely immune to the intense heat surging around him.

"This is the true might of the First Layer of the Blood Arts. Now punch!"
With his muscles coiled in tension, Calron switched to an

offensive stance mid-movement and instantaneously struck his fist out with all the source energy focused on his knuckles.

The water in front of Calron burst apart into small particles when it came into contact with his fist.

BOOOOM.

A loud explosion echoed throughout the lake while the boiling lake water ferociously sprayed everywhere. The body of water quaked with faint tremors as the water surrounding Calron instantly burst into vapor. Further ahead at the lake, dead fish began to slowly float on top of the water with their insides being cooked under the boiling lake.

At the edge of the now-dry piece of land, a scorching red-skinned boy stood as he heavily panted. There were no traces of moisture around him and clouds of steam continued to rise from his skin.

Even under that extreme heat, the small figure's skin did not blister or crack. All the muscles in the boy's body fervently twitched, as if unable to contain that berserk energy within him.

Struggling to calm his racing heart, the boy stared in shock at his fist.

....

Meanwhile, a blind old man stood gazing towards the lake with his cold gray eyes, and slowly, a faint smile escaped from the corner of his lips.

CHAPTER ELEVEN

Fateful Encounter

puff *puff*

"My fist..."
Calron muttered as he absentmindedly stared at his hand.

Currently, there were a series of strange crimson symbols swirling around the center of Calron's palm. He felt an eerie sensation as the symbols continued to wriggle on top of his skin, as they constantly changed their shape.

"That is the legacy armor of the Prime Inheritors. It is still getting used to your body, so it will move around for a while before finally settling in place."
Elias calmly stated while he approached Calron from behind.

Prime Inheritors? Is that different from a normal Inheritor?
Calron thought inwardly. This was the first time he had ever heard about Prime Inheritors, so he was curious how they were related to the regular Inheritors.

"Prime Inheritors are the main successors of the legacy and the ones who the legacy deems to be the most worthy of its power. Since the Blood Legacy has chosen you to be the next Prime Inheritor after me, it bestowed you that armor."

Elias said with a gentle smile.

Calron turned to glance at his hand again while wondering how the symbols were even supposed to protect him. This tiny thing was supposed to be armor? It barely even covered his hand.

"Do not look down on those symbols, Calron. They might be small now, but as you gain a deeper mastery over the Blood Legacy in the future, the symbols will continue to grow until they cover the entirety of your body. With your current cultivation, even those tiny symbols on your palm would be able to hold off against an attack from a genuine sixth rank cultivator!"

"What? This tiny thing is so powerful?"
Calron exclaimed in a disbelieving tone.

He highly doubted that this seemingly fragile series of symbols could genuinely take an attack from a sixth rank expert, but Calron kept those doubts to himself.

Seeing the unconvinced look on Calron's face, Elias did not know whether to laugh or cry. Any Inheritor would gladly chop off one of their limbs to obtain a legacy armor, but his disciple did not even put it in front of his eyes.

Giving a defeated sigh, Elias continued.

"Never mind the armor, take a look around you, Calron. Do you notice any changes?"

Elias asked with a teasing smile on his face. He was amused because Calron had not even realized the destruction he had caused in the lake.

"Huh, what the-"

If Calron's jaw were not attached to his mouth, then it would have fallen onto the ground at that moment.

The previous surrounding water around him had completely evaporated. The lake had receded about ten meters back, leaving behind an entire area of dry ground with near-boiled fish flopping around.

If someone had never seen the lake before, then they would never think that this part of the dry ground once used to be full of aquatic life.

"The punch...it was the punch that did this. Master, that punch was too powerful. What is it called? Aren't I so impressive? Hehe."

After the initial shock had passed, Calron puffed up his tiny chest and boasted about his physical might. This was the first time that he had ever unleashed such a powerful attack, and which young kid did not dream of becoming strong and powerful?

Thus, Calron shamelessly gloated over this moment of triumph.

"Hmph, you think this is powerful?"

Suddenly, Elias stepped his right foot back while he leaned his whole upper body slightly forward. Immediately, he punched the air in front of him.

Elias's fist moved excruciatingly slowly, and it appeared almost as if he was simply extending his arm rather than punching.

BOOOM!

The sound of a loud explosion abruptly reverberated throughout the lake.

The sound of this explosion was much louder than the one Calron had previously made. However, the shocking fact was that the lake was still calm as ever, and not even a single ripple had formed on the water.

Elias continued to perform his extremely slow movements as each of his punches flowed in its own rhythm. The transition between every movement was perfectly executed, and almost as if the first punch had never even ended.

The punches might appear to be moving at a snail-like pace, but in fact, they were extremely fast.

Calron was currently seeing just the afterimages of the punches, rather than the actual movements. It was simply because Calron's eyes could not follow his Master's real speed.

A string of explosions continued to resonate throughout the area, but Calron still did not see anything bursting apart or being destroyed. The fish continued to swim as usual, however, some of them seemed to try to stay away from Calron. It was as if they had seen the way Calron had previously cooked their friends.

With each passing explosion, the intensity behind the punches only seemed to get more powerful. Finally, Elias came to rest as he exhaled a long, deep breath.

"That, my boy, is the true power of the technique you just performed. Strength is not destruction, Calron, and by destroying the area around you, you only show a lack of control in your power. It is wild and uncontrolled, and that kind of power will only backfire on you later on. Control. That is true strength. Destroy what you want to destroy, but leave everything else intact."

Elias somberly stated, as his gray eyes pierced into Calron.

Calron was always taken aback at the uncanny accuracy of his Master's gaze whenever he looked into his eyes, and if he did not know any better, then he would have never thought that Elias was truly blind.

Calron's eyes shined when he heard his Master's words. This was his first step into the world of Martial Arts, and it was at this moment after seeing his Master perform, that Calron's thirst for perfection took root within his soul.

"Master, this disciple will follow your words."

Seeing the childish eagerness on the boy's face, Elias could not help but smile at his student's enthusiasm. Calron's actions reminded him so much of when Marcus had started to learn Martial Arts. Thinking back about his nephew, a tinge of sorrow flickered across his face.

"Um, Master, how did you do that? I heard the explosions, but your fist was moving too slowly."

Hearing Calron's voice, Elias abruptly returned from his brooding and composed himself before responding.

"What I was punching was not a target or an object, Calron. I was punching the very air around me. To punch something that has no physical form or shape is the basis of controlling the very core of your power. Those explosions were precisely the air bursting apart under the pressure of my fists."

Elias did not explain any further, as he wanted Calron to understand this technique on his own, or otherwise, in the future, his disciple would rely too much on others. It was better for the boy to learn on his own, as that was the only way his fighting potential could grow.

"This style of punching is a technique of the First Layer of the Blood Arts. Training in this style will temper your body and muscles to better control the strength of your attacks. Take a rest for now, Calron. I can see that you exhausted a lot of your energy from the previous attack. You have the whole day off tomorrow, so go try making some new friends. Power means nothing if you do not have someone to care for in this world."

Elias addressed the boy amicably, as he turned to slowly walk back into his hut.

Calron desperately wanted to try executing the punches again, but he knew his Master was right and he should let his body recover before training again. Too much strain on his body without proper rest might stunt his future growth.

"By the way, Master, what is the name of this technique?"
Calron called out just as his Master was about to enter his hut.

Elias slowly tilted his head back while he stated quietly.
"It is called the Formless Fist."

…………………….

After exiting the Artifact's dimension, Calron began trudging back to his hut.

"Huh, the symbols stopped moving."
He noticed the strange symbols that were previously worming around his hand, now stood completely still as they formed a crimson print on the palm of his hand. Gingerly stroking the symbols with his other hand, Calron's palm felt cool to the touch.

There were a total of three different symbols etched into his palm. The first two were shaped like a sickle with varying sizes, while the third symbol was akin to that of an icicle or a needle. The bigger sickle's ends were directed towards the tip of Calron's fingers, while the smaller one faced the opposite direction.

The remaining needle-like symbol was in the dead center of the big sickle as it faced the same direction.

The three symbols did not touch each other, but at the same time, Calron got the feeling as if they were a complete single entity. Within a few seconds, the symbols started to gradually fade away until only a faint outline of them remained on Calron's palm.

Shaking off the thoughts of these mysterious symbols, Calron continued walking back to his hut.

"Hmm, maybe I should get some food...I'm feeling hungry..."
Calron began muttering, as he swiftly changed his direction towards the gathering hall.

"I wonder what Gretha has cooked for today. Hehe, I bet she will give me an extra serving."
While Calron drooled at the thought of the delicious food he would soon eat, a commotion seemed to form in front of him.

SMACK
A lump of a compact figure crashed at Calron's feet.

"Haha, that's what you get for not paying your respects towards me, trash!"
A large boy arrogantly spoke down at the crumpled figure on the ground, while a group of boys howled with laughter behind him. The large boy at the forefront was around ten years old, and it was clear that he was the ringleader of the group.

The large boy stood at least a foot over Calron and appeared to be more like a sixteen-year-old teenager than an actual twelve-year-old kid. His abnormal amount of muscles bulging through his robe didn't help either.

From his attitude and the expensive-looking robes, Calron assumed this boy must be the spoiled son of a rich household, as commoners like Calron did not have the luxury of nutritious food, and were usually weak and thin.
Calron stopped in his tracks and gazed at the sorry figure of the

beaten-up boy below him.

It was a chubby kid.

A trail of snot was dripping from his nose, and his swollen face was scrunched up as if he was desperately trying to force back his tears. Both of his eyelids were completely bruised black from the beating, and it was obvious that the fat boy was currently in a great deal of pain, but Calron could not help but contain his laughter as he continued to look at the chubby boy.

It was just that with his eye bruised black, the fat boy resembled a cuddly baby panda. Calron imagined that most of the older girls probably would not be able to keep their hands away from trying to pinch this cute, chubby boy's cheeks.

The strange kid was roughly around the same age as Calron, but was even shorter than him. The most striking feature about the fat kid was his piercing arctic-blue eyes.

The panda boy's eyes faintly reminded Calron of someone he had met before, but he just could not recall it at that moment.

Seeing a stranger had appeared before him, the weird kid glanced up at Calron, his eyes lighting up with a trace of cunningness.

"Big brother!"
Calron was astounded when the panda kid addressed him as his brother.

Big brother? I've never met this chubby kid before, so why the hell is he calling me his big brother? We are both at the same damn age.
While Calron was still pondering this, the fat kid quickly pounced on him.

"Big brother, these goons are bullying me! Please teach them a lesson."

After saying those words, the fat kid rushed behind Calron in a flash and stood there with his tiny chest puffed up like a plump peacock. Although the panda boy looked quite chubby, he was surprisingly very nimble on his feet.

Calron was at a complete loss for words. He had never seen a fellow as shameless as this fat boy, and it was quite obvious that the boy did not even know who Calron was, but still wanted to make him into a scapegoat to escape the beating from the bullies.

"Hey loser, who is this brother of yours?"
The large boy asked as he intimidatingly stared at Calron.

There was an evil glint in his eyes like he had just found a new prey and looking at Calron's simple robes, he was just a commoner, so even if the large boy bullied him, no one would bat an eye.

"Mister, I don-"
Calron began explaining when the panda kid behind him rudely interrupted.

"Hmph, you are not even worthy of knowing my big brother's name. Piss off!"
The fat kid boasted with his chest still puffed up.

At this moment, Calron wanted to grab the fat kid and slap his face until it was swollen, as he was just digging a deeper and deeper grave for Calron.

Being insulted by the fat kid in front of his lackeys, the large boy instantly fumed in anger as he now turned a smoldering look toward Calron. The sound of cracked knuckles reverberated in the air.

The large boy began slowly walking towards Calron, and wisps of orange-red essence began to gather around him and coalesced into a bright flame flowing within both his fists.

"Hey, is Chax really going to fight that skinny kid? He already reached the fifth rank a while ago, so that kid has no hope of surviving... pity that the loser met Chax today."

While various whispers floated up between the disciples, Calron focused intensely at the threat at hand.

Calron was furious at the fat kid at this moment. He only came to the gathering hall to eat some delicious food, but he was now being forced into a fight.

The only way he could contend against the brute in front of him was to either use the Azure Lightning or the Blood Legacy, both of which were forbidden. Calron could not take such a colossal risk in front of so many disciples. He would have to find another way to escape.

crackle
Tendrils of yellow essence coalesced around Calron while bolts of golden lightning crackled around his body.

Silence.

Finally, a disciple at the back spoke.
"A lightning elementalist. The rumors were true. The school had indeed accepted one of them as a student. Isn't this just making us lose face in front of the other schools?"

After that, a bunch of new whispers circulated among the surrounding disciples.

Chax currently had a huge smirk crafted on his face. He had been hesitant before when he noticed the complete confidence on the fat kid's face, as there were several geniuses in the school that liked to shroud themselves in mystery and dress in common attire.

These geniuses did not care about their appearance and were completely immersed in their training. Seeing the lightning gather around Calron, Chax no longer hesitated, and with a sinister smile on his face, he quickly charged toward Calron.

However, the person who had the biggest shock was the fat kid.

"Wah? This boy was a lightning cultivator? I thought I sensed a powerful aura around him...tch, if only big sister were here, then Chax would not dare to make trouble for me."

While the fat kid continued to mumble, his once puffed-up chest had now completely deflated, as he miserably sat down on the ground and began mindlessly plucking the grass near him. He knew that he would get an extra beating from Chax after he was finished with the lightning boy, as he was the one who had caused all this drama.

....

"His movements are slow and sloppy. He's also breathing too heavily while focusing purely on strength and not technique. I think he will most likely punch with his left arm, a straight jab. No, it will be a side swing."

Calron unknowingly began muttering under his breath as he analyzed Chax's movements. His normal golden lightning might be weak, but in matters of Martial Arts perception, Calron was in a completely different realm from Chax.

There were only a few more seconds left until Chax would reach him.

Taking in a deep breath, Calron suddenly released his essence as well. The previous thin bolts of golden lightning started to slowly grow thicker and thicker as they wildly crackled around his body.

Calron had learned this trick of increasing the power of the golden lightning after practicing the second stage of the Thunderbird technique, and it gave him utter control over his essence.

* * *

In a flash, Chax's fist had almost reached Calron's chest. It was a side swing, just as Calron had predicted. Crossing his arms just before Chax's fist was about to impact against his chest, Calron hardened the muscles on his arms. Right then, a vicious gust of wind and flame erupted from their brief contact.

Crack

A small figure violently flew back and painfully collided against the tree. Sounds of bones being broken could be faintly heard in the background.

"Urgh!"
Calron spat out a mouthful of blood on the ground as he gingerly clutched his broken arm.

Even with his cultivation of the third rank, it was impossible to contend against Chax. Blood slowly dripped from the corner of his lips, but the murderous gaze within Calron's eyes remained undiminished. Wild killing intent emanated from his body, that even caused the nearby Chax to shiver slightly.

What is with this brat? He's still conscious after taking a direct hit from me? That attack contained more than half of my strength. If others knew about this, then I would be mocked for the rest of my life.
Chax thought inwardly as he glared at the injured boy in front of him.

Meanwhile, the rest of the gathered disciples eagerly waited for Chax's next move. They thought Chax was just playing around with the lightning kid. Otherwise, how could Calron still be standing after taking a direct hit from him?

The panda kid's mind was in complete shambles.

He was the one standing the closest to Calron, and he clearly saw the power contained within Chax's punch, but even more surprising was the fact that the lightning boy had actually withstood it with just his bare arms.

Out of nowhere, the fat kid sensed a foreign killing intent around him, and shockingly, it was coming from the lightning kid. The chubby boy had never been so terrified before, and that fear was not born from logic, but it was a fear that came instinctively whenever a prey met its predator.

However, within that fear, a seed of admiration grew. The chubby boy had always been treated like a nobody ever since he was born. His mother was a servant in a rich household and was impregnated by the Lord there. Ostracized by his very father, the only one who truly cared about him in this world was his big sister.

Although they were not born of the same mother, she had never mistreated him and always brought him all kinds of delicious food and sweets. It was only because of her insistence that he could even join the school, and the fat kid had promised himself that once he grew up, he would repay the kindness and protect his big sister.

Looking at the back of the boy in front of him, the fat kid felt his heart ignite in flames of hope. He had always cowered from bullies and took a beating every day, but this strange boy had actually dared to fight back with such tenacity.

....

Meanwhile, Calron, completely unaware of the thoughts going through the fat kid's mind, had his focus solely on the large brute in front of him.

Calron felt a cold rage burning through his veins, and he sensed the Azure Lightning trying to force itself out from his body in order to seek vengeance. This was Calron's first proper fight, and although he wanted to act rashly, he still remembered his Master's teachings: Control your body and control your mind.

133

Seeing the apathetic expression flash across Calron's face, Chax felt his face heating up. This kid was looking down on him.

No one had ever dared to look down upon him before, as he was the son of the city Lord and he had the right to be arrogant. Everyone had told him what a genius he was since an early age and his father even collected rare magical beast cores for him to cultivate with.

He was the pride of the city Lord's family, and now a commoner like Calron, and moreover, a lightning cultivator loser, dared to look at him with such contempt?

Unacceptable.

A violent red wave of essence rolled out from Chax, and his flames gushed out in a wild inferno around him. This time, he was going to put his entire strength into this ultimate attack.

The surrounding disciples gasped in wonder at the sudden change. They could sense the dangerous aura surging around Chax at the moment.

Calron forced back the struggling Azure Lightning and instead drew large amounts of source energy from the Blood legacy pool. Even when consumed with rage, Calron knew that the Azure Lightning would spell an even greater disaster if revealed, so he risked the Blood Legacy instead. At least it was not as easily detected as compared to the Azure Lightning.

With the source energy flooding through his veins, Calron prepared to unleash the punch from the First Layer. Although his technique was not as powerful as his Master, it was still enough to deal with the large brute in front of him.

Chax's fist was almost upon him when Calron forced all the source energy into his right arm.

At that moment, Calron unexpectedly felt a faint tingle from the symbols on his palm.

However, just as the two fists were about to collide against each other, a furious shout abruptly resonated in the air.

"STOP!"

CHAPTER TWELVE

Big Sister?

"STOP!"

A powerful voice suddenly roared throughout the entire area, as it caused some disciples to clamp their ears shut with their hands.

Calron's body was completely paralyzed, as an invisible force constricted his limbs from moving.

Chax was in a similar situation to him, but the larger boy's face remained distorted in anger. Being so close to landing his killing blow on his enemy, and then being forced to stop, only made Chax even more infuriated.

On the other hand, Calron had calmed down considerably, and this resulted from Elias's continuous mental training. Even Calron had not realized until now that his mental fortitude had been slowly getting stronger day by day.

The crowd slowly parted away from the center, while the two figures slowly walked towards the front.

One of the two figures was a middle-aged man wearing an ordinary dark red robe. He had an angular face with slight stubble, and pale hazel-green eyes that were as sharp as the edge of a blade.

The man walked with the stride of a warrior, a series of coordinated and precise steps.

Scowling with irritation as he walked towards Calron and Chax, it soon became obvious that the previous explosive voice had belonged to him. With a sword buckled to his side, the man continued walking toward the two boys.

The other figure walking next to the middle-aged man was much smaller, but the proud, lofty aura around her was in no way inferior to the man beside her. The girl appeared to be around nine or ten years old, but Calron thought she had a mesmerizing face. There was still a childish charm to her, but it was clear as day that once she grew up, she would be a beauty that men would fight wars for.

Her gaze was sharp as broken glass, accented further with her arctic-blue eyes that chilled the heart of anyone that looked into her glare.

The surrounding male disciples all found themselves blushing without control and even their eyes lit up as they admired the beauty of this mysterious girl.

"Goddess... why did no one tell me that there was a goddess in our school?"
One kid passionately spoke aloud.

A female disciple standing behind him smacked him on the back of his head, reprimanding him in a whisper.
"Idiot, that's Lady Felice Axier of the Axier family! Do you want to die by pursuing her?"

"Shit! She's from that Axier family?"
Another nearby disciple exclaimed in shock.

....

Both the new figures did not pay any attention to the commotion caused by the surrounding disciples, and continued stoically walking towards the two youths involved in the fight.

"Chax. I thought I had made it clear last time that you were not to involve yourself in fights anymore. If you want to remain as my disciple, then you will have to obey my commands. Even your father has no say in this."

The middle-aged man scolded the large boy, agitation in his tone.

The man's voice had a rough huskiness to it that made it sound deeper than it really was.

"Master Dane! It was this boy's fault, as he intentionally provoked me and even insulted my family's honor!"

Chax hurriedly replied with a flustered expression, and it was obvious that he was afraid of this Master Dane, so he tried to present himself as the victim instead.

"He's lying. Chax was bullying me and he even beat me up, along with his friends over there. Look at my eyes. They've lost all their cuteness! Which girl would ever take a second look at this bruised face? Thankfully, big brother valiantly stepped in and stopped Chax from hurting me."

The panda kid sharply interrupted Chax and blabbered his version of the story while shooting Calron a mischievous wink.

Although Calron was still furious with the fat kid for dragging him into this mess, he could not remain angry after seeing Rory's playful and childish attitude. An involuntary smile slipped from Calron's face.

"Rory! What are you doing here?"

Panda boy turned around to the voice and squinted his eyes to determine who it was that just spoke. The voice was oddly familiar. His eyes were swollen from the beating he took earlier, so his vision was still blurry.

"Wha-? Big sister!"

The chubby exclaimed, fresh tears pouring down his cheeks all the while he ran towards the girl. Tightly hugging her, Rory wailed and complained nonstop about the abuse he had suffered at the hands of the "demon" Chax and his "minions".

After hearing snaps of the story from her crying little brother, Felice fiercely turned a baleful glare at Chax, and if looks could have killed, then Felice's stare have definitely obliterated Chax right there and then.

Feeling the murderous killing intent directed towards him, Chax visibly paled.

The background of this little girl was utterly terrifying. Even his father as the city Lord would have to pay respects to her if she demanded it, and if he had known that the weak-looking fat kid was the brother of this girl, then he would have never even touched the chubby boy. Why didn't the loser say from the start that he was from the Axier family?

"Your name is Chax, right? Who gave you the right to torment my brother?"

A frosty voice sounded out from the girl as she questioned the petrified larger boy.

Cyan wisps of essence coalesced around the girl as they formed into a whip that slowly spiraled around her. Her ice-cold eyes contained a fury that asked for retribution. Even the air around her had quickly chilled, and the nearby chubby boy felt the frost creeping up on his skin.

"Enough Felice!"

Master Dane bellowed with irritation as his essence cut through Felice's and dispersed it.

"I will decide the punishment for my students, and not you. Chax is a new student of mine and he will join you in learning Martial Arts from today onwards. I was just going to introduce you to him later today, but things seem to have not gone according to plan."

Hearing the last sentences of her Master, Felice was immediately appalled, as her face turned frostier. Her arctic-blue eyes continued to fiercely bore into Chax.

Both disciples knew that this matter would not be settled anytime soon.

"By the way, Rory, who is this person you've been calling big brother?"

Felice lovingly turned to her little brother and asked, while tending to the bruises on his chubby face. It was plain to anyone who could see that this girl dotted heavily on the panda kid.

"Hmm, big brother? Oh, that's him right there!"

Rory said cheerfully as he pointed towards the hidden Calron behind the tree.

Damn this panda. He puts me in a dangerous situation again.

Calron cursed inwardly when the chubby boy pointed toward him.

A few minutes ago, when Calron had seen Felice walking, he stealthily hid behind the nearest tree as that was the only decent place that provided a cover to hide in the present situation.

Unfortunately, the nosy panda boy had already noticed Calron jumping behind the tree. Since the beginning, Felice had not paid attention to anyone except Rory and Chax, so she had completely missed the other person who was involved in the fight: Calron.

Calron recalled the last time when he had encountered the girl, and noticing the proud and arrogant nature of this girl, he knew she would unmistakably have her revenge if given the chance. Especially now that Felice knew he was just a lightning cultivator. If Calron could turn back time, then he would have just ignored those girls that night and continued walking.

Felice languidly tilted her head to look at the figure that her little brother was pointing at.

The smile on her face froze instantly.

"YOU!"

Felice screamed furiously, her calm demeanor dissipating in a moment. Just as she was about to release her essence, her brother quickly grabbed her hand and yelled.

"Big sister, what are you doing? Big brother here risked his life for me. I can't let you hurt him!"

Although Rory had intentionally pulled Calron into his mess and he was only goofing around. In reality, he did not really want Calron to get hurt.

He had initially sensed a powerful aura around Calron, and that was the reason he chose to hide behind him. If he had known that Calron was just a lightning cultivator, then Rory would have probably taken the beating all by himself.

In the past, Rory had always been accurate in sensing the aura of others, and he was confused how he had made a mistake with the lightning boy.

He was a mischievous kid, but his heart was still innocent and pure.

Seeing her little brother start to get teary-eyed again, Felice forced herself to calm down and softly petted his head while she whispered.

"Big sister is sorry, Rory. I promise I won't hurt him, so why don't you bring your 'big brother' over here?"

Despite her gentle voice when she spoke to the chubby boy, everyone could hear the chilliness in her voice when she mentioned 'big brother'.

Rory, oblivious to all of this, happily walked towards Calron. Grabbing his hands, the chubby boy forcefully dragged him towards Felice, actively ignoring Calron's protests.

In the end, Calron resigned himself to his fate and let the boy lead him. Calron's body was still injured from the previous exchange with Chax, so he did not have the strength to resist anymore. Master Dane quietly watched this scene unfold, along with the rest of the gathered disciples.

"What's your name?"
Felice asked with false sweetness in her voice once Calron arrived in front of her.

Hearing the mock friendliness in her voice, Calron shuddered a bit, and he knew that once Rory left his side, the ice demon in front of him would try to force countless tortures upon him.

"Uh, Calron."

"Calron? That's a weird name."
Felice responded as she wrinkled her nose.

This brat. How is my name any weirder than hers? She is just trying to provoke me.
Calron thought inwardly, but kept it to himself. It was not good to add oil to the already burning fire.

Before Felice could speak again, Master Dane abruptly interrupted her.

His low, husky voice slowly reached Calron's ears.
"Boy, who is your Master?

"Boy, who's your Master?"

Calron's mind froze when he heard those words.

There is no way he could've detected the Blood Legacy. I didn't even release the source energy. Maybe he sensed the Azure Lightning? No, that's impossible.
While Calron's mind raced with these thoughts, Master Dane continued.

"You have the heart of a warrior, Calron. Do you wish to become my personal disciple?"
Both Felice and Chax gasped in surprise.

Others might not know the complete identity of Master Dane, but how could his disciples not know his background?

Although Dane knew little about the boy in front of him, he had seen the fight from far away. He initially wanted to test Chax, but he found the smaller boy to be more interesting. Dane only took in Chax because of the insistence of his father and to give him some face, but he had no real expectation from a boy who liked to bully the weak.

It was the valiance of the smaller child that ignited his admiration. To stand in front of a larger and stronger foe without hesitation–that is the heart of a true warrior. Even if the child were an Elemental-Less, Dane would have still taken him under his wing. The path of a warrior had nothing to do with essence.

When Calron heard those words, he inwardly sighed in relief, but his expression remained the same on the outside. He had been afraid that his secret was revealed. However, now he faced an even greater dilemma. He couldn't say that he already had a Master nor could he outright refuse the offer, as that would be far more suspicious.

"Um, can I take some time to think about this?"

Calron asked tentatively. The best option right now was to delay the decision as long as he could until he talked further with Elias. He didn't get a bad feeling from Dane, but he already had a Master to whom already sworn to.

When the others nearby heard those words, they were flabbergasted. This kid was a lightning cultivator, and he had the gall to refuse an offer like that? No Master within the entire school would be willing to take in Calron and yet the kid asked for more time?

Common disciples might not know the complete story, but it was clear that this middle-aged man had considerable authority as even the Axier family had connections with him. The only reason others could think of for Calron to refuse Master Dane's offer was that Calron's brain must have been damaged in the previous fight.

Chax visibly sighed in relief. If Calron had become a student of his Master and a fellow disciple, then that would have just added more to his humiliation. Next to him, Felice seemed to relax as well after hearing Calron's words.

Amazingly, Master Dane was not offended by Calron's decision.

"Take your time, kid. Felice, let's go. It's time for our lesson. Chax, follow me. We still have to decide your punishment for disobeying me."

Dane's husky voice resounded throughout the area. Chax slightly trembled when Dane mentioned his punishment, as he could already imagine the pain he would undergo for the next few days.

"Kid, take this pill. It will heal your injuries faster."

Dane threw a small Vermillion pill toward Calron and walked away without missing a beat.

"Rory, take care of yourself and if you get in trouble again, just find me. I will deal with the bullies."

Felice said warmly while hugging her little brother and followed behind her Master.

"I will, big sister."

Rory whispered gloomily.

A tinge of pain flashed across Felice's face when she heard the sadness in his voice, but she hid it as soon as it appeared. She hurried to catch up to her Master.

Chax gave a final intimidating glare at Calron and he, too, left with Felice. But, just as he was about to pass by Calron, he growled in a voice only the boy could hear. "I'll deal with you in the Ranking Tournament, runt. Let's see who will save you then."

He then arrogantly walked away without waiting for a response.

Following that, the other disciples started to scatter away as well. They had witnessed a pretty magnificent show today and shared the gossip with others who came later and missed the beginning of the spectacle. It was certain that rumors about Calron would soon spread around the school. A few hushed murmurs were about Felice and her famous family.

....

In a few minutes, everyone had left until only Calron, and Rory remained in the area.

Calron looked at the pill in his hand, and not seeing any noticeable defects, popped it into his mouth and swallowed with an audible gulp. The pill immediately set to work, and he felt a cool gush of sensation flow out from his stomach. Evidently, this was a high-ranked pill as Calron immediately felt its rejuvenating effects. He didn't know how effective this pill was in terms of healing his whole body, but at least it temporarily numbed the pain from his injuries.

"So, panda boy, what's up with that sister of yours?"

Calron turned to the chubby boy. From the day he met Felice, she always seemed to get on his nerves. He didn't have much experience with girls, but Felice seemed to differ from what Calron knew about girls in general. All the girls he knew in his village were timid and meek; however, Felice seemed to be the complete opposite. Then again, he barely interacted with the village kids as they all made significant efforts to avoid playing with him.

"Huh, big sister? Well, she's mean to everyone, but she really is nice and kind. It's just that Father d-"

Rory stopped mid-sentence as if he had recalled something.

"Hey! Stop calling me panda boy! It was just that Chax hit me there a day ago and again he targeted the same area, so my eyes are bruised more than normal. Besides, you look more like a panda than I do! I have four girlfriends, and they all tell me how manly I am!"

Calron couldn't hold it in any longer and cracked up in laughter. Rory had a genuine humorous nature in him and it was hard to be truly vexed with the chubby boy albeit his mischievous actions.

This was the first time Calron had laughed this openly after the death of his parents. He didn't realize how long he had been laughing, but he only stopped once he felt his wounds open up again.

Rory blankly stared at Calron and spun around to look at his buttocks, wondering if he grew a tail, seeing how hard the other boy was laughing.

Maybe he never heard a joke in life? Or is it because I'm funnier than I thought? I was kidding about the four girlfriends earlier, but I can try for Lily again. I'll tell her the same joke as I told him... no wait, it would need context. I'll just tag big brother next time and ask him to roleplay with me. He'll definitely agree! Although I should not tell him that Lily rejected me already after I stole her cupcake at lunch.

* * *

Filled with a newfound confidence in himself, Rory puffed up his chest and imagined all the wonderful dates he would go on with his new imaginary girlfriend.

Seeing the way the panda boy was puffing his chest, making him look even more akin to a baby panda, Calron felt another burst of laughter coming but forced it down when he felt his wounds hurting again.

"Hahaha, panda boy, you're hilarious! Your sister called you Rory, right?"

Calron squeezed out the words, holding back his grin lest it reopen his wounds.

He never had a friend of his own growing up and this was the first time he genuinely enjoyed being in someone his age's company.

"Mn, well, my complete name is Roran, but I'll allow you to call me Rory as well."

Rory said with a cheerful smile and extended his hand toward Calron.

Looking at Rory's silly smile, Calron let loose the grin he was holding back. He extended his hand and clasped Rory's firmly while placing his other hand around the chubby boy's neck.

"Since you already called me big brother, you can continue to call me that. Hehe, Rory, how does it feel to be my little brother?"

"Eh? But we are the same age. Why do you get to be the big brother? I'm much more handsome than you! I was definitely not lying about the four girlfriends. I'll introduce you to them later."

Rory whined unconvincingly.

"Well, you should have thought of that before you dragged me

147

into your mess earlier."

Faced with the instant reply from Calron, Rory hung his head in dejection, but he continued to mumble about how he was still cooler.

In an empty courtyard in a small unknown school, the two boys formed a bond that would last for countless years and destiny would remember their names when they would shake the entire continent together.

"Hey Rory, do you like chicken more or beef?"

....

Far in the distance from where the boys stood earlier, an old man in a simple white robe gazed from a high cliff. His long silver hair flung wildly in the wind, but the man paid no attention to it. His gray opaque eyes glowed unnaturally while he scrutinized the whole scenery below him. It was unknown how long he had been standing there.

"This disciple of mine continues to get himself in trouble...sigh."

Elias muttered softly, but there was a faint smile lingering on his face.

"He's grown powerful again, and that technique he used to rapidly increase his essence's intensity must have been taught to him by someone else. That's a high-rank technique and no one in this school knows of it. Such precious techniques... it's not any of the Elders... Haha, this boy has more secrets than his blind old master."

Elias leisurely turned back and sped through the terrain. The interest Dane had in his disciple worried him slightly, but if any issues arose, he would deal with them within the shadows.

"At least he didn't get hurt too seriously. I'll have to keep a closer eye on him." The irony of that last sentence was not lost on him. Releasing a quiet chuckle, Elias sped even more, gliding like the wind with his feet never touching the ground.

CHAPTER THIRTEEN

Beast Within

chirp *chirp*

It was a peaceful morning while the birds sailed through the sky and searched for their morning food. The worms in the ground hurried to dig deeper into the soil before their feathered friends noticed.

In a small hut, enormous waves of essence surged around a small boy of eight years old. From the outside, everything appeared normal and not a trace of the essence leaked. The servants swept the entire corridor without realizing that anything was amiss.

"Phew, I think the essence in my core increased by another dozen drops. This is exhausting, after hours of cultivation, and I only increased my essence by a mere few drops."

Calron sighed while he slowly got up from the mat. If the Voice had been here, then he would have immediately smacked Calron. Those few drops of essence had been refined to its purest state, and even a single drop of that essence contained an astonishing amount of power.

It was already outrageous that Calron cultivated a dozen drops in just a few hours. Unknown to Calron, this method of directly cultivating liquid essence would bring countless benefits to his core in the future.

"Where is this panda boy? He said he'll take me somewhere good, and he still hasn't shown his face yet."

Calron muttered while putting on some clean clothes.

After a few minutes, a red-faced Rory appeared in front of Calron's door.

pant

"Sorry, big brother. I got held up in some important business."

Rory wheezed out the words while resting his arms on his knees. His face was completely red, as if he had just run around the entire school. Sweat dripped from his forehead as Rory continuously rubbed it away on his shoulder.

"Don't lie to me, Rory. You were probably just wolfing down Gretha's food."

Calron said while giving the chubby boy a hard look. Under the intense scrutiny, Rory gradually wilted.

"Ahh, forgive me big brother, but she cooked sausages for breakfast, and you know how long it's been since I've eaten those delicious things."

Rory cried while clasping his hands together before Calron and pleading miserably. After only spending a short time with him, Calron already came to be familiar with Rory's silly antics, so he ignored this matter before another headache formed.

"Forget it, panda boy, let's go. You better take me to this nice place you mentioned later, hmph."

"Don't worry, big brother, I promise you'll not regret coming to this place. Frankly, I'm surprised you haven't heard it before."

Rory inquired with a slight raise of his eyebrows.

"I've only been here for a few days, so, naturally, I don't know much about the surrounding areas. Besides, none of the other disciples were very welcoming."

Calron explained while Rory nodded his head. Although the same was true for the socially awkward Rory as well, it was only by chance that he discovered this place.

"Alright, let's go!"

The chubby boy shouted while dragging Calron behind him.

………….

"Uh…what's this, panda boy?"

Several small strange looking lizard creatures were being grilled on sticks, outside a large booth. The lizards had double-forked tails and didn't seem to have much meat on them. The vendor was a sweaty pot-bellied man who kept rotating the sticks over the grill. His sweat dripped onto the meat, but he didn't seem to care as he kept roasting them.

Calron turned his face away, repulsed, and even Rory seemed a bit embarrassed by the situation. With how much he hyped this place up, the last thing he wanted to show Calron was grilled meat marinated with an old man's sweat.

"Forget about him, big brother. Look around you. Anything you could ever want will be for sale here. Food, weapons, pills, and even cultivation techniques. Isn't it amazing?"

Rory exclaimed, spinning on his heels. He seemed to be really enjoying playing the role of a guide for Calron today.

Calron gazed at the whole marketplace and it was exactly as the younger boy had stated. Vendors were selling all kinds of merchandise with buyers bargaining for cheaper prices while the vendors pretended to be cheated of profits.

* * *

Many strange goods were being sold, but Calron had to agree that everything he could think of was available in front of his eyes. He even thought he saw some caged beasts.

Calron realized they were just at the start of the marketplace and that it went a lot deeper inside with the quality of shops increasing the closer one got to the center.

This place was swarming with people. There were various kinds of people, from merchants to martial artists, just loitering around the shops. Calron even spotted a few disciples from the Red Boar School. Giving a final disgusted gaze at the sweaty man grilling lizards, Calron started walking forwards with Rory following behind.

Rory continued his non-stop prattling on the different types of exotic food that were available here, while Calron paid close attention to what was being sold in the market. If he had any money, then he probably would have been tempted to buy almost half of the items he saw in the past few minutes.

All of a sudden, Calron stopped in his footsteps. Rory realized after a while that Calron wasn't following him anymore, so he rushed back to see what delayed Calron.

In front of Calron were countless bottles of pills. Some were colorful, others were ornate with designs, and the rest were simply dull. Even their shapes varied, as some pills were either spherical or cylindrical, and there were even some that were shaped like a cube.

A fifteen-year-old youth sat behind the counter and lazily stretched across the chair. Seeing Calron's curious gaze, he spoke in a nonchalant tone.

"The colorful ones are five copper squares, the square ones are seven copper squares and the rest are all three copper squares. No discounts. If you are going to bargain, then just leave right now."

Seeing the uncaring attitude of the vendor, Calron was slightly taken aback. He thought the vendor would try to convince him to buy his goods, but it was the complete opposite.

"Big brother, what're you doing here? All these pills look pretty, but their actual medicinal effects are very low. They would not sell real pills for just copper squares. You need to be careful when buying something, as most of them are plain junk. Let's leave!"

The young vendor didn't seem to mind what Rory was saying and languidly gestured with his hands, shooing them away.

It seemed like they were still in the cruddy part of the market as Rory explained that the best goods were closer to the center of the market, but Calron was pretty sure Rory was about to say "food" rather than goods.

Sometimes a few older girls passing by would swoop down and pinch Rory's cheeks as they cried out how cute he was, but Rory would just shrug them off and continue walking.

Stupid aunties! Lily's my true love!

Calron was sure he saw a passionate glint in Rory's eyes, but he left it alone. He had a feeling it was best not to know what went on within the weird kid's head.

He hummed a tune and enjoyed the journey, letting Rory take the lead.

It was thrilling for Calron to see all these new things, so he greedily absorbed all the scenery, smells, and noises. It was a chaotic jumble of sensations, but it felt good to have his mind distracted from cultivation.

Just as both Rory and Calron were walking, an immense crowd seemed to gather at the side of the market.

"Rare magical beast for sale! It's your once-in-a-lifetime chance to buy one! Hurry and bid before your neighbor does!"

A loud, boisterous voice sounded throughout the marketplace. The man was using his essence to amplify his voice. The announcement excited Calron.

"Rory, let's check it out! I've never seen a magical beast before."

"But, b-but we're almost there. It's probably a stupid first-rank beast anyway. What's so special about them?"

Ignoring Rory's whining, Calron simply dragged him toward the crowd. There were hardly any gaps to squeeze through and most of the people were taller than both Calron and Rory, so they could not pass through the cluster.

"Rory, get on the ground. We'll crawl through their legs."

Without waiting for an answer, Calron immediately crouched down and started tunneling through the legs of gathered people, while Rory just stood there with a blank stare on his face. Calron was skinny so he would have no problem passing through other people's legs, but what about Rory?

"Big brother, I hate you!"

With a tearful cry, Rory got on his hands and knees and started crawling behind Calron. Every once in a while, one of the standing bidders would kick Rory in the rear as he passed by them but mysteriously Calron would somehow evade the kicks at the last moment as if he detected them beforehand.

thwak *thwak*

Stifling his tears and curses, Rory continued forward.

While Rory was getting kicked around, Calron had already reached the front of the crowd. As soon as he laid his eyes on the sight before him, his mouth dropped open.

Calron felt an unbelievable awe while gazing at this magnificent creature.

It was truly a beauty to behold.

The beast was like a large white cat with rippling muscles. Its fur glowed with an ephemerality that was difficult to describe in words, and Calron was certain that the fur would be extremely soft as well.

It had thin, aqua-blue stripes swirling around its paws and its eyes shone with the same hue. A gentle aura emanated from the beast that made Calron feel as if the beast was a peaceful creature in the wild.

To see such a beast caged and crudely presented in front of an audience, Calron felt only sorrow and bitterness. There was nothing Calron could do to relieve it of its suffering, as he had neither the money nor the power.

Just then, a wailing Rory appeared next to Calron with footmarks all over his robe and face. The footprints varied in size and shape so much so that one could tell Rory had been brutally kicked by a large number of people in the crowd.

"Big brother, how could you do this to me? You know how sensitive my body is and look at my face now. One of the old women stepped on me mercilessly as she thought I was stealing her purse. Big brother!"
Rory wailed his sorrows while Calron paid no attention to his ranting. His focus was wholly on the majestic beast in front of him.

"This is a rare first-rank beast with a water element! Furthermore, it's still young, so it can be tamed much more easily. Starting bid is ten gold squares, so start placing your bids now!"
The crowd erupted into a chaos of shouts and yells. It had to be understood that a single gold square was enough for a small family to survive for months, and this beast's starting bid was ten times that amount.

This auction was happening outside the market, where there were no rules or authority. The scene turned into utter chaos as everyone shouted their bids. The man auctioning the beast seemed to be overwhelmed as he tried to hear some bids, but then someone from a different location would shout even louder than the previous voice.

Right then,
"SILENCE! How dare you maggots cause a commotion in the market?"

A group of guards came marching, and the leading man, who appeared to be their captain, furiously roared at the crowd. The guards had the city Lord's emblem on their chests, and they walked with unveiled arrogance toward the man on stage. The emblem on their armor was a black bear's head growling to the side.

"Hand over this beast right now! It is illegal to auction any property publicly without the city Lord's approval."
The captain stated loftily.

Hearing those words, the owner of the magical beast visibly crumpled. He had lost many brothers while obtaining this beast, and if the guards were to just take it away, then how will he take care of his dead brothers' families? This was why he had to auction outside the market. The city lord's taxes were infamous for being exorbitant. That was the reason he took a chance and sell it outside their jurisdiction, but how could he have expected that the plan in return, would make him now lose everything?

"Sir, please forgive this lowly person. I will give you all the money I have, but please don't take away the beast! My brothers fought against its mother and lost their lives trying to obtain it."
The man kneeled on the ground and begged the guards.

Seeing the man kneeling on the ground, the captain of the guards just raised his foot and stepped on the man's neck.

"You think I have time to waste on you? Just hand it over, or else I will personally chop off both your hands for breaking the law."
The captain stated stoically.

In truth, this was not a serious matter as many vendors didn't have permits, but the captain wanted to take this opportunity to get that rare magical beast as a pet. Although it was only a first-rank beast, it was still worth decent money, or it could be used to bribe an officer for an early promotion. The beast was pleasing to the eye, so any officer's child would fancy it.

Faced with that threat, the man bitterly cried as there was nothing he could do. The crowd of surrounding people had been watching the scene from the start, and yet not one person objected or intervened.

Calron felt his heart violently surge with anger as he saw the man kneeling in front of these pretentious guards. He was almost about to jump on the stage when he saw the captain step on the heartbroken man, but then he suddenly felt a steely grip on his arm.

"Big brother, you cannot get involved. Those guards have the backing of the city Lord and if anyone fights back, then not only the person involved will get killed, but his family and friends will be held accountable as well. Please endure for now, big brother."
Hearing Rory's frosty voice, Calron was startled. Rory's face was burning in rage and even the surrounding air chilled to a great extent, and the nearby people subconsciously moved away from the chilliness.

This was the same feeling Calron felt back when Felice had released her essence. He didn't sense any essence from Rory earlier, but that bone-chilling aura was unmistakable.

Even Rory's vice-like grip on Calron's arm contained a strength that belied his outer chubby appearance. The chubby boy's arctic-blue eyes had a certain sharpness and intensity to them that Calron hadn't noticed before. So far, he had always seen Rory goofing around or chasing after food, but this was the first time he felt like he saw the true Rory.

No. Roran.

He exuded the same noble aura as Felice, and Calron felt that there was a lot more to Rory than the goofy attitude he showed to the world.

"Sigh...sorry Rory, I should have known better than to rashly head into trouble. It still angers me that none of these people here tried to stop the guards."
Knowing that Calron had calmed down, Rory released his grip and even the aura around him returned to normal.

"Big brother, don't blame these people as they also have no choice. If they objected to the guards, then their lives would be at stake and who would be willing to sacrifice their life for a stranger? It's the way humanity is, and only the strong can change their fates and that of those around them."
Rory muttered sadly to Calron.

Hearing the hint of anguish in Rory's voice, Calron was sure something must have happened to Rory in the past, but he wanted to let Rory reveal his life's story by his own choice, rather than confronting him about it. He had learned after being with Elias that some secrets were meant to be in the dark.

"Sir, please don't do this. The livelihoods of several families depend on the money from this beast's sale."
The beast's owner continued to plead while the captain had his foot on his neck.

Seeing the broken state of the man on stage, many of the gathered crowd felt pity in their hearts, but none made a move to stop the guards.

"You filth. Look at what you did to my shoes. It's dirty now, so obediently lick it clean."
The captain insolently commanded the grief-stricken man, while the other guards behind him snickered quietly.

"Captain Gar has way too much fun these days. Remember the old blacksmith a few days ago?"
"Oh, wasn't the Captain interested in his daughter? Hehe."

The guards shamelessly bantered, and since they were being openly loud, the rest of the crowd could hear them clearly as well.
Other than feeling disgusted by them, there was nothing else they could do but quietly watch.

"You. How d-"
Seeing that he was just being kicked around, the man finally realized that no matter how much he pleaded, the guards would still take away his beast. Feeling both rage and humiliation, he got up and furiously released his essence.

Wisps of pale green essence coalesced around the man, and a roaring gust of wind swirled around his fists.

As the man tried to free his neck under the captain's foot, he felt a bloodthirsty aura above him.

"A lowly peasant like you dares to disobey me? I was giving you face till now, but instead, you return my grace with insolence!"
The captain bellowed with rage and unsheathed his sword. An extremely violent sword aura oppressed the trembling man on the ground.

Feeling helpless, both Calron and Rory suppressed their growing fury, but the clenched fists belied their state of mind. They could only watch helplessly as the rest of the crowd.

They felt shame for not doing anything for the man and pity for his dead brothers' families, but to whom else could they complain? These guards were supposed to be the law.

SLASH
A trail of warm blood splattered across Calron and Rory's faces.

CHAPTER FOURTEEN

Broken Weapon

Feeling the warm blood on his face, Calron felt his mind go numb.

This was the second time someone else's blood was on his face and he detected the source pool inside him burst with excitement. The Blood Legacy was thirsting for more blood and it ignited Calron's urge to kill.

Fighting the new instincts inside him, Calron bit his lower lip to draw pain to distract himself from the bloodlust. Elias had warned him before that it was extremely difficult to restrain the Blood Legacy once one started killing, so he had cautioned Calron to remain alert whenever it activated itself.

Meanwhile, Rory had tears pouring down his face. This was the first time he had seen someone die in front of him, and his soul shook from the intensity of the grief he felt for the poor man's death.

"Damn this bastard. He got his disgusting blood all over my uniform."
The captain spat while looking at the corpse on the ground.

"Take that cage and let's head back to our station. I need to change out of this filthy uniform."
Hearing their captain's instructions, one guard picked up the cage

and the rest soon followed behind the captain. The beast inside the cage mewed softly, but put up no further resistance.

Seeing the guards depart, the rest of the crowd slowly dispersed. A few servants came on stage to retrieve the corpse and to clean the stage of blood.

"You kids should not have watched that. Here, wipe away the blood from your faces."

An elderly woman chided the boys while handing them a piece of rag. Sights like these were common for her, but looking at the tear-stricken face of the chubby one, she felt her heart ache for his lost innocence.

The other skinny child's expression slightly confused her, but she didn't bother to dwell on it.

"Uh, thank you ma'am. I'll take my friend somewhere else."

Thanking the old woman, Calron gently dragged Rory away from the gory scene. Taking the rag, he carefully wiped the blood off Rory's face and used the other side of the rag to clean his own face.

"Hey, Rory, are you alright?"

Calron softly whispered to Rory after finding him a spot to sit.

"Huh? Yea, big brother... I just didn't expect that he would brutally kill him in front of this many people. I'm fine, don't worry, big brother. This was not my first time witnessing someone's death."

Rory responded sluggishly after wiping his tears away on his sleeves.

"Let's go. There is still that place I wanted to show big brother."

Rory exclaimed with false cheer, dragging Calron behind him. Calron knew Rory forced the lightheartedness, but they both needed to forget the gruesome sight from earlier, so he said nothing.

After treading through the various shops, they arrived at an upper district that appeared to have a lot more wealthy people wandering around. The shops were also more ornate than the ones Calron had seen previously at the start of the market. There were a greater number of guards stationed here.

"Big brother, this place is called the "Crown District". This is the only place within the entire Vernia city that sells luxury items like high-ranked cores of magical beasts, top elemental techniques, and even previous weapons of famous cultivators."

Rory's words sparked Calron's interest.

Cores? I'm not interested in them for now and Teacher probably has better cultivation techniques anyway, but I do need a weapon. I wonder how long Teacher will take to recover, I wish he were here to advise me on what weapon I should train in.

While Calron pondered this, Rory jumped up in excitement.

"Big brother. There is the thing that I wanted. Hehe, this is my one lifelong wish and if I fulfill it, then I wouldn't mind dying the next moment. Let's go!"

Seeing Rory's outburst, several passing customers gave weird looks towards them, but Rory did not seem to care. Drool was seeping down the corner of his mouth and suddenly Rory ran towards a shop several meters away.

"Hey Rory, wait!"

Calron cried as Rory was sprinting over.

This was the first time Calron had seen Rory ever put this much physical effort into anything, so after his initial astonishment, he soon ran after him while laughing hysterically. The reason for Calron's laughter was the way Rory was running.

Rory had both his arms pointing back while his upper body was leaning forwards. His chubby legs zigzagged through the crowd and at one point; Rory bumped into a little girl of three years old and snatched away the biscuit she was eating. The little toddler erupted in tears as her mother comforted her and spewed curses at Rory at the same time.

Far behind, Calron cracked up a grin and rushed to catch up to Rory.

As soon as he arrived near Rory, the scene he saw stunned him.
It was a food stand.

Various kinds and cuts of meat were displayed elegantly at the side, while several youths were running the front of the shop by taking in orders from customers. There was a sizable waiting line, so their dishes must be high in demand; however, Calron did not understand why there would be such a fuss for food.

Locating Rory near the line, Calron walked towards him. Rory was literally drooling at the sight of meat cooking nearby and initially paid no attention when Calron tapped him on the shoulder. Calron poked him in the side.

"Eh? Oh, it's big brother. Isn't this awesome? Look at all that meat! I wish I could stuff all of them into my mouth, but big sis only gave me a few silver squares."
Rory lamented while looking at the three silver squares in his hands.

"What? You actually have silver squares, and you still don't think that's enough? Punk, you want me to smack you?"
Calron exclaimed while pretending to smack Rory.

For Calron, silver squares were a currency that was only for the wealthy. A poor family only needed bread and some meat for survival, as what use were luxurious items when even their daily survival was at stake?

Calron had never known the feeling of starvation, as his parents would sacrifice their share of what little food there was, so he would not have to sleep hungry. Recalling memories of his parents, Calron felt his heart throb in anguish, but he forced himself to forget those memories.

"But these are the meat of high-ranked magical beasts. The one I want is that cut of Flame-tailed Buffalo, a third-rank magical beast. Its meat is supposed to be juicy and tender, and I heard one disciple talk about how it just melts in your mouth. Don't you think that sounds like the meat of your dreams?"

Seeing Rory talk so passionately about this meat, Calron felt like slapping himself on the head. He had been wondering from the start why Rory had been so focused on reaching this place, and after knowing the reason, he didn't know whether to laugh or to cry.

This Rory had told me he would show me something good, but he just wanted to eat some new delicious foods. Damn this idiot. He only thinks about food all the time... sigh.

Calron could only complain inwardly, as anything said to Rory at this point would just fall upon deaf ears. He should've guessed from the beginning that this was the chubby boy's goal.

"I'll just take a look around. Rory, meet me here in an hour, alright? I don't know this area well, so if you leave without me, I'll tell Gretha to not give you dinner."

Faced with the threat of no dinner, Rory twisted his face towards Calron and nodded his head vigorously.

"No need to worry, big brother. I promise I'll stay here and wait for you. Even if I get hungry, I'll still wait."

Calron smiled at Rory's sudden change of attitude. He learned anytime you threatened Rory with the loss of a meal, he would listen to any demands you'd make. Shaking his head with a smile, Calron turned around and left.

....

After leaving Rory, Calron wandered the Crown District for a while. He saw many shops that sold items from high-ranked pills to rare jewels. He wanted to enter the shop selling the magic beasts' cores, but the shopkeeper refused to let him in.

"Brat, go look somewhere else! This place is not for some runt like you."

The shopkeeper gestured for Calron to move along, albeit with some annoyance.

Slightly dejected, Calron continued to explore the district. Some shopkeepers were nice and let him come in, but most were conceited and refused to let Calron near their shops.

"You'll dirty my shop, piss off, kid!"

Calron ignored those kinds of shopkeepers, and after a while, decided to return to Rory as it was almost the time he said that they should meet.

However, just as he was about to turn around, he felt a slight tingle from his father's locket in his chest.

Calron abruptly stopped moving.

This was the first time after his awakening that he felt the presence of the locket again. He thought it had merged completely into his body, but at this moment he could feel that the locket was still there, lodged firmly on top of his ribs.

He felt faint tremors radiating from it and was befuddled about what the movement of the locket meant. It was not painful, but it certainly felt strange to have something unknown vibrate inside his

167

body.

Not knowing what else to do, Calron started walking back towards the meat shop where Rory was.

The further he went, the fainter the tremors became until they completely vanished. Feeling as if the locket was trying to tell him something, Calron stopped walking towards the meat shop and instead returned to the place where the tremors initially started.

The tremors once again returned and steadily increased as Calron moved forwards. He used the intensity of the tremors to guide his path, changing his direction when the tremors slowed or moving forward when they increased.

After five minutes of sweating and running around, Calron finally reached the place where the tremors felt as if the locket would soon pop out of his body.

Throughout the entire journey, Calron had been running everywhere like a lunatic, going in one direction for a while and a second later, abruptly changing his path again. The people watching Calron thought he was possessed and silently moved away as soon as Calron ran in their direction.

Panting out of breath, Calron looked at the shop in front of him.

It was a broken-down and miserable-looking place. Calling it a shop was too generous, as it seemed more like a shack than an actual store. Glancing around him, Calron saw he was back near the outskirts of the marketplace, where he had first seen that sweaty man roasting lizards.

Most of the shops here seemed like they had seen better days, but the one in front of Calron was the worst by a large margin. Seeing as he had no choice but to enter, Calron anxiously stepped into the store.

cough

A cloud of dust erupted as soon as Calron stepped inside, evoking a series of coughs.

"Who are you, boy?"

A rasp voice of an elderly woman sounded in the empty store.

"Um, I'm Calron. I just came here to look around."

Calron hesitantly replied. He was not sure if the store was open to customers or not.

"Kekeke, look around to your heart's content, child, but I doubt you'll find anything of worth. The guards already took away every precious thing I had."

The woman said in a forlorn voice as she walked towards Calron.

Hearing the click-clack sound of a stick against the floor, Calron looked around until he finally saw an elderly woman approaching him from the side.

Her back was hunched as she rested her body's weight on the thin wooden staff. It was surprising that the thin stick did not bend in the slightest.

A pair of dull brown eyes stared at Calron, observing his face and clothes.

"There are only some broken swords and other defective weapons left. My husband was a talented blacksmith when he was alive, but those bastards even took away his blacksmithing tools."

The old woman wistfully voiced to Calron.

Facing the emotionally wrecked woman, Calron felt sympathy in his heart. This woman was already aged, and who knew how long she had left to live, but even in those last few moments of life, she had nothing but anguish and pain.

"Grandma, is there anything I could do for you?"

Calron inquired while looking at the elderly woman with sympathy. He never knew his grandparents, but he felt close to this elderly lady.

"Child, you are not even ten years old. What could you possibly help me with? My only wish is for that cursed city Lord to die the most miserable death!"

The old woman rasped with silent savagery. However, after seeing the dejected look on Calron's face, she added softly.

"However, this place could use a good cleanup before I close its doors. Child, these old bones don't have the same energy they once used to. Would you help this grandma out?"

"Yes. Just leave it to me, grandma."

Seeing the spirited boy in front of her, even the old lady could not help but crack a smile.

"There should be a broom and some other tools back there, so go knock yourself out."

The elderly woman cackled while staggering towards a nearby chair.

Meanwhile, Calron rushed to the back to retrieve the broom. The tremors had returned to soft vibrations, but Calron had a feeling that what the locket wanted him to find was definitely inside this shop.

Grabbing the broom, Calron immediately set to work. He swept around the place with the energy only an eight-year-old would have. Seeing him madly sweep back and forth, the old woman would occasionally burst into a fit of chuckles.

As Calron was sweeping, he was paying close attention to the changes in his locket. That was the reason he intently swept every nook and cranny of the place. Just as he moved to the back corner of the shop, he unexpectedly felt the locket shaking wildly.

His heartbeat started to rapidly accelerate with anticipation.

As Calron's eyes surveyed the area, the only items he could find were pieces of broken equipment and weapons. There were several discarded swords with bent or fractured blades, while the rest varied from incomplete axes to broken bows.

Calron felt his spirits suddenly doused with water. He thought he would find an extraordinary object that was hidden, something that even the guards had failed to see, but he did not expect to see an assortment of rejected weapons, things that even a beggar would not look twice at.

Noticing that Calron had stopped moving, the old widow looked over and saw that he was just staring at the broken pieces of weapons.

"Those were the failed works of my husband and some other stuff he found when he was a young traveling blacksmith. You can take them all if you want, I was going to throw them out."

The aged woman said indifferently while returning to her seat.

Who would want this junk? I thought there would be something good here... could it be that the locket meant something else? No, but I definitely sensed that it wanted me to come here. Why doesn't it respond now?

Calron's mind unceasingly reflected on these thoughts.

"Kid, I'll get you something to drink. It's already been an hour since you started and you must be thirsty by now. Just finish up the back and you can take some rest. It's not like anyone will come here."

The old woman's hoarse voice rasped behind Calron.

Muttering a simple acknowledgment, Calron's gaze remained fixed on the scene in front of him.

Out of utter desperation, he started touching all the weapons to see if the locket responded in any way. He started with the spears, or what remained of the spears, and felt around for any hidden mechanisms.

Slightly exasperated with no actual results, Calron moved on to the next spear.

....

After a few minutes, Calron had reached the pile of broken swords and he still hadn't received a response from the locket. Growling in frustration, Calron flung the broken sword he was holding to the ground.

"Ouch!"
Calron yelped after feeling a sting on his finger. The sharp edge of the broken blade nicked him.

A globule of blood formed at the tip of his forefinger, and Calron placed the finger in his mouth to stop the bleeding.

"Damn this stupid sword."
As he bent forward to grasp the pommel of the sword, Calron felt an unexplainable urge to look at the object next to the blade.

It was a simple recurved bow with slightly sharp ends. It had a snapped bowstring, so it essentially looked like a curved stick with two dangling strings. The body of the bow appeared to be made of metal and covered with slight scratches and nicks. Its body was wrapped with rust and it seemed more like a discarded piece of metal than an actual bow.

Confused why a bow would be made of metal instead of wood, Calron picked it up.

Crackle
Torrents of Azure Lightning rushed from Calron's body and fluctuated around the room in a frenzy.

This was the first time the Azure Lightning had erupted with such intensity.

The lightning ricocheted into the surrounding weapons, as a small thunderous explosion burst from each of them until only ashes remained in their place.

Calron was watching this entire scene with a stunned expression. He had no control over the Azure Lightning, and it currently seemed to have a will of its own.

At last, all the lightning gathered and formed into a single sinuous body of bolts that spiraled around Calron like a large electric azure snake. For the first time ever, the lightning took up a form.

Feeling the sudden heat from the center of his chest, Calron knew that the locket had awoken once again, and the sound of thunder reverberated through the room.

CHAPTER FIFTEEN

Thunder's Hand

crackle *crackle*

The long electric snake continued to shoot out small bolts of lightning while Calron numbly stared at the scene in front of him. He was right in the center, with the electric snake coiling around him.

The lightning around the snake seemed to get thicker and thicker by the moment until an ear-piercing roar resounded throughout the room.

BOOOM!
The total mass of lightning collapsed into the broken metal bow and a shrill cry of an animal penetrated Calron's mind.

The bow slowly rose in the air out of its own accord, and waves of blue lightning bolts surged around it. A faint glow emitted from its body, as the rust slowly peeled away just like a snake shedding its skin, revealing a dark onyx metallic body.

When the dark metallic body of the bow appeared, a baleful aura spread around the room at the same time and nearly choked Calron, until the locket transmitted a surge of protective energy around him.

Within the crackling of the blue lightning, thin threads of faint pitch-black lightning also rippled around the bow.

The metal appeared to be absorbing the bolts of lightning as the essence slowly decreased by the second. Meanwhile, the metal bow continued to mutate.

Suddenly, the bolts of blue lightning violently expanded in a second and were then vigorously absorbed back into the bow. The previous azure glow around the room disintegrated along with the protective energy surrounding Calron.

Silence.

Calron let out the breath that he had been subconsciously holding the entire time. The scene he witnessed now seemed more like a dream than reality, especially considering the vicious aura that he felt before the locket intervened.

Calron was captivated by the enigmatic bow before him. It had an alluring presence that was impossible to ignore. Upon closer inspection, he could detect faint traces of patterns emitting a dim azure glow that snaked around the bow. The most noticeable fact about the dark metal bow was that it did not even have a bowstring now.

Calron was apprehensive about touching the metal, but he felt the locket subtly compelling him to retrieve it. His hands trembled as they drew closer to the dark bow on the floor.

At that moment, the sound of glass shattering echoed throughout the entire shop.

"Wha- what was that?"

The old widow asked with a quivering voice, emerging from the back

Her dull brown eyes were wide open as she dumbly gaped at

Calron and the dark onyx bow on the floor. Her mind shuddered as she recalled the baleful aura she had felt a few minutes ago in the kitchen.

It seemed as if all the despair and misery of the world threatened to devour her fragile soul. The cause was clearly that strange bow. Something as nefarious as that bow should not exist in this world.

The only thing that saved her life was the distance between her and the evil weapon. Noticing that Calron was unfazed by that deadly aura, a hint of fear seeped into the old woman as she inwardly questioned if the boy was truly human.

"Uh, grandma, I-"
Not knowing what to say, Calron fumbled around while trying to think of a way to explain what had just happened. What worried Calron the most was whether she saw the Azure Lightning released from his body or not.

"Boy, get away from that vile thing!"

In the end, Calron was still a child, so the old woman found it hard to believe that all the destruction and the lightning she saw was from this boy. She naturally concluded that the entire cause of this was the black bow. If she had known that Calron was a lightning elementalist, her earlier assumptions might have been different.

Calron realized from her words that the old woman believed the whole mess was because of the black bow, and he could not help but feel slightly relieved. However, he had another dilemma on his hands. If he purposefully took the bow now, then it would gather too much-unwanted suspicion.

Coincidently, Calron felt the locket heat up again, but this time, a series of images flashed inside his mind. This sensation felt very similar to the time when his Teacher had transferred the second stage of the Thunderbird technique directly to his soul.

The images disintegrated as soon as they appeared, but the information remained inside Calron's head.

He discretely clenched his fist with the finger that had been injured before and used the pressure from his other fingers to reopen the wound. Just as he felt a slight wetness within his fist, Calron moved on to the next part of his plan.

"Sorry grandma, I don't know what happened. I was just looking through the weapons, and when I touched the metal bow, it suddenly started shooting off lightning. Look, this is where I touched it."

Before the elderly woman could stop him, Calron touched the dark onyx bow with his injured hand, and in a blink, the bow vanished completely .

"Where did it go? Boy, move aside!"

The old woman frantically searched for the dark weapon, but could not find any traces of it at all. The boy couldn't hide it as the thing was almost as big as him and the kid seemed to be just as surprised as her.

That was close. I thought she almost saw through me at the last second. Why do I always get pulled into the most troublesome situations? So, its name is Thunder's Hand, huh? Thankfully, the locket told me how to bind it with my blood, otherwise; I doubt I could've taken this bow anywhere. I wonder what this locket truly is. I've never heard of any object being able to convey its thoughts to others.

Calron pondered, while the old woman continued to search for the missing bow.

"Uh, grandma, I need to leave right now. I told my friend to wait for me and it has already been way past the meeting time. It was nice meeting you."

Seeing as there were no signs of the bow, the elderly woman simply sighed and rasped at the boy as he began to leave.

"Go, go. It's not good manners to be late."

As the boy left the store, the old woman slowly picked the broken shards of glass up from the floor.

"Blood?"

The old widow whispered as she saw the drops of crimson blood on the floor, and unintentionally gazed at the door from which the boy had just left.

....

In a crowded district, inside a small meat shop, a lone chubby boy sat at a table by himself. He had a look of despair on his face as he continued to stare at the streets, looking for that one familiar face.

"Where is big bro? It has already been hours since we were supposed to meet, and he still hasn't shown up."

Rory quietly murmured to himself and, after a few moments, his stomach growled.

"I'm starving. I already spent all my money on the Flame-tailed Buffalo... that meat was so delicious, I must come here again after big sis gives me some more money."

As Rory dreamed of more meat, he felt a tap on his shoulder.

"Sorry, Rory. I got lost on the way back..."

Calron sheepishly said while scratching his head.

"What!? You got lost? How can you be lost for hours? And couldn't you just ask someone for directions?"

Rory burst out emotionally.

For the past few hours, the constant smell of the succulent meat roasting tortured him. With no money and being forced to stay at the shop by Calron, he could only silently cry tears and curse his luck.

Knowing he didn't have a good excuse, Calron hurriedly stated. "Rory, let's go back. I'll give you half my share of dinner."

"You promise?"
Rory inquired, slight suspicion creeping into his voice.

"Would I ever lie to you?"
Calron realized his blunder the instant he said those words, as Rory glared accusingly at him.

After fervently apologizing to Rory and with future promises of more food, Calron finally appeased him.

Soon, both boys started walking back towards the Red Boar School as they each recounted their tales of the day. Rory unceasingly described the taste of the "dream meat", while Calron told Rory about some of the fascinating items he saw while wandering around.

Without a doubt, Calron decided to keep the incident with the dark onyx bow to himself.

He did not have the chance to summon it again after leaving the old woman's shop after seeing how many people were around, so he waited until he reached his hut to further inspect Thunder's Hand.

. . . .

The sky imperceptibly turned dark, and the weather dropped in temperature, causing the two boys to shiver uncontrollably.

At last, the gates of the Red Boar School appeared in sight, and both Calron and Rory rushed to get indoors for warmth.
Their breath turned foggy when they exhaled, and Rory glanced at Calron, giving the boy a withering scowl, blaming him for the situation that they were in.

Calron purposefully ignored Rory's stare, but he felt a bit guilty, as it certainly was because of him that they were so late.

"Huh, who's that, big brother?"
Rory whispered when a hazy figure appeared unexpectedly within their sight.

The figure was still a few meters ahead, but the light fog in the air obscured all defining features of the man, revealing an unrecognizable silhouette. Both Calron and Rory failed to distinguish the identity of the figure.

An uneasy atmosphere lingered in the air when it became clear the human-like shadow switched directions to approach the anxious boys.

Within the fog, the shadow continued walking in their direction.

Seeing the figure approach them, Calron felt slightly nervous, as he had come to learn by now that misfortune seemed to follow him everywhere.

Even Rory seemed jittery under the current atmosphere. He could instinctively feel that someone with a powerful aura was coming towards them.

clack *clack*
The sound of a wooden stick hitting against the ground echoed in the quiet road.

"Eh? I've heard that sound before...could it be?"
Just as Calron muttered to himself, a figure soon emerged from the fog, revealing his features.

"Master!"

Calron exclaimed when he saw the wrinkled face of Elias illuminated under the moonlight.

Elias's silver hair was neatly tied in a ponytail, and his white robe glowed with the same luminance as the gentle moon above. The fog dispersed away as he stepped out of it and continued to walk toward Calron and Rory.

Seeing his Master, Calron was both elated and confused. His Master did not like to come out in public and he had often reminded Calron to keep their relationship completely hidden from others.

This was the only reason why he still had not disclosed anything about his Martial Arts training to Rory. In the sparse time they had spent together, both boys had unknowingly developed an unbreakable bond. They did not know much about each other's past or history, but their souls were naturally drawn to each other by mysterious threads of fate.

Rory was the most shocked out of both of them. Calron had just called this old man in front of him, "Master", so how could he not be surprised? Furthermore, the man was completely blind.

Even in the dark, Rory could distinctly see Elias' opaque gray eyes, and besides, who didn't know the crazy blind cripple of the school?

"Big brother, did you just call him 'Master'?"
Rory spluttered hesitantly next to Calron.

Realizing his blunder, Calron felt foolish, as he had unknowingly revealed the deeply kept secret between him and Elias. Glancing towards his Master to see his reaction, Calron felt mollified by Elias' next few words.

"It's fine, Calron. He would have found out eventually. Besides, I need him to know now."

Elias said with a slight smile as he finally arrived in front of the two boys. Baffled by his Master's words, Calron just stood there while pondering what Elias meant.

"Roran, I can cure you of your sickness."
Just those few words uttered by Elias shook Rory's world.

Never mind the fact that the man already knew his name, but his sickness was a closely guarded secret that not even the entire Axier family knew.

Rory's hands trembled as he subconsciously staggered back a few steps.

"H-How did you know?"
Rory asked with a quiver in his voice. His sickness was his greatest weakness and if others found out what it actually was, he would be treated worse than before.

Paying no attention to the nervous changes in Rory's behavior, Elias responded calmly.

"Because I am the same as you."

....

"Report."
An icy voice commanded the man kneeling in front of the dais.

"My Lord, Master Dane has agreed to take the little lady under his tutelage for the next few years. We have talked with the School Head, and Master Dane should have no trouble staying at the Red Boar School during that duration."
The assassin stated in a stoic voice.

"How did Felice take the news?"
A frosty voice inquired, as its owner slowly stood up from his

seat. The tall man turned towards his side and looked out the window, while the assassin continued to kneel on the floor.

A pale full moon gently floated in the starry sky. Below, the calm wind embraced the leaves on the trees as they softly swayed in the night.

"Little lady was most pleased when she found out that Master Dane would tutor her in Martial Arts. His reputation is indeed quite renowned."

"Hmm, I'm glad."
The moonlight shone on the man's face, revealing his gray hair and trimmed beard. A pair of piercing cobalt eyes gazed at the scenery outside the window, as several creases appeared near his eyes.

"How is he?"
Almost imperceptibly, a soft whisper sounded from the gray-haired man.

Noticing the abrupt change of tone in his Lord's voice, the kneeling man knew to whom his Lord was referring.

"He is well, my Lord. He gets bullied often, but his spirit never wavers. As per your orders, we won't interfere unless his life is threatened."

"Does he get to eat good food?"
The Lord asked with a slight smile on his face, which the kneeling man obviously could not see as the tall man was facing away from the assassin.

Not understanding the humor in the gray-haired man's question, the assassin did not know how to respond.

"Yes, my Lord, the school provides meals for all its students."

"Haha, I doubt that rascal would be satisfied with such plain food."

The Lord laughed as he started reminiscing about the memories of his son growing up.

Meanwhile, the assassin kneeled there with his mouth wide open.

He had never seen the Lord laugh so openly. Lord Mort was known for his cold and domineering personality, as the powerful man rarely smiled or laughed.

As if remembering something, the assassin added.

"My Lord, recently he has been spending time with a new friend."

The gray-haired man turned his head slightly at the new information.

"A friend, huh? I hope you stay well, my son..."

The Lord muttered so delicately that even the assassin could not hear the last few words.

....

Standing at the side, Calron was utterly confused about the conversation between his Master and Rory.

Sickness? I don't see anything wrong with Rory, and he seems perfectly fine to me. What is Master talking about?

While Calron's thoughts raced around in his mind, a different scene was occurring between Rory and Elias.

"Yes, Roran, I'm also an Element-Less."

Elias stated serenely while his opaque gray eyes gazed at Rory with an unnatural glow. Under that intense scrutiny, Rory doubted if this man was truly blind.

Silence.

Calron was befuddled. *Rory was an Element-Less?*

Calron thought back to all the time he spent with Rory and realized that he had not once seen him release his essence. Even when others bullied him, Rory would never fight back, and Calron had always assumed that it was due to Rory's inherent nature, but it seemed now as if that was far from the truth.

However, Calron also recalled the moment today at the public execution when Rory released an ice-piercing aura. *What was that then?*

Rory had his eyes wide open as he stared in shock at Elias. He had been secretly hoping that this strange old man would be mistaken, but this man indeed knew his secret. How?

He turned his head and looked at Calron's stunned face. Feeling isolated and alone, Rory hung his head in dejection.

"But yours is a unique case, Roran. You still have your core within you. Only your spiritual veins were forcefully harmed. If the pathway from your core to your veins can be reconnected, then you will no longer be an Element-Less."
Elias stated in a serious tone.

Hearing the old man's words, Rory felt a seed of hope sprout inside his heart. Would he really be able to cultivate? He had long given up on any shred of desire to ever feel the touch of essence.

When he was five years old, Rory was afflicted with a deadly illness out of the blue and then bedridden for several weeks. The healers of the family claimed that he was poisoned and could never awaken his element. It was because the pathways to his spiritual veins were broken and mangled. This turned the entire Axier family upside down when the news was released.

Back then, Rory was too young to realize what that meant, but as he grew older, he understood why he was so different from others. He subconsciously thought of himself as weak and gave up on trying to fight back against the bullies.

He was what they called an Element-Less.

"Y-you're telling the truth? Can I really awaken to an element?"

Rory felt as if his heart would burst with uncontainable joy at this moment. Although he liked to goof around and appeared to be unconcerned by the bullies, in the deepest depths of his soul, he thirsted for power. This once long-extinguished desire had now reignited again into a blazing inferno.

"Yes. If your physical body can transform anew, then all of your spiritual veins will be regrown and connected to your core again."

When Calron heard those words from the side, he felt his heart beat wildly against his chest.

He had a feeling that he knew what his Master's next words were.

"Roran, you will be the second Inheritor of the Blood Legacy."

CHAPTER SIXTEEN
Rebirth

"Roran, you will become the second Inheritor of the Blood Legacy."

Silence.

The scene of an old man benevolently gazing at an eight-year-old child seemed to have frozen in space. The dark ebony hair of the child contrasted with the long silvery hair of the old man underneath the soft moonlight.

A surge of wind embraced them as their hair fluttered wildly in the night's dark and even the stream of time ceased to flow.

Calron's heart violently thumped against his chest as he fixedly stared at his Master, and then his friend.

"What is your answer, my child?"
Elias faintly breathed out the words as he broke the standstill in time.

"I don't know what the Blood Legacy is..."
Just as Elias was about to respond, Rory continued with a fierce determination on his face.

"But if it will give me the power I want, then even if I have to sacrifice everything, I will accept it."

Hearing the intense tenacity in Rory's words, Elias let out a low, admiring laugh.

"Child, you will do just fine. With your determination, you will soon be able to grasp the power of the Blood Legacy. Both of you, take some rest and meet me early tomorrow morning. I will give you what you desire, Roran."

"And take this. It will let you safely enter my home."

Elias stated evenly as he flung a small wooden token toward Rory. It was the exact wooden disk that he had previously given to Calron to enter the area inside the Artifact.

"Calron, take care of him till then."

With a brief glance towards Calron, Elias vanished into thin air.

Both boys stared stupefied at the scene.

It was not the fact that Elias had mysteriously disappeared into thin air, but it was that his speed was so fast that their eyes could not even keep track of his movements.

After Elias left, there was an air of awkwardness between the two boys.

"Uh, big brother, I..."

Rory tried to fill the silence, but he did not know what to say.

Calron guessed what seemed to trouble Rory, and he gently responded.

"Rory, it's fine. Everyone has their secrets to keep, and besides, it makes no difference to me whether or not you are an Element-Less."

"Do you mean it?"

Rory asked with a bright smile on his chubby face.

He had been worried that Calron might see him differently after finding out his secret, as who would want to befriend a loser who couldn't even use essence? He had previously seen Calron's stunned face when the old man revealed his secret, so he thought Calron may have felt deceived by him.

Although it had been only a short while since he met Calron, Rory had never felt so close with anyone in his life besides his big sister. If Calron had broken off their friendship, then Rory would have been utterly devastated.

Seeing the range of emotions flicker on Rory's face, Calron jumped onto Rory's back and ruffled his hair playfully.

"You idiot! Do you think I would stop being friends with you just because of that? Who else would steal my food if you were gone?"

As Calron joked and teased him, Rory laughed as he tried to get Calron off his back.

"That's not true. I would never steal food from someone. Please don't ruin my reputation, big brother."

Rory tearfully cried as Calron started tickling him.

"Eh? What about that biscuit you stole from the three-year-old girl this afternoon? You even pushed her!"

Rory tried to hide his face in mock shame, but burst out giggling without a pause.

"Haha, that little girl was acting so smug while munching on that biscuit, so I just wanted to taste it a little bit."

Shaking his head, Calron joined in, laughing as well. Only Rory could ever justify himself for stealing food from a little girl.

During the fateful night, two youths were bent over laughing hysterically as they reminisced about the scene from earlier in the market. They had completely forgotten all about the cold, the dark, or any other worries, as they simply cherished each other's company.

....

"Rory, meet me at my hut tomorrow morning and we'll go together to Master Elias's place."
Calron stated after recovering from the fit of laughter.

"Alright, big brother. By the way, what is the Blood Legacy? I have heard of the other legacies, but never about one that follows the path of Blood."
Rory asked curiously, while tilting his head to the side.

"Umm, I'll let Master explain it to you, even I don't know much about it. However, you need to learn to control your emotions once you receive it, as this legacy has a vicious bloodlust whenever it senses blood around you."
Calron stated while whispering the last few words.

Rory was even more curious about it, but decided to wait until tomorrow morning to learn more from his new Master.

Both boys now ran towards the Red Boar School and they finally entered the courtyard. The guards at the gates admonished them for staying out so late in the dark, but eventually let them off with a mellow warning.

Before the boys were about to go their way to their respective huts, Rory asked a last question.
"Big brother, is Master truly blind? I could swear he was gazing right into my eyes when he was talking."

"He is blind, but Master has a technique that lets him see essence or some other type of energy around him. I don't really know much about it, but no one can conceal anything from Master's eyes. That is probably how he knew about your core as well."

Nodding his head, Rory shouted out a quick goodnight to Calron and happily strolled toward Gretha's kitchen. Calron said he was tired, and that he wanted to take some rest.

However, the real reason was that Calron wanted to further explore his new bow. Rushing towards his hut, Calron closed the door behind him as soon as he entered.

After making sure that no disciples were wandering outside, Calron willed the bow to appear. In the blink of an eye, Calron felt the heavy weight of the bow in his hands.

The dark onyx bow was surprisingly heavy, and Calron immediately placed it on top of his bed when he realized he could not bear its weight.

It must be understood that after Calron's breakthrough to the third rank, he was much stronger than a normal person and could even lift a huge chunk of steel if he wanted, but this dark bow was even heavier than steel.

The bow appeared to be absorbing all the light near it, which seemed to make its metallic body even darker than the depths of an abyss. The only trace of light was in the strange patterns coiled around it, glowing a faint blue hue. The contrast between the dark onyx body and the blue azure light made the bow seem unnatural and out of this world.

What confounded Calron was that the bow did not have a bowstring attached. So how was he supposed to even use it?

Calron touched the bow, feeling the smooth and pristine texture of the metallic body. It was astonishingly glassy, making it seem brittle, but Calron knew that was an illusion. Not even a hint of a blemish remained on the metal. Moments after Calron touched the bow, he felt his lightning essence hurriedly tremble with uncontainable excitement.

Curious why his essence was reacting in such a way, he slowly released the lightning around him.

Suddenly, the golden lightning surrounding Calron rushed into the dark bow.

As the dark onyx metal absorbed the essence, the faint blue glow around it switched to a pale yellow color and slowly a thin thread of golden lightning coalesced at one end of the bow and gradually connected to the other end, forming a bowstring made of lightning essence.

Amazed at the sudden development in front of him, Calron felt his heart racing as he tried to contain his excitement.

It was obvious that this dark bow was not ordinary and previously Calron had felt slightly dismayed as he could not figure out how to use it, but seeing the current scene, Calron realized this bow required essence.

He had heard of legendary weapons in children's tales that required a cultivator's essence, but it was his first time seeing such a weapon with his own eyes.

Gathering his strength, Calron used his entire body to pick up the heavy bow and took a few moments to steady himself.

With his heart pounding against his chest, Calron finally drew the lightning string.

fizz

The lightning thread completely disintegrated into thin air as soon as Calron drew it slightly.

"Huh?"

Calron dumbly stared at the bow in his hands. Besides the faint yellow glow, the bow was the same as before, and all the essence it had just absorbed seemed to have vanished as well.

"What just happened?"

Calron was utterly perplexed. Hoping it was a fluke, he gathered a huge amount of essence again and willed it into the dark bow.

The yellow glow of the patterns brightened for a moment as the lightning thread formed once more. The string of lightning bolts appeared to be thicker than before. Reaching to draw again, Calron pulled the essence string.

fizz

Although Calron could draw it slightly more this time, it still disintegrated after a few seconds.

"Hmm, it seems that this bow requires a huge amount of essence to use it."

After realizing what the problem was, Calron sighed with regret.

He knew it was just wishful thinking to hope he could use a weapon that emitted such a profound baleful aura with merely his Spiritual stage strength.

Storing the metal bow back inside his body, Calron lay on top of his bed.

"Thunder's Hand... this bow has some sort of connection with lightning and that mysterious locket. I wonder why my father had this locket in the first place... ugh, if Teacher were here, he could answer some of my questions. How long will he take to recover? I really miss him..."

With a wistful groan, Calron turned to his side and slowly closed his eyes.

Within his dreams, various images flickered, ranging from bloody wars to a gigantic bird with lightning bolts.

Feeling the sun's rays boring through his eyes, Calron stared groggily outside the window.

He then immediately tucked his head back inside his blanket and turned his body to the other side to escape from the sunlight.

Out of nowhere, he felt a massive weight on his legs. It was almost as if a baby elephant had just sat on them.

"Rory! Get the hell off of my bed!"
Realizing that the baby elephant was in fact Rory, Calron bellowed furiously while kicking the chubby boy with his feet.

"Ouch! Big brother, no need to be so mean. That hurts! I already got kicked around yesterday because of you."
Rory mumbled as he rubbed his bottom as Calron slowly got off the bed.

After a quick brush of his teeth and a hurried cleanup, Calron returned to find Rory rolling around in his bed.

Shaking his head, Calron yelled.

"Rory, let's go!"

....

After their breakfast at the gathering hall, Calron and Rory left to go to the forest after giving a quick goodbye to Gretha.

Looking at the two boys leaving together, Gretha smiled with tenderness. The two youngsters were almost polar opposites of each other, both physically and in their personalities. Yet, they seemed a natural harmony of energies.

One was skinny and pale, while the other was chubby and energetic. Calron was a nice boy, but he rarely talked to others and seemed to have a mysterious atmosphere around him. On the other hand, Roran was a cheerful kid who was almost always goofing around or shoving food in his mouth.

Giving a final smile towards the young pair, Gretha went back to her work.

....

In a few minutes Calron and Rory had finally reached the start of the forest, and the whole time, Rory either gasped or exclaimed in wonder at the unfamiliar sights in front of him.

"Master told me this was an artifact that is a special treasure of the Red Boar School. He said the School Head let him use it as his home, so Master doesn't have to interact with others."
Calron explained while the two boys were walking towards Elias' hut.

"Master is so strong. Why does he need to hide from others?"
Rory asked curiously. From his experience yesterday, even though the old man was blind, he was extremely powerful. Just based on the movement skill he saw alone, it was comparable to the Martial Arts of his family.

"I think Master doesn't enjoy drawing attention to himself, and besides, he once told me he would barely be a match against a low Vajra stage expert."

"Hey, big brother! Have you realized something yet? From today onwards, we will be cultivation brothers as well. Hehe, I will show you just how awesome I am."

As Rory playfully boasted, Calron just gave him a smug smirk.

"Rory, you forget that I'm your senior disciple. Master has already taught me some powerful moves. If I could use the Blood Legacy during my fight with Chax, I would have easily defeated him."

Calron proudly gloated while Rory turned a disbelieving look towards him.

"Of course, big brother. And I'm secretly a princess in disguise."

Rory responded sarcastically. He had felt a powerful aura around Calron when he initially saw him, but after knowing that he was a Lightning elementalist, the logic in Rory's mind could not associate Calron with someone strong.

Aware that Rory did not believe him, Calron gave up on trying to convince him and cracked a grin when he thought about how he will give a thrashing to Rory when they sparred.

Rory was completely oblivious to Calron's smug expression.

After a few minutes, the familiar hut of Elias soon appeared within Calron's sight and he grabbed Rory's arm, rushing towards the humble hut.

....

An old man sat seated in a meditative pose.

His upper body was bare as the thick muscles rippled under the sun's rays. There were countless traces of scars spread across his skin, some of which appeared to be caused by claw marks, while others seemed to be clean cuts from a sword.

With his silver hair tied neatly in a simple ponytail, the old man emitted a violent and bloodthirsty aura into his surroundings.

Just as the two boys were starting to feel pressured by the aura, the old man unhurriedly opened his eyes.

"Good, you've come on time. Calron, you can practice your Formless Fist if you want, and I will pass on the Blood Legacy to Roran in the meantime."

"Yes, Master."

Calron responded before he started walking towards the lake. He had decided that the open air and the natural environment might help give better results in his training.

As Calron left, Elias stood up and turned towards Rory.

"Roran, what do you think the Blood Legacy is?"

"Um, big brother told me it had something to do with bloodlust or killing?"

Rory answered with trepidation.

"True, but not completely. The Blood Legacy follows the path of destruction and violence. Although all Legacy Inheritors train in battles and war, their main purpose is to increase the understanding of their Martial path of either their weapon or fist. The Blood Legacy is completely different. There is no justice or virtue in our path. We kill what needs to be killed. Or more accurately, we kill who we want to. We are neither the heroes nor the villains as we simply forge our own paths."

Elias calmly explained to the wide-eyed boy in front of him.

"Our Legacy is not the path of a weapon, but a path soaked in the blood of others. Your greatest battle and obstacle will be controlling that bloodlust and the rest you will understand once you inherit it. There will be no going back after you get baptized in the legacy's blood. Do you still wish to become my disciple?"

Elias kneeled and looked fixedly into Rory's eyes as he softly asked the last question.

Gazing into those unnaturally glowing eyes, Rory felt his heart tremble at the sight.

Clenching his fists, Rory gathered up his determination and returned the fierce look toward Elias.

"My desire has always been to cast away my fate as a cripple and seize my destiny. If this Blood Legacy will give me the power I need, then I will gladly embrace it and walk the path of blood."

Rory responded in a cold, low voice.

Hearing the boy's determination, Elias gave a slight smile.

"Roran, you and Calron will be the future of this legacy. Do not let its fire be extinguished."

With a solemn declaration, Elias slashed his palm with a dagger.

"Kneel."

Rory slowly got on his knees in front of his Master and bowed his head. After a few seconds, he felt a warm wetness on his forehead and he knew it was his Master's blood. Just as the blood dripped into his eyes, he heard Elias' voice.

"From today onwards, you will walk in the path of blood. Destruction and Carnage will be your sworn brothers and follow wherever you go. May the God of War bless and look favorably upon you and give rise to your valor. I, Elias Salazar Xuria, hereby acknowledge you as my Inheritor and pass on my will and Legacy to you. Do you accept?"

"I do, Master."

"The first blood has been shed. From this day on forth, you will walk in the path of blood alongside your brother. Let your transformation begin."

CHAPTER SEVENTEEN

Spar

As soon as his new Master spoke those words, Rory felt a foreign sensation bubbling inside his body.

The blood seeped into his eyes and even entered through the pores on his skin. An intense heat radiated from his body as he felt the new blood merging with his own.

As he closed his eyes in utter agony, Rory doubled up on the ground and groaned in pain. He felt as if his body was being broken apart as his muscles stretched and expanded, while the sounds of his bones cracking echoed throughout the empty forest.

Elias calmly stood there watching the boy as he underwent his transformation. All the Inheritors of the Blood Legacy were subject to the same torturous pain. It was a rebirth of the body, and the new legacy's blood would soon flow inside Roran.

If he could endure the agony, then his mental strength would be further amplified in the future. Without an ironclad will or fortitude, no Inheritor could ever control the Blood Legacy.

Elias had seen various paths of the other Legacies, but his family's Blood Legacy was completely different than all the others. To walk in the path of continuous bloodshed and savagery, this legacy seemed more demonic than human. He had always wondered how his first ancestor had received the Blood Legacy, but there were no records written in his family's history.

"ARGHH!"

Hearing Rory's screech of pain, Elias gazed slightly worried at the chubby boy. It appeared as if things were not going as smoothly as he had hoped when he saw Rory's body convulsing on the ground without control.

I decided to pass on my inheritance to this boy after observing him next to Calron. The boy had broken pathways, and I thought if I fixed it with the legacy, he'd be a valuable companion to Calron.

Did I make a mistake?

....

Hearing Rory's cry of agony, Calron stopped in the middle of his punch and turned his gaze toward where his Master and Rory were located.

Rory seemed to be in more pain than when Calron had gone through his transformation. Calron's hands shook as he kept hearing the gut-wrenching cries of Rory, but he knew he could not interfere in this process.

It all depended on whether Rory could inherit the will of the legacy.

....

Meanwhile, inside Rory's mind, his consciousness was on the verge of collapsing as he struggled to maintain his sanity under that immense pain. Raging torrents of fresh blood rushed into his muscles and bones, merging and mutating his body.

New cells took the place of old ones and the process was repeated countless times. Under the blazing heat released by the legacy, even the fat cells in Rory's body started to slowly evaporate.

A faint crimson mist formed around Rory when the new blood forced the old blood out of his body. His muscles and bones started to rapidly heal and slowly fitted back into place.

Rory's current body was rippling with muscle fibers, as the intense heat of the legacy's transformation had already burned off the fat on him. He appeared to be even more muscular than Calron, and slightly taller as well.

Just then, images flickered inside Rory's head.

A giant of a man stood alone on a desolate plain with uncountable corpses surrounding him. The giant emitted a vicious, bloody aura and his body glowed with a deep scarlet hue. In that instance, the giant turned his head towards him and Rory felt the images shatter like glass.

Suddenly, he spewed out a mouthful of dark blood that was filled with his body's impurities.

Seeing the boy cough up the vile substance, Elias secretly let out a sigh of relief. With the impurities expelled from his body, it will be easier for Roran to absorb the extra blood.

Elias had been previously worried, as unlike normal cultivators undergoing a legacy's transformation, Rory will have no assistance from his core to endure the pain or the torment.

The essence from any element will have a supplementary effect of strengthening the body, so even without cultivating, any elementalist will have a tougher body than one who did not possess a core. This was why Element-Less were considered to be dregs and even lower than Lightning cultivators.

After a few more coughs, Rory sat down on the grass and panted as he inhaled large amounts of air. A puddle of dark, vicious blood spread around him as Rory gazed up towards his Master and asked with a pale face.

"Master, why did it hurt so much?"

Noticing that the boy still had not realized the change in his appearance, Elias looked amused.

"Your body has just gone through a process of complete renewal. The pain was likely greater in your case as you did not have the help of your element. Brace yourself, Roran, the Blood Legacy's source pool will soon emerge within your body now."

Just as Elias finished speaking, Rory's consciousness quivered as a foreign entity invaded his mind.

A pool of dark crimson blood coalesced within Rory's consciousness and expanded continuously until it turned into a violent ocean of blood.

The sight filled Rory with an awe that was indescribable in simple words. This was the same feeling that Calron had felt when he first saw the source pool.

It appeared as if the ocean of thick scarlet blood was surrounded by deep darkness. The blood waves crashed against each other and the tyranny of these waves could be seen just from the intense aura it emitted.

At the edge of the crimson ocean, Rory could see two distinct bridges connected to it. One appeared to be withered and dull, while the other was bursting with an intense azure glow. That bridge was also much thicker and sturdier than the one opposite to it.

Feeling curious, Rory sent his consciousness into the two bridges. Instinctively, he knew that the withered bridge was his Master and he faintly sensed his presence as well. Moving onto the other bridge, Rory detected a profound aura enveloping it and he was unable to enter the foreign consciousness until a mental gate incidentally opened and let him in.

Rory felt a range of emotions from this foreign presence. Initially, there was caution, but after a moment it changed into relief and finally, there was elation.

He knew within the depths of his soul that this was Calron.

Rumble

Right then, the ocean of blood surged in its intensity as the waves madly crashed against each other. Soon, another bridge was slowly being constructed at the edge of the ocean. Feeling a trace of familiarity with it, Rory rushed out of the azure bridge and entered the new path that was being formed.

....

Meanwhile, Calron had stopped his training and appeared next to Elias as looked at the once-chubby kid lying on the grass.

Calron felt his mouth drop at the change in Rory. Calling him 'chubby' right now seemed like a joke, as the youngster in front of him was just as lean as him and appeared to have even more muscle mass.

Calron guessed that if Rory stood upright now, then he would probably be several inches taller than himself. He did not understand why there was such a monumental change in Rory's appearance, but he decided to ponder on that later.

At that moment, he felt an intruder within his consciousness.

After delving into his mind, he realized it was just Rory exploring the newborn source pool within his body. Without pause, he opened his mind's gate for his new blood brother.

....

As Rory entered the new path being formed, he felt his soul tremble.

The source energy from the pool rushed into his body, it drowned him with a euphoric feeling. As his heart raced uncontrollably, Rory began feeling torrents of the source energy flooding into his muscles and the fractured pathways.

Everywhere the source energy touched, the cells would become stronger and the muscles more resilient as their density rapidly increased. The fractured veins inside Rory's body started to regrow like the sprout and, with every approaching second, it reached closer and closer to his core.

As the veins were being nourished by the source energy, simultaneously, the meridians in the pathways began slowly opening with every circulation of the new energy.

From the outside, Elias and Calron could see a crimson glow emit from Rory's skin and they witnessed Rory drawing in the source energy.

When the first tendril of the spiritual veins was about to connect with his core, Rory felt his consciousness tremble with uncontrollable power.

His core shook with a thunderous clap when the final vein connected to it, and in the next moment, a colossal amount of essence was gathering above him.

When Calron and Elias saw the enormous mass of essence above Rory's head, they felt as if their tongues had dried up.

* * *

Shua *Shua*

The massive sphere of essence above Rory slowly orbited around him.

"Hm, that sphere is made of water essence. Looks like this kid will awaken to the water element."

Elias softly muttered next to Calron.

At the side, Calron intently observed Rory's awakening. His own awakening was unusual and bizarre, so he was curious how a normal awakening occurred.

"Master, how long does a normal awakening take?"

Raising a curious eyebrow at his student's question, Elias simply answered.

"It should be over in a few minutes. As soon as he absorbs that essence, his core should be stabilized."

Calron gave a noncommittal nod and focused his attention back to Rory.

It seemed as if his awakening was truly different from everyone else's. Rory did not seem to go through any pain right now, but Calron clearly remembered the agony he underwent when he awakened to the lightning element.

Meanwhile, the water essence above Rory slowly started being consumed in his body like a vacuum. Faint tendrils of cyan-colored essence spread around Rory until finally the whole ball of essence above him was completely devoured.

In a flash, Rory opened his eyes and began laughing wildly.

"Haha, so this is what an essence feels like? Truly amazing!"

Looking at the silly boy's antics on the ground, both Elias and Calron let out a chortle.

"How do you feel, Roran?"
Elias questioned.

"Master, I feel incredible! Huh?"
Just as Rory stood up and was replying to Elias, he realized that his body had completely changed.

Rory only now noticed the new muscles on him.

With a gaping mouth, Rory touched around his skin, and with every passing second, his face grew brighter and brighter.

"This...what happened to my body?"

"Once you inherit the Blood Legacy, it will change the very constitution of your body and since your original physique was much worse than Calron, there were more obvious changes to you."
Elias replied, as he folded his hands behind him.

"Hehe, so that means I'm stronger than big brother, right?"
Rory gloated as he glanced at Calron.

Seeing the look on his new disciple's face, Elias felt highly amused. This will be good practice for Calron, as he will finally understand what it means to be the Prime Inheritor of the Legacy. In the future, it will be Calron's duty to initiate and discipline the new Inheritors.

"Oh? I agree, Roran. Why don't you try sparring with Calron here, then?"
Elias asked Rory, while giving Calron a secret wink to the side.

Seeing the amused look on his Master's face, Calron knew what Elias wanted from him.

Although he did not want to put down Rory's spirits, he could not remain silent anymore and continue to pretend. It was one thing to hide the Blood Legacy from outsiders, but now as Rory was a part of it as well, there was no need to hide his true Martial strength.

Elias knew Calron had been disgruntled with hiding his strength, especially after the conflict with Chax. This spar with a fellow disciple would alleviate some of the pent-up emotions.

Since Rory was just a normal Inheritor of the Blood Legacy, his body was not put under as much stress as Calron, so he should be in his prime condition even after the vigorous transformation.

Giving a wide smile to Rory in front of him, Calron cracked his knuckles as he slowly walked towards him.
"Yo, Rory. Why don't you show me your new awesome strength?"

As Rory saw Calron walking towards him, he immediately started drawing source energy from the legacy's pool.
"Hehe, big brother, I will be more than happy to!"

Rory was completely oblivious to the previous sarcasm in Calron's voice and continued to be arrogant.

Feeling all the physical changes in his body and the surge of power that his newly awakened core provided, Rory felt invincible. However, if he had noticed the mischievous glint in Calron's eyes, things might have gone a bit differently.

Sensing the powerful energy fluctuations around Rory, Calron was momentarily surprised because Rory was unquestionably a lot stronger than an average First rank elementalist, but in the end, that level of power was still nothing against him.

Calron had been diligently cultivating every day since he broke through the Third rank, and he had long ago solidified his base at that rank. In fact, he was now closer to breaking into the next rank.

This kind of cultivation speed, along with his extremely pure liquid essence, was already a terrifying existence within his age group.

Seeing that Rory continued to look down on him, Calron gave a soft sigh.

This Rory... he already loves poking fun at others, and after his awakening, he will probably get into more trouble if I don't teach him a lesson. Besides, this will be good practice for my Formless Fist as well. No matter how much I practice, I just can't seem to control the source energy like Master.

With these thoughts, Calron activated his source energy.

"Huh?"
Within Calron's consciousness, the source pool was surging like a violent ocean.

The blood waves unceasingly crashed against each other and even the blood seemed to be slightly thicker than before as well. The pressure Calron felt from the source pool was much more intense than he had ever felt since he inherited it, and it seemed to be a lot more uncontrollable as well.

Could this have something to do with the addition of a new Inheritor? I'll just ask Master later. I need to focus on Rory first.

After pondering these thoughts, Calron put the strangeness of the source pool aside and willed the source energy to come to him.

shua
A dense bloodthirsty aura emanated from Calron as he drew from the source pool. His eyes turned slightly crimson, along with the rest of his body.

This was the first time that Calron had unleashed the complete power of the Blood Legacy and even he did not know its true potential yet.

Calron was astonished by the raw unfiltered power coursing through his muscles. The power of the source energy had increased by leaps and bounds.

Previously when Rory and his Master were talking, Calron was at a distance away and training his Formless Fist, so it had only been a few minutes since he last used his source energy. However, it had noticeably changed in might after Rory's initiation.

Calron was now sure that this had something to do with Rory becoming the second Inheritor.

Seeing the violent aura around Calron, Rory felt his heart being slowly crushed under its pressure. This was it. This was that familiar aura he sensed around Calron when he first saw him.

However, after finding out that Calron was a lightning cultivator, Rory put it to the back of his mind. Only now did he realize how frightening his big brother was indeed.

In a single breath, Calron moved.

Gathering the source energy within his palms, Calron rushed towards Rory. The most striking scene was that his palms were now emitting a blazing crimson mist. And even the bloodthirsty aura around Calron appeared to have intensified as well.

Realizing that there was no choice but to face the monster he stirred, Rory inwardly shed some tears and prepared to block the attack.

BOOOOM!
A disheveled figure was forced back as a crisp cracking of the bone could be heard while the figure groaned in pain.

This figure was none other than Rory.

As the smoke dispersed, the silhouette of Calron slowly emerged out and started walking towards the miserable-looking Rory in front of him. In the first strike, Calron had gone easy and just wanted to test the toughness of Rory's body.

"Eh? Big brother, I was only joking. How could this junior ever compare himself to you? Why don't we sit down and chat for a while? Remember when I gave you that extra piece of chicken..."

While Rory continued to splutter and babble excuses as he gingerly held his bruised hand, Calron's grin grew even wider.

"Haha, Rory, don't stress yourself out with all this small stuff. This big brother of yours will definitely go easy on you. Come, we're just exchanging some pointers."

Noticing Rory back away from the fight, Calron chuckled with mirth. This kid was too mischievous. He was the one who first provoked Calron, and now wanted to sit down and talk after the very first strike.

Seeing Rory spew one excuse after another, specifically the tale of giving him an extra piece of chicken, Calron did not know whether to laugh or cry at Rory's shamelessness. As if that panda boy would ever share his meal with anyone.

Parallelly at the side, Elias's heart trembled with unease. Were his eyes playing tricks on him? Just now, when Calron attacked, he saw the crimson mist surrounding his palms. Calron should not have been able to evoke the Blood Legacy's crimson mist so soon.

Could it be that this kid...

Without finishing his thought, Elias abruptly stepped forward.

"Calron, end the fight now. It's clear who the winner is, and Roran, you must never underestimate your opponent. Many people will feint their attacks and hide their power. Catching someone off-guard is the easiest way to eliminate an unknown opponent."

Hearing Elias's words, Rory felt his mood dull.

"But Master! I wanted to play around with Rory a bit more."

Unknowingly, Rory shuddered when he heard those words.

"No need. You will have a new sparring partner from now on."
Elias calmly stated to the pouting skinny kid in front of him.

"Eh? Who?"
Right as Calron asked his question, he felt a thick, viscous aura oppressing him.

"Me."
Elias answered with a smile.

CHAPTER EIGHTEEN

Azure Lightning Emerges

As Elias's words echoed throughout the forest, both Calron and Rory stood there with shocked looks on their faces.

They had both seen how powerful their Master was, so they were confused why Elias would want to spar with Calron at this moment.

"Don't worry, Calron, it's just a spar. I only want to see how far you've progressed in your Formless Fist."

After hearing that declaration from his Master, Calron breathed a sigh of relief.

This was his first time sparring with his Master. He wanted to see as well how far he had come since he first started training. The memory of the first time he felt blood on his face was still firmly etched in Calron's mind. If not for his Master intervening at the right moment, then Calron did not know what his future might have been.

Taking a stance, Calron prepared to face off against his Master.
"Please instruct me, Master."

Calron then swiftly drew the source energy from the legacy's pool and patiently waited for Elias. The faint crimson mist returned and was languidly floating around Calron's palms.

* * *

Calron had taken notice of the blood mist, but he forced it to the back of his mind, thinking it probably was because of the strangeness of the Blood Legacy today.

"Good. You're not rash and can think calmly in battle. Get ready."
Elias stated as he observed Calron did not immediately charge into the fight, and grew excited as he saw the crimson mist again, but on the surface, he subtly disguised his facial expression.

With a burst of speed, Elias appeared in front of Calron within a blink of an eye.
Before Calron could even react, the punch was almost upon his body when he eventually noticed Elias move.

Forcefully suppressing the panic he felt, Calron directed all the source energy towards his stomach.

BOOM!
A low thumping sound resounded throughout the area as Calron was hastily forced back a dozen steps. His stomach groaned in pain, but Calron hardly felt any sensation at that moment. His body was running purely on adrenaline, and an intense excitement surged within him as the battle progressed.

This is it. This is the type of battle that I seek. Master is really strong, and that one casual punch would have almost blown me apart if I hadn't used the source energy to block it. Master is completely serious about this, so I will not disappoint him.

Wiping away the trace of blood on the corner of his lips, Calron gave a fierce look towards Elias and prepared to use the Formless Fist.

After that moment, the crimson mist around Calron disappeared and even his aura changed. It was replaced with a calm and serene aura. The Calron right now exuded a serene halo, and even his expression was completely neutral.

"It took you long enough to understand."

Immediately, the violent and bloodthirsty aura around Elias disappeared, and he stood calmly in front of Calron.

"Yes, Master. I gained a bit of an insight while I was practicing earlier, but it was only when you unknowingly forced me into a spar and released that vicious aura that I understood what you were trying to tell this foolish disciple."

"Mm, good. A disciple must always learn through his own strength and not depend on others on the path of cultivation. So, what did you learn, Calron?"

Giving a small smile, Calron explained.

"I realized that the harder I forced the punches, the more violent the backlash I got. I only seemed to destroy my surroundings rather than my target, so I thought there must be a different approach to the Formless Fist. That's when I remembered the calm and serene aura you emanated when you were executing it."

Elias flashed an impressed grin toward his disciple.

Meanwhile, Rory just confusedly stared at the scene while trying to figure out what his big brother and Master were talking about. With every passing minute, Rory realized just how much of his true strength Calron had been hiding, and he felt beads of sweat forming on his forehead when he recalled all the boasting he did in front of Calron earlier.

Although Rory did not know many kids his age, he was sure that Calron was an absolute monster within their class and even comparable to the geniuses of the older generations.

With a quivering heart, Rory realized Calron might be on par with his sister, and she was known to be the youngest genius in the entire country to ever reach the seventh rank of Spiritual stage. Although they had different cultivation ranks, Calron focused primarily on combat whereas his sister cultivated only her essence. In a practical battle, it was unknown who would actually win.

"Let us see how deep of an insight you gained in the Formless Fist. Come."
Elias beckoned his disciple to resume the spar.

"Yes, Master."
At that moment, Calron closed his eyes and slowly reached out to the source pool within his body.

He tried to calm the raging waves of blood and painstakingly drew the source energy into his muscles. He let the energy soak into his muscles rather than giving it a direction to circulate, and for a full minute, Calron remained in this position.

Elias did not interfere, and patiently waited for Calron to make his move.

After a moment, Calron slowly opened his eyes, and his soft voice reached Elias's ears.
"I'm ready, Master. Please prepare."

A tranquil aura spread forth from Calron as he sped towards the waiting old man.

Just as he reached a meter away from Elias, Calron threw out a punch.
The punch moved extremely slowly and at the same time, it emanated a sense of softness, as if the punch was more of a caress than an explosive blow. It appeared as if the punch was accompanying a soft breeze as it flowed along with the wind.

"Eh? Why is big brother punching so slowly?"
Rory curiously muttered as he watched the scene unfold.

However, there was a different expression on Elias's face.

Haha, this kid keeps surprising me at every turn. Not only is his elemental cultivation astounding, but his Martial Art is also similarly shocking. I thought that the crimson mist appearing was just a fluke, but it seems as if he had already achieved a perfect resonance with the Blood Legacy. I wonder how far he will reach in the Blood Arts…maybe he could even inherit the legendary Twelfth Layer.

With these thoughts running around inside Elias's mind, he executed his own Formless Fist as he whispered into the air.

"Let's see how much you truly understand."

Just as Calron's fist was about to touch Elias, a finger abruptly appeared in front of Calron's knuckle and completely thwarted his punch.

Seeing a single finger so effortlessly stop his punch, Calron felt his mouth go dry, but he immediately prepared for the second strike.

As the battle continued, Elias simply defended with a single finger as Calron tirelessly executed punch after punch, however, not once did Elias ever attack.

A series of explosions burst into their surroundings each time they collided, and several trees were even blown away in the aftermath.

Rory had long ago moved away from the vicinity of the battle and watched from the edge of the lake.

"I hope big brother wins. Go big brother!"

When Rory cheered for Calron, the two figures fighting in the middle could not even hear his voice, as they were so intent on their current battle.

"Calron, feel the energy around you. The earth, the wind, and the sky. Focus your mind and understand the rhythm of nature."

Between the exchange of fists, Elias instructed Calron.

Nature? Sky? Wind? What do they have in common? Or is it the balance between them?

As Calron pondered on these thoughts, he continued to throw punch after punch at his Master.

Even though he did not land a single attack, Calron was not discouraged at the slightest, and slowly his punches appeared to be more refined and smoother by the second.

It was just then that a certain thought shook Calron's mind.

How is Master using a finger and emitting the same energy as the Formless Fist? Shouldn't he be using a fist as well?

Calron felt a jolt in his brain, and his heart started wildly thumping against his chest. An excited look appeared on his face, and he cracked a slight smile.

"So that's the secret, huh?"

Calron halted his punches and hastily stepped back a few steps. Calming his breath and relaxing his muscles, Calron commanded more of the source energy to be absorbed and dispersed it within his muscles.

Not only in his fists, but Calron also willed the source energy to circulate throughout his entire body. It was a perfect balance of power.

Detecting the energy fluctuations within Calron, Elias let out a low chuckle.

"Not bad. I thought it would take you longer. Do you see?"

Giving out a bashful grin, Calron bowed slightly to his Master before responding.

"Master, thank you for showing me the correct way. If it's acceptable, this disciple would like to exchange the last round of pointers with Master."

"Haha, your level of perception is truly an ability to fear, my child. Let's end this with the next round."

After speaking, Elias rushed towards Calron and extended his right foot towards him in a kick.

Seeing his Master kick rather than punch, Calron showed no signs of shock but instead gave a content smile.

Calron had realized that the Formless Fist was never about the fist or the punches. It was about the total balance of one's power within a body's foundation and once that was achieved, he could attack with any part of his body that he wanted using the Formless Fist.

Seeing the kick approach his chest, Calron slightly leaned forward and then slowly extended his palm.

Unlike the previous exchanges, this time, a subtle ripple of air spread around Calron's palm, as if his palm was passing through water rather than air.

A few seconds before the fateful collision, Calron closed his eyes and a gentle breeze embraced his palm.

"Your Lordship, a letter from your son arrived a while ago."

A servant dressed in a simple brown robe bowed as he addressed the stocky figure seated on the white throne.

"Hm, what did Chax write?"

The stocky man casually inquired.

The man had a trimmed goatee and a head full of pale blonde hair. A large crest of a growling black bear was imprinted on the chest plate of the armor he wore, and his eyes contained a spark of cunningness that was hard to detect to the naked eye.

The man was slightly overweight, however; it was clear to see that he still retained a lot of muscle and strength over the fat.

"He writes that there will be a tournament at his school within a few months and he wishes for you to be there to watch him participate."

The servant conveyed the contents of the letter.

"A tournament...interesting. Reply to Chax, saying that I will be there and look forward to seeing how much he's grown. Haha, with Master Dane there to guide him, I'm sure Chax will have learned a thing or two."

The stocky man exclaimed boisterously as he gestured for the servant to leave.

Once the servant left, the expression on the stocky man's face brusquely changed.

"What's the status of our men stationed at the Mountain Range?"

The Lord asked in a low voice as he turned his head towards the back of the room.

Out of the shadows, a tall and wiry man stepped forward. He had greasy, thick, dark hair, and his black murky eyes exuded a nauseating feeling to anyone standing close to him.

"We captured three first-ranked beasts safely, but unfortunately, we encountered a fifth rank stone ape in the process of securing the previous beasts and lost several men before finally killing the monster."

The nasal voice of the lanky man whispered into Regis's ears.

"Damn it! Why are we losing men every month? Can't you a bunch of idiots capture a fifth-rank beast without killing it? Where is Warrick?"

Under Regis's roar, the greasy-haired man stood there unflinchingly.

"After we lost that lightning elementalist, things haven't been so easy on the mountains. Lately, the magical beasts are getting more and more aggressive by the day, and I sense that one of them is about to breakthrough into a new realm. Warrick still hasn't returned from the last trip."

The tall man answered in a soft voice. A hint of disdain flashed across his face as he gazed at the stocky man seated on the throne, but it was quickly disguised before anyone could see it.

"A beast is about to breakthrough? Send some scouts to monitor the inner circle of the forest. I want to know at once if something suspicious occurs. And tell Warrick to report to me as soon as he returns. I need to put that lightning boy to work immediately. I don't like it when I'm not making any profits."

As Regis continued his tirade, the lanky man listened with patience.

He knew he could not make this obnoxious Lord see any reason, so he simply kept his mouth shut. As for the lightning kid, what help could a first-rank cultivator provide in the first place? It was better to let the kid grow and then break his mind to make him follow their commands obediently.

As the lanky man was pondering his own thoughts, Regis remained impatient with the current developments.

"Viktor."
Regis calmly stated.

"Yes?"

When the greasy-haired man inquired, Regis coldly commanded.

"I have a mission for you."

……………………..

BOOOOOM!

A loud explosion echoed throughout the forest.

As the smoke dispersed, it revealed two figures in the middle. One was an old man standing with his arms folded across his chest, and long silvery hair fluttering behind him, while the other was a youth of eight years old, with midnight hair and eyes equally dark.

Both figures calmly gazed at each other with no words being spoken.

"You've surprised me yet again, Calron."

Elias broke the silence as he admiringly spoke those words to his disciple.

"It's all thanks to you, Master. This disciple would not have perfected the Formless Fist without your guidance."

Calron answered humbly.

Although Calron had an unbelievable perception in Martial Arts, if it was not for his Master giving him pointers at every exchange, he would could never understand the secret of the Formless Fist this quickly. Calron estimated that it would have probably taken him a few weeks at least to comprehend the aspect of balance.

"Sigh… I never had a disciple with as much of a monstrous talent as you, Calron. It has not even been a few days since you started the First Layer, and you are already ready to break the seal for the Second Layer."

As Elias's voice reached Calron's ears, he felt slightly confused by his Master's words.

"Huh? Breaking a seal? What's that Master?"
Hearing the confusion in Calron's voice, Elias shook his head and continued.

"I forgot that it's only been a while since you inherited the Legacy… the seals are located on the bridge that connects you with the source pool. After your first transformation, the first seal is automatically opened, but for every seal after that, you will need to forcefully break through them in order to access the next layer of the Blood Arts."

After Elias finished his explanation, he beckoned Rory to come over as well.
"Roran, you will need to know this as well, so pay attention."

When Rory came over, he excitedly grabbed Calron's arm and vehemently pumped it with his one hand. Rory's other hand was still injured from the exchange between him and Calron.

"Wah- big brother, you're so awesome! Please teach me that move you did in the end."

Seeing Rory being himself again, Calron sighed and shook off Rory's hand from his arm.

"Alright, I'll teach you, but remember that you can't reveal the Blood Legacy to outsiders, including your sister."

"Eh? But I really wanted to show off in front of my big sister."
Seeing the stern look on Calron's face, Rory sputtered before answering.

"I won't tell her, big brother, I promise."

Hearing the conversation between the two boys in front of him, Elias nodded with satisfaction.

Although he could not see their appearances perfectly, he could see the essence outlining their bodies, and watching them bicker back and forth, Elias unknowingly felt content to see them together.

He could finally be at peace knowing that his legacy will remain alive through these two boys.

"So, I'm guessing that you two don't want to hear about the seals?"
Elias asked with an amusing look on his face.

Slapping Rory on the back of his head, Calron stated quickly.
"Sorry, Master, we are ready to listen."

"Very well. The seals on the Blood Legacy can only be broken once you meet the criteria of the next layer. Since Calron has already mastered the First Layer, he has achieved the level of control needed to break the second seal. The Formless Fist is a technique that requires the perfect balance of source energy within the body to activate, and now that Calron has mastered that balance, he will soon be able to break open the seal."

Intently listening to their Master's explanation, both boys nodded as they absorbed the words being spoken.

Within Calron's mind, he sent his consciousness inside the source pool and towards the azure bridge that represented his path. He was curious as to what these seals that his Master talked about appeared inside the source pool.

As he approached the ocean of blood, what he had not noticed before was that there were exactly eleven steps on all three bridges, and with the last step connected to an endless abyss of darkness.

Focusing his gaze upon the first few steps of his bridge, Calron noticed that only the first step emitted the same azure aura as the rest of his bridge, while all the other steps were dull and plain. There were various symbols etched onto them, but they all seemed to blur whenever Calron focused on them.

So this is where Master said the seals were placed. It looks fairly ordinary. What is so special about them?

Right after Calron inwardly made up his mind, he sent his consciousness into the second step.

Bzzt

A burst of pain surged within Calron's mind and he doubled up on the ground, grabbing his head with both his hands.

Seeing Calron fall on the ground out of the blue, both Rory and Elias rushed towards the fallen boy and tried to shake him up. The instant Elias's hand touched Calron's body, he felt a sharp jolt.

Looking down at the boy, torrents of Azure Lightning bolts crackled around his body.

CHAPTER NINETEEN

Supreme Entities

crackle

An azure bolt of lightning pierced through Elias's hand with almost no resistance, causing the elderly man to be shocked.

Elias knew exactly how tough his body was, and for a third-rank cultivator to pierce his skin so easily, he realized whatever this strange bolt of lightning was; it was out of the ordinary.

Rory had similar thoughts, but he seemed to be a lot more confused than shocked.

"Huh? What is this blue stuff? I thought big brother's lightning was gold?"

Just as Rory posed his question, an agonizing groan was emitted from Calron's mouth.

"Master. What is wrong with big brother?"

Rory wanted to go near Calron, but each time he tried to, an azure bolt would assault him. Unknowingly, Rory felt an instinctual fear whenever the azure lightning drew close to him.

Ever since he had met Calron, Rory had the impression that his perception of the universe seemed to turn completely upside down. Rory sensed that indescribable, mysterious aura around Calron from the very first day he gazed upon him, but it was only after seeing Calron reveal his Martial Arts, that Rory realized the truth about his new big brother.

Watching that berserk azure lightning around Calron, Rory did not know what to think anymore. Let alone the fact that he had never heard or seen an element like Calron's. A normal lightning bolt of an elementalist was nothing compared to the aura of the vicious azure lightning crackling around Calron.

"Calm down, Roran. That thing is protecting him, so it shouldn't be the one causing pain to Calron. Let's wait for a while, and if things get worse, I have a final last resort."
Elias stated in a solemn voice.

Rory did not know what his Master's last resort was, but he could guess from his tone that it would not be pleasant.

Elias forced his racing heart to calm down and tried to keep the intense shock he felt from showing on his face.

Agatha was one of the weaker continents in the vast lands. Here, Heavenly stage experts were treated like Gods and exalted beings, whereas on other affluent continents, they were only the most common of cultivators.

Unlike Rory, Elias had traveled to other continents besides Agatha and had a lot more experience of the world outside, so how could he not know about the special elements that existed under the heavens?

These were children blessed by the laws of the world, and each one would grow up to become an emperor among humans. Only the most sacred and exalted families gave birth to these children, as the blessing of the heavens was an inheritance of blood and not luck.

Elias recalled the stories of people with special bloodlines who awakened to a supreme element, and he could not help but tremble in fear as he realized what trouble it would bring to Calron if this was revealed to the outside world.

The other heaven's blessed children were born in large powerful clans or sects, but what about Calron? He would have none to protect him, and Elias's own power was pitiful compared to the might of the large clans and sects.

However, in all his travels, Elias had never heard of a special bloodline existing under the lightning element. Even in the Royal Xurian Library, only four types of special bloodlines existed.

Elias finally came to understand some mysteries surrounding this eight-year-old boy, as his godly talent in cultivation and Martial Arts did not befit the limitations of the lightning element. This also explained why the boy was always so hesitant to talk about his rapid breakthrough to the third rank.

Knowing that the boy had been bearing this burden on his small shoulders the entire time, Elias felt a deep sorrow within his heart. After losing everything and everyone he had, the boy now had to force himself to keep even more secrets, having no one to share his burden. As his Master, Elias regretted that he was not able to help his disciple sooner.

Giving a sad smile to the pain-stricken boy on the ground, Elias patiently waited with Rory for Calron to wake up.

....

Within Calron's mind, a wave of raging azure bolts crackled around the bridge as it tried to contain the backlash from the Blood Legacy.

After Calron had touched the second seal, a tsunami of source energy attacked his mind and tried to forcefully extinguish his consciousness; however, at the exact moment before the collision, the

Azure Lightning burst forth and repelled the violent energy.

Calron cursed in agony at his stupid mistake. He realized that if he had willed his source energy to approach the seal, things might have gone differently. The seal on the second step thought Calron was an intruder and maliciously attacked him.

To break the second seal, his Master had stated that one must balance the source energy completely within the body and then slowly peel away the seal, but Calron had foolishly rushed into it without thinking.

If not for the Azure Lightning stepping in at the correct moment, Calron's mind would probably have disintegrated.

Gazing at the surge of lightning crackling around the bridge, Calron felt intense gratitude for the Azure Lightning. He did not know why it chose him or even what it was, but each time he was in a life-threatening situation, the Azure Lightning would always protect him.

After gathering his will and focusing his thoughts, Calron slowly drew the source energy to his body and circulated it with a perfect balance of power. Within the realm of the Blood Legacy, this control seemed to come easier to Calron than outside.

Calming his breath, Calron then directed his source energy to strike the second seal.

As he barraged the seal with his source energy, Calron felt the symbols on the second step gradually erode away as a glimmer of mist rose from it.

That mist appeared oddly familiar to him, and after Calron scrutinized it in more detail, he came to a realization.

It was identical to the crimson mist that emitted from his palms when he had previously attacked Rory.

Intently focusing on breaking the seal, Calron once again rushed into the seal with renewed ardor.

However, after a while, Calron felt tired and mentally drained. Calron's mind was already exhausted from the seal's initial onslaught against him, and with the second seal increasing its pressure on him, a trace of despair grew within Calron's heart.

Just as he felt that all hope was lost, a torrent of azure lightning crackled around him and swiftly merged with his source energy.

The lightning appeared to be almost absorbing the source energy, as its body got thicker and thicker by the second. The core of the lightning bolt was still an azure color, but the entire outside membrane was now a bolt of dense, blood-colored lightning.

The lightning had not completely merged with the source energy, but even their small fusion radiated an immense surge of brutal power.

Right then, the new Azure-Crimson Lightning fiercely crashed into the second seal and pierced straight through the symbols.

It was as if the seal did not dare to resist in the slightest and willingly surrendered itself to the savage lightning in front of it.

After a moment, the second step emitted an azure glow similar to the rest of the bridge. The illumination brightly flashed for a brief second before reverting to normal. The bridge now had two steps under its control, leaving the rest of the steps dull and lackluster.

As soon as the seal was broken, Calron felt the second step quiver for a moment, after which it released a dense, blood-colored mist.

The mist floated lazily around the step for a while before eventually swarming into Calron's body.

229

Calron did not resist in the slightest, as he knew that this was part of the Second Layer of the Blood Arts. When the last wisp of the mist entered his body, he felt a notion of familiarity with it, absorbing flashes of information on what the mist truly was.

It was a movement-type skill called the Blood Mist Step.

This skill would let the user drift similarly to an ethereal mist and prevent enemies from grabbing the user's real body. It was incomparably swift, leaving a trace of the blood mist whenever the user moved from one place to another.

Once mastered, The Blood Mist Step would subsequently make the physical body of the user explode in a smoke of crimson mist on command, and then reform the body within a few seconds, allowing it to cover short distances.

Although it was not teleportation, its speed was almost comparable to it.

Turning his attention back to the scene in front of him, Calron knew his hands were shaking from anxiety.

Watching the source energy revolve around the Azure Lightning, Calron felt his heart trembling from the pressure it currently emitted. Calron realized that if he called back the lightning into his body right now, it would utterly destroy him.

The current power of the lightning was not something a third-rank cultivator like Calron could safely handle. He was just glad that the lightning was his protector and not his enemy.

After seeing the second seal break, Calron should have been elated, but the next scene astounded him. It seemed as if his soul would collapse from the constant jolts he felt today, but Calron just reaffirmed his determination to survive this obstacle.

The Azure-Crimson Lightning roared savagely within the source pool as a frightening aura immediately burst from its surroundings. Even the bridge seemed to tremble under its might.

Calron's mouth dried up when he suddenly realized what the lightning was about to do.

With a definitive explosion of thunder, the Azure-Crimson Lightning thrust directly into the third seal.

A burst of crimson light flashed through the source pool.

The roar of thunder echoed in the background as the Azure-Crimson Lightning continued to drill into the third seal.

Unknown to Calron, the second seal had long ago started breaking apart, which was clear in the traces of the blood mist that appeared when he was sparring Rory.

Although he was only in the first layer previously, Calron was able to summon the crimson mist despite the usual restriction. No one could break the legacy's rules.

Unless it was willed by the legacy itself.

This was the reason Elias was baffled earlier when he saw the crimson mist, as that meant that the Blood Legacy was helping Calron of its own will.

However, the situation was different with the third seal. The Blood Legacy did not yet deem it worthy of Calron for the time being. The third seal's symbols were a lot more intricate and complex in design, and considering the difficulty the Azure-Crimson Lightning seemed to have, it was noticeable that the third seal would not break so easily.

Calron was utterly lost in what to do at that moment. The Azure Lightning had never listened to him and did things of its own accord.

231

He wanted to leave his consciousness and return outside, but he discovered that no matter how hard he tried, he could not leave the vicinity of the source pool.

Resigned to his fate, Calron just watched the battle between his lightning and the third seal. He could instinctively sense that the Azure Lightning was getting impatient.

crackle
Without warning, a flood of source energy from the pool was sucked into the Azure-Crimson Lightning at a rapid pace.

The lightning grew even thicker and in an instant; it took on an illusory form of a gigantic snake beast. This electric snake differed greatly from the one Calron saw during the dark bow's mutation, the main being that this snake had thick blood-red lightning crackling around it.

The electric snake had a pair of long vicious fangs, with small lightning bolts sparking near them. A bloodthirsty aura emanated from its body as it spiraled above the third seal.

The lightning was no longer a mix of azure and crimson, but a complete blood-red color.

However, that was not the only change happening inside the Blood Legacy.
The third seal also started to briskly absorb the remaining source energy, which was on par with the pace of the red lightning.

The ocean of blood within the pool bubbled at an alarming rate and the waves crashed furiously against the darkness as it tried to put up a resistance against the two entities that were draining its power.

As the electric snake reared its fangs in preparation to strike, the intricate symbols on the third seal glowed zealously.

An image flickered on the steps of the bridge, a figure marginally smaller than the lightning beast coalesced behind the third seal. It was humanoid and appeared to be a giant with bulging muscles.

The giant wore nothing besides a scarlet loincloth and plates of armor wrapped around its wrists and ankles. Numerous scars covered its body like a map, and its skin glowed with an unnatural ruby glow.

When Calron was staring at the muscular giant behind the seal, he had a feeling of familiarity, as if he had seen a similar existence to the giant before.

The long, rusty mane of the giant obscured its face. Without a break in momentum, it crouched to prepare a charge against the lightning beast. The giant's muscles coiled like a thick rope, bulging almost abnormally.

Calron kept scrutinizing the giant. However, despite his best efforts, he could not recall ever seeing other race besides the beasts or humans, so he concluded it was just his mind playing tricks on him.

Casting aside his doubts, Calron intently watched the scene unfold before him.

This was a battle between two supreme entities and who knows when else Calron would ever get a chance to witness a display such as this one again? Besides, by watching this battle, Calron might understand a bit of the lightning element that existed inside of him.

RUMBLE
Seeing the giant obstructing its path, the red electric snake let out a shrill screech and expanded until it exceedingly towered over the giant and viciously struck the brute.

A cloud of thunder roared behind the blood-red snake.
A trace of hesitation flashed across the giant's eyes, but none could

see that expression as its mane completely covered the giant's face. With no other choice but to confront the reptilian monster, the giant braced himself and crossed his muscular arms in front of his chest, an intense scarlet glow erupted from its skin.

"Hssss!"
A cloud of hot steam rose from the giant's skin, followed by a profoundly dense aura.

"AGHHH!"
As the giant fearlessly roared, a suffocating aura rushed out from him and pressed down onto the entire surroundings, including Calron.

As the suffocating pressure strangled Calron, he could not move a single finger. Forced to the ground, Calron kneeled with one knee as he desperately tried to resist the dense aura of the giant.

Drops of sweat formed on Calron's forehead and they slowly dripped onto the ground, the pressure only building by the second. Right when Calron felt he would lose consciousness, a gentle stream of energy entered his body bit by bit.

The foreign stream of energy slowly entered his core and ignited the liquid essence stored there. With a faint tremble, Calron sensed a flood of essence seeping into his body from the core and restraining the suffocating aura that was pressing down on him.

The azure-golden liquid essence soothingly coated his muscles, as the oppressing aura of the giant was slowly expelled from Calron's body.

RUMBLE
As the red electric snake's fangs penetrated the giant's chest, the entire source pool quivered as the blood waves madly crashed into each other. It felt like the start of a massive earthquake.

The giant miserably groaned in agony but remained standing firmly against the electric snake as it menacingly gazed into the slits of the reptile's eyes.

There was a large burned scorch mark on the giant's chest as traces of blood seeped from the sides. However, the giant remained standing defiantly.

puff *puff*
Panting and out of breath, it was clear to see that although the giant stopped the first blow of the blood-red snake, it had done so at a colossal price to its own life.

On the verge of its last breath, the giant clenched both his fists until his skin cracked under the pressure, and blood slowly dripped onto the ground.

The hair on the giant's head parted as it revealed two bloodshot eyes glaring at the monster in front of it. Even in its dying breath, the giant continued to proudly challenge its fated enemy.

As if almost admiring the courage of the entity in front of it, the red electric snake gathered as much of the source energy as it could summon from the nearby pool, and prepared a last strike against the defeated giant.

Watching this scene, Calron felt his fighting spirit surge within his heart. This was a true battle. He thought he had experienced a battle when he fought against Chax, but compared to what he just witnessed, their fight seemed more like a squabble.

With his heart racing wildly, Calron fixed his gaze upon the two existences in front of him.

After a few seconds, the giant abruptly dropped to the floor, his knees crashing into the ground. Even while kneeling, the giant continued to fiercely glare at the red snake, without a shred of submission on its face.

With the cloud of thunder echoing throughout the source pool, a series of blood-red lightning surged around the electric snake. It sprung into motion and bolted toward the half-dead giant.

As the two supreme beings collided, a flare of bright scarlet light flashed in the darkness, causing the giant to silently explode into small fragments of dust.

The symbols on the third step glowed for a moment and gently faded away, revealing a third azure step.

The blood-red electric snake then shrunk down to a single small bolt once the battle ended, and a stream of source energy dispersed from it into a faint crimson cloud.

Restored to its original form, the azure lightning rushed towards Calron and quietly returned to the core inside of him.

However, unknown to Calron, traces of small fragmented dust were also absorbed into his body, along with the azure lightning.

....

Concurrently, a few hours ago, Elias and Rory had dropped to the ground on one knee as they tightly clutched their chests.

They had felt the Blood Legacy violently crashing inside their consciousness, and their whole bodies quivered when they felt two powerful energies clashing within the source pool.

"Master. What is happening? My chest hurts..."
Rory wheezed as sweat formed on his forehead.

Elias was in a better state, but he still felt the intensities of the two auras clashing within the Blood Legacy.

"Th- That can't be possible. Why did that thing appear on Calron's bridge? It's too early."

Elias mutely whispered to himself.

How could he not know what that giant was? Elias had the most shocking talent in the Blood Legacy from his family, considering he was the Prime Inheritor before Calron.

That giant only appeared when the Inheritor was ready to break the third seal, but Calron was nowhere near powerful enough to break the third seal as it required the strength of a Vajra stage expert.

Could it be that this child broke the third seal?

Just as Elias felt his mind go numb, the auras of the two entities abruptly vanished without a trace and his heartbeat gradually returned to normal.

Even Rory to the side softly breathed a sigh of relief as he felt the pressure vanish.

At that moment, Calron opened his eyes.

CHAPTER TWENTY

Titan's Fury

shua

Calron's eyes abruptly opened as he gazed at the familiar forest around him.

He saw that both his Master and Rory were just gaping at him, and remained stunned in their places.

"Ugh...Rory, what happened?"
Calron let out a groan of pain as he slowly got up from the ground.

From the moment Calron had been inside the source pool, he had no idea about what had occurred outside, including the fact that his secret was revealed long ago.

Realizing that Calron was asking him a question, Rory got out of his daze and rushed towards Calron.

"Wah, big brother! You scared Master and me when you suddenly started screaming like a little girl!"
Seeing that Calron was alright and back to normal, Rory felt his heart at ease and started to jokingly poke fun at Calron.

"You punk! Do you want me to give you a thrashing again?"
Calron teased as he playfully punched Rory on the shoulder.

Noticing that Elias still had his eyes in a stupor, Calron softly whispered into Rory's ear.

"Oi Rory, why is Master so shocked? His eyes also seem a bit unfocused..."

Hearing Calron's question, Rory casually responded.

"Ah, I don't know. He's been like that ever since that blue stuff started crackling around you. By the way, big brother, what is that strange blue lightning? It tried to attack both me and Master when we approached you."

As Rory chattered obliviously, Calron felt his heart pounding violently against his chest when Rory mentioned the Azure Lightning.

thump

thump * thump*

It seemed as if all the sounds in the world had been muted except for his pounding heartbeat. A surge of blood rushed towards Calron's brain as he felt himself breathing harder and harder by the second.

Calron was experiencing a panic attack.

He did not know what to do, as the Azure Lightning was his greatest secret and now that it had been revealed, he did not know how his future would pan out.

Calron's mental fortitude had been getting stronger by the day due to both his cultivation and training. However, faced with the current panic he felt, all those mental barriers came crashing down, simply leaving behind an anxious eight-year-old boy.

"Huh? Big brother, are you alright?"
Seeing Calron promptly tense up, Rory worriedly shook him out

of his daze.

In Rory's mind, the Azure Lightning was just something that exuded a powerful essence and seemed different from normal lightning, but he did not understand the future implications of the discovery of such a unique element.

"Master..."
As Calron forcibly calmed his racing heart, he softly called out to Elias. His main priority right now was to explain the situation to his Master.

Hearing the voice of his disciple, Elias turned his head towards the source of the voice and quickly got up on his feet once he realized it was Calron.

He rushed towards Calron and grabbed him firmly by the shoulders.
"Calron, my child... is this what you have been hiding from me?"

Uncontrollably, tears formed in Calron's eyes as he looked at the gentle expression on his Master's face. This was the first time he had cried since the Voice left him, but with all his mental barriers down, he felt extremely vulnerable.

"Seeing as you were so careful in keeping that secret, I assume you know what the presence of that element means?"
Elias continued in a gentle tone.

Watching his disciple in such an emotional state, Elias comforted Calron by slowly patting his head. Elias knew Calron had awakened to his element shortly after his parent's death, so until now, Calron had probably been alone and not able to share his secret with anyone.

That burden was enormous for any grown man, let alone a child who had yet to reach his tenth year.

sniff
"Yes, Master. I know that I must not reveal it to others."
Calron softly responded.

Seeing that his Master was calm and collected, Calron started to steadily regain his composure.

Calron had initially not wanted to reveal the existence of the Azure Lightning to Elias, as the Voice had told him not to divulge it to anyone, and since his cultivation Teacher was not present, Calron did not want to do anything without the Voice's approval.

Realizing that there was nothing else he could do to remedy the situation at hand, Calron decided to no longer hide the Azure Lightning from his Master. Besides, he knew he could trust Elias and even the Voice wouldn't have objected.

"No, my child. I mean, do you know what that lightning is?"
Seeing the confused look on Calron's face, Elias continued.

"There are some heavenly elements in this world which awaken to children with special bloodlines when they turn eight years of age. I don't know much about those unique elements, but one thing is for sure, they are all a domineering power under the heavens."
Hearing the explanation from Elias, Calron was stunned.

He knew that the Azure Lightning was special, but other than that, he had almost no knowledge about why the lightning chose him or what it was. However, from Elias's words, it appeared as if it was because of his bloodline, so that meant that it had to have come from within his family.

"Master, my father was a fourth-rank lightning elementalist, but he did not have the Azure Lightning. Why did I awaken to it?"
Calron curiously asked Elias. His father was the only one in his family that had the lightning element, but he never showed any signs of having blue lightning.

"I don't know, Calron. Even in those exalted clans and sects, they might go on for centuries until another child in their family awakens to their bloodline's unique element. Your ancestors must have once been very powerful, as the Azure Lightning clearly belongs to the special bloodlines."

Meanwhile, Rory, who was at the side listening in on their discussion, quietly muttered to himself.

"That blue stuff is that amazing? No wonder big brother was so afraid of others finding out."

Right then, Rory rushed towards Calron and grabbed his hand.

"Big brother, no need to worry. Even if someone comes looking for you in the future, I will take your secret to the grave with me."

Rory sincerely proclaimed.

Seeing the expression on Rory's face, Calron knew that this was one of the rare moments that Rory was completely serious, and he felt glad for having a brother like him.

Even if they were not related by blood, for someone who would unquestionably risk their life for another, Calron would gladly call them his brother.

The boy in front of Calron was no longer the same as the one he had once met, with a sniveling nose and tears running down his plump face. There was no chubbiness in the boy, and even calling him 'panda boy' seemed like a joke, as the current Roran was extremely muscular for an eight-year-old.

However, to Calron, Rory was still Rory. He might have changed in physical appearance, but Rory's mannerisms and mischievous personality could never be taken away.

Grabbing Rory's hand with his own, Calron smiled as he gazed at his brother.

"Thank you, Rory."

The two boys felt an invisible bond tying their fates even closer together as a strong brotherhood was born from that day forth.

....

Seeing the two boys being chummy with each other, Elias felt his heart warm at the scene in front of him. It made him think of his own brother-in-arms and best friend, Solin. Although Elias had an elder brother by blood, the relationship he had with Solin during his childhood was much deeper than that of any family he had.

Knowing that if he pondered more on his past, his mood would turn somber, Elias coughed in an attempt to get the two boys' attention.

"By the way, Calron, what happened in the source pool?"

Elias asked in a serious tone.

Elias knew it had something to do with the third layer, as he felt the giant's energy. He wanted to confirm directly with Calron. Although entering the second layer was surprising for a third-ranked elementalist, it was inconceivable for someone in the Spiritual stage to directly enter the third layer.

"Uh, you see... I tried to..."

Calron stumbled over his words as he tried to explain, but did not know how to unravel everything he saw, as he was confused by the events that took place there as well. Everything had been out of his control, as the Azure Lightning acted on its own and charged into the third seal.

However, Calron did not want to hide anything about the Azure Lightning from Elias, so he recounted from the beginning how he accidentally provoked the second seal, and the Azure Lightning without notice intervened to help him, destroying the second seal in the process.

Elias had an amazed expression on his face, but he let Calron continue his tale.

While Calron was in the middle of explaining when the Azure Lightning absorbed the source energy, Elias felt his hands trembling, however, it was only when Calron finally disclosed the battle between the two beasts, that Elias felt his heart furiously thumping against his chest.

An element that could take the shape of a living beast? Impossible. Essence by itself was something that existed separate from everything else, as even the heavens were subject to it.

"…so after the giant exploded, the blood-red lightning returned to normal, and I could finally leave the source pool."
Calron exhaled as he finished his story.

"Calron, do you know what the third layer of the Blood Arts is?"
Elias inquired with a solemn tone.

As his Master spoke those words, the atmosphere turned heavy. The sounds of birds chirping, the howling of the wind, and even the critters of the insects seemed to fade away. It was as if the world waited for the next words of the blind old man.

Calron and Rory both felt the changes in the surroundings and unknowingly felt their heartbeat slow down.

"The third layer is special, Calron. It's not a technique or a skill."
Every word of Elias seemed to contain an ethereal feeling to it.

A slow and gentle breeze flowed around Elias as he spoke his next and final words.

"It is a domain known as the Titan's Fury."

"Titan's Fury?"

Calron whispered the name.

"Yes, it is the first domain ability of the Blood Legacy. It will create a special area around you that will trigger a mental suppression of any enemies within its sphere and boost your physical strength by a certain factor."

Elias clarified.

"Wow, Master, I want it as well!"

Rory cheered when he heard the impressive ability of the domain.

Turning his gaze towards Rory, Elias strictly said.

"Roran, this domain is not something that either of you can handle right now. Although by some stroke of luck, Calron was able to break through the seal placed on the third step, but under no circumstances are you allowed to activate it. Is that clear, Calron?"

Seeing the firm look on his Master's face, Calron visibly gulped and responded.

"This disciple understands, Master."

"Eh? But why can't he activate it? It sounds so awesome."

Rory ignored the look on Elias's face and continued complaining.

Realizing that he had just taken on a troublesome new disciple, Elias answered with a soft sigh.

"The domain will indeed boost your physical strength, and at the early stages, it will increase your power by at least two times, but at its peak, the domain will increase your power by over ten times your original strength."

Elias pronounced with a fierce fire in his eyes.

* * *

Just as Rory was about to interrupt, Elias forcibly continued.

"However, it comes at a price. The domain will consume your blood as soon as you ignite it and the longer you keep it activated, the faster it will consume your blood. Although the Blood Legacy gives you an extraordinary regenerative ability, if it can't recover enough blood, I don't think I need to tell you what would happen next."

Both boys shuddered as they thought of this ability that could directly consume one's blood.

Seeing the pale looks on the faces of his disciples, Elias shook his head and continued.

"I did not think I would have to talk about this domain this early... logically speaking, Calron should not have been able to break that seal, as it requires the strength of a Vajra stage expert or above. Once you're at the Vajra stage, your body would have naturally been able to endure the physical strain of the domain without endangering your life."

Hearing those words, Calron asked a question.
"Master, I thought the domain only consumed blood? It puts strain on the body as well?"

"Calron, the blood in your body is the essence of life. It sustains your muscles, bones, and your entire existence. If your blood were to slowly drain away, it will affect your physical condition as well. However, if your body was already strong to begin with, you could endure the strain of the blood loss caused by the domain."

Nodding his head at the response, Calron sincerely replied to Elias.

"Master, unless I'm in a dire situation, I promise I will not activate the domain."

Knowing that was going to be the best he would get, Elias sighed in resignation.

"Hmm, Master, can I also ask you a question?"
Rory interrupted for the second time with a mischievous glint in his eyes.

Seeing the boy's expression, Elias slightly hesitated, but he knew the boy would not give up until he got his way, so he nodded his head in consent.

"Since I still have a long time until I can break the third seal, big brother will get to enjoy the domain way ahead of me. I only request that my most esteemed Master show this poor disciple what the domain looks like."
Rory finished with an elaborate thump to his chest.

Calron sighed from the side as he shook his head at Rory's idiocy.

This kid... He's already learned to manipulate people with flattery and praise.
Elias's eyes twinkled as he pondered these thoughts in his mind.

"Interesting proposition... I have a better idea. I will show you the domain once you master the Formless Fist. I think Calron only took a few days to perfect it, so it shouldn't take too long for you as well."
Elias said mirthfully and gave a discreet wink to Calron.

Hearing Elias's words, Rory sulked at his failed plans and muttered to himself.

As if suddenly remembering something, Elias interjected.
"I almost forgot. You both will have the Ranking Tournament coming up in a few months, so you need to prepare immediately."

"Huh? I heard about a tournament for the disciples before, but do we have to participate? I don't think I can win against the other disciples without using the Blood Legacy or the Azure Lightning..."
Calron lamented.

He had learned from the recent fight with Chax that it would be extremely difficult to win with merely his physical body. Although Calron had a much stronger constitution than others his age, compared to the immense power other's elements provided, there was not much of an advantage.

However, things would be completely different if he could use either the Azure Lightning or the Blood Legacy. Within the entire school, no student could contend with him if he used his true strength.

"Hmm, I think it would be fine if you use the Blood Legacy just a bit."
Elias said with a slight upturning of his lips.

"You mean…"
Calron dumbly stared at his Master.

Was Elias really letting him use his true strength?

"Don't get me wrong, you are still not allowed to use your complete strength, but I will permit you to use just the Formless Fist. With the current level of control you have over the source energy, I assume you will be able to not leak any more than you should?"
Elias inquired with a raise of his eyebrow.

"YES! I mean, I will follow your instructions, Master"
Calron hollered excitedly before regaining his composure.

He could not believe that his Master was seriously letting him use the Blood Legacy in front of others. Although he was only permitted to use the Formless Fist, it would still be unmatched against the other disciples his age.

grumble
A low stomach growl resounded in the area.

Both Elias and Calron turned toward the source of the sound.

An embarrassed Rory stood there while blushing furiously.

"What? I haven't eaten for a few hours and you guys have been continuously talking without involving me, so of course I got hungry. Stop staring!"

Not understanding how their talking would make Rory hungry, both Elias and Calron let out a combined sigh at the same time and shook their heads.

"Hey! Stop doing that... it's freaky."

Both Calron and Elias burst into laughter upon seeing the expression on Rory's face.

After a few minutes of bickering back and forth, Elias finally interrupted the two boys.

"You kids should go get lunch before all the food disappears. Oh, by the way, Calron!"

Elias shouted just as the boys were about to leave.

"Yes, Master?"

Calron curiously responded.

"We will begin your training in the Blood Mist Step in a few days, so come prepared."

With that, Elias turned around and quietly entered his hut, leaving behind a stunned Calron.

"Big brother, what's the Blood Mist Step?"

Rory questioned as he poked Calron on the shoulder.

"Ah? Rory, if the Titan's Fury is the third layer of the Blood Arts, what do you think the second layer is?"

Calron faintly voiced his words.

"You mean..."

"Yes, the second layer is known as the Blood Mist Step."
Calron confirmed to the astonished Rory.

"This is so unfair, why does big brother get all the cool stuff?"
As Rory whined, Calron grabbed him by the arm and dragged him towards the gathering hall for lunch.

The whole way there, Rory tried to glean some information as to what the Blood Mist Step was, but Calron simply evaded all his questions and told him to be quiet.

Just as the two boys were walking towards the hall, the nearby disciples all gaped at Calron and Rory.

Feeling uncomfortable with all the stares, Rory whispered to Calron next to him.
"Hehe, big brother, it seems you got really famous in a few days."
What Rory had not realized was that the disciples were not staring at Calron, but were instead gaping at Rory himself.

Rory completely forgot the drastic physical changes he underwent during the Blood Legacy's transformation.

"You idiot! Look at your current body. The one they're all staring at is you!"
Calron whispered back, as he smacked Rory on the back of his head.

"Eh?"

CHAPTER TWENTY-ONE

Deathly Smile

Ignoring all the stares, Rory and Calron continued to walk towards the gathering hall.

"Hey, isn't that the fat kid... wow, look at those muscles... I remember that lightning kid."

As the nearby disciples whispered amongst themselves, the two boys paid no attention to the gossip and continued their conversation.

"Big brother, after we finish eating here, can you bring out that electric snake? Please?"

Rory fervently asked Calron in a hushed tone.

"Rory, I just told you that I have no control over the lightning. Besides, why do you want to see it?"

Calron said in an exasperated voice.

"Uh...I just wanted to see if it looked delicious..."

Calron stopped walking as he dumbly stared at Rory.

"Rory... it's made of lightning... you can't eat that."

Calron spluttered as he tried to answer Rory. He simply did not understand where Rory got these types of ideas from, or his insane obsession with eating exotic foods.

"Eh? But you said the beast had a physical form, so it definitely must be made of real flesh."

Rory argued, as he tried to convince Calron.

Knowing that he would get nowhere in a conversation about food with Rory, Calron just sighed as he continued.

"I don't even know how to conjure that thing. It always seems to appear whenever it wants."

In truth, Calron had no idea as to how the Azure Lightning worked. Only his Teacher seemed to understand it, but with him currently dormant and recovering his soul, there was no way Calron could question him.

Ever since the locket had been given to him, his future seemed to have taken a detour from what would have been a normal life.

"Ah, forget it. Big brother doesn't understand the passion for exotic cuisine."

Rory exclaimed with a shake of his head.

Rolling his eyes, Calron tugged at Rory's shoulder.

In front of the boys, bustling crowds of disciples were lined up as they waited to receive their meals. A few of them were already busy eating and chattering away with their friends.

The gathering hall radiated a chaotic atmosphere of shouting and scurrying as Gretha and the other cooks rushed to deliver trays of food.

"Rory, I'll go and wash my hands. Save a spot for me in the line."
Calron shouted to Rory over the loud noise in the background.

"Huh? Why do you need to wash your hands? It's a waste of time."
Rory retorted as Calron turned away.

"Hmph, whatever, I get to eat early."
Rory muttered as a thin line of drool seeped from his mouth.

....

After some time had passed, Calron finally came back to the gathering hall as he wiped his still-wet hands on his trousers.

"Well, at least the line is much shorter now."
Calron muttered as he walked over to the queue.

He was gazing around, trying to find Rory in the crowd, when Calron suddenly bumped into someone.

"Ah, sorry."
Calron immediately apologized to the figure in front of him.

The unknown person slowly turned around, revealing a girl of around ten years old.

Her dark red hair fluttered in the air as the strands obscured her snowy white face. Her emerald green eyes sparkled when they landed upon the young boy in front of her, while her red rosy lips moved with no sound coming out.

Not that the girl was mute, but it was that Calron simply could hear nothing, as he was utterly enraptured by the girl in front of him.

Where Felice's beauty was like the fierce blizzard in the Arctic, this red-haired girl's beauty felt like the warmth of a bright sunny day.

The red-haired girl stood at least a foot taller than Calron and was a lot older than him. But none of this seemed to matter to Calron, as he simply stood there in a trance.

Realizing that the boy in front of her was bedazzled, the red-haired girl gently poked Calron on the forehead.

"Huh?"

"I said, are you alright?"
The soft voice of the girl reached Calron's ears.

Shaking himself out of his daze, Calron spluttered out his words.
"Uh… yes, I'm fine…thank you, I should…"

Seeing the little boy blushing arduously as he stumbled over his words, the young girl let out a pleasant laugh and petted Calron's hair.
"Aw, you're sooo cute. What's your name?"

Calron seemed to blush even more when the red-haired girl absentmindedly petted his hair. He knew he should smack her hand away, as she was treating him like a lost puppy, but Calron simply could not bring himself to do it.

"I'm Calron. W-what's your name?
Seeing the boy continue to stutter, the girl gently covered her mouth, trying not to giggle.

"I'm Lora. Nice to meet you, Calron. By the way y-"
The red-haired girl stopped abruptly talking as she felt a hand on her shoulder.

"You shouldn't be talking to a peasant like him, Lora."
A rough voice sounded out from behind the girl as a figure stepped up next to her.

The new stranger was a boy around twelve years of age, with short blonde hair and dark blue eyes. He was slightly taller than Lora, but his thick, muscular frame made him appear even taller.

Although the stranger was not as large or as muscular as Chax, he still had quite an intimidating presence.

"Stop it, Tarth! He's just a kid, and he was talking to me, not you."
Lora furiously scolded Tarth and shot an apologetic glance at Calron.

"This kid is a lightning cultivator!"
Tarth retorted in response to Lora.

"So what? If I want to talk to him, then I will. Back off!"
Although a brief trace of surprise flashed across Lora's eyes, she immediately regained her composure and glared at Tarth.

Watching this scene unfold from the sideline, Calron felt a cold fury surging within him. He was tired of people treating him like garbage just because of his element.

Master has permitted me to use the Formless Fist for the tournament, so it will be alright if I use it just a little bit for this brute right now. Besides, I can always ask for forgiveness later from Master.

As Calron debated on how he will apologize to his Master later, all of a sudden, the muscular boy angrily huffed and stormed away.

Calron missed the discussion between Lora and Tarth, but it seemed as if Lora had threatened the blonde boy with something.

Turning to face Calron, Lora gently patted his head as she stated.
"Well, it was nice meeting you, Calron. I need to get back to cultivating now, so I hope to see you again sometime. Don't worry about what Tarth said, and just focus on your training. I'm sure you will be strong one day as well."

Lora kindly said to Calron. Although her voice sounded sincere, both she and Calron knew that she only said it to make him feel better. It was common knowledge that lightning cultivators could never break through the Spiritual stage.

Nonetheless, Calron smiled at her, as he knew she only meant him well. With a final pat on his head, Lora smiled and walked away.

Coincidently, Calron spotted Rory in the corner of his eye, wolfing down the entire food on his tray.

Calron's ill mood immediately recovered upon seeing Rory's antics. Shaking his head, Calron went ahead and stood in line.

....

"Ah, big brother, that roast was delicious. Are you going to eat that leg piece?"
Rory asked, as he stared at the piece of chicken on Calron's plate.

Already feeling full, Calron shook his head in response, allowing Rory to snatch the last piece of meat.

"Rory, do you think girls are beautiful?"
Calron, lost in thought, asked out of the blue.

"Om nom nom- girls? Well, my big sister is really nice, and she gives me money for snacks.. I don't know about the other girls though..."
Rory said, while continuing to chew his food.

"Never mind, let's go back."
Calron stated as he got up from his chair.

"Noo, I still want seconds!"

"Sigh... I'll go back and start cultivating then. Rory, don't stay here all day and go train. If you want to catch up to me, you'll need to at least master the Formless Fist or reach a higher rank in cultivation."
Calron teased Rory before walking away.

"Hmph, just wait and see, I'll soon surpass big brother."

Rory shouted behind Calron as he continued to gnaw on the chicken leg.

....

Thinking about Lora put Calron in a good mood. He happily whistled as he walked back towards his hut.

He felt like he could finally make a breakthrough into the fourth rank today.

He knew he was already close to the peak of the third rank, but after his recent experience in the source pool, he sensed he had already reached the limits of the third rank.

However, just as Calron entered the corridor of the disciples' huts, he heard a peal of sinister laughter behind him.

"A loser like you thought you could get away that easily?"

"A loser like you thought you could get away that easily?"

Calron stopped midway as soon as he heard the crisp voice. He had expected this outcome, but he had also hoped he would be wrong.

Giving a soft sigh, Calron turned around and faced the owner of the cold voice.

"What do you want, Tarth? I have some important business to take care of, so make it quick."

Calron stated in a chilly tone.

Calron would rather not fight if he could avoid it, as he already had too many restrictions placed on him to not reveal his strength. Nevertheless, if he continued to get pushed around, Calron would return the favor multiple times and then deal with the consequences with his Master later.

Hearing the disdain in the smaller boy's voice, Tarth rabidly gnashed his teeth, burning with indignation.

"Bastard! Let's see how you escape from me now. There is no girl's skirt for you to hide behind this time!"
Tarth raged as kindred energy surged around him.

It was not elemental essence.

Calron was astounded when he realized what that energy was. It was something that he had himself.

It was the power of a Legacy.

Seeing the dumbfounded look on the boy's face, Tarth grew even more arrogant as he coldly laughed.

"A country bumpkin like you has probably never even heard of a legacy. Don't scream for help. I already have the area surrounded by my boys to make sure that no one enters this area. Hahaha!"

Once Calron heard the last sentence, a bone-chilling smile slowly crept across his face, thick killing intent wrapping around him.

Calron's biggest worry was people finding out his true strength, as that would bring further complications to his life, especially if the city Lord found out. However, Tarth had unknowingly paved an easier path for Calron.

Noticing that the expression on the boy's face had changed drastically, Tarth felt his heart shudder momentarily while the thick killing intent gradually drew near him.

Pushing away the doubts about the abnormal aura around the

boy, Tarth regained his vigor as he fiercely bellowed.

"Punk, I will show you the might of a Legacy Inheritor!"

A pale gray source energy discharged from his fists, as the blonde-haired boy simultaneously rushed towards Calron.

Seeing the pale gray source energy, Calron let out a low laugh.

Compared to the vicious source energy of the Blood Legacy, this pale gray energy almost seemed like a joke. Calron did not know the path of Tarth's legacy, but seeing no weapons on him, he guessed it was related to a body-type path.

"The might of a Legacy? Let me give you a little taste of it."

Calron quietly muttered as he deftly drew the source energy from his pool. However, on the outside, not a single trace of the energy leaked.

Although there was no threat of any wandering disciples, Calron still did not want Tarth to know of the existence of the Blood Legacy. He could sense that the blonde-haired boy was not very proficient in using the Legacy, as his energy leaked out everywhere. Hence, Calron knew that Tarth would be unable to detect the source energy inside him.

Just as Tarth's fist was an inch away from his face, Calron smoothly moved to the side, leaving a whistling sound echoing behind Tarth's fist.

Baffled that his fist met the empty air, Tarth glanced around, trying to find Calron.

"Looking for me?"

A deathly whisper sounded out from behind Tarth.

"Huh?"

CRACK

Before the blonde-haired boy had the chance to look behind him, a palm with a colossal amount of strength grasped his hair and viciously struck him against the ground.

....

"Tarth, you're so handsome!"

"No, he's mine! Go away!"

"Tarth, do you think I'm pretty?"

Tarth confusedly gazed around as he tried to understand where he was.

Where am I?

Why are these girls all touching me?

Tarth numbly sat there as the two pretty girls and the woman argued over him. Tarth knew these girls. He had a crush on one of them a few months ago, the other one was a new disciple to the school and the last woman was his teacher who had taught him back home.

"Huh? What are they all doing here? Maybe they all came to visit me."

The woman stroked his blonde hair as she said sweetly.
"Tarth, why aren't you listening to me? Am I too old for you?"

"Eh? N-no way, teacher! You are really pretty! I have always had a crush on you."

For some reason, Tarth felt completely relaxed here, so he openly confessed his feelings.

"Hmph, I thought you said you loved me. Didn't you ask me out a few days ago?"

A brown-haired girl retorted as she turned her head away from Tarth.

"B-but, didn't you reject me?"

Tarth stuttered as he glanced at the brown-haired girl.

"That was before I knew how strong and handsome you were. I wholeheartedly love you now, so say that you love me too."

The brown-haired girl pleaded as she pressed herself against Tarth.

Unable to contain the joy inside him, Tarth blurted out.

"Of course I love you! I still have the sweets I wanted you to try, which you spat out after slapping me..."

Tarth stated enthusiastically, but his voice eventually died down towards the end.

Wait, why would she slap me last time and now say she loves me now out of nowhere?

Before Tarth could think any further, the third girl turned around.

"Hey, muscle brains, can you hear me?"

The third girl's face twisted, warping into the face of the skinny boy he met today.

CRACK

Tarth felt a mind-crushing impact on his face as his head struck the ground again.

"You bastard! How many times do I have to repeat myself?"

Just as Calron was about to smash the blonde boy's face into the ground again, he heard a small whimper escape from Tarth's mouth.

"I'm s-sor... sorry."

Tarth's heart was burning with humiliation as he realized he was completely at the mercy of this brat.

How old was this kid? He appeared to be younger than even his little brother, but attacked with such a vicious killing intent.

This boy was a monster!

Just wait, you little punk. I will have my revenge a hundredfold the next time I see you.

While Tarth's thoughts furiously burned through his mind, Calron continued.

"Curse your stupid muscle brain. Do you know how much time I wasted by trying to wake you up by smashing your head? Who the hell sleeps during a fight?"

Hearing the boy's words, Tarth wanted to dig a hole and bury himself there.

This brat! Did he really continue to smash his head against the floor for the whole time? How vicious! And I was not sleeping, you punk, it was you who struck me till I went unconscious. Does my head look like a bouncing ball to you?

As Tarth pitifully cried out within his mind, he did not dare say those words to the lunatic boy above him.

"Hmm, whatever, my hand hurts now so you can go away. You know, you have an exceptionally thick skull. I had to smash your head over thirty times to wake you up..."

Calron said regretfully, as he gingerly rubbed his arm.

This time, Tarth could not hold his tears any longer.

Demon! You didn't have to smack my head every time! You could have just sprinkled some water to wake me up.
Tarth miserably cried within his mind.

He still did not understand how this skinny kid could completely suppress him to this extent. Let alone his inherited legacy, Tarth's cultivation itself was at the peak of the fifth rank. With his legacy, he could even contend against a cultivator of the sixth rank.

"You can try to bring others after me, but the result will only be worse for you. Next time, I won't leave with just a few smashes to the head."
Calron coldly whispered these words as he bent down next to Tarth's ears.

Hearing the savageness in the boy's voice, Tarth did not doubt for a second what would happen to him the next time he pulled a stunt like this. A kid that did not even slightly hesitate to brutally smash his head would have no qualms about doing even worse things.

"I-I under... stand."
Tarth wheezed out the words as Calron pressed his head against the ground.

"Never try to bully a weak person again...you never know just what they might be hiding."
Calron coldly stated as he slowly stood up.

"Besides, I doubt you would want others to know that you got crushed by a weak little lightning cultivator. Hahaha!"
Calron provoked the defeated bully, as he started walking back towards his hut.

A cheerful whistling tune echoed throughout the corridor.

CHAPTER TWENTY-TWO

Violet-Eyed Executioner

Calron hoped Tarth had learned his lesson, otherwise next time he would not be so lenient in dealing with the blonde-haired boy.

It was finally gratifying to act on his feelings, rather than suppressing his emotions in fear that others would find out his secret. Calron was eternally grateful to his Master for choosing him and teaching the path of the legacy, as without that strength today, he would have been the one with the injuries.

Although the Azure Lightning was a domineering might, it drew too much attention and unless Calron killed every witness that saw his fights, the existence of such an element would only bring him immense trouble in the future. Besides, the blue lightning never obeyed his commands either way.

Calron was still not sure how he felt about killing others. He knew he would have to do it eventually in the future, but he would rather not resort to it unless there were no other choices.

Unknown to Calron, his recent battles and fights were already slowly molding his mind to become sharper and fiercer, as he was starting to be no longer opposed to killing.

Being in an excellent mood, Calron whistled the tune that he once heard from a passing merchant in the village. Although Calron had not whistled in a long time, especially after his father's death, it was one of the few things that he had enjoyed in life.

The village kids were not always nice to him, and they didn't try to befriend him either. The stain of being a lightning cultivator's son was deeply etched in Calron and made the other kids stay away from him.

Faced with this isolation, Calron used to spend his time wandering around the village market and talking to the elderly folk.

The old shopkeepers never scowled at him or treated him like dirt. Calron would always help around at the shops, doing everything from running errands to cleaning the place up, and in return, the shopkeepers would sometimes give him small treats to eat or tell him stories about the legends of the past.

From all the legends, Calron's favorite one was about the Violet-Eyed Executioner.

No one knew where this stranger came from, but he was known to roam the entire continent unparalleled as he vanquished the magical beasts within the human lands.

It was said that in the past, the beasts enslaved humans. They were treated like livestock or cattle for the beasts to leisurely feast upon. Many of the cities were overtaken by the beasts due to their larger numbers. The magical beasts had an overwhelming advantage besides their numbers, they could inherit the memories of their ancestors upon birth. They didn't need a long time to train like the humans to be combat-ready, allowing them to refill their armies quicker than their opponents.

At that time, the humans only had the simplest of cultivation techniques, and against the onslaught of the superior beasts, they were soon miserably defeated.

Only a rare few cities remained under the control of humans, as the vast majority of the lands were rapidly being conquered by the Beast Rulers.

Beast Ruler was a title given to any magical beast that reached the cultivation of the Heavenly stage or more. With countless cities under the control of a single Beast Ruler, it was clear to see the terrifying power that the beasts held back then.

Living in fear every day, the humans desperately fought an uphill battle they knew they could not win. The only path open to them was a life of slavery or a bitter touch of death.

Amidst that agony and desperation, a ray of salvation suddenly appeared in front of the humans.

A mysterious hooded man intervened in one battle the humans were destined to lose and he single-handedly massacred the entire army of beasts along with their ruler.

The hooded man immediately left after that first battle and a few days later, countless stories of a mysterious man effortlessly slaughtering beasts spread across the entire continent.

The only description of the mysterious man that was revealed happened by chance. During one skirmish, his hood accidentally flew back, revealing the striking features of the man.

A nearby wounded soldier at the sidelines etched that memory deep into his heart and he later spread the story around the barracks.

According to the soldier's tale, the mysterious man had his entire lower jaw covered in a veil, but it was his eyes that completely captivated the wounded soldier's mind.

Burning with a celestial glow, the mysterious man's violet eyes bore into the soldier as his heart trembled under the pressure those eyes exuded.

The hooded man's piercing violet eyes blazed with a fierce intensity as he turned away his attention from the soldier and mercilessly butchered the numerous beasts. The scene of the man slaying the beasts as his eyes glowed with an unnatural violet color, later earned him the name of the Violet-Eyed Executioner.

Even the Beast Ruler had only lasted a few seconds longer than the normal beasts against the executioner.

A power that could slaughter a Heavenly stage expert as easily as beheading a pig shattered the minds of the nearby humans.

Could they have the same power as this man?

Within a few months, the entire beast population had been decimated to a mere handful as they frantically escaped to the other continents or the nearby mountains.

The hooded man then headed to the major capital of the human lands and handed a series of scrolls to the people living there. He said the scrolls were different cultivation techniques and that the humans will have to depend on themselves in the future if the beasts attacked.

After he said those words, the hooded man abruptly vanished.

Till this day, none knew his name and even the stories about the Violet-Eyed Executioner were dubious, as most believed them to be tales spun by bored soldiers on the battlefield. However, the truth of the matter would never be known.

Calron did not care whether the legend of the Violet-Eyed Executioner was true or not. He simply wanted to carve his own destiny like the hooded man.

Shatter his fate of being weak.

Shatter his fate of servitude.

Shatter his fate of loneliness.

It had been a long time since Calron thought back to those days and he soon stopped in front of his hut as he reminisced about his life back then.

With a sad smile, Calron slowly entered his room.

....

After a quick clean-up, Calron sat down on the mat in a meditative position and activated the second stage of the Thunder-Bird breathing technique.

"Hmm, I'm almost there..."

Calron muttered to himself. A massive amount of essence was slowly being absorbed into his body.

Meanwhile, within Calron's core, a strange scene unfolded.

Bolts of blue lightning had again appeared around the core as they unceasingly refined every drop of essence that entered the liquid pool within the elemental core.

The golden-azure drops bubbled as the surrounding essence wildly fluctuated around Calron.

A faint sound of thunder echoed in the room as traces of golden lightning crackled around Calron's skin.

"It's starting!"

Calron exclaimed in delight as he saw the changes in his core.

Torrents of lightning essence spiraled above Calron as they were rapidly being absorbed into his body. Within seconds, the new essence was completely refined into the golden-azure liquid and just as Calron felt he had reached his limit, an explosion reverberated throughout the room.

BOOOOM!

A gust of wind expelled from the room as the dust on the floor followed the blast of air, causing a cloud of smoke to form around Calron's hut.

With a series of coughs, Calron forced the smoke out of his room and let out a sudden grin.

"Awesome! I finally entered the fourth rank and with this, I should now be able to contend against Chax with just my physical body. I was at a disadvantage last time, but let's see him try to fight me again. Hehe…"

As Calron excitedly talked to himself, a nearby servant just gaped at him.

What Calron had not noticed was that he was completely covered in dust and subconsciously pumping his fists in the air.

The servant was in the middle of sweeping the corridor when he saw a lunatic rush out of a hut covered in dust as he excitedly yelled and threw his fists around.

The servant did not know whether to be mad at the boy for dirtying the place he had just now cleaned or laugh at the silly antics of the kid.

Sensing that someone was staring at him, Calron turned around until he found a servant just standing there with a broom. Hurriedly regaining his composure, Calron walked up to the servant, and he gave a polite bow while stating.

"Sir, I think there is a little bit of dust near there. Thank you for your hard work."

Before the servant could respond, Calron sprinted toward the Foundation building.

Once Calron dashed away, the servant burst out in laughter, seeing the fumes of dust trailing behind the young kid. The boy had not even realized his comical appearance as he obliviously made his escape.

"Sometimes, life is just meant to be silly…"
The servant muttered as he let out a low chuckle and resumed his sweeping.

As the sun's rays shone in the morning, the young disciples groggily woke up one after another.

In a separate hut, a dark-haired boy of eight years buried his face into the pillow when the sunlight bore into his eyes.

Damn this stupid sun. Why did they have to put a window exactly there? I don't like windows anymore…
Calron annoyingly muttered into the pillow as the bright light disturbed his sleep.

"Sigh… I still have Master's training today, so I better get up."
Forcing himself to climb out from the warmth of the bed, Calron dejectedly stood up.

After a quick cleanup, Calron wore his disciple robes and rushed to the gathering hall to meet up with Rory.

………………..

"Big brother, why are you so happy? You even let me take your chocolate milk and usually, you always smack me whenever I try to."
Rory curiously asked Calron as they were walking toward the forest where their Master lived.

"What? I just didn't feel like having chocolate milk. Why is that so surprising?"

Calron retorted back to Rory.

"Bah! The last time I sneaked one away from you, you viciously grabbed my hand and twisted it backward..."
Rory's voice died down towards the end, recalling that painful memory.

Generally, Calron did not care much about food, but Rory had recently found out that his big brother had a strange infatuation with chocolate milk.

Unlike Rory, Calron did not have the luxury of sweet foods like chocolate, so once he tried the chocolate milk one fateful morning, Calron was immediately obsessed with this godly drink.

"Eh? You're hiding something. C'mon, big brother, tell me! Tell me! Please?"

Faced with Rory's constant harassment, Calron resigned himself as he quietly muttered.
"I broke through to the fourth rank..."

"What? Stop mumbling!"
Rory impatiently stated, as he could not hear Calron's rambling.

"I said..."
Calron mumbled as he purposefully lowered his voice at the end.

"Big brother, I'll forcefully kiss you if you don't tell me right now!"
Rory threatened Calron when he saw that the dark-haired boy was intentionally teasing him.

"I'll punch your mouth if you dare."
Calron said in a low voice, amusement seeing into his tone.

"Hehe, is that a challenge?"

Rory snickered as he nimbly leaped onto Calron's back and wrapped his arms around his neck.

"Dammit, Rory, get off me!"
Calron yelled as he tried to shake off the large boy from his back.

Unlike before, Rory was not the small, chubby kid anymore. He was much heavier than Calron with his newfound muscular frame, so it was difficult for Calron to kick him away. Although he could use the source energy to easily suppress Rory, Calron did not want to use the power of the Blood Legacy on his brother unless they were sparring.

As the two boys rolled on the ground, Rory loudly laughed every time he managed to kiss Calron on the cheek.

"Kekeke, if you don't tell me soon, I think you know where I will kiss you next!"
Rory exclaimed as he puckered his lips in exaggeration while making kissing noises.

"Ugh, you slobbering idiot! I said I broke into the fourth rank!"
Calron shouted next to Rory's ear as he uttered a string of curses into the air.

Flinching at the piercing voice next to his ear, Rory gingerly rubbed his ears as he inquired again.
"So, big brother, what did you say again?"

"Rory, I'm going to kill you now."
Calron stated in a frosty and irritated voice as he wiped away Rory's slobber from his cheeks.

"Haha, just kidding. I heard you perfectly. Wow, big brother, you're so amazing! Although your cultivation is lower than my big sister, I'm absolutely sure that you are no weaker than her with your current power."
Rory sincerely conveyed this to Calron.

Standing up, Rory smiled as he extended his hand to Calron on the ground.

Grabbing his brother's hand, Calron returned the smile as he slowly stood up and patted the dirt out of his robes.

"By the way, Rory…"

"Yes, big brother?"
Rory curiously turned his head as Calron started talking.

"Kiss me again, and I will electrocute you."
Calron stated in a low voice as bursts of lightning crackled around his hand.

"Ah… of course…"
Rory promised as drops of sweat rolled off his forehead.

"Well, as long as you understand, it's fine. Now, let's run, or else we'll be late for Master."
Calron stated as he started running into the forest. Rory soon followed him after he threw imaginary kisses at Calron behind his back.

………………..

"Hmm, so you both are finally here."
Elias calmly stated as he detected his two disciples sprinting towards his hut.

He was seated in a meditative position as Calron and Rory approached him. Elias' cloudy gray eyes flashed as they abruptly opened.

"You're late."
Elias said in a serious tone.

"Sorry, Master, it was big brother's fault. He wanted to kiss me!" Rory interjected before Calron could even speak.

Suddenly a bolt of golden lightning erupted behind Rory's bottom and he yelped in shock.

"I think Rory is still sleepy, Master, as he's spouting nonsense. Master, what are we training in today?"

Calron calmly stated without glancing at Rory, who was currently gingerly rubbing his bottom as he glared at Calron.

"Calron, today you will begin your training in the Blood Mist Step. Roran, you will continue to practice the Formless Fist until you perfect it. I assume you still remember the forms and the stances?"

Elias asked with an amused smile on his face.

"Ugh, yes, Master. I will immediately start training. Hehe, big brother, just wait and see, I'll catch up to you!"

Rory enthusiastically exclaimed as he walked off towards the nearby lake to train. Previously, Rory had found out that both Calron and his Master trained their Formless Fist there, so he decided to practice in the same place as well.

As soon as Rory left, Elias instantly adopted a serious tone as he continued.

"Calron, the Blood Mist Step is an extremely dangerous movement skill. The agility and speed it grants are second to none, but the risks in using it are just as high. Although it will not consume your blood like the Titan's Fury, it will force you to draw large amounts of source energy from the pool."

Knowing that his Master was devoid of any humor about this matter, Calron did not speak and intently focused on Elias's words.

"Since the seal has already been broken, you can now send your consciousness into the second step and retrieve the information for its activation. Unlike the first step, the rest of the following steps will have records of the skills and movements. The deeper your connection to the legacy, the more benefits you'll receive. Come to me when you are stuck or need someone to spar with. I think Roran still has quite some time before he can even put up a resistance against you."

Elias laughed as he glanced off into the distance where Rory was currently practicing.

Noticing his Master accurately perceiving Rory's location, Calron had always found it intriguing that his Master's technique let him see without the use of any essence or energy. Taking this time to ease his doubts, Calron hesitantly asked.
"Master, may I ask you something related to your eyes?"

"Hmm, sure. What do you want to know?"
Elias calmly replied.

"How does Master see the world? I remember you saying it was a technique that lets you see, but wouldn't you at least need essence to use any kind of technique?"
Calron curiously asked his Master.

"You've made some logical points, Calron. However, this world does not conform to a specific order. Do you really think mortals could achieve immortality if they followed the order of the natural world? No, there always exist laws, techniques, or objects that defy the will of the heavens."
Elias stated in a somber tone.

"Then... your technique..."
Calron unknowingly had his mouth wide open in shock.

"Yes, it is something that should not exist in this world."
Elias casually stated as he confirmed the suspicion of his disciple.

"Truthfully, few people know about it, even within my own family. Only my father and brother knew about the existence of this technique besides me. Our ancestor had left the secrets of this technique to the head of the Xurian family back then and commanded that it must only be passed onto direct heirs. Since you are the next Prime Inheritor of the legacy, you are the only one fit to be my direct heir."

Elias explained in a calm voice.

Calron felt his heart racing.

A technique that defied the will of the heavens? Calron remembered the Voice also telling him that eventually, he would have to fight against his own destiny to reach the peak of cultivation.

No matter what, it seemed that Calron was fated to defy the heavens.

"Master, I want to learn this technique."

CHAPTER TWENTY-THREE

Blood Mist Step

"Master, I want to learn this technique."
Calron asked with excitement.

"Haha, you are not yet ready for it, Calron. A technique that defies the laws of this world does not depend simply on one's cultivation or strength. You will know the reason for this when you are ready."
Elias softly explained to his disheartened disciple.

"Alright, Master."
Calron answered in a dejected voice.

He knew he was not strong enough to learn a technique that defied the heavens itself, but he had hoped to at least glean some information out of his Master. Calron curiously wondered what the requirement was in order to be considered worthy of this mighty technique.

"Leave that for the future. Right now, you need to focus on the upcoming tournament. If I had a choice, I would make you sit out of it, but the rules of the Red Boar School state that every single disciple must take part, regardless of their cultivation level or age."

Elias started talking as he beckoned Calron to sit in front of him on the grass.

* * *

"The first round will be the preliminary round, where the disciples will be put in exactly fifty batches and have a battle royale until only one person is left standing. After that, the real Ranking Tournament will begin."

Calron interjected.
"But Master, how does the ranking actually work? What about the ranks of those defeated in the first round?"

"If you had been patient and let me finish, you would have already learned the answer."
Elias started with a raised eyebrow and a slight smile on his face.

"Uh, sorry Master, please continue. I won't interrupt again."
Calron exclaimed with a heated face as he hung his head down in embarrassment.

"Haha, don't worry, my child. Impatience is a virtue of youth."
Elias stated with a pat on his young disciple's head.

"Now, where were we? Ah, yes, the ranking system of the tournament. After the preliminary round, only fifty disciples will enter the actual ranking tournament. The rest of the disciples will be unranked. Only the top students of the school will have a rank assigned to them, with the fiftieth rank being the weakest, while the strongest is the one with the first rank. Are you following along with me alright so far??"
Elias stopped to ask his disciple.

"Yes, Master, I'm listening."
Calron enthusiastically responded.

"Good. We only have a few months left before the tournament begins, and you need to rapidly increase your strength if you hope to contend against the other disciples. The major attraction of this competition is not the ranks, but the rewards that are given to the top three ranked disciples."

Elias stated in a serene voice, while Calron eagerly awaited the next words of his Master.

"The disciple in the third place will receive a ninth-rank beast core, and the one in the second place will be given a top-tier elemental sword and finally, for the first place, a rare elixir will be awarded."

Calron took deep breaths as he heard the prizes for the top rankers.

A ninth-rank beast core could be sold for thousands of gold squares, and even the city Lord himself did not possess many cores of that rank. It was simply too dangerous to defeat a magical beast of the ninth rank, making its core exceptionally precious.

The higher one reached in the ranks of cultivation, the more difficult it would be to break into the next realm. With the aid of a beast core, the time required to cultivate could be greatly decreased, as the core will provide an essence much more refined than the one present in the environment.

The second-place prize held little attention for Calron, as he knew that his dark bow was unparalleled in the weapons category and even a top-tier elemental weapon would pale compared to the mighty and baleful aura of the dark metal bow.

However, Calron was perplexed by the prize for first place. An elixir had medicinal properties, so he was not sure how useful it would be for cultivation unless a person got mortally wounded.

"Master, isn't the first-place prize a bit too lacking compared to the other rewards?"

Calron curiously inquired.

"Hmm, is that what you think? What if I told you that the elixir will help one break into the Vajra stage?"

Elias stated in an amused voice as he watched the stunned look on his disciple's face.

"W-what? But that is im-"
Calron stuttered in shock but was quickly interrupted by Elias.

"It is not impossible, Calron. Tell me, what do you know of the Vajra stage?"

"Um, it is when the core merges with your body and completely alters your constitution."
Calron confidently replied.

Hearing his disciple's answer, Elias slightly shook his head.

"You are partially correct. It is not the core that merges with your body, but the essence contained within it. After your awakening, you are in your first stage, as the core allows you to begin your elemental cultivation. However, your body is still that of a normal person. Although you might momentarily make your body tougher by imbuing essence into it during a battle, it is still relying on the essence. Without it, your body would be as weak as a commoner."

Baffled at the new information, Calron paid closer attention to what his Master was saying.

It was completely natural that Calron's knowledge of the cultivation stages would be incomplete, as he had never known anyone with such high cultivation before. He had only gleaned bits and pieces from when the village kids gossiped or when the adults talked amongst themselves.

"But Master, my physical body is stronger than other cultivators for sure."
Calron blurted out.

"True, but that is mainly because of the Blood Legacy and the unique element that you have."

Elias calmly replied.

"Once you enter the Vajra stage, your body will be completely imbued with elemental essence. Your skin's toughness will be comparable to some weaker metals and even the rate of essence absorption will increase enormously. I do not know how much it will increase in your case, due to your element belonging to the special bloodlines, but I assume the changes will be a lot greater."
Elias stated with a slight anticipation in his voice.

This was the first time Elias had encountered a cultivator with a special bloodline, and moreover, it was someone with the unknown bloodline of the lightning element.

"So the elixir will let me directly enter the Vajra stage?"
Calron curiously inquired.

"Not exactly. It will directly convert all your essence into a liquid form. Refining your gaseous essence into a liquid state is an extremely difficult and complicated process. This is the part where most cultivators are unable to break through and remain stuck in the Spiritual stage."
Elias explained patiently.

Meanwhile, Calron stared dumbly at his Master.

Liquid essence? My essence is already in the liquid state…
As Calron's thoughts raced, he did not know whether he should tell this to his Master.

In the end, Calron decided not to, as it would just shock his Master and he had been giving too many of those lately.

"Wow! That sure sounds amazing, Master."
Calron exclaimed in an overly excited voice.

Completely oblivious to his young student's tone, Elias continued.

"Hopefully, that will give you some extra motivation for the tournament. Now, are you ready to learn the Blood Mist Step?"

"Yes, Master."
This time, the eagerness in Calron's voice was completely sincere.

"You can enter the second step right now. Begin your meditation and wholly focus your consciousness into the Blood Legacy. It will direct your path and come find me when you unlock its teachings."
Elias calmly conveyed as he stood up and walked in the direction where Rory was.

His second disciple was a lot more trouble than his first one and needed careful guidance. Elias was worried that Rory would goof off rather than training, and it turned out that Elias was correct in his worries, as Rory was currently dozing off next to the lake.

"Sigh... this brat."

....

Meanwhile, Calron had already closed his eyes, and he was in the center of the source pool within the Blood Legacy.

Sending his consciousness into his bridge, Calron arrived in front of the second step. Seeing the low azure glow from the third step, Calron was tempted to enter it but restrained himself at the last minute. He had promised his Master that he would not enter it unless he had no other choice.

Taking a deep breath, Calron plunged into the second step.

whoosh

A blood-colored shadow darted in front of Calron, exploding into a cloud of crimson mist and reappearing a few meters ahead of its previous location.

"Huh?"
Calron confusedly stared at his surroundings.

Darkness.

It felt like nothing existed in the world besides the black void that surrounded Calron. There were no signs of any life or objects in the vicinity. It was completely pitch black except for the blood shadows darting around as they continuously exploded into bursts of crimson mist.

Not even a hint of a breeze could be felt on Calron's skin as he simply observed the scene before him.

"What is this place? Is that the Blood Mist Step?"
Calron muttered when he saw the blood shadows erupting into clouds of mist.

Knowing that he needed to gain insights into the technique on his own, Calron sat down in a meditative position and put his full focus on the movements of the blood shadows.

The longer Calron gazed at the shadows, the deeper he became immersed in his concentration. He felt like he was absorbing bits of information as small tendrils of the crimson mist entered his body whenever the shadows kept bursting apart.

"Hmm, this seems familiar..."
Calron had already experienced the sensation of the crimson mist before when the Blood Legacy started breaking the seal out of its own accord. Recalling those memories, Calron entered an extremely profound state of meditation.

....

"I'm hungry, Master. Can we take a small break?"

Rory pitifully asked the old man sitting on the large rock in front of him.

"You just took a bathroom break a few minutes ago. Concentrate on your training, Roran."

Elias answered in a strict tone.

Earlier, Elias had been fooled by Rory when the boy had requested multiple breaks for either the bathroom or for drinking water. After continuously leaving, Elias figured out that the boy was simply too lazy, so he forced Rory to train with no interruptions.

With a dejected sigh, Rory continued his training as he unceasingly punched the air in front of him while drops of sweat rolled off his body.

Elias sat on the rock and hummed a slow tune as he watched his second disciple dance in combat.

....

Tendrils of crimson mist constantly drifted into Calron's body as he remained in a state of deep meditation.

On the outside, a dense scarlet cloud was ominously floating above Calron as he slowly absorbed the crimson mist. Unbeknownst to him, the number of the blood shadows in the surrounding area was steadily decreasing the more Calron continued to absorb the crimson mist.

Soon, Calron's skin glowed with a faint red hue as traces of sweat formed around his body.

Not only was he absorbing the crimson mist into his body, but Calron was also inhaling the blood mist into his lungs.

After a few minutes, his skin turned completely red, and hot steam sizzled over him. Intense pain shot across his body, leaving Calron to cry out a hoarse roar.

His blood felt like it was slowly being boiled, and his body temperature rose to an abnormal degree.

"This is what Master warned me about."
Calron rasped as he struggled to maintain his consciousness.

There was simply a gargantuan amount of source energy within his body at that moment, and Calron could not safely control it.

"DAMN IT!"
Gathering every shred of willpower he had, Calron bellowed furiously into the darkness.

shua
Right then, his palm began heating up, and a series of symbols revolved around his hand. A bright light flashed as it revealed a large translucent shield behind the seated Calron.

The shield had three distinct symbols etched into the center, and they were identical to the symbols that were imprinted on Calron's palm.

"The Legacy Armor..."
Calron softly whispered in the darkness as he speedily regained control of the blood mist.

....

hisss
A fist viciously struck the empty air as a sound of a small explosion trailed behind it.

"Haah... Hah... I did it!"

Rory panted and tried to steady his breath, dropping to the ground in exhaustion.

"Good job, but you are still far away from perfecting it. I guess that is good enough for a day's training."
Elias gently said while looking down at his weary disciple.

"Calron should be done as well... I hope he can endure it."
Elias quietly murmured as he gazed in the distance toward his other disciple, who was currently entranced in meditation.

At that moment, a deafening explosion reverberated throughout the forest.

Both Rory and Elias swiftly headed toward the source of the sound and were shocked at the scene in front of them.

There was a tornado of crimson mist encircling Calron. The boy had his eyes closed with a faint smile tugging at his lips.

Seeing the sight of the crimson mist spiraling around his disciple, Elias let out a small sigh of relief and a moment later, an elated grin spread on his face.

"I think I'm becoming numb to the number of shocks this disciple of mine continues to throw at me."
Elias said while letting out a low chuckle and walking towards Calron.

Rory had his mouth wide open at the sight of the crimson tornado in front of him and immediately stood up from the ground.
"Wah, big brother is simply too amazing!"

Just then, the tornado instantly calmed down and dissipated into the air, revealing the complete figure of a dark-haired boy.

Calron turned his head as he noticed his Master and Rory

approaching him.

"Seeing that silly smile on your face, I'm assuming it all went well?"
Elias asked with mirth.

"Yes, Master. This disciple has successfully learned the basics of the Blood Mist Step."

"Good, good. I'm curious how you endured the pressure of the second step. Was it your Azure Lightning that aided you?"
Elias curiously inquired his young disciple.

"No, Master... It was this thing that you previously said was extremely powerful."
Calron replied as he showed his palm containing the three distinct symbols.

"Haha, I forgot you had inherited the Legacy Armor. So, do you still think it is a useless ability?"
Elias asked in an amused tone.

"N-no, of course not. How could something that Master said was powerful ever be useless?"
Calron stammered out the words, his cheeks reddening.

He remembered a while ago when he had complained to his Master about how useless the symbols were, and today, Calron experienced its powerful defensive ability.

"Well, what are you waiting for?"
Elias stated with a mischievous grin on his face.

"Huh?"
Calron was utterly confused at his Master's behavior.

"Let me see just how proficient you are in the Blood Mist Step."

Elias responded as his grin turned even wider.

In a flash, Elias disappeared from his spot, leaving a trail of crimson mist behind him. With his instincts kicking in, Calron immediately activated the Blood Mist Step and moved a step back.

Unlike Elias, Calron had not yet learned to move large distances with the Blood Mist Step, so the most he could do was move a single step.

Fortunately, Calron evaded his Master's fist by a hair's breadth and counterattacked with his palm.

Right when Calron's strike was about to land on Elias, his Master gracefully vanished again. However, this time, Calron was prepared for it and a part of his arm turned into a cloud of crimson mist and elegantly reappeared behind him, where his Master stood there with a surprised look on his face.

With a sly grin, Calron launched another strike against his Master hoping he would catch him off guard.

Seeing his disciple adapt so quickly to battle and the technique, Elias was momentarily shocked but he quickly regained his composure.

"Still too early for you, my young disciple."
Elias calmly stated as he exploded in another burst of crimson smoke the instant before Calron was about to strike.

Within a second, Elias reappeared next to Calron and had his finger placed firmly against Calron's neck before the boy could react.

"Not bad for your first try."
Elias whispered as he gave a proud smile to his disciple.

Hearing his Master's praise, Calron beamed with happiness.

"I will catch you next time, Master."

"Woah, I want to learn that cool trick as well!"
Rory interjected when he realized that the spar between his brother and Master had ended.

"Hmm, you have not yet perfected the Formless Fist, so master that first, and then you can learn the Blood Mist Step, Roran."
Elias gently voiced as his second disciple jumped in excitement.

Smacking Rory on the back, Calron stated in a serious tone.
"Master, I think I'm ready for the tournament."

CHAPTER TWENTY-FOUR

Change Of Heart

The sounds of sparrows chirping and the sweeping noise of a broom resounded in the disciple lodgings. It was still a bit early for the disciples to wake up, so they were all comfortably sleeping in their warm beds.

A lone, dark-haired boy inside a small hut was seated on a mat as he deeply immersed himself in meditation.

Faint tendrils of golden lightning bounced around his skin as waves of essence floated above him.

The dark-haired boy no longer appeared to be as skinny as he was a few months ago. Cords of dense muscle covered his body, giving him a lean constitution but not making his appearance overly bulky. His face had also lost some traces of its chubbiness, making his jaw seem more angular while emanating a feeling of fierceness.

After months of intense training in both Martial Arts and cultivation, the dark-haired boy currently had a completely different aura and composition from before.

shua

Calron sharply opened his eyes, golden lightning flickering across his pupils.

Taking a deep breath, Calron ended his cultivation and slowly stood up.

Grabbing the towel on his bed, he went outside his hut and gazed at the empty courtyard.

"So, today is the day that it all begins."

Calron murmured as he glanced towards the horizon.

In the past few months, Calron had grown by several inches, and he was now just as tall as Rory, or maybe even slightly taller. Whereas Rory had a much more muscular frame, Calron was leaner, with thick whipcord-like muscles.

Both brothers had been vigorously training for the tournament and the changes were evident. It was finally time for the Preliminary Round.

Wiping his sweat with the towel, Calron deeply inhaled the fresh morning breeze as he waited for the sun to completely rise.

This was a new hobby that Calron had recently adopted. For some unknown reason, he felt serenely peaceful when he watched the sun slowly rise, giving life to yet another day.

After the sun reached its peak, several disciples exited their huts to get ready for the day. Calron went back inside and commenced his preparation for the first round of the tournament.

. . . .

"Big brother! Big brother! Here!"

A cheerful Rory jumped up and down as he waved both his hands in the air to get Calron's attention.

The Preliminary Round was set at the school's Arena. Throughout the year, the Arena would be mostly empty, and only during the rare occasion of a duel or a big ceremony would the Arena be opened. Until a few weeks ago, Calron had not even known that a stadium as large as the Arena existed within the school.

Seeing Rory over in the crowd, Calron gave a wide smile and rushed forward to meet his brother.

* * *

"Yo Rory! Are you ready to finally showcase your awesome talent?"

Calron teased Rory as he locked his arms around Rory's neck.

There was a large crowd of disciples gathered around the entrance of the Arena, as they excitedly chatted about the battles they would participate in, and then later watch their friends' battles. Although few had the hopes of reaching the top fifty ranks of the tournament, the Arena was a perfect place to showcase their talent and cultivation prowess.

For the disciples who had not yet been taken under the tutelage of a Master, the tournament would be the perfect opportunity for them to gain a Master if they performed well in the battles.

It was a tournament where everyone competed to be acknowledged as the most talented and powerful.

"Eh? How could I possibly be considered talented, when big brother will participate as well? Wouldn't everyone be taken aback once they witness a lightning elementalist destroy the top students?"

Rory answered in a mock pitiful voice as he gave a quick wink to his brother.

"Hahaha, you don't have to worry. I will intentionally lose in the first round."

Calron stated as he continued to walk towards the Arena.

"W-what!? Why would you do that? You could easily reach the ranks of the top fifty, so why would you want to lose in the Preliminary Round?"

Rory was confused. The two brothers had both been zealously training for months and right before the tournament would start, his brother announced out of the blue that he wanted to lose in the very first round.

"Sigh... Rory, this whole thing is pointless. What do you think will happen once I reveal my strength? Although Master has permitted me to use the Formless Fist, would anyone here be able to take even a single punch from me? It just doesn't interest me anymore."

Calron lazily replied as folded his hands above his head.

In truth, within the past few months of training, Calron had already broken into the fifth rank. Just with his physical body alone, he would be able to easily defeat any cultivator of the sixth rank.

With the average strength of the Red Boar's disciples being at the third rank, it would hardly be a challenge for the current Calron to defeat any of their outer disciples.

A few months back, Calron had been eager to show off his strength in the tournament. However, after a few weeks, he realized he would achieve nothing by gaining that much attention. On the contrary, it would draw the eyes of his enemies sooner.

"But there will be other elites of the outer disciples. I remember my big sister telling me that there were some outstandingly strong disciples in the school. If big brother reaches the top ranks, then you will be able to fight them and, at the same time, receive the reward for the top three placements."

Rory exclaimed in a passionate voice.

"Uhh, fine. I'll try it out, but if it gets boring, I will just quit and leave."

Calron conveyed in an exasperated tone.

Although he had been training continuously for the past few months, it was not for the tournament, but to beat his Master. At the end of the day, he was still a kid and was tempted to show off a bit.

Calron had sparred countless times with Elias, and not once had he ever come close to defeating him or landing a strike against him. Battles with his Master always excited Calron and ignited the raging battle spirit inside him.

What was the point of a fight where one's heart did not violently pound against one's chest? Or when the blood did not boil with unrestrained excitement?

* * *

Calron was only participating in the tournament because it was a rule of the Red Boar School, otherwise, he would not even have entered the Preliminary Round.

The reward for the first place did somewhat rouse Calron's curiosity, however, it was not enough for him to waste his time by fighting multiple battles. His essence was already in the liquid state, so the elixir would hardly be of any use to him.

"Big brother is so lazy. Whatever, that means I get to shine instead. Hehe!"

Rory boasted as he puffed up his chest.

Within the past few months, Rory had rarely been lazing around and trained with just as much intensity as Calron. He had broken into the third rank and cultivated his essence according to his family's secret arts.

A while ago, Felice had found out that her brother had mysteriously awakened to an element. After being stunned and speechless for a long time, she soon burst into tears as she tightly hugged her little brother.

Without the slightest hesitation, she had discreetly handed out Rory the Axier family's cultivation techniques and made him promise to not reveal it to anyone.

Currently, only Calron and Elias knew exactly how much of a freak Rory really was.

....

Finally reaching the inside of the Arena, both Calron and Rory gaped at the sight in front of them.

The Arena was simply massive.

There were thousands of chairs and booths surrounding the stadium and a vast crowd of disciples wearing different colored armbands.

There were also several older men and women, who Calron guessed were the current Masters of the disciples there.

* * *

Unfortunately, since it was secret that both Rory and Calron had Elias as their Master, they would not be having anyone to wish them good luck besides themselves. However, their Master had promised that he would watch from within the audience.

Walking towards the stand where the other disciples were receiving their different colored armbands, Calron and Rory hoped that they would not receive the same colored armband.

It would be a cruel twist of fate if they were placed in the same batch for the first round, as that would mean that only one of them could reach the top fifty ranks.

"Good luck, big brother."

Rory whispered next to Calron.

"You too, Rory. Hold nothing back, even if we are pitted against each other."

Calron whispered to Rory, as he gave him an optimistic wink.

"Name?"

A detached voice sounded from the stand when Calron and Rory approached the front of the line. A fat pot-bellied man sat in a chair that was too small for him as he lazily handed out the colored armbands.

"Calron."

"Hmm, registered under... the City Lord."

The fat man abruptly sat up straight when he saw who the sponsor of the boy was.

Noticing the pot-bellied man's frenzied actions, Calron did not know whether to laugh or cry. If the man knew the real reason the City Lord sponsored him, then he doubted the fat man would be so respectful.

Enjoying the frenzied actions of the man, Calron responded.

"Yes, that would be me."

"Alright, you are in the seventh batch. Here is your armband. Best of luck."

The pot-bellied man sincerely said as he handed out Calron a black armband.

Patting Rory on the back, Calron stepped to the side and dragged the band along his arm.

"Hey look! That loser lightning elementalist has the same colored armband as us. Keke, how unlucky for him."

A nearby disciple gleefully cheered when he saw Calron wearing the black-colored armband.

Irritated by the voice, Calron lifted his head and looked up towards the group of disciples in front of him.

Calron's eyes widened in surprise as his eyes locked with the person who stood at the front of the group.

After not having seen that person in such a long time, Calron's initial surprise soon turned into amusement.

"Yo, Tarth. Is your face still hurting?"

Calron shouted, noticing that the boy at the head of the group was the blonde muscular boy he clashed with a few months ago.

Seeing the dark-haired boy whom one of their group members had just called a loser now arrogantly greeting their leader, the surrounding disciples were all stunned.

"Hey, boss, why is that peasant talking to you that way? Did he mistake you for someone else?"

A short boy with copper-colored hair asked, looking at Tarth.

Meanwhile, Tarth felt his heart trembling with fear.

This child demon had to be in the same batch as me? Curse my stupid luck. How will I ever show my face again if I lose in the very first round?

"Boss?"
Another boy next to Tarth nudged his shoulder.

"Shut up and walk away! Don't insult that kid again. He is a wolf in a sheep's skin."
Tarth fiercely whispered, as he started scurrying in the opposite direction without taking a single glance at Calron.

"Huh? What's wrong with the boss? Let's just follow him."
Giving a last look of disdain at Calron, the other boys trailed behind Tarth.

Shrugging his shoulders, Calron started a low whistling tune as he patiently waited for Rory to return with his armband.

"Tarth! Where the hell did he go? I just saw him here a few minutes ago. Tarth!"
A sweet, melodic voice sounded in the area.

Hearing that voice, Calron felt his heartstrings tug violently.

thump
thump *thump*

It's her.

Calron's heart pounded wildly against his chest as he tried to steady his rising heartbeat.

It had been a long time since he last saw her, and she only seemed to have grown more beautiful. Her soft red hair fluttered in the wind as it partially obscured her charming face and snow-white skin.

Wearing a dark emerald dress and a yellow armband on her right arm, Lora surveyed the vicinity to find Tarth. With a slight scowl on her face, she angrily exhaled as she realized that the boy she was looking for was not anywhere near.

A few meters away, Calron furiously blushed as he thought of how pretty she looked when she was mad.

In the past few months, thoughts of Lora did not come to him often, and when they did, Calron forced them out of his mind to focus on training.

However, physically seeing her just a few steps away from him, Calron was drained of every drop of willpower he had.

Calron wanted to shout out her name, but the words died out in his mouth. He wanted to walk over to her, but his feet refused to obey his commands. With his heart racing against his will, Calron closed his eyes, and he tried to regain his composure.

"Hey! The cute boy with the black armband."
The familiar sweet voice of a girl echoed in Calron's ears.

"Huh?"
Opening his eyes, Calron saw Lora walking towards him with a bright smile on her face as she energetically waved her arm around.

"Uh, H-hi."
Calron greeted back with a shy smile on his face.

If Rory had seen his big brother behave like this, then the next few weeks would have been torture for Calron, as Rory would have unceasingly teased him.

"I never saw you again after that last time, Calron."
Lora said in a soft voice when she arrived in front of him.

"Yea, uh, I was busy with training, so I never hung around the gathering hall."

Calron sheepishly responded as he scratched his head.

"I wish I trained more as well... but unfortunately, my talent is only average. Sigh, I don't think I have any hope of winning the elixir..."

Lora said in a forlorn tone as she quietly gazed at the Arena.

Calron's heart raced as he saw the sad expression on Lora's face.

"You want the elixir?"

Faced with Calron's abrupt question, Lora turned her head back to the dark-haired boy as she gently stated.

"Yes, I'm afraid that the elixir is the only hope I have to break into the Vajra stage. Tarth promised me that he would try to win it for me, but he vanished now. He is stronger than most disciples, so he should have a decent chance of reaching the top ranks."

Noticing the black armband on the boy's arm, Lora exclaimed in surprise.

"Oh. You're in the same batch as... Tarth."

A trace of pity flashed across Lora's eyes, but she hid it quickly before Calron could notice.

However, with Calron's enhanced instincts and perception, how could he not detect the change in Lora's expression?

A bitter smile crept over his face, as he unknowingly clenched his fists.

It was one thing for the others to call him weak, but for the girl he liked to also see him as weak, it crushed Calron's heart.

Sensing that the surrounding atmosphere had become somewhat heavier, Lora tried to lighten it up.

"I'm sure you will do fine, Calron. Besides, a boy as cute as you can easily win the heart of any girl, so make sure you find yourself a cute little disciple in the tournament."

Lora teased as a cheerful laugh escaped from her mouth. Giving a quick kiss on Calron's cheek, she walked away.

Meanwhile, Calron just stood there in a daze.

Gingerly touching the cheek the girl had just kissed, Calron felt a silly grin spread wide on his face.

"Hahaha, she kissed me! She actually kissed me!"

Calron felt all the blood in his body rush towards his brain as an uncontainable joy emerged from his heart.

Feeling giddy, Calron simply stood in the same spot for the next few minutes with a sheepish grin on his face.

Meanwhile, Rory had just arrived, and as he was searching for his brother when he noticed Calron was just standing in the center of the crowd with an idiotic grin on his face. His left hand kept rubbing one side of his cheek.

"Eh? What's wrong with big brother?"

Rory curiously muttered as he arrived next to Calron.

Seeing his big brother so unresponsive, Rory felt a splurge of mischievousness.

"Hehe, this is the perfect time to take revenge for the previous electrocution."

Puckering his lips, Rory smacked a big kiss on Calron's other cheek.

Silence.

Slowly turning his head, Calron realized Rory was currently

kissing his cheek in the same spot as Lora.

"Rory… you are dead."

A guttural growl erupted from Calron's mouth as bursts of lightning crackled around his body.

Hearing the noisy commotion, the surrounding disciples all turned to stare at the spectacle unfolding before them.

"Uhh, big brother, wait! Wait! We will be disqualified if we fight outside the Arena!"

Rory blurted out as he saw the furious expression on Calron's face. He did not know whether or not a rule like that actually existed, but Rory would do anything at this moment to escape the wrath of his big brother.

He knew Calron did not like it when he kissed him, but Rory's mischievous heart could never suppress itself whenever an opportunity presented itself.

Realizing that he was causing a commotion, Calron restrained his anger and willed the lightning back into his body.

"I swear, the next time you kiss me, I will burn every single morsel of food that will ever enter your mouth."

Calron declared in a frosty voice.

However, Calron knew deep within his heart that Rory would never stop with his pranks, no matter how much he threatened him. Calron's mental fortitude had already become sharper, but Rory still kept his immaturity.

Giving a quiet sigh, Calron inquired.
"So, where is your armband?"

"Hehe, don't worry, big brother. We are not in the same batch."
Rory declared with a bright grin as he took out a blue armband

from his pocket.

"Phew. Well, Rory, you better make sure that you reach the top fifties. Hopefully, we'll get to fight against each other there."

Rory's mouth dropped open.

"B-big brother, you will fight seriously?"
Rory asked with an excited quiver in his voice.

Solemnly gazing at the disappearing figure of the red-haired girl, Calron slowly nodded his head as he whispered.

"Rory, I just found a reason to win."

CHAPTER TWENTY-FIVE

Arena

The sound of a loud horn reverberated throughout the entire Arena.

The disciples all stood erect as they tried to figure out the cause of the horn.

"ALL DISCIPLES ENTER YOUR DESIGNATED AREAS NOW!"
A booming voice of a man echoed in every person's ears.

"Big brother, let's go!"
Rory cried out as he dragged Calron and rushed toward the center of the Arena.

The other disciples also burst into motion as they bid their masters farewell and searched for the areas designated by the color of their armbands.

The closer Calron approached the center of the Arena, the more awe he felt. The Arena was simply enormous.

It was circular with a series of booths allocated at its sides for the audience. The stadium itself, which was in the center of the Arena, was filled with sand.

Surrounding the stadium were smaller circular marked areas with different colored flags. An Elder stood within each of these smaller circles and patiently waited for all the disciples to arrive.

"Rory, I think my batch is here."
Calron said as he located a black-colored flag next to a circular area.

"Mmn, big brother, good luck. If you quit the tournament before you fight me, I will never talk to you again."
Rory seriously stated as he firmly clasped Calron's hand.

He knew that if Calron got bored midway, he would simply quit and leave without caring about the consequences. However, unknown to Rory, Calron had another reason to take part in the tournament.

"Haha, Rory, don't worry. I promise that I won't quit. I will win this tournament at all costs."
Hearing his brother's passionate exclamation, Rory nodded in relief and bid Calron farewell as he went to look for his own area.

Turning his head to look at the area designated for the disciples with the black armbands, Calron observed his competition.

There were around twelve to fifteen disciples in his batch, all of various ages. He spotted Tarth and his goons talking to the Elder, but Calron paid them no attention.

Sensing two other disciples besides Tarth, with the cultivation of the sixth rank, Calron knew they were the ones he would have to watch out for. However, it seemed that most people in his batch were relatively weak, with the best of them only at the third or fourth rank.

If anyone had heard Calron's thoughts at that moment, they would have spat out blood.

A child who had already reached the third rank at such an age would be considered an outstanding talent in the city, but Calron did not even put them in front of his eyes.

It must be understood that the average soldier in the city of Vernia had the cultivation of the seventh rank, while the commoners were mostly around the fifth rank. However, they were all adults. The ones in front of Calron had barely even started going through puberty.

"Tsk, this is lame... if not for that reward for Lora, I would not even bother being here."

Starting a small whistling tune, Calron walked towards the circular ring.

As Calron neared the other disciples, looks of disdain flashed across their eyes when they saw the dark-haired boy casually whistling without any worries. Calron's confidence stemmed from the fact that although he didn't have the cultivation to directly fight against the City Lord, he at least had the capability to escape using his blood arts.

"That lightning trash... How arrogant! He looks so carefree, but he'll probably surrender as soon as the fight starts. Hehe, let's make sure that we give him a beating before the Elder stops us..."

One of the fourth-rank cultivators in Calron's batch muttered when he saw Calron whistling past him.

When Calron heard those words, he slowly turned his head to face the disciple who just ridiculed him and flashed a vicious smile.

Seeing the lightning boy's focus drawn to him, the fourth-rank cultivator felt a mysterious unease well up within his body as he saw that sinister smile on the boy's face.

"Alright, you bunch of maggots! Listen up!"

The voice of the Elder interjected, his essence amplified voice drawing everyone's attention.

Unlike the gentle and calm Elder Calron had met on his first day, the one in front of him was the complete opposite.

With a head devoid of any hair, the middle-aged Elder chewed on a twig as he gazed at the surrounding disciples in contempt.

"Only the disciples with the black armbands may enter this ring. If you were assigned a different color, then leave before I kick you out."

Pausing to see if there were any outsiders, the baldhead Elder continued.

"All you punks, get ready to enter the ring! Also, remember, if you want to surrender, just remove your armband and wave it in the air. If a punk attacks you after that, I will personally make sure that not even that punk's mother will recognize his face after I'm done with him. Understood?"

The bald man fiercely bellowed towards the gathered disciples.

Calron liked the bald-headed man. Although the older man was extremely rude, there was a certain honesty in his actions that reflected his integrity.

"YES, ELDER!"

The disciples all loudly shouted.

"Good. Enter the ring and only begin once you hear the horn."

The bald Elder stated as he stepped out of the ring and stood at the side.

The disciples all rushed towards the ring as they hoped to strategically position themselves with their friends so that they had a higher chance of being the last one standing.

Although the Preliminary Round was a battle royale where disciples were supposed to fight against each other, most of them usually formed packs early on, to make sure they reached the final stages of the battle. Even though this was a despicable act, it was technically not against the rules of the battle, so the Elders did not stop this behavior.

Seeing the others sprint towards the ring to get a slight advantage, Calron just shook his head and lazily started walking towards the ring. Relying on other people's strength to achieve victory was the mindset of weak cultivators, so naturally, Calron detested it.

Noticing the unusual behavior of the dark-haired boy, the bald Elder raised his eyebrow but did not make a single comment.

"Interesting, either he is very confident or very stupid. Let's see."
The Elder quietly uttered to himself, as his curiosity peaked.

By the time Calron had arrived near the ring, almost every single disciple was already in their desired position and eagerly anticipating the start of the battle royale.

Just as Calron stepped into the ring, the sound of a loud horn exploded in the air.

Whoosh
The disciples all burst into action as several groups clashed against each other. Besides a rare few youths, almost everyone was in a group.

"Sigh... I'll just wait here until there are only a few left and then join in on the fun."
Calron stated as he languidly sat down on the ground.

Seeing that scene, the bald Elder spat out the twig in his mouth.

"What the hell is wrong with this kid.? And what is with that position?"
The bald man exclaimed when he saw Calron lazily sprawled on the ground, while the other disciples were fighting around him.

Initially, Calron was just sitting upright on the ground; however, he soon felt his backside ache against the hard ground, so he simply laid his whole body down. With his right arm supporting his head and one of his knees folded, Calron continued to whistle as he watched several battles unfold before him.

Originally, none of the nearby disciples had bothered Calron, as they all knew he was a weak lightning cultivator, but seeing his completely carefree attitude at this moment, they all felt an intense rage within their hearts.

"Bastard! We are all fighting here and he's just whistling there like an idiot. Brothers, let's teach this loser a lesson."
One of the fourth-rank cultivators of the group shouted as he rallied the nearby disciples to deal with Calron.

Most of them ignored the fourth-rank cultivator as they continued with their fights, but several individuals joined him as they felt mutual irritation at the lightning elementalist's behavior.

Seeing that he had a decent amount of people behind him, the fourth-rank cultivator gained a lot of confidence and started arrogantly walking towards the whistling Calron.

"Bastard, get up and fight!"
The fourth-rank cultivator yelled as he spat towards the side and glared disdainfully at the laid-back Calron.

"Hmm?"
Calron turned his head as he stopped whistling and noticed a small group of disciples all angrily shooting daggers at him.

"Did I do something to you?"
Calron inquired with extreme politeness.

"Huh? No, this is a fight! How dare you look down upon this

tournament with this blatant disrespect?"

The fourth-rank cultivator was a bit taken aback by Calron's politeness, but he quickly regained his composure and retorted his reasons for confronting the dark-haired boy.

"Disrespect? How have I disrespected this tournament? I have been peacefully minding my own business until you came along with those idiots wagging their tails."

Calron responded in a frosty tone as his mood quickly changed. It was refreshing to finally give these pompous noble kids a taste of their own medicine. Calron had been acting aloof on purpose. Elias had taught him that in a real battle, the one who was underestimated had the highest chance of launching a surprise attack.

"Y-you dare insult us? Lightning trash like you actually dares to talk back to us?"

The fourth rank cultivator stuttered as he replied.

In that instant, the rowdy group suddenly felt a bloodthirsty aura around them, and initially, they thought it was the lightning boy in front of them, however, those thoughts soon vanished as they realized that it was simply impossible.

"Trash? I think that I'm starting to get irritated by that word..."

Calron coldly stated as he slowly stood up.

Straining and cracking his muscles, Calron released his vicious killing intent in waves and addressed the disciples in front of him.

"COME!"

It was time to let loose the beast.

"COME!"

Hearing the fierce roar, the disciples felt their hearts tremble violently.

"W-what is this feeling? Is this coming from that loser?"

The disciples behind the fourth-rank cultivator gasped, as the bloodthirsty killing intent started to slowly suffocate them.

This feeling was akin to when one met an extremely powerful cultivator; however, none of them could believe that they could get this feeling from a boy even younger than them.

"Surround him!"

The fourth-rank cultivator shook himself from his daze and commanded the others to follow his orders.

The disciples were clearly in disarray under the oppression of Calron's killing intent, so they hurried to follow the commands of their self-assigned leader.

Seeing the bunch of disciples rushing to surround him, Calron patiently waited, steadily increasing his killing intent.

"Haha, you guys are pathetic. Did you not just call me a loser? Why do you need so many people to deal with a nobody like me?"

Calron taunted as an intense aura radiated from him.

"S-shut up! T-this is just to make sure you don't run away! That's right, we are only doing this to contain you, haha..."

One of the nearby disciples yelled with false bravado, a quiver in his voice.

"Understood. Let's see how well you contain me."

Calron coldly stated as he disappeared in a flash from his spot and rushed towards the disciple who had just spoken.

CRACK
"ARGHH!!"

Everyone stood still as they gaped at the current scene in front of them.

Calron was calmly holding the poor disciple's hand in a twisted position, and it was clear from the previous cracking sound and the gut-wrenching cries, that the disciple's wrist was guaranteed to be broken.

Calron remained standing in that position as his pupils fiercely bore into the disciple's eyes.

"Who is the loser?"
Calron's chilly voice resounded in the vicinity as he turned his head to glare at the other disciples surrounding him.

"The next one to insult will get the same treatment as this idiot."
Hearing the dark-haired boy's threat, the fourth-rank cultivator felt his hands tremble.

Impossible! He is only a lightning cultivator, so how is it possible for him to suppress us to this extent? This must be a dream. Yes, I'm dreaming!

While the fourth-rank cultivator's thoughts raced about, some of the surrounding disciples suddenly removed their armbands and waved them in the air as they openly surrendered.

They knew from the start that one of the sixth-rank cultivators would win this round, so there was no need for them to risk an injury just to be defeated in the end. Seeing the cold savagery of the boy that they had all previously called a loser, the disciples all felt beads of sweat forming on their foreheads.

The only reason these disciples had participated in the first place, was to attract the attention of some of the Masters in the school through their fighting ability and techniques. There was no point in continuing a fight if there was nothing to gain.

It's that they never thought a lightning elementalist would be their downfall. Weren't all lightning elementalists only able to paralyze their opponents? Why did this child demon have such ferocity then?

Seeing some students wave their armbands, the bald Elder nodded and let them exit the ring.

However, the bald Elder's gaze remained fixed on Calron.
"This kid... is not so simple."

Unlike the children, the Elder detected traces of a legacy.

....

On the side, Calron did nothing to obstruct the surrendering disciples from leaving. In truth, he did not wish to fight these disciples, as they were all extremely weak when compared to him. However, Calron detested any insults directed at him, causing him unable to contain his rage. His whole family had suffered abuses from the villagers, and he had enough of it.

Letting the disciple's hand go, Calron turned around and faced the remaining disciples.

Currently, there were only three people left, including the fourth-rank cultivator. Although the fourth-rank cultivator had also wanted to leave, he knew he could not, as he was the one who had invited everyone to attack Calron in the first place. Wouldn't he just lose face if he surrendered now?

"I don't like your clothes."
Calron's voice turned icy as he abruptly stated.

"Huh?"
The three remaining disciples were all confused by Calron's statement.

Without a halt, Calron disappeared in a blink and reappeared next to the disciple who was wearing a pale gray robe.

riiip

Calron tore away the disciple's robes without care, leaving the boy standing there in his underwear. The disciple felt like crying with embarrassment at the public humiliation.

The others watching the scene did not know whether to laugh or to cry. How did this battle royale suddenly take such a comical turn?

This was no longer a fight between cultivators, but public shaming. It looked more like kids teasing each other at the playground rather than a tournament for combat elementalists.

A loud roar of laughter emerged from the side of the ring.

It was the bald Elder.

"Bahaha, I don't think I have ever seen a fight like this in all my history of judging the Preliminary Rounds. Good job, kid! Hahaha!"

The bald Elder bellowed as he laughed again at the sight of the red-faced disciple standing there with only his underwear.

The remaining two disciples all shivered as they watched the scene of Calron rudely ripping apart their fellow brother's robe. There was no dignity in this fight. They would rather surrender now than face this kind of humiliation.

How would a cultivator ever show his face to others after being stripped naked in front of everyone?

"Ah, little brother, how about we end this here? Look, the other battles have nearly ended as well. We can team up and finish them. What do you say?"

The fourth-rank cultivator spoke with a slight trace of hope in his voice.

He would rather break his arm than go through that public

humiliation.

"Eh? Why should I? Besides, I think I don't like your robe as well..."

Calron lazily stated as he shot a mischievous smile at the fourth-rank cultivator.

This bastard. How are these robes any different from what he's wearing? These are the normal robes for the outer disciples. This is just plain bullying!

The two disciples pitifully cried out in their minds as they heard Calron's words.

Not daring to upset the mood of the little monster they had provoked, the fourth-rank cultivator was just about to remove his armband to surrender, when he suddenly felt a steely grip on his arm.

"Shouldn't you remove your robes first before taking off that armband?"

A frosty voice softly spoke into his ear.

"H-how did you-"

riiip

Even while his robes were being ripped away from his body, the fourth-rank cultivator still could not understand how the lightning boy had so quickly reached him.

With tears on his face, the fourth-rank cultivator ran away from the ring in complete embarrassment. Sounds of laughter echoed behind him, which only seemed to make his tears flow faster.

Wuuwuu, how could anyone be so heartless? What Master would ever bother taking me as their disciple after that public stripping and humiliation?

The fourth rank cultivator thought as he inwardly cried.

"I'm tired now, so I'll let you go. Scram."

Calron said as he gazed at the last remaining disciple.

As if he had just heard the voice of salvation, the last disciple quickly removed his armband and rushed toward the edge of the ring.

Calron felt a bit self-conscious with all the current attention, so he just wanted to end the farce there. Hearing the laughter from the people watching the battle, Calron turned around and gave a sheepish smile as he scratched his head.

"Hehe, does anyone want these robes for a copper square?"

Hearing Calron's words, the audience burst into another fit of laughter.

"Hahaha, what is with this kid? I can't stop laughing... is he selling those robes now? Hahaha."

The crowd erupted in a peal of roaring laughter as they watched the current scene in front of them.

Although there were still a few other battles happening within the ring, they were completely ignored and everyone seemed to be more interested in watching the amusing dark-haired boy.

clap *clap*

"You should have been a jester instead of a cultivator. Anyone could defeat those weaklings, so how about having a battle with me?"

A pacifying voice reverberated within the ring.

CHAPTER TWENTY-SIX

Jester

"Hmm, jester? I think I enjoy being a cultivator more. After all, it's a lot more exciting, don't you think?"
Calron responded without turning his head to face the stranger.

Hearing the arrogance in the dark-haired boy's voice who was not even bothering to face him, the stranger let out a low growl as he released his essence.

"Sigh... this was why I did not want to participate. Everyone has such big egos here."
Calron lazily turned around as he faced the stranger.

Hearing Calron's words, the nearby audience felt like knocking their heads against a wall, as from the beginning of the round, it was Calron himself who was looking down on everyone else.

The stranger was a skinny boy around the age of twelve, with long, dark green hair and coppery skin. His feminine features made him appear more beautiful than handsome, and if not for hearing his voice, Calron would have thought that the boy in front of him was a girl.

"Yo, are you a boy or a girl?"

Calron asked with a curious tilt of his head.

The effeminate boy emitted a dense aura as he yelled furiously.
"I'm a boy, you idiot!"

"Eh? Really? You sure don't look like one to me. Drop your pants, let me see."
Calron said in an unconvinced tone.

".............."

The crowd just stood there with their mouths open. This kid had completely changed the whole tournament. First, stripping the disciples of their robes and now asking another cultivator to drop his pants in front of everyone. This was simply too nonsensical.

"Y-you're joking, right? Just fight me!"
The feminine boy stammered as he tried to get his words out.

The dark-haired boy in front of him had utterly destroyed his calm demeanor.

"We can fight later, but right now, I want to see if you're really a boy. C'mon, just show it!"
Calron stated with no intention of fighting whatsoever and eagerly waited for the feminine boy to follow his request.

Unlike the twelve-year-old feminine boy, Calron was still eight years old and inexperienced in the different aspects of man and woman. Although he was brutal when it came to battles, he had not yet learned about the dignity of a man.

"You bastard! How shameless!"
The feminine boy roared with a wave of furious anger on his face.

A light green essence coalesced around him as a violent burst of gust erupted beneath his feet.

"Enough of this pathetic joke. After I defeat you, I will only have one more opponent to beat to reach the top fifties of the ranks."
The feminine boy coldly stated as he rushed towards Calron.

"Huh? Only one? If I'm the second last, who's the last one left?"
Calron asked as he looked around the ring.

It was true.

Besides himself and the feminine boy, there was another disciple nervously standing in the ring. His eyes met Calron.

"Haha, so it's Tarth. Wait for me until I confirm whether this guy here is a boy or a girl, and I'll fight you next!"
Calron laughed as turned his head back to face the feminine boy.

"I guess I'll just have to see the truth for myself."
Calron said as he slowly cracked his knuckles.

Unlike the previous weaklings he had stripped naked, the green-haired boy in front of him was a genuine sixth-rank cultivator.

It was finally time for the Formless Fist to appear.

....

Meanwhile, Tarth was sweating profusely as he saw the battle unfold before him.

I knew this bastard would be one of the last ones standing. He's only gotten crueler since I last met him.

Tarth inwardly thought as he glanced at Calron. At least Tarth was not publicly stripped naked in front of the entire audience like the other two. It was better to get his head smacked a hundred times, than lose his dignity in front of such an enormous crowd.

Tarth shuddered as he thought of what would happen to the feminine boy if that little monster caught hold of him.

"Little girly brother, I sincerely hope that you escape from that demon's clutches…"
Tarth quietly murmured.

…………..

Outside the ring, another figure hastily appeared as he pushed through the crowd to see the battle in the ring designated to the black armbands.

The figure was quite muscular with a childish glint in his eyes. Upon his right arm was a pristine white colored armband that radiated within the crowd.

Seeing the pure white colored armband on the boy's arm, the crowd quietly let him pass without obstruction.

"Hehe, I wonder if big brother won in his batch as well."
Rory muttered as he arrived at the front of the ring.

"… Drop your pants, let me see!"
A familiar voice echoed in the ring.

"Eh? Big brother wants to see someone's legs?"
Rory was utterly confused as to what his big brother was talking about. It was a battle royale, so why would he want to see someone drop his pants?

Seeing his opponent, Rory exclaimed.
"Woah, what a pretty lady!"

"That's not a girl, son. He is a boy, just like you."
An elderly man next to Rory whispered.

"Huh? That's impossible. She's definitely a girl. So, that's why big brother wanted her to drop her pants... YEAH, DROP YOUR PANTS!"
Rory abruptly bellowed from within the crowd.

"What is with this year's tournament? There are idiots everywhere... yes, but nothing can compare to that child who stripped his seniors naked ... yeah, that was brutal..."
The people near Rory quietly gossiped while shooting glances at the nearby Rory and Calron, who was standing in the middle of the ring.

....

BOOOM!
The sound of an explosion reverberated throughout the ring.

As the smoke dispersed, it revealed two figures with their fists touching each other.

"How?"
A soft, quiet voice emerged from the feminine boy's mouth. Only the person in front of him could hear his words.

"A lot of chocolate milk?"
Calron sheepishly responded as he gave a quick wink to the green-haired boy in front of him.

"Hahaha, you are a funny kid... unfortunately, I lost this round. Can you tell me the real reason for your strength?"
The feminine boy asked in a sincere voice.

"Hmm, maybe later. But, drop your pants first, I still want to see."
Calron asked in a persistent tone.

"Y-you would really humiliate me like that."
The feminine boy asked in an unbelievable voice.

"Well, it's fine if you don't want to."
Calron said as he gave out a small sigh.

He honestly wanted to confirm his doubts. His childish curiosity made him oblivious to the social norms between people. Added to that, Calron had no friends growing up, since all the village kids avoided him like the plague.

Unlike the disciples from before, this feminine boy only wanted to fight him to test his strength and not because he thought of Calron as a loser like the other disciples.

This kind of fighting spirit was worthy of Calron's admiration.

Hearing the words of the dark-haired boy, the feminine boy felt extremely relieved. He had tasted the strength of Calron's fist and knew that he was no match.

If the others knew just how strong the lightning kid was, they would have spat out blood in shock. This child defied all stereotypes about lightning elementalists.

What confused the feminine boy was that even towards the last moment of the strike, he had not detected a single trace of essence from the boy in front of him.

"Hey, what's your name?"
The feminine boy asked softly.

"Calron."

"Calron? I like that name. I'm Aryn, by the way."
The feminine boy replied as he gave Calron a slight smile. Removing his black armband, Aryn slowly exited the ring.

Silence.

The audience was speechless after the previous fight. A sixth-rank cultivator had lost to a lightning cultivator? This was unequivocally unbelievable.

Before the crowd could dwell any further on their thoughts, a loud voice echoed within the vicinity.

"This is the last battle. Both of you, get ready."
The bald elder conveyed through his booming voice.

The crowd felt their hearts racing as they waited in anticipation for the last and final battle of the first round.

thump *thump*

The winner of this battle would immediately enter the top fifty ranks of the disciples and have the chance to become one of the elite students of the Red Boar School. Witnessing the intense battle earlier, the crowd sat up straighter in their seats, their anticipation building.

Right then, Tarth turned towards the elder and removed his armband as he firmly stated.

"I surrender."

"I surrender."

Silence.

The crowd mutely watched the current scene unfold before them. A sixth-rank cultivator had surrendered before the fight had even started.

"What kind of battle is this?"

Some members of the audience complained as they did not get to see the finale.

"Batch forty-two's battle has ended, and the winner is... Calron!"
The bald Elder announced when he saw Tarth had removed his armband.

Although he was also disappointed at not being able to watch more antics of that hilarious lightning boy, he still had to follow the rules of the tournament.

"Calron... so that is the funny boy's name... "
The crowd muttered amongst themselves as they etched Calron's name into their minds.

"Let's see how he does in the actual ranking battles. Every single one of those disciples should be the strongest of their batch, so he won't be able to con his way through the second round."

Members of the crowd whispered as they eagerly awaited the second round of the tournament. Although they found the lightning boy amusing, they had still not seen any display of power from him.

"Disciple Calron, come in front to receive your new armband."
The bald Elder stated in a serious tone.

"Uh, yes."
Calron hurriedly replied as he got out of his daze.

He was completely taken aback when Tarth suddenly surrendered. Calron was hoping for a decent battle, and he did not understand why Tarth would surrender out of nowhere.

Unbeknownst to Calron, his past incident with Tarth had deeply scarred the blonde-haired boy and given birth to an instinctual fear within him.

Slowly walking up to the bald Elder, Calron patiently waited as the Elder took out a pearl-white armband from within a small wooden box, and presented it to Calron in front of the crowd.

"Regardless of what happened today, you are the final one standing and thus the victor of this batch. Congratulations, and this is the armband that will let you compete in the top fifty ranks. Good luck."
The bald Elder said with an amused smile on his face.

"I will help myself then."
Calron casually stated as he picked up the white armband and placed it on his right arm.

"Woohooo! Big brother won!"
A loud cheer suddenly erupted from the audience.

"Rory?"

………………..

"He won… he actually won."
A red-haired girl in the audience quietly whispered with utter shock on her face.

What surprised her even more than Calron winning was the fact that Tarth had willingly surrendered.

Having known the obnoxious boy for several years, Lora knew just how much pride Tarth had, and for him to do something like this, there must be another reason.

How could Lora know that Calron had already miserably beaten up Tarth before?

"Pfft, I still can't believe he ripped someone's robes off in a battle."
Lora softly murmured as she burst into a fit of silent laughter.

....

"The second round will begin shortly, so quickly go to the main stadium and register under that white armband. You will then get your entry number and be officially recognized as the contender for the top fifty positions."
The bald Elder stated as he gave a rough pat on Calron's shoulder.

"Yes, Elder. I will take my leave now."
Calron replied as he rushed to meet up with Rory.

"Big brother. I knew you would win. Look, I won too."
Rory excitedly yelled as Calron approached him, while simultaneously showing his white armband on his right arm.

Unlike Calron, Rory had no restriction on revealing his element. After his battle had started, Rory viciously attacked every disciple near him regardless of their cultivation, until only disciples of the fifth and sixth rank remained in the ring.

Just with his cultivation of the third rank, Rory had completely suppressed everyone.

He easily defeated even the fifth-rank cultivators, and only the last sixth-rank cultivator had given a slight resistance under Rory's brutal onslaught.

The reason for Rory's overwhelming strength hid within the Axier Family's cultivation secrets. How could the cultivation techniques of such an influential family that even the city Lord of Vernia himself would have to pay respects to, be so simple?

Rory's display of power alarmed the audience, and right after he was declared his batch's winner, several Masters approached Rory to make him their personal disciple. In the eyes of others, Rory had won purely with his cultivation whereas Calron used his words to taunt his opponents. Despite both of them winning their respective batches, only Rory received the praise.

Evading their requests with stupid responses, Rory quickly left his ring and returned to watch his big brother's fight.

"Haha, I knew you would win, Rory. By the way, did anyone become suspicious of you?"

Calron gave a low chuckle as he saw the excited Rory, and quietly asked his question.

Both Elias and Calron knew Rory cultivated his family's secret arts and the astonishing might he had. Rory had even once challenged Calron to a spar after receiving the Axier family's techniques from his sister.

Rory had hoped to at least deal a serious strike against his brother; however, by just using the Blood Legacy, Calron had easily suppressed him.

Within the past few months, not only had Calron increased his cultivation, but he had also become much more proficient in the control of his source energy and the Blood Mist Step.

"Hehe, of course not, big brother. I used my brains and smartly evaded all their questions."

Rory responded while puffing up his chest in pride.

If Calron or Elias had heard some of the idiotic responses that Rory gave to the other Masters, they would have banged their heads against a brick wall.

"Hmm, alright, let's go to the stadium. The second round should begin soon."

Calron cheerfully said as he pushed Rory to walk toward the

center of the Arena.

....

Meanwhile, within the audience, a blind old man was currently sitting as he gazed into the crowd in front of him.

Tapping his wooden stick against the ground, the old man slowly walked.

"I sometimes forget that he is only eight years old, Haha."
Elias softly murmured as he gave out a small laugh.

He had watched the fight of both his disciples, but he had been focusing more on Calron's battle so that no accidents that might happen. Unlike Roran, if Calron had a sudden burst of rage while fighting, there would be fatal repercussions for those around him. Let alone the chaos the knowledge of his special bloodline would cause.

This was the first time that Calron would fight in public, so Elias had been extremely worried about his first disciple.

However, contrary to his concerns, Calron had astounded him by the antics he displayed in front of everyone.

"I just hope this does not become a habit. I will have to talk to him later about a person's sensitive body parts, so he understands why he can't ask anyone he meets to remove their pants. Haha…"
Elias gently said, as he could not hold back his laughter.

....

"Alright, so 'Calron' has been registered in the top fifty ranks. After the tournament has been concluded, your rank will be assigned to you."
A young lady in her twenties strictly stated as she handed back Calron his white armband.

"You are the fifteenth in line for your duel, so please wait at the contestants' booth."

The young lady declared in a serious tone.

Before Calron and Rory had reached the main stadium, sounds of a battle could already be heard and they knew they were late.

Rory had stopped in the middle of their walk to go to the bathroom, so Calron was forced to wait for his brother.

Fortunately, all fifty batch winners must participate in the second round, so they were allowed to be registered after a quick scolding from the organization's Elder.

"Hehe, I'm the third in line for the duel, so I will get to fight before big brother."

Rory excitedly claimed as he dragged Calron to the contestants' booth.

Just as the two brothers entered the booth, a relieved voice sounded in their ears.

"Rory, You made it!"

A blur in a blue dress suddenly rushed towards the boys, as she happily hugged Rory.

"Big sister!"

Rory exclaimed in a similarly joyous tone.

Meanwhile, Calron just silently backed away. He knew that Felice still held a grudge against him, so he did not want to give her any chance to act on him.

"Hmph, how did a bunch of losers like them enter the top fifties? Sigh... this school is seriously lowering their standards."

A deep, rumbling voice echoed in the booth.

Seeing the familiar figure, Calron felt his blood boiling as he restrained the rage he felt welling up inside him.

Calron could never forget the first time someone dealt him a vicious blow and drew his blood.

"Chax."

With a savage growl, a bloodthirsty aura emanated around Calron.

CHAPTER TWENTY-SEVEN

Entering The Stage

"Piss off. Who do you think you are, to have the right to challenge me? If not for my Master stopping me back then, I would have broken every single bone in your body."

Chax fiercely roared as he released his essence.

Waves of scorching flames suddenly flowed around Chax's hands, and the surrounding disciples were all forced to step back under the intense heat.

A sinister glint flashed in Chax's eyes as he prepared to rush towards Calron.

Seeing the large boy aiming for Calron, Rory joggled his sister aside as he released his own essence into the air. Rory's face was completely distorted in anger as he stepped in front of his big brother.

A cyan-colored essence coalesced around him, and the temperature in the room seemed to have dropped by several degrees.

It was a bizarre environment, with one side being scorching hot and the other side being freezing cold.

"Who the hell are you?"

Chax halted his attack as he turned to glare at Rory.

This was the first time he had seen Rory after the previous incident and Chax did not recognize the current Rory, as he was entirely different from the Rory that Chax last remembered.

Before Rory could respond, a firm hand grabbed his shoulder.

"Rory, come back. This is not your fight."
Calron hoarsely voiced next to him.

"But big broth- "
Rory abruptly stopped as he felt Calron's hand tighten its grip on his shoulder.

"Sigh... alright, big brother."
Withdrawing his essence, Rory slowly stepped back.

However, he continued to emanate an aura of hatred towards Chax.

Calron did not want Rory to fight this battle, as he could clearly sense that the current Chax was not as simple as before. His current cultivation was at the seventh rank or possibly even at the eighth rank.

The difference between the fifth and sixth ranks might not be great, but the closer one reached the peak of the Spiritual stage, the purer their essence would be. It was at the seventh rank that the essence within one's body would go through a qualitative change.

Although Rory might be able to defeat cultivators in the fifth and sixth ranks, he would be no match for a genuine seventh or eighth-rank cultivator.

It appeared as if Chax had used a lot of resources to gather the required amount of essence to break into the next rank of cultivation.

This would not be surprising, as his father was the City Lord and had plenty of beast cores to provide for his son to cultivate.

"Chax, stop this fight right now! You know very well that we are not allowed to engage in battles outside of the tournament."
Felice stated in an indifferent tone.

Initially, she had not wanted to involve herself as Chax was unmistakably going after Calron, but when her little brother stepped in, she was forced to intervene as well.

Unlike others that tried to stop Chax, Felice had a strong background that even Chax would not dare to provoke. Even if Rory was her brother, the two held vastly different positions within the Axier family. For whatever reason, Rory was cast aside, leaving Felice as the generation's heir.

"Sigh... yes, I forgot about the rules... "
Chax replied in an overly sincere tone as he slowly stepped back away from Calron.

The nearby disciples all breathed out a sigh of relief when they heard those words.

However, in a flash, Chax abruptly turned around and flung a huge ball of flame toward Calron.

The blistering ball of flame traveled at an insane speed and was almost upon Calron before anyone had even realized that Chax had attacked.

All time seemed to stop.

The fiery glow of the flames was reflected in Calron's eyes. The blazing ball of flame drew closer and closer toward Calron's face.

From the intensity of the heat, Calron knew that even with his physical body, he would take considerable damage if he did not use the full power of the legacy.

However, before he could even activate the Blood Legacy, he felt his core brusquely quivering with violent energy as the Azure Lightning threatened to come out.

Calron tightly clenched his fists as he tried to force down the lightning. He would much rather risk revealing the Blood Legacy than his Azure Lightning.

Torrents of blue lightning flashed across Calron's pupils.

Knowing that he was powerless to stop the lightning, Calron resigned himself to his fate, as a tenacious expression spread across his face.

"Hmm, is someone being a naughty boy?"
A gentle and pleasant voice thundered throughout the booth.

In slow motion, the figure of an old man coalesced in front of Calron.

Although the old man appeared to be moving leisurely, his speed was so shockingly fast that even Calron did not detect him till the very last moment.

The old man had a striking pair of bright sea-green eyes and his medium-length gray hair was tied back in a neat ponytail. Although his face had signs of aging and slight wrinkles on the skin, his eyes fiercely penetrated the souls of every disciple there.

"Admirable... to have such proficiency in a fourth-rank technique like this Solare Blast."
The old man cheerfully stated as he caught the giant ball of flames in his hand.

Meanwhile, Chax just stood there with a dazed expression on his face.

This old geezer was a hidden expert!

It was obvious that this old man had the cultivation of the Vajra stage, or else how could he so easily nullify Chax's attack?

From the old man's white robes, it was evident that he was not an Elder of the school, but an outsider.

"If Serina had not come to me in time, things might have turned ugly... "
The old man whispered to himself, as he then turned to look at Calron.

"Boy, are you alright?"

"Yes, sir, thank you for stopping that attack."
Calron calmly responded to the elderly man.

The Azure Lightning had quietly disappeared on its own once the danger to Calron's life vanished. Thankfully, the sudden appearance of the ball of flames and its bright light had drawn all the attention, so no one noticed the strangeness of Calron's lightning.

The old man was a bit taken aback by the calmness in the boy's voice, but he turned his head to gaze into Chax's eyes.

"I don't care whether your father is the City Lord. You will obey the rules of the tournament, or I will personally disqualify you. Is that understood?"
The old man spoke in a serious tone as his eyes pierced into Chax's.

"Y-yes."

Hearing those words, Chax immediately realized who this old man was.

The old man was the tournament moderator.

The Red Boar School always hired an external group to mediate the tournaments. This was to ensure that the battles and duels all stayed fair and none of the teachers or masters gave a biased judgment.

To be a Moderator, one had to have a very high cultivation.

"Lord Jarin, the next round is about to begin."
A tall and stunningly beautiful woman walked towards the old man as she reported to him.

The woman's dark maroon dress tightly hugged her body, as it accentuated her curves and voluptuous figure.

Some of the older male disciples in the booth drooled at the sight of the gorgeous woman.

"Eh? Serina?"
A strange look flashed across the old man's eyes, as the intense aura around him completely vanished.

"How about giving me a kiss for good luck, eh?"
The old man sweetly asked as he quickly arrived in front of the beautiful woman.

A scowl emerged on the woman's face as she saw the dirty look in the old man's eyes.

"Lord Jarin, the Captain has asked you to mediate the next round. Please report to him."
The woman responded in a brusque tone.

It was clear that this was not the first time the woman had to deal with the degenerate old man in front of her.

"Well, how about a quick hug then?"
The old man was completely undeterred in his advances, as he spoke with a lewd expression on his face.

The nearby older disciples all felt like slapping the old geezer for his shamelessness.

Just a moment before, they all had admiring gazes towards the old man who exuded such a calm and powerful aura, but seeing his attitude completely switch, only one word seemed to echo in their minds.

Pervert.

A loud horn buzzed throughout the entire arena.

"Lord Jarin, the first duel has just ended. Please make your way to the stadium before the Captain gets angry."
Serina stated in a strict tone as she glared at the old man.

"Alright, alright, I'm going."
The old man responded as he started walking past the beautiful woman.

"Ahh!!"
Serina suddenly yelped as she grabbed her behind.

"Hehe, I'm suddenly feeling very motivated."
The old man abruptly exclaimed as he vanished from the booth in a blink of an eye.

"Damn that geezer! This is the third time today that he has pinched my butt. I will report it to the Captain when this tournament is over."

Serina furiously muttered as she then walked out of the contestants' booth.

The disciples all stood numbly at the side with their hearts in turmoil.

"I thought the Moderators were supposed to be high-ranking officials... what's up with that perverted geezer then?"

"Hey! The second duel is starting! Who are the ones fighting?"
As the surrounding disciples all chattered amongst themselves, Felice abruptly turned towards Rory and gently whispered.

"Rory, you will fight the duel after this. I don't know who your opponent is, but you have to be careful. If you feel you cannot win, just surrender before you get hurt."
Hearing his sister's words, Rory obediently nodded back.

"Alright, big sister."

Meanwhile, Calron was pondering within his thoughts:
That ball of flame was too dangerous. That bastard is definitely in the eighth rank. I can't let my guard down around him...

Chax had a cunning and despicable personality, which was clear when he attempted a surprise attack on Calron when his guard was down.
Shaking his thoughts of the large bully, Calron turned to Rory.

"Rory, let's go watch the fight. You are next after this duel, so you need to check out your competition."
Calron stated as he rushed towards the stadium.

Rory immediately followed behind his big brother after saying a quick goodbye to Felice.

....

"Are the two participants ready?"
A familiar voice loudly echoed within the stadium.

Calron and Rory both looked toward the source of the voice and found the old man from earlier standing in the middle of the stage.

The calm and powerful aura around him had returned, and if the two boys had not witnessed the previous scene in the booth with the old man harassing the beautiful woman, then both of them would also have deep admiring gazes like the rest of the people around the stadium.

"Hey, isn't that the perverted old man we just saw in the booth?"
Rory abruptly shouted into the crowd as he turned towards Calron.

"You idiot!"
Calron suddenly plunged Rory's head down before the old man could notice them in the crowd

Just a second later, the old man had turned his head around as he scrutinized the crowd to find the source of the voice. A tint of embarrassment could be seen on his face as he lightly coughed to regain his composure.

Seeing the two competitors nod their heads in agreement, the old man vanished from his original spot and reappeared at the edge of the stage.

"BEGIN!"
The old man roared with a booming voice.

The disciples on the stage burst into motion as they

simultaneously released their essence.

One of the two disciples was a girl around ten years old, with dark brown hair and a petite body. Scarlet tendrils of essence coalesced around her as waves of flames erupted behind her.

The other disciple was a boy, who was similar in age to the girl but appeared to be much older because of his larger frame, which overshadowed the petite body of the girl.

A burgundy-colored essence coalesced around the boy as his fists morphed into a rock-like appearance. They had the shape of human hands, but the texture was akin to a dense slab of rock.

The crowd gasped in astonishment when they saw the technique and stepped closer to the stage as they eagerly waited for the battle.

"I wonder which family that boy is from? To comprehend such a complex earth-attributed technique at that age is simply amazing."

As the audience all chattered amongst themselves, the male disciple rushed towards the girl in front of him as he prepared to strike his fist.

Seeing her opponent make a move, the petite girl patiently stood there as her eyes continued to bore into her opponent. There was no sign of fear or alarm on her face, as she stoically remained standing in the same position.

A trace of worry flashed across the boy's face, but he paid no heed to it when he realized he had almost arrived in front of the petite girl.

Clenching his fists tighter, the boy drew his right arm back, and just as he was preparing to launch his blow, the flames around the girl abruptly surged as they covered her entire body.

Watching the current scene unfold, the crowd all shouted and cheered in excitement. This was the reason they all came here for.

Passion.

Vigor.

Adrenaline.

These youngsters were the future of their city, and the more talented each one was, the more their city would benefit. These disciples all trained with extreme perseverance, and the tournament was the place where they could showcase their talents. How could the crowd not be excited when they saw these youngsters fight with such passion?

BOOOOM!
Waves of flames dispersed around the girl as it slowly revealed her clutching the stony hand of the boy, just inches away from her body.

A look of shock flashed across the boy's eyes, but he immediately regained his composure and raised his left leg in an attempt to kick.

"You are certainly strong, but this fight needs to end now."
The petite girl fiercely stated as a slow smile spread across her face.

In the next second, a raging torrent of fire flowed around her body, and it viciously rushed toward the boy.

The boy tried to escape from the petite girl's grasp, but he could not shake her grip off.

"H-how is your strength so strong.?"
The boy whispered in panic.

It was understandable that the boy would be shocked, as with his earth element, he had a much stronger vitality and strength than any other cultivator of the same rank.

He sensed from the beginning that the petite girl had the same level of cultivation as him, the seventh rank of the Spiritual stage, so how could she be so much stronger than him?

A faint orange-colored energy separated itself from the girl's flames.

"You're an Inheritor!"
The boy exclaimed in surprise, as he noticed the unique aura of the orange-colored energy.

It was no wonder that he could not break free. The girl in front of him was an actual Inheritor of a legacy.

"Haha, I admit defeat."
The boy calmly stated as he nodded his head towards the girl.

Releasing her grip on the boy, the petite girl withdrew her essence and source energy back into her body.

Giving a slight bow to her opponent, the small girl spun around and exited the stage without speaking a single word.

"The winner of the second duel is... Alicia."
The old man's booming voice reverberated in the audience.

"Wow! Big brother, that was so amazing! I can't wait to enter the stage."
Rory excitedly spoke as he stared at the stadium with a bright twinkle in his eyes.

"Haha, calm down, Rory. They will call you onto the stage soon. Just surrender if your opponent is someone really strong."
Calron softly advised Rory, as he swung his arm around the large boy's shoulder.

"I will, big brother."

Just as Rory finished replying to Calron, the old man's voice suddenly sounded again.
"The disciples assigned to the third duel. Please step forward."

"Big brother, wish me good luck."
Rory whispered as he prepared to go on stage.

"Go crush your opponent, Rory."
Calron softly said as he clasped his arm around Rory's wrist.

Giving a huge grin, Rory leaped onto the stage.

"RORY! GOOD LUCK!"
A voice shouted from the back of the audience. The owner of the voice tried to push apart the crowd to reach the front of the stage, revealing her petite figure. Felice waved her hand to get her little brother's attention.

Seeing his sister, Rory enthusiastically returned the wave as he turned to face the old man.

"Hey, perverted old man. I'm ready."
Rory stated while a stupid grin covered his face.

Meanwhile, Calron just smacked his head against his palm as he muttered to himself.
"I knew he would do something like this."

The crowd was similarly astonished when they heard Rory shout. How could such an influential and prestigious man be a pervert? They thought the boy was simply playing a joke.

"You brat! How dare you call me a pervert?"
The old man furiously yelled when he heard Rory's shout.

"Eh? But weren't you touching that nice lady back in the booth?"
Rory innocently responded to the old man.

"I-I was just talking to her… anyway, if your opponent doesn't arrive in the next few minutes, you will win the duel by default."
The old man stated with an intense blush on his face. He was quite embarrassed about having been called out by a child in public.

Right then, a cruel and sinister voice sounded out from the audience as a figure slowly stepped forward onto the stage.
"No need to wait anymore. Let's begin."

Seeing the figure step on the stage, Calron felt all the blood drain from his face.

CHAPTER TWENTY-EIGHT

Behind Scenes

---A few hours ago---

"Lord Regis, the tournament has started."
A middle-aged Elder in black robes stated in a respectful voice.

Standing in the courtyard was a stocky man, who was surrounded by an entire brigade of guards.

The guards all wore pitch-black armor that had the red insignia of a bear. Their appearances were completely different from the usual guards stationed around the city, so it was clear that this was an elite group of soldiers.

Hearing the unhurried voice, the stocky man turned around as he faced the Elder of the school.

"Why hasn't Orlon greeted me yet?"
A calm voice sounded from the city Lord.

"The school Head is currently still in cultivation and hasn't returned from his previous destination."
The Elder responded in an apologetic tone.

It had been years since the Head last came to the school, and many Elders of the Red Boar School were worried about his disappearance. The Head would occasionally communicate and send orders, but none of his messages contained any hints of his location or when he would return.

"Hmm, very well. Where is my son?"
Regis inquired in an unsatisfactory tone.

Considering his noble title, it was beneath him to be welcomed by a mere Elder, but since he only came to watch his son fight, Regis let such matters slide.

"Chax has received the white armband for his victory in the first round, so he should be preparing to enter the duels for the second round."
The Elder answered in a polite voice, as he sensed that the city Lord was slightly disgruntled at the absence of the school Head.

"Let's go to the stadium then. It's better than standing around here."
Regis stated in a brusque tone as he gestured for two of his guards to follow him.

"The rest of you stay here. I will be back after Chax wins the tournament."
After those final words, Regis started walking with two black armored guards behind him.

Seeing that the city Lord had not even waited for him, the middle-aged Elder could only sigh in resignation as he walked behind Regis as well.

Watching the intimidating guards and an Elder of the school quietly walking behind a stocky man, the nearby disciples and servants all stopped what they were doing and simply stared at the awe-inspiring scene.

Most of them guessed, from the overbearing attitude and the insignia on the guards' chest plates, that the stocky man in front of them was the city Lord himself.

Although the city Lord had a disdainful look on his face, the regal and oppressive aura around him was unmistakable.

For the disciples and servants who had previously met the Red Boar School's Head, the pressure that the city Lord emanated was akin to the Head's aura.

No one knew the real cultivation of the city Lord, but he had to be at least above the fifth rank of the Vajra stage. Equally impressive were the two guards marching behind the City Lord.

The cold and merciless gaze in their eyes combined with the sharp movements that they executed as they walked, all made the hearts of the surrounding disciples quiver with excitement.

They all hoped that one day they would become as strong as those elite guards and serve the city of Vernia by keeping its peace.

After a few minutes, Regis and his group finally reached the Arena.

"Follow me this way, Lord Regis."
The middle-aged Elder stepped forwards as he guided the city Lord into one of the ornate booths erected close to the center of the stadium.

Seeing that he was given a prime location for viewing, Regis gave a nod of satisfaction as he entered the booth allocated to him.

"The second round should begin shortly. If you need anything else, I have a servant stationed outside the booth that can cater to your every need."

The Elder politely stated while giving a slight bow, and exited the booth.

As soon as the Elder left, a shadow stealthily darted into the City Lord's booth.

Without turning around, Regis quietly asked.
"What is the news on the boy, Viktor?"

The shadow coalesced into the figure of a tall, wiry man as he slowly spoke.
"There are many rumors about the boy floating around the school. It seems your son has a bit of a history with him."

"Chax? Report to me about their encounter. Leave nothing out."
Regis turned around to face Viktor, and he asked in a serious voice.

For a full five minutes, Viktor recounted the rumors and gossip about the fight between the two boys.

CRACK
The sound of a wooden table being splintered loudly resounded in the booth.

"That little bastard dares to fight back against my son? A slave should behave like a slave."
Regis furiously roared as faint traces of essence leaked out from the pores of his skin.

Viktor silently stood there as the city Lord fumed with anger.

This bloody moron! Is a person supposed to quietly take a beating just because it's your son? Such a despicable family...
As Viktor's thoughts raced through his mind, his outward expression did not change in the slightest.

"I want you to kidnap the boy after the tournament ends. It is obvious that he is no longer just in the first rank of the Spiritual stage."

Regis muttered in a chilling tone.

"Is that wise? He clearly has someone teaching him, as there is no way the boy advanced on his own in such a short period. It's better to wait until we have more information on his master."

Viktor advised in a neutral voice.

"I did not hire you to give me your opinion. Do as you are told, unless you want me to replace you as well."

Regis slowly stated as his eyes fiercely bore into Viktor.

"Very well, I'll do it."

Viktor calmly stated as if unfazed by the city Lord's scrutiny.

Within the blink of an eye, his figure formed into a shadow and silently darted out of the booth.

"I do not trust him, my Lord."

One of the black armored guards said in a steely voice as he gazed at the booth's exit.

"Neither do I, but his element is useful."

Regis softly declared as he entered the balcony of the booth and took his seat.

Knowing that the city Lord did not wish to further talk about Viktor, the guard silently followed behind him.

The booths were set up such that they all stood a few feet higher from the ground, so they had the best visibility of the stadium. The distinguished members who were given a booth were all high-ranking officials and guests of the school.

Many of the officials and guests seated in the adjacent booths gave a respectful nod or slight bow to the city Lord.

Returning their greetings, Regis turned his head towards the stadium as he calmly observed the current duel.

His mood had completely shifted from before, as he eagerly waited to see the development of his son, Chax.

Regis had called in many favors to convince the renowned Master Dane to take his son as his disciple, and it was finally time to see the results.

"What rank of cultivation do you think Chax has reached?" Regis asked without shifting his gaze from the stadium.

"I think the little lord should be around the eighth rank by now. The beast cores you sent last month had accelerated his growth." The nearby guard quietly answered.

"Good, good. By the way, when does Chax enter the duel? I do not want to waste my time by watching these talentless punks fight." Regis muttered in a low voice, as his fingers impatiently tapped the side of his chair.

"Little lord should enter right after this duel is over. He was registered for the third duel." The guard promptly replied as he sensed the impatience of the city Lord.

".... disciples assigned to the third duel. Please step forward." The old man's voice echoed within the audience.

"Haha, Chax's fight is soon about to begin." Regis exclaimed in an excited voice.

After a few seconds, a large boy immediately stepped on the stage.

"Hmm, that must be Chax's opponent. A pity… he is nothing compared to my son."

Just as Regis was muttering to himself, a familiar voice resounded in the stadium.

Chax had just entered the stage.

"No need to wait anymore. Let's begin."

When the figure slowly stepped on stage, Rory sensed the intense pressure exuding from Chax.

Feeling his hands faintly tremble, Rory tightly clenched his fists to steady his nerves.

Dammit, dammit, dammit. Why did it have to be him.? There is no way that I can fight against Chax. Maybe I should give up…

Rory's thoughts frantically raced in his mind as he debated on what to do next.

Turning his head to look at his big brother, Rory saw the pale-faced Calron worriedly gazing at him.

Seeing the expression on his brother's face, Rory felt the turmoil in his heart slowly resolve. This was his chance to do something for Calron, and besides, how could he simply surrender to someone who constantly looked down upon his big brother?

"Hehe, how can the little brother be a coward if the big brother is so amazing? If I give up now, I can never catch up to big brother."

Rory softly muttered to himself, as he gave a small smile to Calron, and then turned to face the opponent in front of him.

…………………..

"Rory… no, don't do this…"

Calron whispered to himself as his heart violently pounded against his chest.

"He looks up to you… I don't know why, but he adores you like his own blood brother."

A gentle voice sounded out from behind Calron as he felt a soft hand on his shoulder.

Felice slowly stepped next to Calron while she continued speaking.

"He told me he wanted to be as amazing as his big brother, and it was his motivation to train relentlessly. Even now, he wants to fight to prove his strength to you."

Felice softly said as her eyes got misty.

How could she not know what her little brother was thinking? If it was not for Chax constantly oppressing Calron, why would her little brother continue to stand his ground against someone of Chax's strength?

"Rory…"

Calron clenched his fists until the veins on his arm popped.

"Just watch him. Rory is not as weak as you might think."

Felice gently whispered with a slight smile on her face, as she withdrew her hand from Calron's shoulder.

Tilting his head to look at the girl he was once extremely weary of, Calron did not know how to feel about the current Felice.

Calron realized that this was the first time that he had truly talked to Felice. Her previous cold and heartless exterior had completely vanished, as it left behind a girl who was simply worried about her little brother.

Although Felice spoke in a light tone, Calron could still detect traces of worry on her face.

"Rory, you better not lose."
Calron murmured as he turned his attention to the stage.

....

"The heavens must favor me, to make you my opponent for this duel."
Chax loudly stated as he gave a low chuckle.

Rory remained silent, as he knew words would just be wasted on the arrogant boy in front of him.

"What happened? You were pretty impatient to fight me back in the booth. Don't tell me that you're afraid now because that lightning trash isn't behind you?"
Chax continued to taunt Rory as he walked toward the center of the stage.

Hearing Chax insult his big brother, Rory's expression abruptly changed as his eyebrows knitted together in a fit of furious anger.

"You can insult each other as much as you want, but wait till I give you the permission to start your duel."
The old man's voice echoed in the stadium as it was amplified with essence.

"Are the two participants ready?"
The old pervert inquired as he looked at the two disciples.

"I'm ready to give this punk a thrashing."
Chax fiercely growled as his eyes bore into Rory.

"I am ready."
Rory replied to the old man in a firm tone.

"You may begin."

The old man suddenly bellowed as he stepped away from the stadium.

Immediately, Chax released his essence as a fiery wave of scarlet flames coalesced around his body.

Cracking his knuckles, Chax laughed out loud.

"You still haven't told me your name. Well, whatever, it's not like it matters."

Hearing the large boy continue to taunt him, Rory remained still for a while, and then suddenly released his own essence.

A wild, howling wind viciously screamed in the air, as bursts of arctic blue essence circulated Rory.

A cold freezing mist exuded from his body, as the temperature abruptly dropped by several degrees. Ice formed beneath Rory's feet, as his expression slowly morphed into a chilling anger.

Seeing the two contrasting forms of essence behind the boys, the crowd felt their heartbeats race in excitement.

From the threats exchanged between the two boys, the intensity of the flames around Chax, along with the bone-chilling mist around Rory, the audience knew that this would not be a simple duel.

Meanwhile, Chax knitted his eyebrows in doubt as he sensed the cold and frosty aura around Rory.

"Why does he give off the same feeling as Felice... "

Chax had still not realized that the person in front of him was Felice's little brother and a member of the Axier family. The chubby Rory back then, and the athletic Rory in front of him were polar opposites.

"Hmm, seems like you have a few tricks up your sleeve, but it won't make a difference. Your cultivation of the third rank is simply too pitiful."

Chax calmly said, as he put aside his doubts and focused on the duel.

"Shut up!"

Rory stated in a low, frosty voice.

This was the first time that Rory spoke since the duel had started.

The current Rory was contrary to the one that used to goof around and play pranks on Calron. This was a rare side of Rory that emerged once he had awakened his element.

How could Rory be so simple? The Blood Legacy coursed through his veins just like Calron.

The path of blood and carnage was their true inheritance.

Subconsciously, the Blood Legacy had added fuel to Rory's rage, as his skin started to slowly emit a faint crimson hue.

In the audience, Calron felt his heart wildly thumping against his chest.

"The legacy is activating within Rory."

Although the change in Rory was very difficult to detect, how could Calron not sense the Blood Legacy?

Calron had a much stronger mental fortitude than Rory, so he could mildly control the bloodthirsty urges of the legacy. Rory, on the other hand, was just getting used to the Blood Legacy.

"Curse this tournament! Rory, surrender NOW!"

Calron sent a furious mental message from the source pool and towards Rory's bridge. This was the first time that Calron had tried to mentally communicate through the Blood Legacy, but he had no other choice at this moment.

The crowd was howling and cheering with excitement as they encouraged the two disciples on stage to fight. Calron's voice could never reach Rory over the yelling of the crowd.

Calron knew deep within his heart that it would not work, as Rory was already too immersed in the legacy's bloodlust.

Fervently hoping that his brother would hear his message, Calron intensely watched the scene in the stadium.

....

WHOOSH
A torrent of flames blazed behind Chax as he abruptly rushed towards Rory.

"Your time is up, punk!"
Chax loudly roared, while his fists exploded in a surge of scarlet flames, as he prepared to strike at Rory.

Seeing the large boy advance toward him, Rory let out a similar roar as he charged toward Chax as well.

A mist of ice-cold essence violently burst out from behind Rory as his fists suddenly emitted an arctic blue gas.

The stage quaked with faint tremors as the two forces were about to collide against each other.

BOOOOM!
A gust of violent wind spread from the center of the stage as the two fists collided.

Immediately after the first collision, another explosion sounded out.

BOOOOM!
BOOOOM!

The crowd all numbly watched the scene in front of them.
The voices and the cheering from the audience abruptly stopped.

BOOOOM!

"W-what is this?"
A disciple in the crowd muttered in a quivering voice.

"I can't watch this anymore... this is too sick..."

BOOOOM!

Except for the sounds coming from the stage, the whole Arena had turned completely quiet.

Within the crowd, a teardrop suddenly splashed against the ground.

CHAPTER TWENTY-NINE

Retribution

splash

splash *splash*

Silence.
The entire world seemed to be frozen in place.

A lone girl stood within the audience as tears streamed down her pale cheeks.

"Rory... "
Her heart was crushed as she saw the mutilated state of her little brother. A feeling of desperation suffocated her mind as she felt her heart numbing to all emotions.

She wanted to feel angry, but besides the soul-crushing pain in her heart, she could not muster up the will to feel any anger.

Her heartbeat slowed down as she continued to gaze at the broken figure of her little brother.

Rory's right arm was twisted, and fragments of his bone stood out against the dark crimson blood covering his body.

Multiple cuts and wounds were scattered across his body, and even his clothes were completely shredded apart, with his split skin clearly visible.

Blood seeped out from the corner of his mouth and nose as it slowly dripped onto the stage.

splash
Her knees started quivering as she continued to see the sight of her brother in that state. Felice recalled their childhood memories and the countless times that Rory had tried to gain the attention of her parents, but only to be rejected and ignored, time after time.

However, his eyes never lost their luster, as her little brother continued to hope that one day, he would have a family that accepted him.

As each drop of blood dripped from Rory's body, Felice felt the life of her little brother slowly drain away...

....

"Big sister, look at these pebbles! I collected them all for you."
A cute chubby boy with dark black hair excitedly shouted as he ran towards a little girl with equally dark hair.

The little girl stood taller than the chubby boy, her ice-blue eyes twinkled in happiness when she saw the boy running towards her.

"Rory, quiet down. The guards might hear you, and then they will tell my mother. She was already quite furious when she saw me giving you candy yesterday."
Felice quickly shushed down the chubby boy as he arrived in front of her.

However, the joy in her face and eyes remained unperturbed.

"Hehe, it's alright. Big sister, look, this is the prettiest stone I found. It's blue, just like your eyes!"
The chubby cheerfully said as his arctic blue eyes shined with life.

"You are so cuuute!"
Felice suddenly exclaimed as she grabbed the chubby boy and tightly hugged him while pinching his cheeks with her other arm.

"Keke, aren't I so handsome?"
The chubby boy proudly boasted as the little girl continued to hug him.

"Of course, Rory will always be the one I love the most!"
The little girl softly stated as she petted the boy's hair.

"I love big sister as well!"
The small chubby boy cheerfully responded as he rubbed his head against his sister's belly.

"Hahaha, Rory, stop! That is tickling me, hahaha!"
The merry sound of two children laughing and giggling filled the empty garden as the gentle breeze embraced them.

"Big sis... why does stepmother hate me so much?"
The chubby boy suddenly asked as he sat down on the grass.

A sad and lonely expression flickered across his face as he gazed into his sister's eyes.

The little girl felt her heart twist with pain as she saw the forlorn look on her brother's face.

"I don't know, Rory... I've asked her many times, but she refuses to answer."
Felice gently replied as she looked into her brother's eyes.

"I... I just want to have a family. Can you tell her I promise to be good? And I will also not play pranks or eat her food. I just don't want to live alone in that hut anymore. It's so lonely..."

The chubby boy tearfully asked the little girl, as he sobbed between his sentences.

"Oh, Rory..."

Felice felt her eyes moisten as she sensed the pain and anguish contained within her little brother. He had spent his whole life alone without the love of a mother or a father.

The little boy only wanted to have a family, and he did not understand why other people hated him so much.

He had cried outside the doors of the Axier mansion many nights, but no one ever opened the door for him.

This heart-wrenching pain would crush the soul of any child, but the little boy continued to hope that one day, his family would accept him.

"Rory, I will always be your family."
A soft whisper echoed in the gentle breeze.

....

Chax was holding Rory by the neck as his legs dangled above the ground. A sinister smile was spread across Chax's face as he cruelly gazed into his opponent's eyes.

Rory desperately struggled to break free, but his strength was slowly being depleted as his breath was constricted by Chax's chokehold.

"B-big brother... I tried... cough cough... I'm just not... as cool as you... "

Rory rasped with a slight smile, as he felt his consciousness start to slowly fade away.

Calron and Felice were the only family he ever had, and what Rory regretted the most, was that he could not even slightly deter Chax.

Rory recalled the first time he had met Calron, and in a way, it was because of him that his big brother got involved with Chax.

I hope big brother will not be mad at me...
And then, Rory's consciousness faded away.

....

Seeing the mangled body of his opponent desperately struggling to escape from his grip, Chax felt a sick sense of pleasure as he saw the helplessness in Rory's eyes.

Since he was a kid, no one had ever dared to oppose him on account of who his father was, but here was a nobody who had defiantly stood against him.

"Now, only that lightning trash is left."
Chax gleefully snickered as he looked into the audience to locate Calron.

Just as his eyes were scanning the crowd, he felt a dense killing intent directed at him from the corner of the stadium.

This was unlike anything Chax had ever felt before.

Even with an enormous distance between him and the audience, Chax felt suffocated as his nerves went wild with panic.

With his hands trembling, his grip on Rory's neck loosened up a bit. Rory's broken and injured body abruptly collapsed onto the stage with a deafening thud.

Rory's body lay completely still.

At that moment, the suffocating pressure on Chax intensified by several degrees, and he felt as if a predator had just started its hunt.

....

Meanwhile, the nearby crowd slowly backed away from the stranger who was currently emanating such a dangerous killing intent. They felt their hearts tremble with fear when they realized just how young the boy was.

The nearby Felice abruptly snapped out of her daze, as she also felt the intense bloodlust near her.

"Y-you... "
Felice's heart started to rapidly pound against her chest as she saw the twisted expression on the boy's face.

He was no longer the calm and collected boy that she had previously seen.

Thick, bulging veins popped all across his body as a dark crimson mist floated around him.

The scent of fresh blood polluted the air, and the nearby crowd felt their minds quivering under the savage aura released by the boy.

No one knew what that crimson mist was, but from the pungent smell that filled the entire vicinity, it seemed as if it was real human blood.

Before they could even contemplate this any further, the boy suddenly bellowed out with a mighty roar.

"TI.....TAN'S..... FURY!!!"

* * *

splash

As Rory's blood slowly dripped onto the stage, a surge of pain suddenly shot through Calron.

Calron had never felt such a bond with anyone else in his life. Watching his brother bleed before his eyes awakened a primordial rage inside of him.

He and Rory were kindred souls. They had shared the same torment of not having a place where they belonged, and although Rory constantly goofed around and annoyed Calron, deep within the depths of his heart, Calron enjoyed having Rory pester him.

Rory was the only one that Calron had ever felt such closeness with, and he had not realized until this moment just how much effect that boy's presence had in his life.

Seeing his brother's current mangled body, and the broken arm with pale white bone showing, Calron felt an intense hatred and wrath welling up within his body.

He slowly observed all the countless cuts and wounds spread across Rory's body.

The blood continued to drip on the stage, as Rory desperately tried to break free of Chax's hold. Just as Calron was about to rush to the stage, Rory stopped moving.

Time stopped.

Calron breathed heavily, as his heart violently thumped against his chest. A colossal amount of blood surged through his veins, as an intense killing intent emanated from Calron.

A guttural growl sounded out from his throat as he felt the concrete beneath him cracking apart. A fiery heat circulated inside his body, as Calron's skin flushed with a crimson color.

He no longer looked like a human while exuding that savage aura which was akin to that of a wild beast. His skin shimmered with a blood-colored glow.

The crimson mist orbited around Calron, as the domain of the Blood Arts was activated for the first time.

Completely unaware of the changes happening to his body, Calron growled through his clenched teeth.

"TI.....TAN'S......FURY!"

....

High above the Arena, and on top of a cliff, an old man stood with an enraged expression on his face.

CRACK
A huge boulder next to him disintegrated into dust as his fist struck the large rock.

A vicious aura suddenly radiated from his body, as his long white hair wildly fluttered in the wind.

"THESE BASTARDS!!"
Elias furiously bellowed, as his opaque gray eyes burst with an unnatural light.

Seeing his disciple beaten on the stage, Elias felt an uncontainable fury welling up inside him. This scene was very similar to when his nephew was slaughtered back then, and Elias did not have the heart to watch another disciple of his being killed in front of him.

However, just as he was about to leap towards the stage, the source pool inside the Blood Legacy trembled vigorously.

"No...No... NO! This can't be happening. CALRON!"

....

Deep within Calron's consciousness, a series of images flashed across his vision.

A crimson giant with bulging arms stood alone on a deserted plain, as countless corpses surrounded him. It was not clear whether the giant actually had crimson skin, or if it was just the blood of the corpses.

Calron could only see the back of the giant and no matter how hard he tried, he was unable to gaze at the giant's face.

Patterns of symbols were wholly etched across the giant's skin and they faintly glowed with a pale light.

The symbols were surprisingly identical to the one Calron had on his palm.

"Boy, do not regret this."

A hoarse whisper sounded out from the giant, as in the next moment, all the images shattered within Calron's mind.

An intense surge of source energy rushed into him as he felt his muscles and bones being completely imbued with a crimson glow.

A profound strength seemed to enter Calron as he sensed his body grow stronger and stronger by the moment. Even the experts at the peak of the Spiritual stage would hardly be a challenge for the current Calron.

Every fiber of his being was emanating the source energy of the Blood Legacy.

However, after a single second, Calron felt a sudden jolt of pain shoot through his body.

His blood was being consumed by the legacy.

"ARRRGGGHHH!!!"

A gut-wrenching scream erupted from Calron's mouth, and then a faint illusion of a massive crimson giant coalesced behind him.

It stood around twenty feet tall, with plates of armor covering its chest, wrists and ankles. Besides a loincloth covering its private parts, the giant had no other clothing on it.

The giant suddenly raised its head and mightily roared towards the heavens.

The nearby crowd all stared in shock as they saw the changes in the boy, and their hearts trembled with fright when the illusion of a crimson giant appeared behind Calron.

None of them knew what that creature was, but they could feel the intense pressure it exuded.

Meanwhile, Felice's mind was completely numb with shock as she saw the current Calron. With his red skin and savage aura, the boy no longer appeared to be human, and instead seemed like the very incarnation of a devil from the depths of hell.

Before she could regain her composure, Calron vanished from his spot in a flash.

Only a faint cloud of crimson mist remained where he had previously stood.

....

Chax felt his whole body trembling uncontrollably as he closed his eyes in an effort to steady his nerves.

Right at that moment, he heard an ear-splitting roar of a savage beast.

Before he could even open his eyes, a scorching palm with frightening strength gripped his neck in a vise.

Chax opened his eyes in surprise and stared into the distorted face of Calron.

"W-who are y-you?"
Chax asked in a shaky voice.

"This is my retribution."
A cold and frosty voice whispered into Chax's ear as he felt his body being lifted into the air.

Holding Chax's body by the neck, Calron viciously smashed his head into the ground.

BOOOM!

Pressing Chax's neck into the ground, Calron bent down as he whispered into his ear.
"This is for justice."

Grabbing Chax's right arm, Calron maliciously twisted it until it popped out of its socket.

Chax let out a blood-curdling screech as a burst of pain exploded within his mind.

Tightly gripping the dislocated arm, Calron exerted his pressure until sounds of the bone cracking could be heard in the surroundings, along with Chax's miserable cries of pain.

A spray of blood burst forth, as the entire arm from the elbow to the wrists was completely crushed into a mesh of fractured bones and flesh.

Under the domain of the Blood Legacy, Calron's physical strength was amplified immeasurably and with just his bare hands, he could crush the bones of an eighth-rank cultivator.

The illusion of the crimson giant had disappeared a while ago, but Calron did not even realize it, as he was utterly immersed in torturing Chax.

Gazing at the still figure of Rory, unbidden tears formed within Calron's eyes as he firmly clenched his fists, and turned to glare at Chax.

With the crushed arm still within his grip, Calron let out a loud roar as he suddenly ripped apart the arm from the elbow down.

"ARGHHHH!"
A soul-crushing cry of pain erupted from Chax's mouth as he felt the torturous agony of his limb being torn out.

"This is for vengeance."
Calron coldly whispered as he stared into Chax's eyes.

…………………..

In the booths above the stadium, a chaotic scene was unfolding.

"What is that thing behind that little bastard?"
Regis loudly exclaimed as he abruptly rose out of his chair.

Even from here, he could detect that the aura around that thing was extraordinary, and he had never heard of a technique that could bring out such a realistic illusion with its own signature aura.

"Stop this tournament and bring that runt to me! NOW!" Regis bellowed as he turned towards his two guards.

He could see that the lightning boy was not so simple, and he wanted to seize him before anyone else made a move.

After this day, the boy would not remain in the Red Boar School as the various officials present today would certainly try to capture the boy for their own purposes.

A young lightning cultivator that could turn his skin to an astonishing crimson color, and bring out such a violent and bloodthirsty aura, would be the fascination of every influential power in the city.

Turning his head to gaze at the stadium, Regis was pleased with the performance of his son and loudly applauded as he beamed with pride.

No one in the younger generations could contend against Chax.

His son was a rare genius.

Just as these thoughts were racing within his mind, Regis got up to exit the booth to congratulate his son, when a blood-curdling scream echoed in the entire Arena.

"ARGHHHH!"

Swiftly turning around, Regis rushed to the edge of the balcony as he saw the soul-crushing scene below him.

His son was being tortured by the red-skinned boy.

Before Regis could even comprehend the situation, another gut-wrenching scream echoed on stage, as Chax's limb was savagely ripped apart from his body.

"YOU LITTLE BASTARD! KILL HIM!!"

The roar of the city Lord reverberated into the sky, as the entire crowd below felt their hearts shake with terror.

CHAPTER THIRTY

Shadow Corps

—In the Axier Mansion—

"My Lord... we just received an instant transmission from the Red Boar School."

A figure in a pitch-black outfit stated while kneeling on the floor.

Standing in front of a large ornate window was a tall, gray-haired man with a stern expression on his face.

"Hmm, did Felice want something?"

The gray-haired man inquired as he continued to gaze at the scenery outside the window.

"Uh... no, my Lord... it's about your son."

The assassin stumbled over his words, as he did not know how to report the news of this recent calamity.

Hearing that it was about his son, Mort abruptly turned around as his eyes pierced into the kneeling assassin.

"Speak."

A voice, devoid of personal touch, reverberated in the room.

Knowing that there was no choice but to relay the information, the assassin started recounting in detail as he inwardly cursed his captain for making him the bearer of this tragic news.

Kacha
A bone-chilling mist spread around the room as the glass on the windows abruptly froze and started to slowly crack under pressure.

The temperature in the room dropped to dangerous levels, and the assassin started to uncontrollably shiver as he felt the frigid energy piercing into his skin.

A wrathful expression covered Mort's face, as he icily whispered.
"Order the guards stationed in the school to stop the tournament and to protect my son at all costs. If Roran dies, then even the Gods themselves will not be able to save Regis!"

"Y-yes, my Lord."
The kneeling assassin stammered as he skirred the room.

If he had stayed even a second longer around that bone-chilling mist, then his limbs would have been completely frozen.

"Selia... for you, all these years I have kept my own son apart from me. But from this day forth, Roran will become my legitimate son and heir to the Axier Family."
Mort solemnly stated as a dark crystal suddenly appeared in his hands.

"Mobilize the Shadow Corps. We are leaving for the Red Boar School."
Mort strictly commanded, and a quick response was immediately sounded out from the dark crystal.

"We are ready, my Lord."
With an explosion of a thick frosty mist, Mort vanished from the

room, as a whisper echoed within the entire Axier Mansion.

"I am coming, my son."

....

"YOU LITTLE BASTARD! I'LL RIP YOUR HEAD OFF!"

Regis furiously bellowed as he leaped out of the balcony and released his essence in mid-air.

A long stream of flames erupted behind him as it enveloped his entire body.

Seeing the enraged city Lord nearing them from the sky, the crowd below all started sweating profusely as they cursed their fates for coming to the tournament.

The City Lord was infamous for disregarding the lives of commoners, and with his son in such a miserable state, they all knew that there was a very high chance of dying in the aftermath of this impending battle.

A few seconds after Regis had leaped off the balcony, the two guards behind him had immediately exited the booth and sent a quick transmission to their brothers, while they rushed towards the stadium.

Unlike the city Lord, they could not leap off the balcony from such an immense height, as they were still in the Spiritual stage, so their bodies did not have the same toughness that the experts in the Vajra stage had.

"Surround the gates of the school and make sure no one leaves or enters its premises!"

One guard sternly yelled into a crystal in his hand.

....

"ARGH!"

Calron suddenly dropped to one knee as a searing jolt of pain exploded within his veins.

His vision became blurry, as the domain was slowly consuming his blood. Calron knew he was reaching the end of his strength, and it was only the thought of protecting Rory that allowed him to maintain consciousness.

Ignoring the wailing Chax on the floor, Calron painstakingly crawled towards Rory as tears streamed down his face.

His skin was also starting to slowly revert to its normal color as the domain withdrew back inside Calron.

"Rory... brother... I'm sorry, I couldn't save you... cough."
Calron morosely whispered as he uncontrollably sobbed on the floor.

Grasping Rory's hand, Calron tilted his head towards the sky as he mustered up all the strength he had.
"YOU TOOK MY FAMILY! YOU STOLE MY CHILDHOOD! AND NOW, YOU TOOK AWAY THE ONLY BROTHER I HAD! DAMN YOU!"

Gasping with a lack of breath, Calron collapsed on top of Rory.

"Big... broth...er..."
A faint whisper suddenly emerged from Rory's mouth.
Hearing that familiar voice, Calron felt his heart thumping against his chest as he abruptly opened his eyes to confirm that Rory was still alive.

"Rory!"
Calron wiped away his tears as an immense feeling of elation spread throughout his body. Firmly grasping Rory's hand, Calron slowly smiled as he realized that Rory was still alive.

"YOU FILTHY LITTLE SHIT!"

A furious roar suddenly erupted behind Calron as Regis landed onto the stage with a loud explosion.

Seeing his father arrive, Chax felt a surge of hope within his heart, as he knew that he could get his revenge now. Never in his life had he been this humiliated, and today's memory would scar him forever.

Calron would have to die for him to ever be at peace.

"Father… "

Chax hoarsely whispered, as he tried to stand up. His throat was completely parched from the screams and cries evoked under Calron's torture.

"Son… I will destroy these two for you, so hang in here."

Regis fiercely declared as he turned to face Calron and Rory.

Flames unceasingly flowed on top of his body as an oppressive aura surged around him. The pressure it exuded immediately forced Calron to the ground and prevented him from making a single movement.

"I will slowly skin your flesh and make you scream until even your ancestors will hear your cries of agony, and only then, when your soul is on the verge of insanity, will I take your life."

Regis coldly stated as he strolled towards the two boys.

Calron knew he was no match for a Vajra stage expert, especially after activating the Titan's Fury, and he realized that there was nothing he could do at this moment. If not for his tremendous willpower, Calron would have long ago collapsed from the strain of using the Blood Legacy's domain.

Calron's current blood quantity was at dangerous levels, and if he even attempted to activate the Titan's Fury again, then his body would immediately crumble apart.

Regis raised his arm, and a large ball of scalding flames gathered within his palm.

The ground beneath Regis cracked apart from the intense heat radiating from him, but he showed no signs of stopping.

Rory clasped Calron's hand as he struggled to sound out his words.

"Big broth... er, you sh... ould lea...ve."

"Haha, Rory, if we die today, I will make sure to at least take out as many of these bastards as I can."

Calron fearlessly stated as he saw the guards with the bear insignia on their chest plates slowly gather around the stage.

The crowd slowly stepped back as the black armored guards completely encircled the stage as they waited for their Lord to issue orders.

Just as Calron resigned himself to his fate and was about to summon the Azure Lightning, a sudden surge of bright cyan essence erupted within the crowd.

"Lord Regis, you will step down from that stage immediately or I will personally kill your son right now!"

A cold and frosty voice echoed around the Arena, as Felice started to slowly walk towards Calron and Rory.

Previously, when she had seen her brother move and confirmed he was alive, Felice immediately regained her composure while an elated relief spread within her, but before she could even rejoice, she saw that the city Lord was preparing to attack her brother.

"Who the hell are you?"
Regis angrily asked as his eyes bore into Felice.

Out of the blue, a series of shadows flashed across the stage.

As Felice was about to respond, a tall figure in an assassin's outfit stepped in front of her.

Facing the city Lord, the assassin icily stated.
"Any further threats against the Axier family, and you shall forfeit your life."

— A Few Hours Ago —

"Captain, why did you stop me from interfering in the battle? It is my duty as the Moderator to stop such things before they get to this stage."
Jarin angrily muttered as he stood next to a middle-aged woman with dark blonde hair.

Her gray eyes calmly gazed at the brutal scene unfolding in the Arena, and not a hint of emotion flickered across her face.

"One of those boys is the son of the city Lord of Vernia, and judging from that unique frosty essence, the other one seems to be connected with the Axier family. It is best not to get involved in the conflicts of these two powers."
The middle-aged woman serenely replied as she continued to observe the chaos on the stage.

Next to her, Jarin bitterly gazed at the defeated boy as he tightly clenched his fists.

………………………..

"Sir, we just received a transmission from Lord Mort."
A tall man in assassin's garb urgently turned around before he angrily stated.

"Stop wasting time and quickly report the Lord's orders!"

The tall assassin had been inwardly raging from the very moment that Rory was beaten, and if not for the massive crowd present in the Arena, he would have intervened long ago.

Very few people knew Lord Mort's deep affection for his son, and this tall assassin was one of the few that knew this fact.

Lord Mort's commands were to keep an eye on the boy and to only intervene if his life was threatened. However, the Lord had also ordered that the Shadow Corps should never reveal themselves to the public.

How could they have possibly known that a situation like this would arise in front of such a large audience?

With those two orders clashing against each other, the tall assassin could only wait for further orders before acting. If it were not for Lady Selia's insistence on ostracizing the boy, then the assassin would not have had to wait for more orders to act in this situation.

"Lord Axier has commanded us to protect Roran at all costs."

The subordinate hastily informed the tall assassin.

"Haha, finally! Order the third squad of the Shadow Corps to follow me immediately!"

The tall assassin roared, as a ferocious smile spread across his face.

"Little lord, we are coming."

....

Arriving at the Arena and inspecting the state of their Lord's son, the Shadow Corps felt a blazing fury ignite within their hearts.

Unlike the normal guards of the Axier Family, the Shadow Corps were under the direct command of Lord Axier, and their allegiance only extended to the direct heirs of the family.

There were many sub-branches in the family, and the formidable might of the Shadow Corps was what helped the main family maintain their influence.

Because Lord Mort had officially claimed Roran as his son, the boy now had the right to inherit the family throne after his father.

"Quickly, give that elixir to the little Lord."
The tall assassin commanded when he saw that Rory was in a dire state.

A figure flashed next to Calron and Rory. He immediately kneeled and poured the contents of the glass container into Rory's mouth.

Both Rory and Calron made no move to stop the figure, as they knew that the Shadow Corps were the only chance they had of surviving today.

Just seconds after Rory ingested the unknown elixir, his wounds started to rapidly heal in front of Calron's eyes.

The flesh around his right arm expanded and contracted as it straightened the bone back into place, and the blood vessels and arteries started slowly to reconnect to his body.

Within a few minutes, Rory's entire body was completely back to normal.

Seeing that the elixir had healed the boy, the kneeling assassin let out a sigh of relief.

A famous individual on the continent of Agatha had concocted that elixir, and it was known as the Elixir of Rejuvenation. It could instantly heal mortal wounds of any cultivator below the Vajra stage.

The preciousness of the Elixir of Rejuvenation was many grades above the elixir that was being awarded to the first-place winner of the tournament. How could an elixir that could bring someone back from the edges of death be comparable to a mere cultivation aid?

Seeing that Rory was no longer on the verge of death, the nearby Shadow Corps and Felice all inwardly felt their nerves calming down. It was unknown what would have happened to this school if Lord Mort had arrived here and found his son dead.

Rory slowly stood up and helped Calron next, as they watched the Shadow Corps confront the city Lord of Vernia.

"Any further threats against the Axier family, and you shall forfeit your life."
The tall assassin icily stated as he glared at Regis.

Noticing that the shadow technique these assassins used was similar to Viktor, Regis immediately guessed as to whom they represented.

"I'm sorry, but I don't think I have offended any members of the Axier fam-"
Suddenly Regis felt his heart quiver in shock as he gazed at the arctic blue eyes of Rory and his dark hair. Noticing the similar features in the girl that had just threatened him, Regis felt his soul instantly collapse.

No, no, no! How could I have not realized who they were? The signs were all there. Shit!
Regis furiously cursed inside his mind as he faced the current dilemma.

Although Regis had a much higher cultivation than the tall assassin, who was merely in the second rank of the Vajra stage, it was the power behind the Shadow Corps that truly frightened him.

The current Lord of the Axier family was an expert in the Saint stage.

If he wanted to, he could single-handedly destroy the entire city of Vernia.

"I would advise you to take your son and leave immediately. Lord Mort will arrive here soon."
The tall assassin calmly stated to the numb Regis.

Hearing those words, Regis knew he had no further choice but to back down in this matter. However, just as he was about to order his guards to retrieve Chax, Regis glanced at Calron from the corner of his eyes.

"Very well, I will immediately leave this school right now, but I assume you have no problem with me dealing with that boy? He is not part of the Axier family."
Regis slowly spoke as a sinister smile spread across his face.

Unlike Rory, Calron did not have a major power backing him, and Regis doubted that Lord Mort would even care about others as long as his son was unharmed.

Before the tall assassin could even respond, Rory shouted in a fierce voice.
"If you try to hurt my big brother, I will fight you!"

Rory knew that the current Calron was drained of energy and there was no chance of him resisting the City Lord.

"Hahaha, I might be apprehensive about your father, but even he would not dare to cause trouble for me without a valid excuse. That slave there belongs to me!"
Regis roared as he suddenly rushed towards Calron.

"STOP HIM!"

Felice abruptly yelled as she activated her movement skill and darted towards Calron as well.

Hearing the command of their little lady, the Shadow Corps immediately burst into motion as they obstructed the path of Regis.

"I do not wish to fight against you. Just let me take the boy and I will leave right now."

Regis coldly stated as bursts of flames ignited on his body.

Just a second later, Felice arrived next to Calron as she frantically whispered.

"You need to leave right now. Without Father here, we cannot hold out against the city Lord for long."

"Big sis, how can you tell big brother to suddenly leave? Where will he go?"

Rory sadly replied, as he gazed into Calron's eyes.

Patting Rory on the shoulder, Calron gave him a slight smile.

"Rory, you are the first brother I ever had, and I'm glad that I met you in this life. Take care."

Calron softly whispered into Rory's ear as he tightly hugged him.

Rory wept as he hugged Calron even tighter.

"Big brother, please don't leave me! You are the only brother I ever had as well!"

Rory sorrowfully cried as his tears dripped onto Calron's back.

"You idiot! Who says we won't ever meet again? Fate has brought us together once, and it will bring us together again."

Calron whispered as stepped back from Rory and gave him a sad smile.

"Big brother…"

Tightly clenching his fists, Calron slowly drew a faint trickle of source energy for a last burst of the Blood Mist Step.

Inwardly screaming with pain once it activated, Calron turned around and gazed at his brother for the last time.

With tears flowing down his cheeks and a slight smile on his face, Calron's body exploded into a burst of crimson mist.

CHAPTER THIRTY-ONE

Destiny

cough *cough*

Calron suddenly doubled up on the ground as he spat out a large amount of blood.

Turning his head around to look behind him, Calron saw the distant figures of Rory and the Shadow Corps surrounding the city Lord, as they prevented him from moving.

Calron was forced to use the Blood Mist Step multiple times to make sure he was at a long enough distance away from the Arena.

With barely even the strength to use it once, Calron had risked a great deal by activating the Blood Mist Step multiple times.

cough

Calron excruciatingly spat out another mouthful of blood on the ground, as his hands trembled with exhaustion.

He had decided to head towards his Master's home because the Artifact was his safest bet, as it only permitted people with the wooden token to enter. If Calron could safely cross the invisible barrier of the forest, then he had a much higher chance of surviving today.

However, just as he was about to turn his head back around, he suddenly saw multiple figures darting toward him.

They were the black armored guards of the City Lord.

Feeling his heart pound against his chest, Calron painfully contracted his muscles as he immediately sprinted toward the forest.

The guards were still of a distance away. However, they were rapidly gaining ground, and unlike Calron, they were in their peak condition.

With his quivering knees, Calron forced himself to continue running as he desperately hoped that his body would not fail him right now.

Taking another quick glance behind him, Calron saw that the black armored guards were almost upon him, as only a few meters separated him from them.

Just as he felt that all hope was lost, Calron spotted the familiar sight of the forest's entrance.

However, the guards were now only two meters behind him, and Calron could hear the distinct rattling of their armor and the heavy stomps of their legs against the ground.

"I decided long ago to shatter my fate of weakness, so I refuse to die here!"
Calron furiously roared, as he gathered every last drop of strength and willpower that he had, and charged into the forest.

A sensation of a gentle tingle rippled through Calron's body just as he crossed the barrier. Stopping after a few steps, Calron panted laboriously in order to regain his breath.

Feeling his nerves start to slowly calm down, Calron raised his head as he prepared to look back at the black armored guards.

thump

thump *thump*

His heartbeat began to wildly accelerate when he saw the guards were all grinning at him as they stood outside the barrier.

"Teon, bring it out."
The guard at the forefront shouted as he turned towards another guard behind him.

Teon slowly stepped forwards while holding a strange translucent gem in his hands.

"Did you really think that we didn't know about this artifact? I don't know how you were able to enter it unobstructed, or even know of its existence, but none of that matters now."
The guard at the forefront calmly stated, as his eyes cruelly bored into Calron.

How could the city Lord not know about the Red Boar School possessing an artifact? Regis had long ago prepared a countermeasure against it, as he knew the school's Head disagreed with many of his ideals, so he had secretly paid an enormous sum of gold to get this mysterious gem that could bypass the barrier of low ranked Artifacts.

Hearing the words of the guard, Calron felt his entire body quivering uncontrollably.

He had thought that he was finally safe from danger, but fate seemed to have other plans for him, as even his safe location was soon about to be compromised.

Suddenly, all the nearby guards released their essence into the air.

The various tendrils of essence merged into a multi-colored wave and poured into the translucent gem that Teon was holding.

A bright multi-colored glow immediately illuminated the entire area, as the gem appeared to be bursting with raw energy.

"Teon."

Knowing it was time for the next step, Teon slowly brought the gem closer and closer to the barrier until it made contact.

BOOOOM!

The invisible barrier around the forest rippled for a brief moment before it returned to normal.

BOOOOM!

Another explosion sounded out, as Teon pushed the gem further into the barrier.

CRACK!

A tiny crack suddenly appeared at the top of the barrier, and upon seeing that result, the black armored guards frantically increased the intensity of the essence that they were pouring into the gem.

Meanwhile, Calron dumbly stood there as he observed the inevitable collapse of the barrier.

"Is this what the heavens have destined for me?"
Calron whispered, as his soul drowned in despair.

yawn

"Stop making that loud noise, kid. Can't you see I'm trying to sleep here?"

A grumpy voice groaned from within Calron's mind.

"Teacher! You're back!"

Calron exclaimed as a surge of joy spread throughout his body.

"Huh? Calron? Wait, I awoke already? That's impossible, I sh-"

A jolt of shock burst out from within Calron's mind, as he felt the Voice's astonishment.

"Y-you are in the fifth rank already? Even with the Thunderbird's technique, it's still impossible!"

The Voice yelled in an astonished tone.

The Voice realized that he could only make such a quick recovery because of Calron's rapid advancement in cultivation. Their souls were merged so the higher the boy's rank, the quicker he would heal.

CRACK!

"Teacher, I will explain everything later, but can you somehow deal with those guards?"

Calron frantically asked his Teacher, when he saw that the barrier was soon going to shatter.

"Goddammit, kid! Why do you always chase after trouble?"

The Voice angrily scolded, as it realized the precarious situation they were currently in.

"Tch, it's more like trouble follows me, rather than me chasing after it."

Calron sulkily responded to the Voice.

Even though they were in a dangerous situation, just knowing that his Teacher was back made Calron ease his worries a bit.

"It doesn't matter, you brat! Just stop involving me in them! Hmph, looking at the current state of your body, you would be lucky to even land a slap against them. Just run for now. I need to keep thinking."

The Voice advised as he urged Calron to run.

Wiping away the traces of blood from his mouth, a determined expression etched itself on Calron's face, as he knew that there was no other choice.

KACHA

The shattering of the invisible barrier loudly echoed throughout the forest as the guards let out a victorious yell.

"I swear on my parents' grave that if I survive this day, I will return to exterminate Chax and his entire wretched family."

Calron savagely whispered while glaring at the guards, and then abruptly burst into a sprint towards the inner forest.

Seeing that the boy was escaping again, the guards furiously bellowed as they immediately followed behind Calron.

"I will strangle that little bastard with my hands."

The guard at the forefront infuriatingly yelled as he activated his movement skill to charge at Calron from behind.

"I do not remember giving you permission to enter this area."

A cold voice resounded in the forest, as a figure slowly walked towards the guards.

With his silver-white hair wildly fluttering in the wind, Elias leisurely stepped towards the group of guards, his gray eyes shining with an unnatural glow.

"It has been a while since I was this angry."

Elias frostily stated as a crimson mist floated around him.

"Who the f**k are you, old man?"
One guard arrogantly spoke, as he sensed that the stranger in front of him was not in the Vajra stage. For these elite guards, only someone in the Vajra stage could threaten their existence. In fact, the guard could not even detect a trace of essence from the stranger.

"Have you ever seen a demon?"
Elias calmly asked, as he completely ignored the talking guard.

"This shitty old man, how dare you ignore me?"
The guard furiously yelled as he stepped towards Elias.

"Youngsters these days truly do not know how to respect their elders... sigh."
Elias softly muttered, as the aura around him abruptly intensified, and an extremely dense killing intent spread through the air.

"A demon exists within all of us... the only difference is that I choose to embrace it."
Elias coldly whispered, as his body exploded into a smoke of crimson mist.

Before anyone could even react, a severed head softly thudded against the ground.

thud

A headless corpse slowly collapsed on the ground, while a severed head rolled a few yards away. The nearby guards felt their hands trembling with horror as they witnessed the current scene.

"W-what just happened now?"
One of them numbly muttered as he gazed at the dismembered head of his fallen comrade.

"Shit. This old geezer is a Legacy Inheritor!"

An older guard at the back yelled out with a slight quiver in his voice, while slowly stepping back.

Hearing that the old man was an Inheritor, the rest of the guards started sweating profusely as their hands and knees trembled.

"So, which one of you wanted to strangle my disciple?"

Elias frostily stated, as drops of fresh scarlet blood dripped from his hand, while he continued to slowly walk towards the remaining guards.

Before anyone could make another move, Elias again exploded into a burst of crimson mist and suddenly appeared behind another guard.

"I will make sure your brothers will join you soon."

Elias darkly whispered into his victim's ear as he thrust his hand into the guard's chest.

cough

The guard excruciatingly coughed up a mouthful of blood, as he slowly dropped onto the floor, never to move again.

"S-send a t-transmission to the city Lord!"

A frantic voice sounded out from the guard, as he desperately tried to run away.

Just as the guard moved, Elias flashed in front of him with a cruel smile on his face.

"Going somewhere?"

Another spurt of blood sprayed into the air, as the guard's corpse silently thudded onto the ground.

Only three more guards were left standing as their knees

miserably shook in fear.

They had all thought that they had finally completed their task when they finally caught up with the boy and saw the hopeless look on the child's face. Now, under the intense aura of this old man, they all cursed their fates as they realized that their lives were in the hands of this old man.

"Do you have any children of your own?"
Elias icily asked, as his eyes bore into the oldest appearing guard.

"Y-yes, one s-son and a daughter."
The older guard replied in a shaky voice.

Hearing the older guard's answer, a howling wind erupted out from behind Elias as heavy pressure oppressed the three remaining guards.

"When did our hearts become so cruel that we seek to kill each other's children?"
Elias softly whispered as the pressure around the three guards continued to increase until their knees crashed onto the ground and drops of sweat formed on their foreheads.

"The day we kill for pleasure is the day we lose our humanity."
Elias calmly said as he walked closer and closer to the three kneeling guards.

Just as he arrived in front of them, the guards clasped their hands around their necks as the pressure from Elias suffocated them.

"P-plea... se... h-have... mer... cy."
One guard despairingly rasped, as tears flowed from his eyes.

"Mercy does not exist for people like you."
Elias evenly stated as a bright light flashed from his gray eyes.

"ARGHHHH!"

Miserable cries of agony sounded out in the forest, as the surrounding grass was slowly being stained with dark blood and the smell of blood seeped into the air.

Hearing the gut-wrenching screams behind him, Calron stopped and glanced behind him.

"Master..."

Calron tried to yell, but only a hoarse whisper came out.

Calron had been in a daze the entire time as his body slowly took one step at a time. His mind was drifting in and out, and even the Voice was completely muted in his head.

Only the loud cries of the guards had brought Calron out of his daze. He leaned against a nearby tree and panted as he desperately tried to remain conscious.

All emotions and sensations had left his body, only a ferocious will to survive remained.

Only a few meters separated Calron and his Master, so Elias could still faintly hear the hoarse whisper of his disciple.

Elias immediately activated the Blood Mist Step as he rushed toward his disciple.

"Calron."

Just as Elias arrived in front of Calron, the boy unexpectedly fainted from exhaustion.

Seeing the current state of the boy, Elias felt a furious wrath welling up inside of him. Calron's lips were parched and various wounds covered his body from the strain of going past his body's limits. Using the domain of the legacy and constantly activating the

Blood Mist Step, it was a wonder that the boy was even alive.

A sudden light illuminated the surroundings as Elias's eyes glowed mysteriously.

Gently touching the closed eyelids of the boy, Elias softly whispered.
"I had hoped to pass this on to you at a happier time, but current circumstances leave me no choice."

Soon, an intricate and ancient symbol formed on Calron's forehead.

Within a few seconds, a celestial white glow emitted from the symbol as it slowly faded away.

"It is done."
Elias whispered as the glow within his own eyes dimmed.

"Master?"
Calron softly rasped, as his eyes slowly opened again.

His complexion had become healthier, and even the wounds on his body healed at a slow pace.

Although the healing effects were not as miraculous as Elixir of Rejuvenation, Calron at least regained a bit of his vitality and stamina.

"YOU LITTLE SHIT! YOU REALLY THINK YOU CAN ESCAPE?"
A furious echo resounded throughout the forest as the ground shook with tremors.

Calron's eyes abruptly opened in panic as soon as he heard that familiar voice.

"Haha, I guess we are truly having a shit day, eh, Calron?"

Elias asked in an amused voice, as he gently gazed at Calron.

"Master! That's the city Lord. We need to escape now!"
Calron frantically shouted, as he quickly got up on his feet.

"Huh? What happened to my body?"
Calron stated as he curiously touched his body.

"You will soon learn of it later. I need you to follow my instructions carefully now, Calron."
Elias sternly spoke as he deeply gazed into Calron's eyes.

"Run to my hut, and underneath the mat, you will find a large inscription pattern etched on the floor. Immediately place a drop of your blood on it, and it should activate. I had been saving it for an event like this, but I had hoped that it would be me that would have to run and not you."
Elias gingerly said as he ruffled Calron's hair.

"Master, what will that inscription pattern do?"
Calron hesitantly asked as he felt his Master was hiding something from him.

"It will take you to the Desolate Mountains. Now, GO!"
Elias hastily stated when he felt Regis was drawing close.

"Master, what about you-"
Calron started talking, but was immediately cut off by Elias.

"Child, do not worry about me... I have lived a long and satisfying life... just do not forget about me... "
Elias softly whispered as he lovingly gazed at Calron.

"M-Master? What are you talking about?"
Calron's voice trembled as he realized what this meant.

With tears blurring his vision, Calron suddenly rushed toward

Elias and tightly embraced him.

"Haha, you need to go now, child. A whole new life awaits you..."
Elias tenderly spoke as he patted Calron's head.

Another loud roar reverberated throughout the forest as Regis furiously bellowed.

Breaking the embrace gently, Elias pushed Calron towards his hut.
"GO!"

With tears streaming down his face, Calron gave a deep bow to Elias as he ran towards the hut.

Seeing that his disciple had left, Elias's aura switched as the vicious and bloodthirsty killing intent returned.

Just as a blazing figure wrapped in flames appeared within his sight, Elias savagely roared.

"TIT...TAN'S... FURY!!!"

....

Meanwhile, Calron sadly stood in front of his Master's hut as he realized that this was the first time he was ever entering it.

Turning his head around to look behind him, Calron gazed at the distant trees with a forlorn expression on his face.

"Master... "
Wiping his tears away, Calron slowly entered the hut.

The room was bare and empty besides a bed and a mat. There were no further possessions in the entire hut. Elias had never bothered with worldly materials, and that was reflected in his home.

Walking towards the mat, Calron gingerly swept it away as it revealed a large circle with various patterns etched onto it. They vaguely resembled the symbols on his palm, but Calron was uncertain. However, the inscription pattern on the floor was undoubtedly related to the Blood Legacy.

"Kid, are you ready?"
The Voice abruptly asked in a serious tone.

Biting his palm, Calron slowly placed his hand over the large circle as a single drop of blood splashed onto it.

shua

A dim scarlet glow filled the room, as the patterns on the floor seemed to come alive.

"Life will be hard from here on forth, Calron. You will be alone, without the warmth of friends or family."
The Voice somberly stated to test the boy's resolve.

"Who says that will be my fate? I will create my own destiny."
Calron firmly responded with a determined expression on his face, as he took a step into the inscription circle.

"Haha, that's my boy! Let's go!"
The Voice happily yelled, as he urged Calron.

"The Desolate Mountains, huh?"
Calron softly whispered to himself as he finally stepped into the circle.

A bright crimson light suddenly burst from the hut until it slowly faded away and revealed an empty room.

CHAPTER THIRTY-TWO

Epilogue

The melodious sound of a flute echoed throughout an isolated small mountain.

Surrounded by lush green trees and grass, a boy of thirteen years old was seated on the grass as he leaned against a large rock. Wearing only a pair of shorts made of animal fur, the boy was bare-chested.

His fingers rhythmically moved as the mesmerizing sound of the flute resonated in the air. The music was calm and soothing, as it exuded a feeling of both warmth and loneliness.

The long black hair of the boy obscured his entire face, and only his lower jaw was visible as he gently continued to play the flute.

chirp

Suddenly a clutter of soft footsteps could be heard in the area, as a series of small animals curiously observed the strange human with their large innocent eyes.

Their tiny ears all perked up as they reveled in the beautiful and enchanting music. They wanted to approach closer to the human to listen better, however; they were still wary of the boy playing the flute.

One of the furry animals in the group was a wolf pup with pitch-black fur. Its fuzzy fur appeared to be extremely soft, and its twinkling eyes brightly gazed at the mysterious human.

The wolf pup cautiously sniffed the air around the stranger, and sensing that nothing was abnormal, it slowly prowled towards the boy while crouching to the ground.

The other small animals carefully observed the human and remained on high alert so they could warn their wolf friend to escape if the human tried to attack.

After a few moments, the small wolf pup finally arrived in front of the stranger and curiously tilted its head to look at the boy's face.

A slight smile slowly formed on the boy's face as he noticed the cute antics of the wolf pup. Continuing to play the flute, the boy ignored the small beasts surrounding him.

After sniffing the human's skin, the wolf pup finally felt assured that the stranger was not dangerous and jumped onto the boy's lap. It blissfully laid down while closing its eyes and enjoyed the melodious music.

Seeing that the stranger had no malicious intent and that their wolf friend was safe, the other small animals rushed towards the human and cheerfully played around him. Baby birds fluttered their wings clumsily as they practiced flying, while the other four-legged creatures playfully wrestled with each other.

A pair of small furry tigers ran around the large rock as they tried to bite each other's tails. Meanwhile, a black bear cub lazily spread itself next to the human boy and laid its head on its paws before it dozed off.

The parents of these animals had all left them as soon as they were born. Life was harsh and cruel in the Desolate Mountains, and every beast would have to struggle on its own to reach the peak of cultivation.

Most of the beasts surrounding the boy were all common beasts, but there were a few magical beasts mixed in with them. As babies, they all stuck together until they could fend off for themselves.

ROOAARR
Suddenly, the deafening cry of a colossal beast reverberated throughout the small forest.

Hearing that roar, the small creatures all scurried away in panic. Even the bear cub rushed to hide itself behind a tree and protected the smaller animals within its embrace.

The strange human boy abruptly stopped playing the flute and set it on the grass beside him. Reaching out his hand, he gently petted the quivering wolf pup until it calmed down and tentatively licked his palm.

The boy tenderly smiled at the cute wolf pup on his lap.

CRACK
The sound of a large tree splitting apart echoed within the forest, as the atmosphere instantly became dark and tense.

The large beast was still some distance away, as none of the creatures could currently see it.

Gently picking up the wolf pup, the boy set it on the ground while he slowly stood up on his feet. Tilting his head toward the direction of the large beast, the aura around him gradually changed.

crackle
Faint bolts of Azure Lightning spread across his body, while his

long dark hair wildly fluttered in the wind, revealing his face.

A pair of striking gray eyes pierced into the large beast when it just entered the small forest. The gray eyes resembled that of a blind man, yet it was obvious this boy could see.

The large beast fearfully took a step back as soon as it felt the bloodthirsty aura around the human.

In the following second, the boy's gray eyes suddenly flashed with an unnatural white glow. A savage grin spread across his face while a single bolt of blue lightning flickered across his pupils.

crackle

Continue to Read "***Book 2 - Desolate Mountains***" here:

https://www.amazon.com/gp/product/B01I8BZDEA

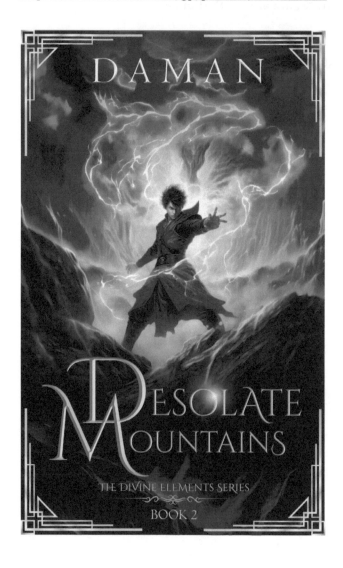

This series was self-published by the Author, so it heavily relies on the readers for their support as there is no large publishing company behind.

The series is first written in a web novel format with new chapters releasing every week, before it's published on Amazon. To read the latest Book 5, support the Author by subscribing to his Patreon and get early access to the chapters.

Patreon not only allows the Author to continue writing, but gives our amazing readers early access to the books before they are published. This means that you don't have to wait for a year to read the next book in the series and can start enjoying today!

Patreon: https://www.patreon.com/daman

Make sure to follow the Author's Page on Amazon to be notified on future books:

https://www.amazon.com/stores/author/B01CLUJ3JA/about

Twitter - https://twitter.com/TDE_Team

Email - damanknightley@gmail.com

Made in United States
Troutdale, OR
11/28/2023